Not Alone: The Final Call

CRAIG A. FALCONER

Not Alone: The Final Call
© 2019 Craig A. Falconer

This edition published May 2019

ISBN: 9781098662981

For the long shots.

Part 1

TIME BOMB

*"Honesty is the first chapter
in the book of wisdom."*

Thomas Jefferson

THURSDAY

V minus 99

LAKE MAGGIORE
ISPRA, ITALY

"Hashtag blessed," Emma Ford said, turning her back to Lake Maggiore and pretending to take a sunset selfie as the third day of her pre-honeymoon began its slow fade into night.

With her phone and all of the couple's other digital devices locked away for the week as part of an all-out ban on news and outside communication, Emma's mind was as happily empty as her hands.

Laughing loud and long, Dan McCarthy rose from his poolside sun-lounger and joined her to make the most of a picture-perfect view he would never get used to. The luxurious villa, owned by their good friend Timo Fiore, couldn't have been nestled in a better location and truly was the ideal place for the happily engaged couple to spend a week away from the incessant attention that followed them around in the real world.

With only this one beautiful sunset remaining before sunrise ushered in the first anniversary of Contact Day, the timing of Dan and Emma's romantic retreat was anything but coincidental.

Their need to escape this time around, while strong in Dan's mind, had certainly been less urgent than prior to their previous trip to Italy. Back then, when he had been pushed to breaking point by intense and often hostile scrutiny over his decision to leak a series of controversial documents which seemingly exposed a top-level government cover-up of extraterrestrial visitation, the trip had felt necessary to protect not only Dan's sanity but also his physical safety.

Things had then gotten a lot more difficult and a *whole* lot more complicated before they got any better, but Dan's relentless pursuit of the truth ultimately led to the epoch-defining moment when extraterrestrial beings walked on Earth in full view of hundreds of people and dozens of cameras. Three hundred and sixty-four days had passed since that moment, and not all of them had been easy.

Dan's highly public contact with the Messengers had evidently been enough to land him a reluctant place in humanity's hall of fame and, even less welcomely, it had also cemented his position as a prophet in the eyes of many.

But the direct *result* of that contact — the Messengers' agreement to divert the course of the colossal comet *Il Diavolo* away from Earth and prevent an extinction-level impact — took the public's adoration of Dan to even higher levels.

Much to his own unease, many of the celebratory events scheduled to mark the anniversary of Contact Day were instead terming it *Salvation* Day. More uncomfortable still, the vast majority of messianic adulation was directed squarely at Dan rather than at the benevolent but far from all-knowing aliens he had successfully persuaded to act.

"You just need to remember that this is the hardest it's ever going to be," Emma said, correctly sensing the direction of Dan's thoughts. "This is the first anniversary. Every year from now on, it'll be less and less of a huge deal."

As well as having far more experience of dealing with media attention than Dan thanks to a decade spent at the top of the public relations industry, Emma also had a degree of distance from the worst of it given that she hadn't been present at the Birchwood drive-in when the Messengers finally showed themselves.

Emma's earlier contact with them in Lolo National Forest, during which *they* had asked *her* for help regarding the placement of an engraved plaque designed to calm growing tensions on Earth, had been public knowledge ever since Dan desperately revealed everything in an effort to draw the Messengers back to Earth to stop the comet before it was too late. This ensured that she too remained a subject of often-overwhelming public interest, as well as often-exhausting interest from all kinds of governmental and international agencies.

The pressure on the couple to take part in one particular anniversary event had been almost crushingly overwhelming, but Dan stood firm in his insistence that his days in the spotlight were all behind him.

The level of global esteem in which Dan was held, not to mention the level of authority his views on this topic understandably carried, gave his words unparalleled weight. Without doubt, even a single negative word from Dan could have utterly torpedoed the fledgling and highly controversial Global Contact Commission's attempts to position itself as the sole legitimate point of future diplomatic contact with the Messengers, or indeed with any other extraterrestrial race.

It took an outright threat of this nature for Dan to get the GCC's powerful members to stop bothering him, with the likes of US President Valerie Slater and the organisation's Chairman William Godfrey ultimately deciding that it was better to accept his position as a neutral observer than to keep aggressively pursuing his endorsement when doing so might have pushed him towards a hugely damaging public disavowal.

Dan hoped Emma was right — that this first anniversary *would* be the hardest — and he nodded slowly in acknowledgment of her efforts to ease his mind.

"Do you think they're watching us?" he asked a few minutes later, catching her by surprise as the night's first stars became visible.

Emma hesitated. "I think they're watching Earth," she eventually replied. "But I don't see why they'd be watching *us*."

Again, Dan nodded very slightly. It wouldn't have bothered him if he knew they *were* watching him — there might even be a degree of comfort in it — but nor did he think there was any reason they would be.

In the past three hundred and sixty-four days, Dan McCarthy had experienced as much and as little contact with the Messengers as everyone else on Earth: none at all.

He hadn't had any dream-time visions, he hadn't made any sleep-walking trips to the cornfield at Stevenson Farm, and most happily of all he hadn't felt any searing pains in the back of his neck.

The neck scar where such pains had previously been felt, and which was initially brought about by the Messengers having twice physically connected a cable-like communications interface to Dan's person, was now almost completely invisible. There would have been no 'almost' if the scar hadn't been the focal point of so many of the occasionally invasive medical tests Dan still endured at the hands of government doctors every month, but to the best of his knowledge the doctors and analysts had never learned anything meaningful from their obsessive study of the scar.

The sound of a car pulling into the long driveway at the front of the house tore both Emma and Dan's eyes from the stars, but there was no concern in either of their expressions. Christophe, Timo's driver of many years, had left an hour ago to procure a pair of wireless headphones Emma had requested to replace the old ones that had quit on her the previous day. For security reasons she couldn't receive any deliveries at the house or leave the premises, as per Timo's cautious insistence, and Christophe was glad of having something to do.

"That'll be the headphones. Do you want to do day two of your goals thing?" Dan asked, referencing the decades-old personal development program Emma had found in Timo's media drawer. The ancient program was CD-based and could be played via the TV's Blu-ray player, which allowed her to listen without breaking the 'no personal devices' rule that was in place primarily to keep Contact Day related news at bay. The TV signal had also been disconnected at their request, so there was no scope for slip-ups even if curiosity got the better of her.

The headphone problem had prevented Emma from listening to the second seminar early in the morning like she had the previous day with the first, but she told Dan she would just write the day off and get back to it when morning came again.

She walked through the house and out to collect the new headphones from Christophe, who politely asked if that was all she needed for the night.

Emma always felt more than a little awkward being waited on like this — it was neither something she was used to nor something she particularly *wanted* to get used to — but Christophe was a personal friend of Timo as well as an employee, and he clearly enjoyed his job. This perhaps had something to do with the flat 100,000 euro salary Timo paid him despite only utilising his services for a month or two each year, and Christophe's level of salary was likely why he insistently refused to accept tips.

Emma warmly expressed her thanks and confirmed that she didn't need anything else, at which point Christophe turned the key to bring his limousine-like car back to life. A news reporter's voice blared through the open window, coming in mid-sentence:

"… know that tensions here in Buenos Aires were already extremely high, but the tone of these latest comments from Chinese Premier Ding Ziyang is likely to draw a firm response from Chairman Godfrey. At a time when the regular citizens of Earth are unified in relief and gratitude over what happened on that fateful day in Birchwood one year ago tomorrow, the political chasm between East and West appears to be reaching a point where, sooner rather than later, something really does have to give. For ACN Radio, this is Norman Holt."

"Forgive me, Ms Ford," Christophe said, shutting the radio off as though suddenly becoming aware he'd been listening only when the news report ended. "I know you have both been trying to stay away from all of this."

Having been similarly entranced, Emma blinked and exhaled sharply right after the report ended, regretting that she hadn't covered her ears or asked him to hit mute as soon as it began. "Not your fault," she said, smiling and waving him off before she walked back to Dan and the majestic lake view.

For Dan's sake, Emma kept the news report and its implications to herself. The imminence of Contact Day nevertheless made this night different to the two they'd enjoyed in Italy so far, with an unspoken understanding that each of them both did and didn't want to talk about it.

They opted not to, finding effective distraction in the enormous master bedroom.

Sometime after 2am, however, Emma accepted defeat in her battle to fall asleep over the ceaseless pondering of her mind. She got up, quietly enough not to wake Dan, and unpacked her new headphones.

The sight of the house's locked safe provided a challenging distraction, a siren call for her to check her phone — just once — to see exactly what was going on with China. The radio reporter's comment that tensions were high was an understatement if ever she'd heard one, and an escalation was the last thing the world needed.

But a promise to Dan was a promise she couldn't break, so her phone stayed where it was and she instead connected the wireless headphones to the TV and placed her CD inside the Blu-ray player. She poured a drink and stepped out into the mild Italian night, leaving the outside door open so Dan would immediately know where she was if he woke up concerned by her absence from the bedroom.

The energetic voice of her new favourite motivational guru quickly distracted Emma completely from all thoughts of Buenos Aires and Beijing, but the goal-setting workshop that began after a few minutes proved to be the most challenging she'd ever undertaken.

This was no real negative, though, only reflecting how many of Emma's old goals had been met and how many of her old dreams had come true. Even the section on wishes for friends and family wasn't easy, mainly since her sister Tara was now doing so well as a fashion designer having failed to push herself to fulfil her potential for so long. Emma eventually settled on the wishes for Tara to find some balance in her personal life and for Dan's father Henry to one day walk again; but even in the energised mental state she found herself, the latter seemed particularly unlikely to come true.

Even the one intention that Emma had never shared with anyone besides the paper she'd used during previous goal-setting sessions was now three years ahead of schedule having once looked distant: her intention to be happy in a committed relationship and ready for a child by the age of 35.

Emma smiled widely as she considered how far she'd come in recent years, and even more widely as she thought about how many happy years with Dan lay ahead.

The motivational guru continued on with some tips about the most energising foods and the benefits of nutritional planning, and Emma took keen notes whenever something struck her as a good idea.

But because her headphones so effectively blocked out all external noise, Emma didn't hear the sudden thud that came from Dan's bedroom.

She continued obliviously, jotting down new meal-plan ideas as they entered her mind.

And because her sun-lounger was facing the starlit lake rather than the house, she didn't see the shadows of the two tall figures opening the bedroom door and going inside to take him away…

V minus 98

Early in the Argentine evening, a long row of American news crews lined up in front of the huge GCC compound to shoot their live reports for the prime-time bulletins.

Many of them had stood on this very street multiple times in the past during the building's days as the headquarters of the similarly named Global Space Commission, but little else felt the same.

For unlike then, the GSC's successor organisation — headed once again by the United Kingdom's William Godfrey — was 'Global' in name only. Two particularly high-profile absentees, namely the governments of China and Russia, staunchly opposed the GCC's creation and had vowed upon its announcement that they would not stand idly by while certain Western leaders tried to unjustifiably position themselves as the default representatives of humanity as a whole.

The GCC's grand opening was set for the following day, and not by accident. Opening the doors on Contact Day made more sense than doing so at any other time, Godfrey insisted, and his key supporters agreed. Since that announcement, the Chinese and Russian governments had hastily announced plans of their own for a similar organisation to be known in English as the Earth Liaison Forum, and they dealt a blow to

Godfrey's aim of a smooth GSC-GCC transition by formally launching the ELF a week before the GCC's long-announced date.

The ELF's opening had been a grand spectacle, with an enormous parade and full red-carpet treatment for leaders of participating nations. No majorly surprising defections had occurred so far, but Cuba's presence at the ELF brought the organisation's reach far too close to American soil for President Slater's liking, and Godfrey was well aware that some other countries with tumultuous recent relationships with Western powers were also wavering.

Beijing's charm offensive included an open doors policy that welcomed states who were already members of the GCC, without insisting that they withdraw. GCC Chairman Godfrey, fully aware that they were trying to bait him into a similar concession, doubled down and insisted that any countries who formally recognised the ELF would be barred from the GCC. He was able to do this without fear given the unconditional support of the United States, owing to the enormous military and economic benefits its allies were loath to give up for the sake of abstract principles of international inclusion.

No one was foolish enough to think that the ELF's leaders were motivated by anything other than geopolitical concerns, in any event, and it did remain true that their nations' absence from the GCC table was through their own choice; Godfrey had repeatedly reaffirmed that no one had been unconditionally excluded from the GCC and that no one ever would be.

The crux of the split had been Godfrey's uncontested election as the new organisation's Chairman, a decision which most major Western leaders saw as a sensible way to ensure continuity following the disbandment of his Global Space Commission. Chinese and Russian officials, having felt very much like they were equal participants in the GSC's inner circle in name only during the Il Diavolo crisis, refused to participate on such terms.

Latent political divisions, never far beneath the surface, were once again on open display as two competing organisations now stood ready to present themselves as the sole legitimate point of diplomatic contact between humanity and all intelligent extraterrestrial races.

"Ding Ziyang's language reached a new level earlier today," a Canadian reporter spoke into his camera, raising his voice to ensure it came across clearly over the hubbub of a hundred others doing the same. "Particularly alarming was Ding's description of Chairman Godfrey's recommitment to the GCC's exclusion policy, and his insistence upon inaugurating the GCC on the anniversary of Contact Day, as *'two delib-*

erate acts of hostile and provocative Western aggression'. Tonight, a map of the world coloured to represent GCC-ELF divisions, like the one our viewers can see on their screens now, bears an all too familiar resemblance to the Cold War world my generation grew up in. This isn't what we wanted for our children, and the primary question you have to ask as night falls in Buenos Aires is a simple one: what must the Messengers make of all this?"

The reporter's cameraman outstretched his hand twice to indicate that he still had ten seconds left.

"And *then*," the reporter continued, ready to wrap it up, "then comes the question that naturally follows: if the Messengers ever make their return, where are they going to land? When the aliens are looking for our leader, where do they turn?"

Few expected to find an answer to these questions anytime soon, and *no one* expected that the Messengers' next intervention on Earth would come not in Buenos Aires or Beijing, but a small town in northern Italy.

V minus 97

Although Dan had never set foot in Buenos Aires, several of the city's landmarks were familiar to him from the countless news reports that had originated there since the fateful day when a supposedly alien sphere was discovered in the ocean off Miramar.

The sight in his dream, however, was all new.

He recognised the famous Gravesen signage on the building before him and thus knew that he was looking at one of the high-end chain's luxury hotels, but his knowledge of the surrounding area ended there.

Just as pertinently, he had no idea as to why he was there.

I'm not here, he thought. *It's just a dream.*

And then it hit him: he was lucid. It wasn't a dream at all.

Like only one prior occasion, when a vision of Lolo National Forest had prompted Dan to send Trey there to record an imminent happening that turned out to be an uncloaked alien craft's overhead flight, Dan was in full mental control of a dream-like first-person experience.

Frightened, excited and confused all at the same time, Dan endeavoured to look around for clues. He tried to focus his energy on finding out precisely what the Messengers were trying to tell him, rather than wondering why they were communicating with him again at all — and particularly in such a roundabout way.

Suddenly remembering the other element of his Lolo dream, Dan glanced at his wrist. He was wearing a basic digital watch, just like in real life, but its screen showed 11:15am above the following day's date.

He made a mental note of the time and date then resumed looking around for the main clue; for the main reason the Messengers were showing him this, however the hell they were doing it; and for some suggestion of what he was supposed to do when he woke up.

A deafening hail of gunfire coming from inside the building shut off Dan's thoughts in an instant, prompting a fight-or-flight rush of adrenaline to flood through his veins. He felt his heart pounding, sure that these sensations were genuinely physical ones, and took a step towards the building.

I'm not here for nothing, he told himself. *And besides, everyone knows you can't die in a dream… or a vision… or whatever the hell this is.*

Two employees from the reception desk emerged through the front door and sprinted past Dan without so much as a second glance. *"Run!"* one called.

And run he did — in the wrong direction.

An incongruously calm police officer intercepted Dan before he reached the door and told him in no uncertain terms that he had to retreat, not only for his own safety but to prevent the escalation of a developing situation which risked turning into a tragedy of a kind unseen in well over fifty years.

"What's going on in there?" Dan asked, addressing the officer directly and unsure whether any kind of reply would come, let alone a useful one.

"They've taken hostages," the officer said, settling that issue. "President Slater and the Japanese Prime Minister are surrounded."

Before Dan had any time to vocalise the obvious question of *who* had taken hostages, an all-too-familiar flag was unfurled from a window on the top floor of the hotel to answer it.

Jet black with a small blue circle at its centre, the flag was the calling card of the so-called *GeoSov* movement whose members rejected any kind of future contact with extraterrestrials and had already proven willing to engage in terroristic methods to forward their aims. This version of the flag had a conspicuous arrangement of dot-like white markings in one corner, not too unlike the constellations of stars seen on many national flags.

I can't die when I'm not really here, Dan thought to himself, sidestepping the officer and making a dash for the door. *I have to see exactly what's happen—*

As Dan reached the doorway and attempted to step across the threshold, he collapsed like he had been shot. His hands immediately grasped the back of his neck, trying desperately and violently to claw out something that wasn't there.

Just when the pain reached a crescendo and Dan felt a momentary sensation of passing out, he opened his eyes and saw the vast bedroom he had fallen asleep in a few hours earlier. He was lying on the floor and his neck hurt — it hurt like hell — but the worst of the pain was behind him. He weakly placed his hands on the bed and pulled himself to his feet, calling for Emma as he did so.

She didn't reply.

"This doesn't have to be difficult," a strong American voice boomed from the bedroom's doorway.

Dan froze in fear.

"If you come with us peacefu—"

"Emma!" Dan yelled, piercing the air with quite possibly the loudest sound he had ever made.

But sitting out by the pool, even with the external door open, she heard nothing beyond the motivational words pouring into her ears via her noise-cancelling wireless headphones. The commercial for the premium headphones promised that buyers would get what they paid for, and it now seemed as though Dan was about to pay for Emma's selection in the worst possible way.

He turned around and saw not one mountain of a man but two, neither of whom were wearing any badges or discernible uniforms. Their clothing was dark, with the light making it difficult to tell black from navy blue or perhaps even a deep grey, and their expressions were even darker.

Dan was standing now, lamenting his utter lack of apparent options rather than trying to choose between any. But just as had been the case in his remarkable dream-like vision a few moments earlier, Dan's mind was quickly made up by a harrowing development directly in front of him.

For beyond his two bedroom intruders, Dan saw a third man outside — moving straight towards Emma as she sat gazing out over the lake with her back to the danger that was rapidly coming her way.

Dan's legs drove him forward before his mind had any chance to point out that there were two hostile figures standing in the way, and one of the men roughly grabbed hold of him after only a few urgent steps.

Dan could only watch in helpless horror as the man outside reached Emma and put one hand over her mouth while unceremoniously forcing her from her sun-lounger with the other. Her headphones fell to the ground, bouncing to a watery death in the shimmering pool.

With his own ears having been uncovered all along, Dan heard Emma's muffled attempts to call his name only too well. In instinctive and protective reaction to the harrowing sound, he recklessly smashed his head into the nose of the man who had been holding him. The man let go, and Dan seized a momentary opportunity to firmly kick his colleague in the groin.

"I'm coming," he called, now free and desperate to reassure her. He proceeded as recklessly as he had in the dream, with no concrete plan of what exactly he would do when he reached the unflustered third man who was in the process of carrying her away.

It didn't even come to that.

Before Dan came face to face with the third intruder, a fourth tackled him from an unseen position and slammed him into the ground. The force of the impact between his head and the floor dazed Dan to the point of near unconsciousness. As he lay there helplessly, the only physical feeling he was aware of was the weight of the much larger man pinning him to the floor.

"What did they tell you?" asked the fourth intruder, releasing his weight and gently slapping Dan's face to try to bring him round. "What was the message?"

Dan's eyes opened wearily, with a distinct feeling circling in his aching head that they wouldn't be open for long. These men were very clearly not friends or allies of any kind, but the impending incident he had been warned of in the dream was so explosive and so time-sensitive that Dan's conscience was positively screaming for him to choke out the words.

He could only impotently watch through heavy eyelids as Emma, putting up a brave but futile fight, was carried past his fallen body towards the front door. Dan knew for certain at this point that whoever these men were, they were not to be trusted; if they were willing to be so needlessly rough with Emma now, there was no way he could safely expect them to return her unharmed if he volunteered the knowledge they so clearly wanted.

The knowledge granted to Dan in the dream-time message was the only leverage he had, and his scrambled mind wrestled with the uncomfortable possibility that this leverage was the only thing keeping the pair of them alive.

"Tell me!" the man demanded, anger crossing his face as he positioned a firm hand under Dan's chin and pressed against his throat. "What did they want you to know?"

As Dan McCarthy felt the darkness coming, he forced out one final sentence with as much energy as he could muster before slipping into unconsciousness: "I'll tell you fucking nothing."

V minus 96

"I wish *I* was in Italy," Tara Ford sighed, slowly spinning the base of an empty wine glass between her fingertips. "Henry, how come no one ever takes *me* to Italy?"

Clark McCarthy, gazing out of New Kergrillin' Bar & Grill towards the eerily quiet drive-in lot, was the only other person left at Tara's table. His father Henry and their friendly old neighbour Mr Byrd had long ago made a move to the restaurant section of New Kergrillin', enjoying the free leftovers from the expensive afternoon buffet that had been laid on for political and media dignitaries.

"You do know it's just been the two of us for the last hour, right?" Clark asked with a grin.

With New Kergrillin' closed to regular customers and no bar staff present, Clark had been on barman duties all night and could now see that it was time to cut Tara off. As a guest of honour at the pre-lockdown afternoon event, she had been on the free wine for almost six hours and had handled it well, all things considered, but enough was enough.

"Hey, don't blame me that you're starting to look like your old man," she replied with a wide grin of her own.

Clark let out a dry chuckle. "Well, I'd say you're starting to look like your big sister but that would be too much of a compliment since I know you're shooting for Emma every time you sit down in front of a mirror."

"You're lucky this glass is empty," Tara gasped, pretending to splash its long-gone contents in his face. Her heavy eyes fell closed for a second or two, until she caught them in the act and blinked herself awake.

"Do you want to call it a night?" Clark asked.

She shook her head. "The house is empty. Except for old Rooster, I mean. It's *people*-empty."

"Exactly; he'll be missing you. Come on, I'll get your coat."

"At least I know *he's* never gonna leave me for someone else," Tara mused, rising to her feet and walking steadily in the sensible shoes she'd chosen in experienced anticipation of how the night would end up.

Clark handed Tara her $600 coat and kept his thoughts on her last comment to himself. He cared about Tara, but it was difficult to make the same points over and over again without them sounding like lectures. Emma had tried countless times in the past few months, repeatedly telling Tara that any man who left someone else *for* her was certain to do the same *to* her at some point, but the trappings of success and her move to Colorado Springs had seen Tara fall into all-too-familiar patterns of excess. It had happened during her modelling days in New York and it was happening again now, with Emma and Dan at times struggling to keep her in check.

Clark had promised he'd keep an eye on Tara while they were in Italy, and he had stuck to his promise diligently.

It was like she was a different person at night, as Tara herself had put it, but she was yet to have the epiphany that the emptying of wine glasses had something to do with this.

Amid a rocky period in personal terms, Tara's career as a fashion designer was going better than ever, with each month breaking her previous sales record and each new line's success bringing her ever closer to full creative control. What had begun as a branding relationship following a short-lived but attention-grabbing modelling career was now a hands-on project for Tara, who while grateful that her sister's level of celebrity had helped her get a foot in the door was very pleased to be making a name for herself with something that stood alone.

A few weeks earlier, after one particularly messy night following a break-up that made waves in the online world of celebrity worship, Emma had invited Tara to come and stay in Birchwood for a while to gather her head and get back on top of things emotionally. Everyone agreed that some time in the relative tranquility of Birchwood would be good for her, and so far it had been.

This one night of blowing off steam wasn't going to do any harm, especially when she was out with Clark rather than the usual string of enablers and hangers-on who followed her around in the city, but it had clearly reached its natural end-point.

"Okay, we're heading home," Clark called to the only other three people inside the cavernous New Kergrillin', an alien-themed venture named in honour of the Messengers' unlocated home world known commonly as New Kerguelen.

The voice of its owner, Phil Norris, beckoned Clark into the restaurant area. "This shrimp ain't gonna keep and the three of us can't eat it all," he called. "You want to take a tub of it home?"

"Why did you order so much?" Clark called back.

"I thought rich guys loved shrimp," Phil replied. "Shows what I know, huh?!"

"All the cash you've made from this place," Clark said, "and you'll still never fit in with the old money. Can't buy class!"

Phil laughed. "Clark, if sliced cucumber and sparkling water is what passes for class these days, those assholes can keep it!"

V minus 95

"Dan McCarthy?" a disbelieving security officer spoke into his phone, sure he must have misheard. "You're bringing him *here*? Do we have clearance to—"

"This is under the radar," a far firmer voice replied down the phone. "Do you know what that means? Make sure the entrance is clear so no one sees us coming in. We can't ask for clearance without explaining how we know he's been contacted, so don't even *think* about taking this up the chain. Understood? If this goes wrong, it's *your* ass."

The line was dead before a reply could come.

V minus 94

Drive-In
Birchwood, Colorado

Already, shortly before midnight on the eve of Contact Day's first anniversary, as Clark stepped out of New Kergrillin' he could both see and hear signs of the unique day that lay ahead.

The drive-in lot itself was completely empty, falling squarely within a temporary lockdown zone instituted by local and federal law enforcement to prevent the dangerous levels of overcrowding that would have doubtlessly occurred if no such action had been taken. Having been the site of the Messengers' uncloaked landing a year earlier, the drive-in was *the* focal point of the world's attention.

The temporary lockdown extended beyond the town limits and was going to cost Phil Norris untold revenue in lost sales from not only New Kergrillin' but also the various independent stores that filled his U-shaped lot and kicked back a significant percentage of their profits in exchange for such sought-after positioning.

Phil couldn't be too upset, however, since in the aftermath of Contact Day he had feared that the entire lot would be seized by the government given its unparalleled significance. It had in fact only been out of commission for around two months, during which time all manner of tests were conducted in the key areas. These included the spot where the alien craft touched down, the lines where the Messengers placed force-field-like walkways to keep the awestruck crowd at bay, and the three distinct spots where Dan, Clark and an on-duty police officer had been involuntarily immobilised.

While the lot which had housed hundreds of media personnel during the days of the IDA leak and on several more occasions since then was now entirely empty, the media appetite to get as close as possible was stronger than ever. Inevitably, the edges of the curfew zone were now media encampments all of their own; and with only one way in and out of the small town, Birchwood felt somewhat like an area under siege.

Helicopters whirred in the distance and a general hubbub from one side of the curfew zone made its way into Clark's ears as he led Tara outside. He could understand why Dan and Emma had decided to get away from everything; things were crazy enough for the regular citizens of Birchwood, let alone the town's favourite son who had been under crushing pressure to formally endorse the GCC's position as the legitimate representative of humanity in any future contact scenarios.

Dan had been accused of selfishness by some who thought that his silence reflected his desire to position *himself* as humanity's continued point of interplanetary contact — an assessment that could hardly have been further from the truth — while others had leaned upon Richard Walker-era soundbites in accusing Dan of being a double-agent working secretly with Chinese and Russian officials to undermine the GCC.

Most fantastically of all were the supposedly serious suggestions that Dan may have been compromised by the aliens and used as something between an avatar and a puppet to forward their own machiavellian plans. This didn't hold up to a lot of scrutiny given that the Messengers had unconditionally saved Earth from cometary destruction, and most dismissed the memetically spread theory for what it was: an attention-seeking ploy by an anti-contact group of planetary isolationists known as the GeoSovs.

Any understanding of the GeoSov movement had to begin with an understanding of its predecessors who had come in the form of the so-called Antidotalists and Welcomers. The Antidotalists, now consigned to history, were a nihilistic eco-terrorist organisation who decried humanity as a scourge on Earth's fragile ecosystem and conducted deadly attacks on targets such as life-extension researchers and agricultural experts in an effort to keep humanity's numbers down. Rather than fade away, the Antidotalist movement had essentially morphed into the

Welcomer movement as a means of staying relevant following the discovery of Il Diavolo.

As the name suggested, the humanity-hating Welcomers actively *welcomed* the comet and did all they could to sabotage the GSC's defensive efforts. Their most famous attack came in Colorado Springs, where Emma Ford and Timo Fiore were seriously injured during a press conference officially scheduled to announce the latter's plan for a last-ditch effort to change the comet's course. Ever since the events of Contact Day, a hard core of Welcomers had once again rechristened themselves — this time as *GeoSovs*, pertaining to their view that the Earth should and must be sovereign and free from extraterrestrial intervention.

Some high-profile GeoSovs, all of whom consistently distanced themselves from violent attacks carried out in the group's name, were extremely well spoken and skilled in the art of personal marketing. TV stations, always looking for controversy, gave a platform for these individuals to share watered-down versions of their positions. Too often, the GeoSovs were allowed to come out of interviews and discussion panels looking like victims whose views were being unfairly dismissed by a corporate elite who they claimed couldn't be trusted not to sell humanity down the river.

Much had been written in discerning publications about the fact that the GeoSov movement had somehow managed to whitewash its past, what with the Antidotalists' calls for forced depopulation and the Welcomers' attempts to doom humanity having apparently been relegated to mere footnotes in the mainstream media now that future contact was the topic of hot debate, but few people read such articles. For the vast majority who got their information from TV news and social media channels — where the highest-profile GeoSovs were particularly effective at gaining attention among the young — there wasn't necessarily an automatic mental connection between the GeoSovs and their direct predecessors.

Every attack blamed on the GeoSovs was held up by the group's leaders as *"yet another false flag operation"* designed to discredit their innocent goal of keeping Earth free from alien intervention. The language of false flags and shadowy elites was more effective than ever after everything that had happened in the past few years, given that Dan McCarthy had fought against an often hostile media and ultimately exposed a meta-conspiracy so grand that no one could ever have believed it without seeing the truth with their own eyes.

In a world where the entire planet could fall for an alien-related hoax which ultimately came true, the GeoSov movement understood that presenting itself as an underdog in a battle against the ill-defined *"powers that be"* was the key to winning hearts and minds.

Serious commentators who wrestled with the question of what exactly the GeoSovs' endgame might be came up short of finding an answer. Like the flat-Earth theory which had recently seen an unexpected revival that baffled experts in related fields, no one could be sure whether the mouthpieces of the GeoSov movement truly believed what they were saying or if they were knowingly and skilfully deceiving a cohort of citizens ready to believe anything that contradicted the so-called establishment position.

Each conspiracy theory that came true made the ground more fertile for the next; and ever since the biggest one of all was *decisively* proven real on Contact Day, a new favourite was that future contact with the Messengers would occur to the detriment of everyday humans and benefit only the same elites who had lied about so much for so long.

Dan had been relentlessly baited by the GeoSovs for months, keeping quiet largely because he knew it was impossible to win an argument with people who didn't care about the truth. But the more airtime the GeoSovs received and the more they called Dan out, the more it weighed on his shoulders.

His continued popularity among the general public remained unquestioned, but his silence over two particular accusations was beginning to raise questions. The first of these was that he was secretly working as an intermediary between the Messengers and the political elites he had once persistently claimed to despise. The second, and even more fanciful, held that the reason he was no longer vocally standing up for common people's interests was that his body and mind had been taken over by the Messengers during their physical contact a year earlier. Dan saw this second accusation for what it was: a way for the GeoSovs to reliably secure the kind of mocking responses they needed to fuel and sustain their ridicule-based victim mentality.

It was all so convoluted and, as far as Dan could tell, so utterly pointless. The whole GeoSov issue didn't make sense however he looked at it, so he tried not to think about it too often.

Clark, meanwhile, had long thought that the media was playing a dangerous game in presenting certain GeoSovs as serious commentators or figures of fun at worst, and much of the pre-anniversary preparations he had been involved in with his colleagues at the police precinct focused on ensuring that no GeoSov-backed attacks would derail any anniversary celebrations.

Clark's role in the police force kept his mind occupied and was welcomed by all; the presence of someone so well liked by the public helped with community relations, even around Birchwood where such things didn't tend to be problematic.

Tonight, however, not even the good citizens of Birchwood itself would be allowed near the drive-in once 4am rolled around and the security operation shifted into maximum gear. Clark took a long look around the lot before he got into his car, stone cold sober. Tara climbed into the passenger seat.

"What's the hold up?" she asked, tired and cold.

Clark looked across to the far side of the lot, remembering the landing like it was yesterday. He would never forget the fear of being frozen on the spot as the Messengers inserted a sharp communications cable into Dan's neck and he would never forget the relief that flooded through his veins when they left and Dan was okay. The next relief that had come with the confirmation that they had diverted Il Diavolo's path was like nothing Clark could ever have imagined, so total in its calming effect over his nervous system, and after all of that he was fresh out of ideas as to how anyone could *possibly* question the Messengers' motives, much less his brother's.

Dan had been through too much, and Clark sometimes wondered why the Messengers didn't just come back and put everything straight. He knew there was no reason to believe they would care about something as socially constructed as an anniversary celebration, but he allowed a small part of himself to hope that they just might show up again — that they just might show up to tell the GeoSovs to fuck off, to tell the GCC and ELF nations to stop their dick-measuring contest and get around a single table, and to tell Dan that they could and would reach out to him again if they ever had to do so.

That final point was one that kept Dan up at night, out of fear that the invasive government tests he and Emma underwent every month might have damaged whatever it was that made their necks hurt when the Messengers were close and wanted to communicate.

Dan knew better than anyone how committed the Messengers and their mysterious Elders were to the principle of 'minimal necessary intervention', and it concerned him greatly that another public appearance might be considered too major and destabilising an intervention given the growing divisions between East and West. With fading confidence that more discreet contact would still be possible after his neck had been invasively tested so often, Dan's mood often dropped danger-ously when he considered this for too long.

The vast majority of the world idolised Dan McCarthy, but Clark didn't envy his life for a single second.

"Clark," Tara called, "you told me we were going home..."

He looked in at her shivering in the front seat and realised how long he had been ponderously staring across the vacant lot. "Sorry," he said, getting in without further ado and immediately handing her his jacket to cover her legs beyond the point where her own coat stopped.

"Such a gentleman," she said, gladly accepting it.

Clark laughed as he turned the ignition. "I've been called a lot of things, sweetheart..."

"Me too, but no one ever calls me sweetheart."

Clark glanced sideways and saw Tara looking at him quite intently. "Then I guess we'll call it quits," he said. "And remember, I'll come next door tomorrow morning and then we're gonna stay inside all day, until the anniversary is over and everything is back to normal. Do you want me to let myself in if you're still asleep?"

"I want you to stay with me tonight," Tara said, very straight-forwardly.

"Uh..."

"In a different bed, obviously," she added quickly. "I'm in the spare room so you could have theirs or the couch. It's just, I'm really not built to be on my own, Clark — even when things are okay. But lately they're not... lately I'm not doing so good. I went to a doctor and he gave me—"

"I'll stay," Clark interrupted. "You don't need to tell me anything else. You *can*, but you don't need to."

"Thanks," Tara said, a small and unusually insecure smile briefly crossing her lips. Ironically, given that she was wrapped up in two coats and most of her appearance was hidden by the low light, she somehow looked far more exposed in Clark's eyes than was normally the case. He knew her well, *way* beyond the caricature of the always smiling and ultra-successful fashion designer cum media darling that the public saw when they looked at her, but he had never seen her seem so... vulnerable.

"Just remember that *no one* is built for the lives we live," he said, "and especially yours. This media attention isn't normal. The secret we had to live with last year wasn't normal. Being Emma's sister isn't normal, and neither is being Dan's brother. They get back in a few days but even before then, you're not on your own, okay? We've got Mr Byrd, my dad, Phil… and that's just right here in Birchwood. People are with us all across the world."

"Don't forget we've got each other, too," she said, almost inflecting it into a question.

"Always," Clark nodded, his voice firm. "Wherever this ride takes us, we're in it together."

V minus 93

CASERMA FLORENZI
MILAN, ITALY

Dan McCarthy didn't know where he was or how long he had been unconscious from the concussive effect of a rough tackle to the ground. All he knew was that as he looked around the nondescript office in which he had been placed, none of the several faces he saw were Emma's.

"What did they tell you?" a man asked when he saw Dan's eyes opening at last, his voice familiar. His nose was covered in a thin bandage, stained by the blood Dan had drawn with a well-placed headbutt.

The other men were all dressed similarly and all but one appeared to be in their late twenties or thirties. The exception, less burly and clearly a few decades older, waved a hand to silence his younger colleagues.

"I know you must have a head full of questions, Mr McCarthy," the older man said, "and I want to begin with an apology for how things turned out at the lake house. My name is Frank Livingston and I work for an agency of the United States federal government. We're currently sitting in a US military installation called Caserma Florenzi, which was the closest secure site we could utilise for this important meeting."

"Meeting?" Dan echoed, disdain and incredulity dripping from his voice in equal measure. "You're going to pretend you called me in here for a meeting instead of abducting me for whatever the hell this really is?"

"Mr McCarthy, the—"

"I'll talk just as soon as Emma is here and just as soon as these assholes are gone," Dan interrupted, glaring at the other men who had been party to the aggressive home intrusion that landed him here. "The only thing I'm telling you now is that when you finally do what I say and your bosses find out what I know — and when they find out what my knowledge can *prevent* — they're going to hope you've been treating me well. And trust me when I tell you that President Slater will have a particular interest in this."

"Ms Ford is perfectly safe and unharmed," Frank insisted. "She's only a few rooms away and is currently being questioned in a very friendly manner."

Dan couldn't contain a reactive snicker. "Listen, Frank... if that's even your real name. We can sit here and lie to each other for as long as you want, but I'm saying nothing until Emma is sitting next to me and your goons are gone. And even then, I'm not telling *you* anything. I'll talk to President Slater and I'll talk to Harris, but I'm not talking about this with anyone I don't know."

"That's not how this works," Frank said, trying to maintain a non-confrontational and sympathetic tone. "Dan, if I can call you Dan...?"

Dan threw his hands up in an uncaring shrug.

"Well, *Dan*, I don't have a direct line to President Slater and I'm not sure which Harris you're referring to."

"The Harris who showed me around the research base on Contact Day," Dan expanded, fairly confident that Frank's ignorance was an act. "Who else? The Harris I've seen every month since then for my medical checks. You know, those invasive government tests I *voluntarily* undergo every single month?" Dan glared at the younger men in the room — his captors, as he couldn't help but see them.

Frank nodded slowly in understanding. "Ah, *that* Harris. Again, Dan, I wouldn't know how to reach him even if that was an option. As you can imagine, in his line of work a high degree of secrecy is—"

"Michael Joseph Harrison," Dan announced robotically, as though reading from a cue card. "Resident of 1644 Jade Terrace, Santa Fe, along with his wife Susan and their two children, Layla and Owen. Born June 16th 1970, graduated from—"

"Enough," Frank boomed, flustered for the first time and returning the interruption with more than a hint of concern creeping through his forceful tone.

"*Is* it? So you don't care that I know where he works? You don't care that I know he took me to the secret underground base at Heron Lake, the one that *no one* is supposed to know about? With the greatest respect, Mr Livingston, I can't tell you too much more without knowing exactly what level of clearance you have, but I *can* tell you the facility is located at latitude thirty-six point sev—"

"All of you out," Frank interrupted once more, even more forcefully than before and this time facing his younger colleagues as he delivered the order. As soon as the room emptied, a look of new-found intensity crossed Frank's face. He balled his fists and pressed them into the table, staring intently at Dan. "And *you*. No more games, McCarthy. I tried to be nice about this..."

Although his heart felt like it was fixing to jump out of his chest, Dan fought to maintain an air of detached composure. He drew upon memories of the hostile crowds and questioners he had faced in the past, from Marco Magnifico to Joe Crabbe, and remembered all the times Emma had impressed upon him the importance of conveying strength even if strong was the last thing he felt.

Affecting nonchalance, Dan pushed his chair backwards, crossed his arms, and placed his feet on the table.

"Who the fuck do you think you are?" Frank yelled.

Dan uncrossed his arms then put his right hand behind his back and into the waistband of his underwear, delicately unclipping something. The item he produced look like a tiny piece of individually wrapped candy. He wasted no time in unwrapping it to reveal a blue capsule.

"I'm the guy who the Messengers just warned about what the GeoSovs are going to do tomorrow," he said, holding the capsule an inch from his lips and keeping his shaky voice as assertive as he could. "And if you don't bring me my fiancée right now, there's going to be nothing anyone can do to stop it. This isn't a negotiation, *Frank*. You give me what I want or I give you nothing — that's what this is. But tell me... how much blood can those hands of yours take?"

Frank stood up straight and narrowed his eyes, as though studying Dan for telltale signs of a bluff. There were none. "Take that away from your mouth," Frank said. "I'll bring her in."

Dan lowered his legs from the table but kept the capsule right beside his mouth, actually moving it slightly closer to emphasise the point that he wasn't going to cooperate until Emma was safely at his side. He glanced at his watch. "The clock's ticking..."

Without another word, Frank left the room. He didn't slam the door or look back in anger, but his frustration was evident.

Alone in the office, Dan placed the small blue capsule into his pocket for safe keeping.

Rather than cyanide, as Frank had apparently and understandably assumed, the capsule in fact contained a tiny state-of-the-art tracking device; and if Dan ever had cause to bite into it, an emergency notification would reach his brother Clark's phone to reveal his exact location.

There was a spare still attached to his waistband, just in case one was ever unclipped by accident, and thinking about this led him to remove the first from his pocket and gaze at it more pensively than ever.

Despite Frank's claim that they were at 'Caserma Florenzi', Dan couldn't truly be sure where he was and he certainly couldn't be sure what was going to happen next.

Hearing footsteps approaching the door — it was impossible to tell whether there were two feet or four — Dan placed the capsule between his molars and crunched. He immediately spat it out and saw that it had opened successfully, exposing the tiny and now-activated tracker.

He put the tracker back in his pocket and sat up straight, as ready as he'd ever be for whatever was coming next.

V minus 92

"Against their will?" President Slater barked incredulously into her phone, which had been handed to her at 40,000 feet by a trusted aide as she made her way to Buenos Aires. "I don't care how you know he was contacted! I care that you *took* them, using force, and now you're wasting time asking my permission to reunite them! *Of course* reunite them, you stupid…"

Slater trailed off, leaning forward and pinching the bridge of her nose between her thumb and forefinger. It was proving difficult to stop her mind from jumping into worst-case scenarios of what could happen next when the world found out that federal agents were treating Dan McCarthy and Emma Ford like criminals, but that was just one of many problems raised by the news she'd just received.

If Dan really had been contacted again, particularly on the eve of worldwide Contact Day anniversary celebrations and the GCC's inauguration gala, the list of the kinds of disruptive and destabilising events that might follow was almost endless.

Much, of course, depended on the nature of the message he had received; if his insinuation that its content was related to an imminent

GeoSov attack turned out to be true, she very much wanted to hear all about it.

There was however no doubt in Slater's mind that Dan would have shared it voluntarily — despite their differences in the past, he had never been one to act out of spite — and that only made things more frustrating.

The reckless actions of the agents who seized Dan and Emma angered her immensely, since this was one issue that could have been easily avoided. And without knowing *exactly* what the supposedly GeoSov-related message pertained to, she quietly hoped that *it* would prove easy to deal with, too.

In a matter of hours she would be on the ground with William Godfrey, and the scope of their discussions was clearly no longer going to be limited to the topic of how to best navigate the growing war of words between Buenos Aires and Beijing.

Every little development that painted the United States in a bad light gave ELF nations another stick with which to beat the GCC, but a development like this was unprecedented. If news got out that the Messengers had reached out to Dan McCarthy and that American agents had violently seized him before he could tell another soul, the time for words would be gone. As President Slater knew only too well, the time for protests and quite likely riots would be upon her... and that was without even thinking about the reputational damage such a story would deal to the GCC and all of the geopolitical ramifications that came with that.

"I don't need you making my life any more difficult than it already is," Slater said, "so just give Dan exactly what he wants, record exactly what he tells you, and give me a report immediately. Emma isn't stupid and we know they don't want any public attention; this situation doesn't have to get any worse, and it doesn't have to get out. And before you question the two of them together, bring some Italian personnel into the room. I don't want this mess being all about us, understood?"

The man on the other end of the line, Frank Something-or-other, confirmed his understanding and launched into a bumbling apology for the way things had been handled so far, but Slater hung up midway through it.

Why tonight?, she lamented internally. *Of all the goddamn nights... why did it have to be this one?*

V minus 91

Emma ran into Dan's arms as soon as the door swung open, giving him no time to meet her halfway or do anything except smile at the confirmation that she was okay.

"Is it true?" she asked him, running a gentle finger over the back of his neck. "They're back?"

"Close enough to send me a message," he said. "It was the dream kind, like when I saw the triangle that led back to Lolo."

Emma turned towards Frank, the only stranger present other than a junior-looking Italian officer of some kind who looked greatly out of his depth. Immediately, Frank closed the door.

"You're going to ask how we knew," he began, "so I'll save everyone a few minutes and tell you that a small device was implanted in Dan's neck during one of his monthly tests back home. It was designed to alert us to any unusual sensations of pain... in other words, it was designed to immediately alert us to any contact events."

"You put something *inside* me?" Dan asked, enraged at the violation.

Frank nodded curtly. "And it worked."

"But when I woke up, your goons were there," Dan went on.

37

"*Instantly.* Have there been agents hiding outside my house every night, all this time, in case the Messengers contacted me again?"

Emma was shaking her head, disgusted at the thought of how closely they had evidently been surveilled.

"We've been monitoring you for your own good!" Frank replied, raising his voice. "Dan, like it or not, your safety is a national security priority. We can't allow you to fall into the wrong hands, and we can't allow you to do anything that might lead you into trouble. Sleepwalking, venturing into cornfields in the middle of the night... as our established point of contact, your wellbeing is *extremely* important to us."

"And who exactly is '*us*'?" Dan blasted. "The US? The GCC? Because something tells me your bosses won't be calling Ding anytime soon to tell him the Messengers are back. Something tells me that *my* interests aren't really what you care about here. You know, there's a reason the Messengers go through me: because they don't trust any of you! And why would they? *I* don't trust any of you *Men In Black* wannabes, and we're not just the same species and the same nationality — my taxes pay your damn salaries!"

Frank shrugged. "What do you want me to tell you? That the content of your communications with the Messengers, one-way or two-way, *isn't* an important national security issue? We're all adults here, Dan, so let's be real about this."

"So what about me?" Emma asked. "Do I have one of these pain-tracking chips in *my* neck? Let's be real about that."

"You do," the man admitted.

Emma looked squarely at Dan. "Tell him nothing. Until these microchip implants are out, tell him nothing."

"Does Harris know about the implants?" Dan asked, surprising even himself by caring.

"No," Frank said. "As your personal liaison, he knew no more than necessary about anything. But speaking of Harris, how did you know so much about him? He can't have told you any of it, and I'm sure you understand the security implic—"

"Stop changing the subject," Dan interrupted. The real answer was relatively mundane — he had covertly placed a tracking chip on the collar of Harris's blazer during one of their monthly meetings in Colorado, and before long it very straightforwardly showed Dan the location of the man's suburban home and top-secret workplace. There was a hint of hypocrisy in the fact that Dan had tracked Harris's movements but would have felt betrayed if Harris had been party to the reverse process, but no one could deny that attaching a basic tracker to a piece of clothing was a world away from medically inserting a pain-measuring device beneath an unknowing target's skin.

And mundane or not, Dan wasn't giving Frank any answers.

"Bring me a phone so I can call Timo and find a doctor he trusts to get these things out of our necks," Emma said. "Because we're serious: until they're out, Dan's telling you nothing."

Dan gulped and pulled her in close, whispering as quietly as he could that the message was very time-sensitive and had to reach President Slater as soon as possible.

"Forget Timo for now," Emma decided, aiming the words at Frank. "Get Slater on the line. Dan will talk to her."

After five minutes that felt like fifty, Frank returned once more with a phone in his hand. Dan had told Emma nothing in the interim, understanding that sharing the content of his dream would have risked making her a target for some potentially questionable interrogation methods.

Dan looked at Emma as Frank held the phone out, as though asking if she would mind doing the first of the talking.

She took the phone. "Hello?"

"Ah, *Emma*," President Slater said, slightly surprised. The two weren't on the friendliest of terms given everything that had happened in the last few years, including a few tense stand-offs and a fruitless midnight raid on Dan's home that still had Slater in his family's bad books, but Emma could see why 'Ms Ford' might have felt overly formal.

"First of all," Slater continued, "let me apologise for what you've been put through. The first I heard about any of this was when I received a call asking if Dan's request to have you by his side could be granted. I didn't authorise any of this."

"Did you authorise the chips they put in our necks?" Emma asked. "Or the twenty-four-hour surveillance we've been under for the past year?"

"I do know that you've been under close surveillance, but at no point did I sign off on sub-dermal implants to track your pain levels. I learned of those implants during the phone call I just mentioned, when I asked how the agents could be absolutely sure Dan really had received a message. But Emma, you know better than anyone that I don't make every decision at every level. I apologise again for how this has been handled, but as for what we can control right now, I gather Dan wants to tell me something?"

"He does," Emma said, taking the apology for what it was worth but seeing no need to acknowledge it. "But would you mind telling Frank and his friend to give us the room?"

Frank scoffed at the notion and shook his head in disbelief. But when Emma handed him the phone, his expression quickly confirmed that the unwanted order had indeed come. He didn't argue, clearly and understandably less used to dealing directly with the President of the United States than Emma had become in recent years. He left the phone on the desk and sulked out of the room with the bewildered Italian officer he'd brought along to ensure some form of international presence as per Slater's earlier order.

Dan looked at the phone for a few seconds before picking it up, then wasted no more time in getting to the point. "I would have told you this right away if those guys hadn't taken me like they did," he began, "because this is the most urgent message I've ever gotten."

Emma stood anxiously beside Dan, currently as unaware as Slater of what he was going to say next.

"Are you in Buenos Aires yet?" he asked.

"Almost," Slater replied. "Why?"

"Will you be staying at the Gravesen?"

"No…"

Dan hesitated, more than a little surprised by this. "Uh, well, are you scheduled to be there tomorrow morning at eleven?"

"How do you know that?" Slater asked, an automatic question to which she already knew the answer.

"And you're supposed to be meeting with the Japanese Prime Minister, right?"

The sound of President Slater gulping came through the phone. No verbal reply was needed.

"Listen to me," Dan implored. "If you go to that meeting, you'll be taken hostage by the GeoSovs. I don't know how in the hell they're going to pull it off, but they are. And they'll unfurl a huge flag from a window on the top floor, on the right as you look up from outside. That's all I know. It came to me in a dream — or I should say the Messengers *showed* it to me in a dream — and when I tried to run into the hotel, the pain got so strong that it woke me up and knocked me out of bed. Before I could make sense of anything, your goons grabbed hold of me and—"

"They're not *my* goons," Slater said, her voice far hollower than

40

usual. "But Dan... thank you for sharing this. I'll see to it that your implants are removed whenever is convenient for you. We both know that you can't go back to leading a normal life, but please don't be under any illusions that I think things have been handled acceptably so far. I'll also let you know what our security services find during the full sweep of the Gravesen that I'm about to order. Would you like us to arrange a flight, or do you want to stay for the rest of your week in Italy?"

"We can't stay here after this," Dan said, "but after what just happened I'd rather get Timo's staff to arrange a flight with a pilot I trust. Thanks all the same."

"Very well. Thank *you*, Dan, and please know that I'm sorry for all of this. Before you go, could you pass me over to Emma for a second?"

Dan handed the phone to Emma and gazed at the wall in a fuzzy kind of overwhelmed relief. He had gotten the message across to the person who needed to hear it most, but he would never get used to the fact that he was in a position to be conversing directly with President Slater. He didn't *like* her — he couldn't like someone who had ordered a raid on his home during his last stay in Italy — but in recent times he had come to *dislike* her a lot less than was once the case.

And Slater's tone, one of something like fearful gratitude, added a very human element to a woman whose position often made her seem untouchably detached from the real world of feelings and vulnerability. Her final direct apology, the '*I'm sorry*' rather than the previous dancing-around-the-words attempts to express regret for the actions of others, hit Dan particularly hard. He was never going to *not* tell Slater that her life was in danger, but he now felt a surprisingly warm gladness that he had.

"Of course he understands that," Emma spoke into the phone, rolling her eyes as Dan watched on. "Yep... okay... obviously. So you'll let us know what happens with the sweep of the hotel and you'll definitely make sure none of these ground agents bother us again? Uh-huh? Good. Well, just stay safe, okay? The last thing the world needs right now is something happening to you."

Emma walked to the door and opened it, handing the phone to Frank before closing it again and returning to Dan.

"What was the part about me understanding something?" he asked.

"She just wanted to make sure we know that this has to stay quiet. For now, *all* of it; even the fact that the Messengers are close. At least until tomorrow passes without any trouble, that has to stay between us. And the part about the planned hostage-taking... I think that one's going to be a *forever* kind of secret, okay?"

"I've kept bigger secrets than that," Dan said, grinning slightly despite the gravity of the topic.

Frank burst back into the room a few seconds later, evidently frustrated at having been kept out of the loop but with no choice but to obey a direct order from his commander-in-chief. "I'll take you back to Fiore's place," he sighed.

"Sure thing," Dan said.

Frank held the door open as they exited the room. "Am I *ever* going to find out what the Messengers told you tonight, or is this the kind of thing I should hope to never hear about again?"

"The second one," Emma said.

Frank glanced between them, as though seeking a second opinion.

"What she said," Dan confirmed. "On this one, no news is good news."

FRIDAY

V minus 90

More than anger, more than resentment, and more than indignation, the overwhelming emotion in Dan McCarthy's mind was relief. Having watched Emma being roughly dragged away by a then-mysterious stranger just hours earlier, he counted his lucky stars as he now watched her sleeping soundly in Timo Fiore's private jet.

They had flown this exact route once before, with Clark, immediately after the sphere had been found off Miramar to seal the deal for a hoax Dan had fallen for and inadvertently sold to the rest of the world. The lie had long since come true, what with Dan ultimately admitting he had been duped by Richard Walker but later being contacted by the real Messengers. Best of all, those real Messengers' well-timed public arrival on Contact Day had gone on to convince the world beyond any doubt that he was telling the truth and had never deliberately misled anyone.

It all felt so long ago… or at least it *had*. Until his dream-like vision of President Slater being taken hostage, thoughts of Kerguelen and Miramar and Lolo were beginning to feel like distant memories. There was the hostile attention from idiotic GeoSovs and the far more common adoration from everyone else, but in Dan's internal and domestic lives, at least, things had been returning to something approaching normality.

But the vision changed everything; and even though the resultant run-in with shadowy federal agents left a sour taste in Dan's mouth, that vision was all he could think about. That the GeoSovs would try something on the Contact Day anniversary came as no surprise, particularly when Godfrey had opted to formally launch the Global Contact Commission on that very day. Dan didn't want President Slater to get hurt — out of basic human compassion as well as a rational fear of the chaos that would follow the worst-case scenario of her political assassination — and he was relieved to have been able to warn her in time.

What he was even more relieved by, however, was that the Messengers had been able to warn *him* in time. His fears over the continued viability of whatever it was in his neck that made him receptive to the Messengers' interventions had been eased, despite his concerns over the invasiveness of his monthly medical tests having been proven well-founded with the revelation that government doctors had indeed planted a chip of their own under his skin.

Along with Dan's relief that the Messengers had *managed* to contact him sat the perhaps even greater relief that they had *wanted* to. They were still keeping an eye on Earth, quite clearly, and were still willing to intervene when the likely consequences of not doing so were deemed sufficiently destabilising. In human political terms it didn't get much more destabilising than the potential assassination of a sitting US President, and the timing would have amplified things even further.

A huge part of Dan wanted to see the Messengers again and ask them the million questions that still filled his mind, but the rational part of his brain reminded him that any such meeting would only come as a result of a necessary intervention; and since any earthly development that might provoke another intervention would likely be anything but positive, he considered it unwise to wish too hard that he would see his extraterrestrial friends in the flesh again anytime soon.

A phone call came in from Clark well into the flight, so much later than expected that Dan initially didn't understand why he sounded so concerned. As soon as Clark mentioned the emergency tracker showing Dan's location at the time of its activation as a military complex in Milan, the memory came back.

Dan downplayed the issue for now; Clark would hear everything, of course, but there was no sense in angering him with it yet. An equal consideration in Dan's mind was that this had to stay quiet for the sake of national security and international stability, and that the validity of these kinds of abstract reasons wouldn't be as easy to impress upon Clark over the phone as they would be in person.

When Clark asked what the hell Dan had been doing at a military complex in the middle of the night, all Dan could do was say it was a long story he would tell when he got home but that there was nothing to worry about in the meantime. He likewise explained that the decision to come home early hadn't been made because of any major problem, but because of something that was happening in Buenos Aires that he didn't want to talk about right now.

When Clark pushed for details, Dan changed the subject by lamenting how useless Clark would have been if there *had* been something to worry about, since it had taken him several hours to look at his damn phone and see the emergency location update.

Dan ended the call by asking how Tara was, knowing she'd been going through a rough time but having been out of touch with the world for several days. Clark said she was sound asleep at home and doing fine; he neglected to mention that he was there too, watching late-night TV on the couch while she slept in the bedroom.

Keeping the full story from Clark — for now — brought into Dan's focus the broader point that the whole episode would be kept quiet by the countless people who were going to need to know about it. Frank Livingston and his young colleagues in Italy already knew about the contact event, while all of the security staff involved in the full sweep at the Buenos Aires Gravesen would clearly have to know what they were looking for, if not necessarily why.

The news of a foiled hostage-taking plot against President Slater was never going to see the light of day for obvious reasons, however, much less the news of direct alien involvement in its foiling.

Dan, contemplative in his high-altitude solitude while Emma caught up on some sleep, considered that this point confirmed his old deeply held belief once and for all: the government really *could* have covered up alien contact or visitation, had they found out about it before he broke the story.

After all, he thought, *that's exactly what they're doing now!*

V minus 89

Ford Residence
Birchwood, Colorado

"You okay?" Clark groaned, yawning halfway to life after being roused by Tara opening and closing doors. He looked across the living room and saw her leaving the kitchen with a ludicrously over-filled glass of red wine.

"Just thirsty," she said, a slight but somehow uncertain grin on her face.

At least she was drinking it from a glass rather than the bottle, Clark thought to himself, and she wasn't trying to hide it. Despite these rationalisations, though, when taken alongside everything else he'd seen in recent days this was still far from a soothing sight.

"You gonna tell on me?" Tara asked, as though trying to mask a serious question with a mocking tone.

"Just try to get some sleep, okay?"

"I remember when you were fun, you know."

Sitting up straight, Clark pointed at her as she carried the glass into her bedroom. "If you can look in a mirror and tell yourself that's fun, we've got less in common than I thought."

Tara turned away and re-entered her bedroom, slamming the door behind her.

Clark shook his head at the ceiling and tried to get comfortable again.

Emma and Dan couldn't get home soon enough.

V minus 88

Private Jet
Milan to Denver

Sleep would come to Dan eventually — this was an inevitability during a long flight which followed a night as restless as the one he'd just endured — but not before he caught the last few minutes of a special ACN report on William Godfrey's imminent return to a position of unmatched political power.

The resolute Englishman, former Chairman of both the Global Shield Commission and Global *Space* Commission, was unquestionably the greatest political survivor since the late Richard Walker. Just like Walker had repurposed his Interspace Defense Agency to keep up with changing times, Godfrey had succeeded in repurposing himself as the obvious candidate for a leadership role in three successive supranational organisations.

The Global Contact Commission, in one sense, was smaller than its predecessors. It was certainly true that a significant portion of the world had aligned with the China-led Earth Liaison Forum rather than the predominantly Western GCC, and Godfrey made no attempt to pretend otherwise. In another sense, however, this element of competition made his role at the GCC the most important of his life. For just like a country, a planet could have no more than one true leader. Godfrey considered it his calling to represent Earth in any future contact scenarios, and he had never before been more determined to win a bloodless war than he was to win his stand-off with Beijing.

Emboldened by the economic, military and cultural strength of his GCC's unwavering core members in the shape of the United States, United Kingdom, European Union and Japan, William Godfrey would stop at nothing to see the ELF fall and Ding Ziyang come crawling for a seat at the GCC's table in Buenos Aires.

The special report closed with a replay of a speech Godfrey had made mere months earlier while contesting a leadership election with his arch rival Diane Logan, prior to the idea of the GCC first being floated and back when his immediate focus was regaining his position as Prime Minister after the GSC's collapse. Godfrey won that particular contest at a canter, surprising no one given the gravitas that came with his worldwide prominence in recent years, but it had since been claimed that he knew he would be quitting almost as soon as he stepped back inside Number Ten.

He had known about the international plans for the GCC and had known he would be asked to lead it, this highly plausible theory held, and his participation in the leadership election was a message to the wings of his party who remained loyal to Logan or, even worse, to the risible John Cole.

Cole, Godfrey's handpicked successor when he first stepped down as PM to lead the Global Shield Commission, had resigned in disgrace following uproar at his self-serving decision to leak news of Il Diavolo's collision course with Earth. His hand had been forced by Godfrey's calculated decision to expel his own nation from the rechristened Global *Space* Commission; few survived making it onto Godfrey's bad side, and Cole's political career appeared to be completely over. The last Godfrey had heard, he was somewhere in Africa or the Middle East using the weight of his former office to cash-in on the desperation of political and business leaders seeking to add an air of Western legitimacy to whatever projects needed it most.

Dan hadn't previously seen or heard anything about the supposedly famous Godfrey speech that was about to air — he did his best to stay away from politics, year round — so he thought he might as well pay full attention given that he had nothing else to do and his mind was already firmly back on the GCC-ELF stand-off. If this speech was as relevant to current events as the introduction suggested, it was sure to be interesting.

The speech, given in the House of Commons, began with Godfrey launching a seemingly petty attack on his rival for wearing workmen's clothes during a recent photo op at a building site. Plenty of other British politicians had frequently done similar things in the past and most saw it as a transparent but essential effort to present an 'all in this together' kind of message.

On this occasion, however, Godfrey had pulled no punches in his own evaluation of the incident.

"The men and women on that building site are from a completely different world than Diane Logan," he began, "and they know that better than anyone. Diane was born into opportunity utterly alien to those workers, as was I, and she would do well to stop patronising the hard-working people of our country by pretending otherwise. The difference between Diane and myself is that I will look a citizen in the eye and stand before him as I am — with no apologies and no pretence. When I do so I will dress appropriately for a man of my position, because I was born with certain opportunities and intellectual propensities which imbued upon me the ability to serve this great country as its leader. Diane Logan may have the ability to stand before an honest working man and lie to his face about her being a woman of the people, but I have neither that ability nor a desire to possess it. For I am not a man of the people, I am a *servant* of the people. I am the man *for* the people. I was without question born to be the *leader* of the people — and I make no apologies for stating that fact!"

Much of the House roared in support.

"This leadership contest is a distracting formality that our party and far more importantly our *country* could do without," Godfrey continued. "My Honourable and Right Honourable friends, the matter comes down to this: I was born to lead, and lead I shall."

Godfrey's closing sentence was an instant soundbite. Although seized upon by his opponents as a sign of his detachment and an implication that he believed others were born to slave away beneath him within the confines of an inescapable class structure, the comment went down well in the polls.

The host of the special ACN report interjected at this point to state that many now believed Godfrey had made his 'born to lead' speech full in the knowledge that he would be back in Buenos Aires before long to build the GCC from the GSC's ashes. Dan's tired mind, having missed this point until it was explicitly spelled out, agreed that this was just the kind of thing Godfrey would do; love him or hate him, few could deny that William Godfrey was a grandmaster of political chess in a world where most of his opponents were still learning which pieces could move where.

The very end of the ACN piece showed Godfrey dealing with the single most common question he faced during his effortless leadership victory over Diane Logan: the question of how he could be trusted to lead the country when it was now known that during his time at the GSC, he had actively suppressed data supporting the notion that the Kerguelen bolide event of a year earlier had been alien in nature.

"From time to time, it is in the interests of the public for certain things to be kept quiet while solutions can be sought," he said, addressing the strongly worded question which came from Logan herself. "If you'll forgive my tone, Diane, do you understand what leadership actually entails? Difficult decisions and a weight of responsibility come with the territory you're trying to conquer here, and heavy is the head that wears the crown. Some have leadership thrust upon them, such as my good friend Dan McCarthy. Tell me: was Dan wrong to keep from us what he did? Was Dan wrong to maintain our belief in a hoax perpetrated by Richard Walker and benevolently maintained by our friendly visitors from afar with their delivery of the third and fourth plaques? Of course he wasn't, as all right-minded people already understand completely.

"And on the other side of the line," Godfrey went on, "what of our former colleague Mr Cole, the man who vacated the position we're competing for after disgracing himself and the United Kingdom by revealing news of Il Diavolo's trajectory — something *else* which was being kept quiet for very good reasons of public order? Tell us, Diane: in your black and white world, are we to understand that Dan McCarthy is the villain and John Cole the hero?"

The ACN host reporter returned to the screen for her sign off: "And while few are seeking *John Cole*'s views on this first anniversary of Contact Day, with so much uncertainty about how this GCC-ELF stand-off will play out and just what would happen if the Messengers were to return... it's difficult not to wonder what *Dan McCarthy* must be making of it all."

Trust me..., he thought, sighing as he positioned his body for whatever sleep it could manage, *...you don't want to know.*

V minus 87

GCC Headquarters
Buenos Aires, Argentina

At long last, the day had come.

After the better part of a year of planning, almost all of it under the radar and much of it entirely secret, the day of William Godfrey's formal swearing in as inaugural Chairman of the Global Contact Commission was finally here.

Godfrey hadn't had any formal say in the US security services' sensible decision to close down Birchwood for the day to eliminate the risk of fatal overcrowding, but he was pleased with the decision nonetheless. With the key site of Contact Day's ground zero out of the media's reach, their attention had to turn somewhere else; and Buenos Aires was just the place.

An altogether less welcome security operation at the nearby Gravesen hotel had threatened to derail the inauguration gala before it began, but Godfrey most certainly *did* have a say on the matter of whether the event should go ahead as planned and found ready agreement on this point from President Slater and his other key allies.

When the show was as big as this one, it quite simply *had* to go on.

Until at least the following day, the true nature of what was found at the Gravesen — and more importantly *how* it had been found — would be kept between those who truly needed to know. The items discovered in the room pinpointed by intelligence agents included an array of firearms and a flag proclaiming support for the risible GeoSov movement. Godfrey's in-house security agents informed him of the discovery, revealing that intelligence pointed towards a foiled hostage-taking plot against President Slater and the Japanese Prime Minister, and his understanding was that no other leaders aside from Slater and her Japanese counterpart had yet been informed.

Unsurprisingly, the scale of the early-morning security operation proved too vast to stay under the radar. As far as the media knew, though, it had simply been sparked by a tip-off about a potential time bomb planted within the hotel. The official line held that nothing had been found, with many reading between the lines to speculate that the GeoSovs themselves had called in a fake bomb threat at the Gravesen as a means of disrupting the day's GCC gala given that several guests of honour were staying there.

Now, well into the evening and with many formalities behind him, Godfrey was minutes away from the speech that would formally establish the GCC as the organisation through which many of the world's most prosperous nations had committed to channelling all contact-related efforts.

If the Messengers came calling within the borders of a GCC member state, or if a previously placed artefact was discovered, the matter would immediately fall under the GCC's competence. William Godfrey, leader of leaders, would be humanity's official point of contact.

This in itself was not controversial; indeed, both direct polling and Social Media Meta Analysis had consistently highlighted Godfrey's position as the individual deemed the second most appropriate representative of humanity in a future scenario involving direct contact. Godfrey knew that second place to Dan McCarthy was no bad place to be, even though he ultimately wanted to be in *first* position in the public's collective opinion, and he took heart from the fact that he was head and shoulders above any other Western leader.

Predictably, the data showed that citizens of many countries believed that their elected national leader should take the reins. This was less true in the United States and United Kingdom than anywhere else, due to Godfrey's success in having positioned himself as a relatively safe pair of hands during his challenging stewardship of the GCC's predecessor organisations. When the world needed to be united, Godfrey had done as good a job as the public seemed to believe anyone else could have.

On the issue of future contact, however, global unity was in distinctly short supply. Feelings ran high in China in particular, where it was generally felt that Godfrey would always exhibit a Western bias and discount Chinese interests. Other nations felt similarly, with the Russian President stating that a new organisation with Godfrey at the helm might as well be called the North Atlantic Contact Commission and move its headquarters to Washington to be done with the charade of inclusivity. Before long, dozens of countries with strong economic ties to Beijing and Moscow had formally stated their collective concerns.

Fortunately for Godfrey, he retained sufficient support among Western populations to win the backing of Western *leaders*, and he emerged as the clear choice in an advisory straw poll conducted at the first of several UN meetings dedicated to the new organisation's formation. When Chinese Premier Ding Ziyang withdrew from the discussion process and stood alongside the Russian President to announce a competing organisation to be known as the Earth Liaison Forum, Godfrey didn't blink despite the immediate exodus of several dozen other countries from the GCC discussions.

Instead, he held the situation up to his increasingly tentative backers as an example of what would happen if they allowed their countries to be tied into an organisation with nations apt to behave in such a childish way. The Chinese and Russians had revealed their hand, he said, showing beyond doubt that they were willing to play geopolitics even over an issue as important as future contact. Godfrey warned that any contact-focused international organisation which included such countries, even if it was initially led by a Westerner, would ultimately fall into the hands of a spiteful individual like Ding. The strength of Godfrey's words surprised no one given his historically proven penchant for controversial statements, but they did have the desired effect.

His words echoed a similar concern which had once been expressed by Richard Walker himself. When discussing the possibility of a sovereign one-world government, the old stalwart had insisted that the Cold War had never ended in the minds of the enemies of freedom, and that any supranational institution would inevitably come to be led by an anti-American and Chinese-backed candidate — nationality irrelevant — propped up by the increasing number of small countries who found themselves dependent on Chinese investment and trade.

Today, though, the grand top-floor conference room of Godfrey's GCC building had been refitted to receive political representatives from the countries who mattered: those on his side. There were no surprising omissions from this list, with India being the only nation Godfrey had seriously hoped to be able to talk out of its misgivings. His failure to do so had the frustrating and damaging effect of meaning that the ELF's affiliated countries housed a slight majority of Earth's human population, dealing a blow to the credibility of his 'Global' organisation in the eyes of many.

But the eyes and minds of citizens in *all* countries were currently focused on the right place — Buenos Aires — and as Godfrey began his slow walk to the podium from which he would address them he knew he had one man to thank for the fact that the entire inauguration hadn't been derailed by a disaster that could well have torpedoed the good ship GCC before it even left the docks.

Without Dan McCarthy, things would have turned out very differently.

Godfrey was particularly grateful that Dan had raised the alarm despite having been treated badly by American agents, if reports were true, but the broader point that Dan had been contacted again raised a host of new questions and concerns.

Resentment wasn't quite the right word, but Godfrey had always been envious of Dan's communicative relationship with the Messengers. Dan had fallen into his important role, Godfrey considered; greatness had been thrust upon him. He hadn't spent decades doing whatever it took to climb a political ladder that ultimately led all the way to the top of the GCC, as Godfrey had, and he didn't even seem to *want* the power he had been granted, much less appreciate it.

The silver lining for Godfrey was that if the Messengers' favoured point of contact *had* to be someone else, there were seven billion worse choices than Dan McCarthy. For not only had Dan shared the message he received and in doing so prevented utter pandemonium, he had also kept it out of the news. When it came to the crunch, Godfrey was pleased that Dan knew how to handle things with their effect on long-term stability in mind.

Admittedly, Godfrey did consider it quite probable that Emma Ford, a truly formidable PR expert, was behind Dan's recent history of good decisions. He knew that Emma had likely convinced Dan to meet him publicly in Birchwood before DS-1's lifetime-ago launch, and similarly to attend Richard Walker's high-profile funeral where he and Godfrey had shared a fairly cordial discussion about how much they both detested the crocodile tears of most of the other attendees.

Godfrey and Emma had clashed considerably during his time at the GSC, to put it mildly, but Emma had readily laid personal vendettas to one side in pursuit of the common good.

In this way and this way only, Godfrey's complicated relationship with Emma and Dan wasn't too unlike his relationship with President Slater, another individual with whom he had engaged in brutal public disagreement before they agreed to bury the hatchet when it was in their shared interests to work together.

This had never been more apparent than earlier in the day, when Slater made an executive decision to personally loop Godfrey in on exactly what had led to the discovery at the Gravesen. Before their mid-afternoon meeting, Godfrey had known only one thing more than the public: that a genuine GeoSov plot to take Slater hostage had been foiled.

It was thanks to Slater that Godfrey knew Dan McCarthy had been responsible for the tip-off. It was thanks to Slater that he knew the Messengers were back. And given that the foiling of the plot had saved his GCC inauguration, Godfrey's mind made the somewhat understand-able leap to consider that the Messengers had just quietly chosen a side.

When they wanted to come back for real, he now believed more firmly than ever that they would come to him.

As a grandfather clock chimed on the hour, Godfrey reached his podium. Not quite nervous but certainly feeling a kind of pre-speech excitement he hadn't experienced in a while, he took a deep breath.

Today was the day William Godfrey had been born to see, and the Global Contact Commission's was the throne on which he had been born to sit.

The GeoSovs would be dealt with in good time and the implications of the Messengers' apparent return would be debated long and hard in days to come as other key figures were looped in, but for now nothing else mattered.

Godfrey's stage was set, and the one thing he was not going to do was let anything else get in the way.

V minus 86

Sunrise Palace Resort
Zanzibar, Tanzania

Forty minutes before the sun would wake for the day and rise over the idyllic island of Zanzibar, Hassan Manula made his regular pre-dawn walk to the beach. This was no leisurely stroll, but instead a necessary part of his work at a high-end hotel patronised mainly by wealthy Westerners.

Recent years had seen an increase in Chinese visitors to the hotel as well as the island in general, and Hassan had made an unprompted step to improve his standing among the hotel's management by taking Chinese language lessons on his own dime as soon as this trend became clear. His initiative and commitment to self-improvement *had* impressed the management, quite likely playing a part in Hassan having survived a corporate restructuring which saw several of his long-term colleagues lose their positions.

Through committed nightly practice Hassan had since become fairly proficient in basic Chinese conversation, at least of the kind that tended to arise most frequently between a hotel's employees and its guests. He was also now acutely aware of how the typical needs and expectations of a Chinese family could vary from those of a Western family, to the extent that he had recently been asked to start conducting informal training on this very subject with all new staff arrivals.

To Hassan, the Tanzanian mainland seemed like a far more understandable destination for tourists than the admittedly pristine beach; with its unrivalled safari opportunities, not to mention the dramatic star-capped summit of Mount Kilimanjaro, the country had much to offer that nowhere else could match.

With a private stretch of white sand as photo-worthy as any other and a location off the usual beaten path, Hassan could just about under-stand why guests chose the Sunrise Palace Resort over similarly high-end hotels in other parts of the world. What he had far more difficulty understanding was why anyone would pay that kind of money to lie on a beach *anywhere*.

But, aware that he wasn't paid to ponder, Hassan was very keen to get his work on the beach done before any early-rising guests arrived to secure their spots for a full-day's relaxation of which their unbeatable sunrise view was an important part.

Hassan knew from experience that some guests didn't like to see workers moving the fabric-covered sun-loungers and heavily weighted parasols to their correct locations in accordance with tidal patterns and weather forecasts, apparently preferring to think they arranged them-selves by magic; and with a sick father and a second child on the way, a complaint was the last thing he needed right now. Even as highly regarded as he was among the management, there was no room for any guest-relations problems.

Shining a flashlight ahead of his feet to ensure he didn't step on any wildlife as he crossed the short walkway between the hotel's garden area and the immaculately maintained beach, Hassan reached into his pocket to remove the key he needed to get the first batch of sun-loungers from their out-of-sight storage locker.

But as he walked along the white sand in anticipation of a straight-forward but physically exhausting half-hour's work, Hassan's flashlight beam landed on something that reflected the light back in a way he didn't expect.

What the…

Wondering if it was a piece of plastic film or broken glass, both of which would have to be dealt with immediately, he walked towards the item and repositioned the flashlight to scan the surrounding area.

As soon as the beam moved slightly away from the sea and further up the beach, Hassan got a pulse-quickening sense of the scale of what-ever he had stumbled upon. He stepped up his pace, hurrying towards the huge object, then stopped in his tracks when both its *true* scale and the extent of its reflectivity became apparent.

Everything in Hassan's mind told him to turn around and run — to tell someone what he'd found, and to leave it for the authorities to deal with. But something deeper, whether in his heart or his soul, implored him to stay.

For several seconds, he stood frozen in indecision. He then took a bold step forward and continued until he was just a few feet from the enormous object.

Hassan shone his flashlight directly downwards, revealing an incredible and consciousness-altering detail he had missed from further away.

The sight caused another instance of momentary suspension, but this time — having seen what he just had — Hassan Manula involuntarily dropped both his flashlight and his key and sprinted for the safety of the hotel.

V minus 85

GCC Headquarters
Buenos Aires, Argentina

"The road was long, but here we are," William Godfrey began, proudly addressing a room full of political leaders and media personnel.

The *day* had been long, with countless formalities and photo ops with various national representatives having driven Godfrey to near-exhaustion, but the main event had arrived at last.

Going out live on prime-time American television, the GCC's official inauguration was set to reach viewing figures unseen since Contact Day itself, when billions of awestruck citizens had rushed to the nearest TV to see aliens walk on Earth. Whatever the next few days might bring as the full nature and implications of the Messengers' recent reconnection with Dan McCarthy came to light — and particularly if it leaked to the public once shared among the GCC's full membership — Godfrey knew that the speech he was embarking on now would be quoted for years and decades to come.

"We are gathered here today to formally initiate the cooperative union of our manifold member states," he continued, deliberate in his matrimonial tone. "We are gathered here today in the spirit of breaking down barriers and extending our outreach, not only among our once-competitive nations but also between our new collective and the extraterrestrial beings whose intervention secured our future one year ago today. Indeed, the GCC will serve as the focal point of contact between humanity and any *other* extraterrestrial races we might one day discover."

This implicit point that humanity's prior contact with one race of aliens didn't necessarily increase or decrease the likelihood of future first-time contact with another drew nods from a small group of guests whose presence pleased Godfrey greatly. And although Timo Fiore himself had chosen not to attend and was instead wining and dining at a Contact Day anniversary party in Colorado Springs, the presence of three senior staff from Fiore Frontiere — his privately held space research and exploration firm — was hugely symbolic.

The staff in question were Alessandro Bonucci, Timo's right-hand man, along with the far more famous duo of Louisa Conte and Fransisco Abate. The duo owed their immense name recognition to their official listing as the discoverers of Comet Conte-Abate, better known as Il Diavolo. Only they, Timo, and a handful of others knew that Alessandro had been the true discoverer only too keen to leave the dubious honour of naming a potential planet-killer to his more senior colleagues.

Even before the dissolution of the GSC or the events of Contact Day, there had been serious concerns within several American agencies that Timo might partner with the Chinese. The money Beijing had been willing to throw at space-related research and technologies already posed a huge problem for President Slater's administration, but any link-up between CNSA and Fiore Frontiere would have been cause for immediate alarm.

But now, on the contrary, Timo's decision to recognise the GCC rather than the ELF was a cause for celebration. The support of the space-obsessed world's richest man didn't only strengthen the GCC in budgetary terms, however, but also — perhaps even more importantly — it *hugely* strengthened the GCC's appearance of legitimacy.

With Dan McCarthy and his friends and family in Birchwood diplomatically silent on the GCC-ELF chasm and with no suggestion that they would ever change course, Timo's position mattered.

And in the eyes of a public more sceptical of their political institutions than ever before, Timo was a man whose word still meant something. He was also greatly admired for his bravery in the face of the life-altering injuries he suffered in a botched assassination attempt at the hands of nihilistic terrorists who now hid themselves within the dangerously media-savvy GeoSov movement.

That same terrorist attack in Colorado Springs had almost cost Emma

Ford her life, and both Timo's injury and his close friendship with Dan made him a hugely sympathetic figure across the world.

Dan didn't mind that Timo had opted to publicly pick a side, understanding that he had only done so under a considerable degree of political pressure. Timo would have been able to withstand this pressure had it been merely economic in nature, but the firm message Godfrey ultimately issued wasn't something he was able to ignore.

Essentially, Godfrey calmly told Timo that unless he backed the GCC, its founding charter would include a provision barring any private launches into orbit or the analysis of data from certain kinds of privately held telescopes within its member states' territories. Timo's observatories in South Africa and Italy and his headquarters in Colorado Springs would have been affected by these restrictions, as would his ambitious plans for an orbital laboratory far larger than any before it.

Godfrey framed it as though these were general purpose restrictions and as though he'd had to work hard to convince some unnamed member states that Fiore Frontiere should be allowed to operate at all. All Timo had to do was issue a public statement recognising the GCC's sole legitimacy and to refrain from ever recognising the ELF, Godfrey said, and Fiore Frontiere could continue as normal.

The only thing that made Timo Fiore more sick than the idea of shaking Godfrey's hand was the alternative option of moving his operations eastward and working with an organisation led by countries who seemed determined to engage in direct geopolitical competition with his European homeland.

"We are joined tonight by our friends from Fiore Frontiere," Godfrey said, gesturing to the attendant trio and inviting a polite round of applause, "and their presence is a sign of just how inclusive the GCC wants to be. Timo Fiore is not a head of state or government, and yet he has a seat at our table because of his committed investments in the field of astronomical research. We all know that two of our esteemed Italian guests detected Il Diavolo from a facility Timo built from the ground up and funded for the good of humanity, and I'm sure you'll all agree that their presence here is more than welcome.

"I'm equally delighted that our membership includes so many of the nations who came together when our planet's future looked far less rosy than it does now, and despite my disappointment that we are *not* joined tonight by representatives from certain other countries, I do want to stress that our door is always open. Despite the hollow propaganda with which Beijing has been bombarding the world of late, the GCC is as exclusionary as the sun is purple.

"Allow me to set the record straight: we did not sit around a table and draw up a list of invitees to this party… this party was open to all! We did not and will not exclude anyone; others, unfortunately but not irreversibly, have opted to exclude themselves. And when I say our door is open to all, I do mean *all*. Were I to get a call from an ELF-affiliated state tomorrow, I would welcome them with open arms. But it's often said that when one door closes, another opens. And, out of necessity, that's the case here. To be granted a seat at the GCC's table and pass through our door, any such nation will first have to exit the ELF's and relinquish all participation within that undemocratic organisation."

Godfrey's eyes narrowed all of a sudden as he saw his executive assistant standing at the far side of the room with his arms aloft in a decidedly ominous X shape. Stopping the speech now to find out what was wrong seemed utterly out of the question, but Godfrey had known and trusted Manuel for long enough to know that this wasn't a drill.

As Godfrey considered his next move, however, the ball was taken from his hands by an unexpected development.

"What the hell's going on?" one cameraman asked, his voice loud and clear before a deafening hubbub filled the room as the others caught on.

Gruffly calling for silence, Godfrey heard a clear shout that all phone, data and satellite signals within the room had suddenly been lost. He stepped away from the podium, seeing little sense in continuing a speech that was meant less for the room than the billions of people around the world who could no longer see it, and headed straight for Manuel.

"Don't worry about anything," he calmly announced to the more frightened members of his audience as he walked. "Please wait patiently while these signal issues are corrected. We had intelligence that the GeoSovs might attempt some kind of city-wide technical disruption or cyber attack today, and it looks like our pitiful foes have had a rare and momentary success in that regard. But let's not let them win by losing our composure, shall we? As you were."

This effortless lie about an expected cyber attack came to Godfrey on the spot, and it seemed to do the trick. People were still unhappy and concerned, for sure, but there was no longer a sense of dread that everything had died because of a bigger issue such as a physical attack somewhere else.

"So what's happening?" Godfrey whispered when he reached Manuel; his tone was gentle even in the circumstances, as it tended to be

64

whenever he spoke to one of the few men in the world he truly and unconditionally liked.

"*We* did this, sir," Manuel replied. "We engaged the building's full signal block as soon as the word came in."

Godfrey's shoulders tightened. "When *what* word came in? Don't tell me those bloody GeoSovs really have—"

A quick head-shake from Manuel cut off this train of thought.

"Okay," Godfrey continued. "So what *is* the news? And how did we get it before this lot?" he asked, gesturing to the media pack behind him, all of whom were desperately fiddling with cameras, phones and computers in the hopes of getting some kind of data or satellite signal.

"At this stage, it's intelligence rather than news, sir. This isn't public yet... not even locally."

Godfrey had to fight to keep his cool, frustrated by Manuel's slowness in spitting out the pertinent details but loath to let any anger show when so many eyes were on him. "Locally *where*?" he probed, almost hissing out the question. "What the hell is going on?"

"There's been a discovery on a Tanzanian beach," Manuel said. "Sir... there's been an *alien* discovery."

After slowly and dryly blowing air from his lips, Godfrey grinned involuntarily. "Not just on the anniversary of Contact Day," he mused, "but literally *while* I'm making my inauguration speech. It's a bit on the nose, Manuel, don't you think?"

The man couldn't hide his confusion. "Sir, I don't—"

"It's a distraction, Manuel. A cheap Chinese hoax. I mean, come on... Tanzania? With the money they've spent there, it's practically a Chinese colony by now! I'm almost embarrassed for them; the timing just makes it all so blatantly obvious. Do they really expect anyone to believe that they just happened to dig something up today of all days? Are we *seriously* supposed to buy the story that they just discovered whatever this thing is?"

Manuel gulped. "Sir, if our ground intelligence is correct and this image is legitimate, this isn't something they could have kept under wraps for a single second." He encouraged Godfrey to turn around so they were side-by-side and both facing the rest of the room, then showed him the image on his phone.

Of its own accord, William Godfrey's jaw dropped.

"You see, sir?" Manuel said, his voice shaky under the weight of the words. "They didn't just *find* it... it just *arrived*."

Part 2

ZANZIBAR

"The only true wisdom
is in knowing you know nothing."

Socrates

V minus 84

With Birchwood locked down for another twelve hours and with a hotel the last place he wanted to be after the foiled GeoSov plot at the Buenos Aires Gravesen, Dan McCarthy sat alongside Emma in a small room at Denver International Airport.

This spartan room, bunk beds and all, was normally reserved for individuals facing immigration complications that seemed likely to be solved eventually but to take more than a few hours.

The airport's immigration and security staff all proved extremely accommodating, going out of their way to make Dan and Emma feel safe and welcome, but Dan knew beyond doubt that there were other and distinctly less personable agents lying unseen nearby.

There had been agents lying unseen nearby for a year, he now realised, and the violated feeling of having been closely watched and surveilled for so long was like a film of dirt on his skin. He couldn't shake it and suspected he never would, angrily considering all the private and intimate moments the agents would have seen or heard.

The conspicuous camera on the ceiling of the airport's holding room made Dan and Emma wary to speak much and certainly ruled out any physicality, but pondering their obvious current surveillance only made

Dan think that it had been like this all along; really, the only difference now was that the visible camera made it known.

On reflection, this colossal invasion of privacy bothered him even more than the fact that a government doctor had covertly placed a pain-monitoring device under his skin.

But while these two very different kinds of violations were troubling in their own ways, it did seem clear to Dan that the doctor in question had acted in accordance with political orders rather than the supposedly sacrosanct Hippocratic oath.

His anger was so strong that he was paying little attention to William Godfrey's inauguration speech as it played on the room's surprisingly large TV. The words so far had gone in one ear and out the other, with Emma occasionally adding a word or two of commentary which registered only slightly more fully in Dan's mind.

But as the speech appeared to be nearing its end, the news feed on ACN abruptly turned black.

Dan and Emma turned to each other; whatever was happening, it couldn't be good.

"Well, clearly we're experiencing some kind of technical issue," the news anchor said, his confused face suddenly filling the screen. "I'm being told that *all* feeds from the GCC have been lost, so please do bear with us here on ACN while the tech-heads in Buenos Aires fix whatever has gone wrong. But Chairman Godfrey has covered a lot of ground already, so let's hear the views of our in-studio analysis team on the speech so far. James, what do you make of—"

The sound of the room's door being urgently thrown open tore Dan's attention from the screen.

"Are you okay?" a black-suited agent asked, bursting into the room with an expression on his face befitting a man who had just seen a ghost.

"Uh, yeah..." Emma replied, although the question had clearly been directed primarily at Dan. "What's going on? Why did the feed die?"

The man placed a finger to his ear, concentrating on the words coming through a barely visible earpiece. "It didn't die," he relayed. "It was cut. All signals in and out of the GCC building have been blocked."

Very suddenly and very noticeably, the man's eyes widened in shock.

"What are they telling you?" Dan asked, rising to his feet. "What's happening?"

Holding a finger out to beg Dan's patience, the man listened carefully then spoke in evident reply to an unheard question: "Yes, they're both fine; no indication of any contact. Do we know exactly what this discov... *oh*. Definitely? And do we have a reliable visual? *No?* So when do we expect one? Okay."

"Well?" Dan said.

The agent rubbed his chin, somewhat flustered by the news he had just received and the unexpected position in which he now found himself. "Well... communications in and out of the GCC building were cut to prevent the news I've just heard from reaching any of the media personnel who are attending the inauguration. They clearly didn't want Chairman Godfrey to be caught off-guard in front of all those live cameras, and I can see why. Intelligence from Tanzania is telling us that an alien object has just been discovered at a beachfront hotel complex. I'll be surprised if I can show you an image before it's on that TV, because our intelligence presence on Zanzibar isn't exactly enormous."

Dan, truly stunned by these words, didn't react.

"Zanzibar?" Emma mused. "How random is that? Why would the Messengers put—"

"We don't know that they did," the agent interrupted. "For all we know, this is a deliberate distraction from the inauguration. Tanzania is an ELF member with extremely close links to Beijing."

"You think this could be a hoax?" Emma asked.

The agent nodded. "I think it *could* be, to be clear; not that it *is*. The sun is rising over Zanzibar as we speak and our limited local intelligence confidently tells us that there was no object on the beach when the sun went down last night. So whatever this thing is, it seems to have... *appeared*... sometime in the last eleven hours or so."

Emma looked squarely at Dan. "Did you feel anything?"

Glancing between her and the agent, he said nothing.

"Mr McCarthy," the man said, his tone firm without being confrontational, "I can understand your anger over how certain things have been handled recently. At least, I can *try* to understand. But please: it's crucially important that you tell us if you have experienced any kind of feeling or sensation since leaving Italy, physical or mental, that might point towards the Messengers having planted this object. If I were in your shoes I don't think I would feel too much like cooperating right about now, but I hope you'll understand that this is a very important issue."

Dan held the man's eyes and gave a slow and exaggerated shrug, walking a fine line between defiance and petulance. He then shifted his weight, exaggerating the movement again, and turned back to the TV. "You've been watching me close enough to know that the Messengers haven't contacted me since your buddies kidnapped me last night. So if you don't have anything useful to tell me, feel free to get out of my sight at any point."

"*Dan,*" Emma scorned.

"No, I understand," the agent said calmly. "I would feel violated, too, Dan. But I really do hope—"

"Oh my god!" an interrupting voice blared from the TV. "And this is from a tourist at the hotel? Okay. Well, ladies and gentlemen, I think we have our answer as to why communications have been cut. The following footage has just reached our news desk from the island of Zanzibar, and… well… it speaks for itself."

The agent at Dan's side reached for his phone as it buzzed in his pocket, and his jaw dropped at the sight of the image he had been sent.

"Let me see," Dan said, turning to him.

Dan's firm belief that the supposedly alien discovery would be nothing more than a distracting hoax collapsed in an instant as his eyes fell upon an enormous object so ornate that he struggled to comprehend how any humans could ever have constructed it. When the shaky mobile-phone camera zoomed in as far as it could, showing several local police officers and decidedly foreign-looking officials as they stood around the incredible find, Dan caught sight of a particular series of jewel-like adornments which appeared far more prominent than the others covering the remarkable object. Somewhere deep in the recesses of his mind, he knew he had seen the shape of this conspicuous jewel arrangement before.

Dan had to stifle a gasp when the realisation finally hit him.

Holy shit…, he thought to himself. *It's real!*

V minus 83

Sunrise Palace Resort
Zanzibar, Tanzania

A picture-perfect sunrise provided a serene backdrop to the chaotic scenes playing out on a stretch of sand typically filled with sunbathing tourists.

Already, within an hour of Hassan Manula's discovery of what he could only describe as a monolithic and triangular object from another world, he had been detained for questioning and his find had been concealed from public view. The concealment method he saw from one of the hotel's windows before entering a quiet room for questioning appeared to be very basic, with an enormous tarpaulin cover supported by high metal rods shielding the impossibly ornate triangle from open sight.

Hassan's mind thought of the object as a triangle and he had already heard that word being used by others around him, but the three-dimensional nature of the object made 'triangle' an imprecise descriptor. He would later conclude that 'triangular prism' was more appropriate in a technical sense, but this didn't change the fact that everyone — including himself — would persistently and uniformly call it a triangle.

When initially trying to describe the object in a phone call to the local police, he'd encouraged them to imagine a very wide cylinder that was cross-sectionally triangular instead of circular and which had been horizontally sliced to leave a 'stump' only three or four feet high. As inele-

75

gant as this description may have been, it did paint a fairly accurate picture.

After alerting the police, Hassan had returned to the triangle along with some of his colleagues for a second and better look. The hotel workers thought it was going to be some kind of practical joke, quite understandably, and all were stunned into silence when they saw the scale of the object that had landed — or been placed — in their tiny corner of the world.

The low light prior to the police's arrival restricted how much detail Hassan and his friends could discern. They did however see enough to know that the object, an ornately decorated triangular prism composed of a remarkably black rock-like metal, quite clearly had an inlet groove where a smaller object of the same kind could be placed. There was a further triangular groove within the first, apparently for an even smaller replica, and it appeared to Hassan very much like his discovery was one third of a finished article.

Whether the other two parts had arrived elsewhere or would do so soon was something he couldn't even guess, but the nested Russian-doll like effect was unmistakeable to his eyes. Aside from the very clear physical indentations which suggested that smaller triangles could be placed within this one, there was another indication of incompleteness: the jewel-like studs which adorned the outer edges of the triangle's upper surface stopped at the indented centre. Indeed, the absence of these highly reflective 'dots' was a large part of what made the first indentation so apparent even at first glance.

Hassan's indoor questioning was very gentle, certainly nothing worthy of the term interrogation, and the local policeman who took his sworn statement of how he had discovered the triangle clearly believed him. Unbeknownst to Hassan, however, control of the situation on the beach was already out of the police's hands.

"The hotel's beach-facing security cameras will show me walking out to the beach," Hassan said, "in case anyone needs to see that I really did only find it two minutes before I called you. In fact, those cameras will show the triangle arriving — we will know once and for all where it came from!"

The policeman raised his eyebrows and shrugged. "The cameras were the first thing we tried, Mr Manula. Unfortunately, there was a white flash at around—"

Without a knock, the door swung open very abruptly.

"I think we have kept Mr Manula for long enough," an eavesdropping official interrupted. Hassan looked at the man and saw Chinese features above an ELF emblazoned uniform.

"Of course," the policeman said, deferring in accordance with orders he had already received from his superiors. As per the ELF charter, this fell squarely within the organisation's remit.

"Thank you for going to the police and not the media," the official said, shaking Hassan's hand with a firmness that bordered on aggression and then encouraging him to leave the room. "You made a very wise decision."

These words, although grateful on the face of it, were spoken in a threatening tone that left Hassan in no doubt that his decision *had* been a wise one. Glancing out of the window on his way to the parking lot to get out of there and home to his family as quickly as he could, he saw that the makeshift tarpaulin cover had now been replaced by a peaked tent-like structure that must have been the size of two basketball courts.

Hassan didn't know what would happen if the triangle was still there when the tide came in — its sheer mass would likely anchor it to the spot, he thought — but he couldn't imagine that it wouldn't be long gone before then.

The ELF officials clearly weren't messing around, and he couldn't blame them. Unshakeable certainty filled Hassan's mind that the triangle wasn't just an object... it was a *message*. The first of three parts, perhaps, but a message nonetheless.

And for better or worse, it was in the ELF's hands now.

V minus 82

Three hours after the news came in from Zanzibar, a heated crisis meeting among national representatives at the GCC was drawing to a close. For the most part, these representatives were in fact national *leaders* already present in Buenos Aires for the inauguration, rather than the permanent delegates who were set to reside in the city full-time. As if it was needed, this added an even greater feeling of unprecedented urgency to an already volatile political situation.

The media had been dismissed from the building almost immediately, after a short statement from Godfrey which informed them of the supposedly alien triangle's discovery and of his intention to carefully assess the "remarkably timed incident" before making any further comment. The GCC was officially inaugurated behind closed doors with far more haste and far less fanfare than he had hoped, but right now there were far more important things to worry about.

There had so far been little opportunity for careful assessment given how little footage and how few eyewitness reports of the triangle were available. The speed with which a swarm of ELF agents arrived from the Tanzanian mainland to close down the site at dawn was almost as suspicious as the timing, Godfrey considered, and he wasn't alone in his sceptical cynicism.

Indeed, the majority of the emergency GCC meeting had been spent not debating the consequences and implications of a new gift from the Messengers but rather the most prudent way to respond to what all in attendance assumed to be an obvious hoax. Godfrey, commanding in his seat at the end of the table, insisted that the triangle was "so obviously a cheap Chinese hoax" that he didn't even have to say it. On that point, however, he decreed that for the time being *no one* should say it in public.

Some European delegates disagreed with this course of action in clearly stated but cordial terms, and Godfrey appreciated their candour. He also appreciated their deference to the will of the majority, which was a core principle of an organisational structure in which decisions by consensus could not be counted upon. The GCC charter made it clear that comments directly relating to extraterrestrial contact or visitation would be issued only by the collective once approved by a simple majority of member states. This was an unbreakable tenet upon which the organisation's credibility rested, and it appeared to be facing — and surviving — its first serious test far earlier than anyone could have predicted.

A corollary of the individual member states' commitment to supporting the majority position was Chairman Godfrey's similar commitment to refraining from making any major statements without first seeking and securing explicit majority approval of their general content. A vote wouldn't be required every time he opened his mouth, of course, but any significant political interjection and any change of direction most certainly *would* require such approval.

When the initial decision to avoid calling out the Zanzibar triangle as a hoax had been reached, a victory for wait-and-see diplomacy, Chairman Godfrey rocked the room with a piece of news that came as a revelation to all but two of the gathered representatives. He glanced at these individuals, President Slater and the Japanese Prime Minister, silently seeking their consent to share the information on the tip of his tongue. Both nodded; the timing was right.

"You all know about this morning's foiled plot at the Gravesen," Godfrey said. "Well, *yesterday* morning's, since we're far beyond midnight now. In any case, what you don't yet know — and what has only been 'kept' from you so everything could be fully verified before we risked jumping the gun — is *how* the plot was foiled. On Friday evening in Italy, Dan McCarthy was contacted by the Messengers. On

Friday evening in Italy, the Messengers went *untold* miles out of their way to warn Dan McCarthy precisely where and when the GeoSovs intended to strike."

Sudden silence rather than shocked gasps greeted Godfrey's revelation. He watched with mild interest as delegates looked around and exchanged glances with their closest allies, subconsciously revealing friendships in the way only an unexpected development ever could.

"There are several things we could read into this," their Chairman said, "but the most objectively certain are these: First, the Messengers remain close, keeping a watchful eye on humanity and ready to intervene when they deem it truly necessary. Second, the Messengers quite rightly deemed the safety of our American and Japanese representatives worthy of such an intervention. Third, Dan McCarthy remains the Messengers' preferred point of contact. Fourth, Dan McCarthy remains an individual we can rely upon. He may not have nailed his colours to our GCC mast quite yet, but when push comes to shove his loyalty lies with his country and its allies.

"And stretching objectivity only slightly," Godfrey continued, "allow me to suggest one more thing I believe we can safely conclude. Last year in Colorado Springs, the Messengers did *not* intervene to prevent a near-deadly attack on Timo Fiore and Emma Ford. For one reason or another, their lives were deemed unworthy of an intervention. Of course on the face of it, the potential assassinations of two heads of state may seem like a far more destabilising blow than the deaths of two civilians. But if we cast our minds back to that awful day at the Fiore Frontiere headquarters, we will remember that the hopes of a desperate world were on Timo's shoulders as Il Diavolo drew ever nearer. The attack, even though ultimately unsuccessful, ushered in a night of chaotic rioting and could very well have hastened the decline of civilised society had Dan not bravely beckoned the Messengers to Birchwood in the immediate aftermath.

"I remind you of this point to introduce another: in my view, the Messengers acted not only to prevent two cold-blooded political assassinations but to allow our inauguration to go ahead as planned. The sham that is the ELF will not have gone unnoticed by the Messengers, and they have quite clearly chosen a side. Like Dan, they may not be public in their endorsement — at least not yet. But just like Dan, I know to the depths of my being that I can count on their support when it's needed most. To state my confidence in the simplest of terms: the Messengers *have* never, *would* never, and *will* never give anything to the Chinese or any other enemies of freedom."

The nods of support which greeted Godfrey's words were few but firm; quite clearly, those who approved of his robust language and continued conflation of the ELF with the Chinese government *fully* approved. Some were less comfortable with the tone, perhaps hearing a little bit too much of Richard Walker in the Sinophobic wording.

"I would very much like to convene again tomorrow afternoon once more intelligence on this triangle is in our palms, but for now I shall close with a final comment on the importance of strategic restraint. As you all know, for my sins, I spent a considerable amount of time with Jack Neal before I cut him loose and he scampered away to the side of John Cole — birds of a feather flocking together, as they do."

The assembled representatives were surprised to hear these names spoken, especially Jack's and especially President Slater, who had given the disgraced founder of XPR his break as a political strategist. Jack had lost all of his powerful former clients and allies in recent years, falling firmly out of favour with Slater, Godfrey and Cole and foolishly making an enemy of his former protégé Emma Ford.

Now that Jack was back in the commercial PR game, salvaging celebrity reputations almost as damaged as his own, more than one mind in the room wondered why his name had been deemed worthy of a mention in a meeting as highly charged and important as this one.

"You're probably wondering why I would mention him tonight of all nights," Godfrey went on, attuned to the mood of the room, "and the reason is simple. I'm reminded tonight of the one sensible thing Jack ever told me, which has stuck with me since the day he said it: *you can hide the truth forever, but the lie always gets out.*"

Many of the powerful heads around Godfrey's table nodded in full support. He commanded their respect without having to demand it, and not even those who disliked him in a personal sense were begrudging of his position.

"Friends," he said, "we all know that this is a cheap Chinese hoax. What I also want you to know is that our counterparts in Beijing will overplay their hand and expose themselves before long. To paraphrase a far wiser man than Jack Neal, we must avoid the temptation of interrupting our enemies while they are making this mistake. Reality is on our side and so are the Messengers. For now, all we have to do is hold our nerve."

SATURDAY

V minus 81

Having kept his thoughts on the so-called 'Zanzibar triangle' to himself overnight, aware of his close observation as he was, Dan was overwhelmingly glad when word came in on Saturday morning that Birchwood was open for business once more.

A small exclusion zone was still in place around the drive-in given the reasonable expectation that news of another supposedly alien discovery would bring crowds once more, but residents like Dan and Emma would be allowed to go in and out of town as they pleased.

Right now the only way Dan wanted to think about going was *in*, and Emma shared the sentiment. Their pre-honeymoon had been cut short by a development neither had seen coming, but now that it was over they wanted to get home as quickly as possible. An airport was no place to spend any night, let alone one as politically turbulent as the last, and their small room's TV set had proven too tempting to resist. Because of this they were acutely aware of the growing diplomatic tensions over the discovery in Tanzania, an ELF member state, with talk of an emergency GCC summit having leaked out of Buenos Aires.

Nothing regarding the *content* of the meeting had leaked out, and although Emma was naturally curious she knew this was for the best;

things were shaky enough as they were without any off-the-cuff and potentially regrettable reactions making their way into the public sphere.

As soon as the road in and out of Birchwood reopened, Clark McCarthy set off on the drive to Denver. He insisted this was no trouble and Dan was glad of it, understandably more reluctant than ever to get into a vehicle that wasn't driven by someone he trusted completely. Dan even asked Clark to make sure he drove his own car, which was older than Dan's and lacked some of the 'smart' features which Dan's paranoid mind now worried could be used to remotely immobilise the engine or even take control of the steering mechanism and eliminate him once and for all. Dan didn't know who exactly might have a sufficiently strong interest in trying to get rid of him for this to be something worth worrying about, but such small details didn't stop his mind from wandering.

When Clark called again to say he was outside, one of the airport's regular security staff asked Dan for an autograph before he left. Dan obliged happily enough; the man sounded local, couldn't have been any older than 25, and had been friendly and helpful overnight whenever they'd needed anything. A supervisor stepped in when the man asked for a *photograph*, however, and Dan could only apologise having initially agreed.

Eight security staff flanked the couple as they walked to the airport's exit, which from their current position involved passing through a busy area. The option of waiting fifteen minutes while this area was cleared was offered to Dan and Emma, but neither were willing to entertain the idea of putting so many people through such an inconvenience. The airport really was no place to spend any more time than necessary, as they had both been reminded overnight, and they had no problem with traversing a crowd of people who would be delighted to see them.

For most of the past year, Dan had avoided public areas as much as possible simply to keep himself out of the media in the hope of hastening a return to something approaching a normal life. After what had happened in Italy and Tanzania, however, he knew the days of hoping for such a thing truly were gone. He put on a brave face as one of the security officers opened the door which led them into the large Arrivals area. It took mere seconds for the news of his presence to ripple through the crowd. The effect was visible, along the lines of a Mexican wave, as first every head turned and then every pair of feet approached.

Four of the security officers surrounded the couple more tightly now, with the others using firm words and raised tasers to enforce a buffer of several metres in each direction.

Dan didn't hear any particularly audible comments from the crowd and didn't get the impression that many of them were asking questions about the Zanzibar triangle or anything else. Most were simply smiling and waving, some taking photos and some raising their thumbs in support.

"It's been a while, huh?" Emma whispered, smiling along with their supportive public and momentarily forgetting the storm clouds that were gathering. "Have you missed it?"

Dan chortled. "I wouldn't go that far!"

A line of stores filled the wall to their left, positioned to separate recent arrivals from some of their money and evidently aimed more at the tourist market than the business travellers who still accounted for a narrow majority of the airport's traffic despite a huge rise in visits to Colorado following Contact Day and everything that had preceded it. Dan momentarily wondered if a similar influx would soon hit Zanzibar and wherever else further triangles might turn up, but his attention then fell on one particular store.

It was busy, or at least had been until its customers began flooding towards him, and the italicised 'TARA STYLE' signage made him smile even wider. The huge pictures in each window were eye-catching shots of Tara Ford herself. One showcased a simple yellow party dress and was set against the backdrop of a long-exposure shot of streetlights in a city that looked like New York. The other, a black and white close-up of her face, to Dan's mind evoked thoughts of catwalks and perfume commercials where no one was allowed to smile.

He knew that TARA STYLE — always fully capitalised — was the name of a series of stores aimed at a young, price-conscious crowd. Its upmarket and hair-raisingly expensive counterpart, TARA COUTURE, did have a presence in Colorado but lay to the south in Colorado Springs, with other locations in more traditional fashion capitals such as Paris and London.

Given Tara's level of fame and the depth of her recent association with Colorado, it made sense for there to be a TARA STYLE outlet within the building where Colorado met the world in the same way it made sense for a Scottish airport to contain stores selling expensive tweed and whisky or for a Cuban one to contain stores full of rum and cigars.

The same logic held for the alien-themed gift shop that was also rapidly emptying before Dan's eyes. Its window displayed all kinds of memorabilia and trinkets, from posters of the drive-in to full-size replicas of the 'Welcome to Birchwood: Proud Home of Dan McCarthy' sign that would greet any tourists who made their way towards the small and once-unknown town whenever it wasn't closed off to incoming traffic.

The walk passed without incident and Dan was sitting in Clark's car within a few minutes. Dan and Emma, quickly settling in the back seat, stuck to their plan of not telling Clark anything until they got home. This was less about keeping his mind focused on the road than it was about Dan's desire to tell Henry and Tara at the same time; after almost two years of secrets and lies, all he wanted was for his close friends and family — his trusted circle, his team — to be on the same page whenever possible.

"How are you guys doing?" Clark asked, deliberately low-key in his greeting.

"Glad to be home," Emma replied. "Where's Tara? I thought she might have fancied coming along for the ride to get her out of the house."

Clark turned the ignition to start the engine. "She's still sleeping off last night," he said, not laughing.

"Last night? I thought everything was closed and you were both staying in?"

"Yeah… that doesn't exactly stop her from going to town these days," Clark shrugged. "It was the same at the grill the other night. She's in that kind of *'drinking to feel better'* zone right now, you know? Not drinking to have more fun. I've been staying at your place for the last few nights because she didn't want to be alone, and she usually lives alone so it's not like she's not used to it. You know her better than me, but… I dunno, this seems like it's maybe more than just feeling down about a guy."

Emma sighed, almost sorry she'd asked but naturally concerned. "They *did* just break up two weeks ago," she said, "and she *did* find out he was cheating when Blitz News ran the story. But she seemed to be getting over it before we left. She forced us not to cancel our trip and said she'd be fine staying in Birchwood as long as you'd be around, and it sounds like you have been."

"I *have*," Clark nodded. "And I don't want you to think it's worse than it is or anything. I mean, she's okay… but I'm glad you guys are home earlier than planned. You know, ignoring everything else that's happening right now and *why* you're home early. I think she needs you."

Emma lifted her phone from her pocket. "I'll tell her we're on the way home," she said, getting right to the texting.

Dan, silent in the seat behind Clark, looked out of the window and saw a huge TARA COUTURE billboard featuring Hollywood A-lister Kaitlyn Judd in a subtly pinstriped power suit.

Tara was certainly *doing* okay, but Dan knew that didn't mean anything if she wasn't *feeling* okay.

~

Clark seemed to respect Dan's tired silence for the rest of the drive, which passed fairly quickly thanks to Sunday's typical lack of late-morning traffic.

After lounging in thought most of the way, Dan sat up straight when there were only a few minutes to go.

He looked out with a head full of competing memories as he saw the barely visible turn towards Richard Walker's old place at Stevenson Farm, the site of so many incredible extraterrestrial moments that it would have been a tourist destination rivalling the drive-in if anyone other than the three people in the car and Tara knew about them. Phil Norris now owned the place having bought it at auction after Walker's death, and they still saw no reason to compli-cate Phil's life and ruin his love affair with Stevenson Farm by telling him which political titan used to live in the cottage or which interplan-etary travellers had made more than a single landing in its adjacent cornfield.

Next came the road sign, which was always when the real feeling of being home kicked in. A heavy police presence surrounded the drive-in, and a manned roadblock remained in place on the way to the McCarthys' residential area of town. The attending officers saw Clark's car approaching and raised the barrier in good time, with no need for him to draw to a full stop. He raised a hand in appreciation and continued on.

A minute or so later, the car did draw to a stop as he pulled into the driveway.

"Uh, the door's not opening," Dan said in surprise as he tried to get out. He glanced forward to Clark and saw his expression and body language turn in a decidedly negative direction.

"So..." Clark said, huffing out the word. "Were you ever planning to tell me about this goddamn message you got on Friday night, or are we back to keeping secrets?"

"When the hell did I ever keep a secret from you?" Dan snapped, the words pouring out of his mouth at twice the normal rate. "And what are you even talking about, the Kloster letter way back at the start? Okay...

one thing, for a *few days,* when you were on another *continent* and I didn't want to mention it over the phone. That's your beef?"

"I need to know these things, Dan," Clark said, his tone one of concern rather than anger.

"Open the door right now or I'm smashing my way out," Dan threatened, emptily and emotionally, from a position of frustration and exhaustion.

Clark pressed the button to unlock the passenger doors and folded his arms in annoyance as Dan wasted no time in getting out.

"How do you know?" Emma asked, perfectly calm despite the heated exchange and the surprising question that kicked it off. "I mean, *obviously* we were going to tell you as soon as we got inside, but how the hell do you already know?"

Clark opened his own door, answering as he stepped out. "Godfrey told everyone at the GCC, which meant Timo's three delegates heard. Alessandro called him as soon as he could and he called me. Simple as that."

Dan, having lifted out his suitcase, noticed Clark getting out of the car but hurried into the house without a backwards glance.

"You need to tell me these things!" Clark yelled, striding forward in pursuit.

Emma intercepted him at the door and stood directly in front of him. "Clark, give him a break," she hissed under her breath, surprising him with the insistence of her tone. "You don't have a clue where we've been or the weight that's on his shoulders. There are no more secrets — okay? — but the last person we need any more bullshit from is you. Let him breathe."

"If something happens, I *need* to know," Clark reiterated. "He's my brother!"

"And *he* needs *you;* of course he does. But right now? Well, right now *I* need you to bring Mr Byrd across the street and see if you can get hold of Phil while you're at it. Dan wants to tell everyone at once."

"Tara and my dad already know, too," Clark said.

Emma shook her head. *"None* of you know everything…"

V minus 80

"*Daaaaad,*" Hassan Manula's six-year-old son yelled from the hallway.

Hassan had heard the doorbell and thought nothing of it, but the tone of this call sent a shiver down his spine. His son didn't sound frightened, as such, but he definitely didn't sound like he was looking at someone he knew.

The day so far had been the strangest and least comfortable of Hassan's life, beginning with his accidental discovery of an enormous and apparently alien object and continuing for far too long with a series of tense conversations with all kinds of law enforcement officers and ELF officials. The latter had told him he'd done all that was needed of him and could return home safe in the knowledge that he would be well looked after for having taken the discovery to the police rather than attempt to make himself famous in the media.

Fame was the last thing in the world Hassan Manula desired, and the second-last was any more attention from the agents. His son's tone planted a seed of fear in his mind that those very agents were here, and upon reaching the hallway his eyes confirmed as much.

"Mr Manula," said an unfamiliar man in an ELF blazer. He looked and sounded local and was flanked by two colleagues, both of whom were Chinese and both of whom had been present at the Sunrise Palace Resort during Hassan's initial questioning. They had been cordial enough with Hassan on that occasion, but their presence at his family home was as welcome as an earthquake.

"What do you want from me?" he asked, his voice and legs shaking. "I told you everything. You said this was over. What do you need?"

The local official smiled, not perturbed by words which were clearly coming from a place of concern rather than recalcitrance. "*I* don't need anything," he said gently. "But you *will* have to come with us for a while, because Ding Ziyang would very much like to see you."

V minus 79

When Dan entered his old family home, next door to the house he'd shared with Emma for the past year, the first person he saw wasn't Tara and it wasn't his father Henry. Instead, and very surprisingly, it was Timo Fiore.

The Italian billionaire and GCC associate member, a great friend of the family, beamed a smile that Dan couldn't quite understand given the political instability swirling around the organisation Timo was so deeply involved in.

"They're back," Timo beamed, his familiar soft accent tinging the words. "And this time they visited you at my lake house! Tell me, can I claim contact by association?"

Dan couldn't help but laugh, despite still not knowing why Timo was so positive about it all. The man's lifelong interest in all things extraterrestrial comfortably predated the recent explosion of interest, as evidenced by his massive investment in SETI observatories around the world, and it slowly struck Dan that Timo was simply excited by the Messengers' return in a way that he himself might have been had he not been seized by shadowy agents in the immediate aftermath.

Had there been no Zanzibar triangle to complicate things, Dan

91

figured he might have already been over his unceremonious detention and experiencing an excited state of mind not unlike Timo's. But there *was* a Zanzibar triangle and things were — *again* — stomach-churningly complicated.

"It's good to see you," was all Dan said to Timo, but he truly meant it; after the life-threatening injuries the Italian had sustained in a terrorist attack aimed at halting his efforts to save the world from Il Diavolo, it would *always* be good to see Timo.

"What about me?" a voice asked from the kitchen, catching Dan's attention. He turned and saw Tara Ford, looking as bright as a daisy as she stood in the doorway, all teeth and eyes like the world was perfect. She opened her arms, exaggeratedly wide, and walked towards him.

"Are you doing okay?" Dan asked, worried about her having heard what Emma and Clark were talking about in the car.

Tara pulled back and raised her eyebrows. "Am *I* doing okay? I heard about Friday night, mister. Are *you* doing okay?"

"I'm fine," he replied unconvincingly. "But do you know where my dad is? I want to get everyone together.

"He's with Phil," Tara said, pointing towards the back of the house. "Outside."

Emma emerged through the front door with her suitcase moments later and put it down as soon as she saw Tara.

Tara didn't move towards her like she had to Dan, always more reluctant to show her big sister that she needed her, but her eyes gave away how good it was to be reunited.

Emma did the walking and hugged Tara tightly before placing a hand on her cheek and looking into her eyes, the visual resembling a mother checking a fallen child for injuries more than anything else. "Are you okay?" she asked. "And it's okay to say no."

"What the hell did Clark tell you guys?" Tara laughed, amused by their unusually concerned attention. She pointed a finger at herself and ran it up and down. "Because I know you're not about to stand there and tell me I don't *look* okay…"

It was Emma's turn to laugh now. "Can you believe I was almost starting to miss you?" she said, happily convinced by Tara's faux narcissism that her apparent malaise had been a temporary one after all.

Clark and Mr Byrd entered soon after Emma. "Phil's already here with Dad, out back," Clark announced, continuing straight through the house to get them. "Mr Byrd doesn't know anything at all about Friday, by the way. He wasn't here when Timo told us."

Mr Byrd, the loyal neighbour who had been there for Dan during the earliest stages of the IDA leak when no one else could be, glanced around at the faces in the increasingly crowded living room in an effort to gauge whether the news he didn't know was good or bad.

"Well…" he said in his usual slow, gentle tone, "I *do* know they found a triangle on a beach."

As soon as Clark opened the back door, Dan heard rapid and excited footsteps under the laughter that followed Mr Byrd's comment. Rooster, the affectionate spaniel Dan had rescued from Richard Walker's place after the Messengers took Walker for the last time, raced through the kitchen and into the living room as quickly as his old legs would carry him. He was more excited to see Dan than anyone, but he stopped very suddenly just a few feet away.

Dan crouched to the ground. "It's okay, boy… they're gone. It's just me." He held out a hand which Rooster timidly inched towards. He was fully relaxed and nuzzling into Dan by the time Henry and Phil appeared, but his initial reluctance had given Mr Byrd an idea of what he was about to hear; ever since Dan played the old footage from Lolo National Forest at the drive in on Contact Day, Rooster's ability to sense the recent presence of the Messengers was globally renowned. Indeed, government agents and researchers had performed all kinds of non-invasive tests on Rooster since then, and he had even gone along to some of Dan's monthly check-ups for some scans of his own.

"Okay," Clark boomed, clapping his hands together. "Dan, we're all here. Spit it out."

V minus 78

"Billy, Billy!" a slew of reporters called as they surrounded Billy Kendrick on the sidewalk outside the New York Gravesen.

The only media personnel who ever irritated Billy were those who got physical and invaded his personal space, and fortunately they were few and far between. The sheer size of this pack, however, was a great annoyance in and of itself.

"I'm just trying to get to my cab," the usually affable alien expert said in an impatient tone. "You'll hear from me on Focus 20/20 tonight... can't you wait a few hours? That's if I can get to the damn studio through this rabble."

Amid the hustle and bustle, which did grow increasingly physical as Billy neared his cab and the swarm of photographers fought for one final shot, he heard a particularly loud question about the unconfirmed rumours that Dan McCarthy might also be appearing on the show.

"Where do you people even *get* these rumours?" Billy guffawed. "Of course he's not! Don't get me wrong, it would be wonderful if Dan felt like he could make these kinds of appearances, because we'd all love to hear from him... but do you cockroaches really wonder why he has to keep his head down? Look at you all, and I'm *no one*! Try being Dan for five minutes!"

V minus 77

McCarthy Residence
Birchwood, Colorado

Before opening his mouth to begin an uncomfortable and potentially divisive explanation of what he had experienced on Thursday night, Dan looked around the room and found his eyes settling on the door to the basement. It was inaccessible for Henry's wheelchair so out of the question as a secure discussion area at the moment, but memories of the previous year rattled through his mind.

"How long would it take to fully shield my old basement again?" he asked Phil, in reference to the signal-blocking technology the privacy-conscious prepper had installed during the basement conversion and then removed after Contact Day when Dan realised that his borderline obsessive paranoia was no longer necessary.

Phil gave it a few seconds of thought then turned his palms up in a slow shrug. "The actual work? Eight, ten hours. Sourcing everything we'd need? At least a few days. But I'll level with you Dan: that shielding gave you peace of mind more than anything else. The walls down there are thick as hell and they're under the ground. No one is eavesdropping on you in the basement so long as you have this sealed door and so long as you start keeping all the tech out of there again like you used to. I could hook up the old security centre today if you want it, with feeds from all over town. But in terms of the shielding, the only protection it gave you that you can't get from basic common-sense security practices was the protection against EMPs. If you're worried about that, I can get a Faraday cage for your computer and we can hard-wire a secure connection like you used to have."

Dan rubbed his chin in deep thought. "And next door? We would just need to keep digital devices out and get a better door like I have here, and then Emma's basement... *our* basement, I mean... would be totally secure too?" He quickly glanced at Emma. "If you're okay with that?"

"I guess I'm not *opposed*," she said, clearly not too enthused, either. The day when Dan and Phil had ripped the shielding from the walls of Dan's basement had been symbolic of his post-Contact Day freedom from a time of secrets and pressure, and it saddened Emma that such freedom seemed to be a thing of the past. "But Dan, if you're worried about them listening in, I think that *other* thing is probably the main thing to worry about right now..."

Dan instinctively put a hand to the back of his neck. Sensing everyone else's confusion, he then dived right into an explanation. "The government or some secret agency put a chip in my neck," he said. "I didn't know, but it detected the pain I felt on Friday night when the Messengers contacted me. By the time I woke up, and that couldn't have even been a full minute after it started, there were agents standing in the bedroom. They grabbed me, grabbed Emma, and took us away for individual questioning. I've been under close surveillance all year — and if they can get to me that quickly in Italy, you can be damn sure they've been hanging around here a lot closer than we ever could have thought."

"Jesus," Henry groaned. Like most of the others, he wore an expression of shock.

Clark's, however, was a look of full-on rage. Godfrey had naturally only told the GCC representatives of the contact event and nothing about the forceful detention, so this particular part of the story hadn't reached Birchwood via Timo. "They took you away?" he asked, fury in the words. "So *that's* why your emergency tracker said you activated it at the military complex in Milan, when you told me that was nothing to worry about?"

"Well it wasn't the *main* thing to worry about!" Dan replied, sounding slightly defensive. "It's not the most important part."

Clark breathed very slowly. "Did they hurt you?"

"Not on purpose," Dan said, choosing his words carefully. "They grabbed me and I saw one of them sneaking up on Emma; she was outside with her headphones on. I fought two of them off for long enough to run out of the bedroom, but another one tackled me from the side and my head hit the floor pretty hard. It knocked me unconscious, but sort of *slowly*... I didn't just black out straight away. I guess the guy who tackled me was holding me down pretty hard; I couldn't breathe easily."

"Did he speak? Did you get his name? Any birthmarks, tattoos... give me something to—"

"Clark, it's done," Dan said, cutting off the thought of natural justice that so often seemed to be where Clark's mind went whenever he became aware that someone he cared about had been mistreated.

"Anyway..." Emma interjected. "That's the thing about surveillance and security and everything else... I'm not so sure they really *have* been watching and listening to us all year, in terms of actual eavesdropping. Because we've all talked about a lot of stuff in the past year... all kinds of ideas and theories. All kinds of little things they didn't know about, but which they definitely would have wanted to know *more* about if they'd heard us mention them at all. Do you know what I mean?"

No one said they didn't.

"But about these chips in our necks," she went on. "I have one too, but do you think there's really any way they could hear us... through the skin? I would say no, and from their perspective I can see why it makes sense for them to have something in there to alert them if we ever feel sudden pain — *contact* pain — so I don't see any reason to doubt that was their sole purpose. I understand why they'd want one in Dan's neck more than why they'd want one in mine, but I guess they wanted to be thorough."

"And we're getting them removed soon," Dan clarified. "Slater said so, and she doesn't gain anything from lying to me when all a lie would do is make me angry. She doesn't want anyone to know what they did to me and she knows I'll talk if they piss me off any more than they already have."

Clark grunted out an uncertain reaction. "I dunno, man, she might know how set you are on staying out of the spotlight. Especially if they *have* been watching and listening in all this time, but even if they haven't... the only public comments you've made in the past year have all been about you feeling like you've done your part and wanting to leave everything else to the elected leaders."

Mr Byrd waved his hand slowly, half-raising it like a school child.

"So for those of us who missed the start… you were contacted on Friday and the government knew straight away? That's all we know for sure?"

"That's part of it," Dan said. "I had a vision of the Buenos Aires Gravesen, in a dream, and a policeman in the dream told me someone was inside and had just taken President Slater hostage. The Japanese Prime Minister, too, and my watch in the dream said it was Saturday morning at 11. I saw a GeoSov flag hanging from a window on the top floor. Then in real life, when I spoke to Slater, she said she wasn't staying at the Gravesen but was scheduled to meet him there at that time. And the security services found a GeoSov flag in the exact room whose window I saw it hanging from, so Slater and Godfrey and everyone else know it wasn't a false alarm."

"And *that's* all we know for sure," Emma confirmed.

Dan gulped. "Well…"

Emma's brow furrowed. "*Well?*"

"I didn't want to tell you this next part while the guards at the airport were definitely watching and listening to us, because I'm still trying to make sense of it. And I didn't want to tell you in the car because I didn't want to tell Clark before Tara or my dad. I don't want any more secrets or some people knowing more than others. I don't want *any* of this, but I *definitely* don't want that."

She nodded in understanding.

"Oh, and just quickly on that," Dan said. "Clark, remember the guy who took us to the facility on Contact Day? I know his full name and I told the agents, when I was trying to make sure they knew not to mess with me. I know the facility, too. I mapped his movements with a tracking device, but I didn't tell them that. They don't know how I know, and they might even think the Messengers told me. Anyway, the secret base is out at Heron Lake reservoir and it's completely underground. You know how Billy Kendrick always said it's easier to hide something underground than restrict a huge sector of airspace, especially if you want the very existence of the place to be secret? It's exactly that… the old idea of being able to hide the fact that there's a secret, not just hiding the secret itself."

"Okay, man," Clark said. "That wasn't smart but it's not exactly the most important thing right now, is it? What's the next part that even Emma doesn't know."

Dan spat it out: "I know how much this Zanzibar triangle looks like an obvious hoax, but I think it's real. There was a shape on the flag I saw in my dream, like white dots in the corner of the flag making a kind of constellation shape. It *wasn't* a constellation, I just mean that kind of thing like you see on an Australian flag or whatever. Anyway, that exact shape is pretty clearly visible in the blurry photos we've seen of the triangle. You know those little jewels on it? All the brightest ones that reflect the most light are arranged in the same shape as the arrangement I saw on the flag. In the dream, I think the Messengers were telling me they were going to plant it."

"Why?" Emma asked, one word summing up everyone's feelings.

"I'm just going to admit that I flat-out don't know," Dan said. "And I don't know *why* I don't know. I don't know why they're being so cryptic again. Last year it was because they wanted to guide me to the fourth plaque with enough provenance to make the discovery seem plausible without exposing Walker's hoax, because they didn't want to destabilise Earth anymore than they had to. But now? Everyone already knows they're real. Everyone saw them a mile down the street, standing at the drive-in with a cable connected to my neck and a forcefield holding everyone else back. I don't get it."

"Well, it's a triangle," Tara chimed in. "And we know they like triangles. The first vision you had last year was a triangle in the sky and then it was a triangular shape between the main locations of other stuff that led us to Salida. Remember? What Trey saw at Lolo, the California Fireball, and then Salida. So a triangle does fit in with everything else, is all I'm saying. At least we know that much."

"Hmm, but so does everyone else," Timo Fiore mused, breaking a long and thoughtful silence. "If someone wanted to hoax an artefact, it would probably look like this. With the timing and location so neatly benefiting the ELF, I can't see past the idea of a hoax… either by the ELF themselves or maybe even by the GeoSovs."

"The GeoSovs?" Dan asked, clearly having not even considered this.

Timo shrugged. "Think about it… maybe the Messengers were telling you there was going to be a GeoSov hoax? You saw this constellation-like arrangement in the same dream that told you the GeoSovs were going to try to take Slater hostage, correct? It therefore makes a degree of sense that the constellation was there to warn you that the GeoSovs were going to do *this*, too. Think back to the IDA hoax: Walker set everything up to fit in with the idea that the Nazis dumped that sphere off Miramar. Maybe the GeoSovs are setting everything up to make it look like the ELF dumped this triangle?"

Dan rubbed his eyes in exasperation, not in disagreement at Timo's well-argued point but purely at his own frustrated confusion. The last thing he thought he'd be thinking about once again was whether something was a hoax or a genuinely extraterrestrial find. All over again, he felt sick to the pit of his stomach.

Emma lifted her phone from her pocket and groaned, interrupting a conversation no one was enjoying. Like Dan, she hated Timo's suggestion but reluctantly recognised that it might just be valid. "Focus 20/20," she said. "It's tonight — a Saturday special — and they want you on via satellite."

"Me?" Dan asked. He walked around to look at the list of names on her phone. All were written underneath a politely worded invitation from the desk of the show's much-respected host, Marian de Clerk.

First came Billy Kendrick, a good friend of Dan's and a reasonable man. Next was Joe Crabbe, the one-time shock-jock who was now seen as a more balanced media personality. Thirdly, and certainly most surprisingly, was an unnamed 'GeoSov spokesperson'.

Fourth was Kaitlyn Judd, the famous actress who had already appeared alongside Dan on the show on one previous occasion. People now associated her with aliens, especially due to her starring role in the critically panned movie *The Fourth Plaque*, which had almost ended her career when the final cut ended up being little more than a propaganda piece for William Godfrey's now-defunct Global Space Commission. Most recently she'd starred in a far more successful movie dramatising the approach and eventual deflection of Comet Conte-Abate, titled simply *Il Diavolo*.

Officially, Kaitlyn had been booked to talk about that movie's home media release; she had asked some good questions on her previous appearances, though, and clearly knew what she was talking about. There was no way Dan was participating, but he looked forward to hearing what she had to say as well as how Billy Kendrick and Joe Crabbe would deal with a GeoSov.

It also mentioned that a final guest would be appearing via satellite, and that this was not a reference to Dan who could round the panel out to six if he wished.

"Not a chance in hell," he said, exactly as Emma expected. "I don't even know what's going on, and I'm staying out of the spotlight, anyway."

"Quite right," Clark said, nodding firmly.

Emma nodded too, though far less committally.

"Shutting down a GeoSov once and for all?" Timo said, bucking the trend. "It's enticing, Dan. And we have many hours to prepare…"

"Timo," Dan sighed, "I wouldn't do this if the Messengers themselves came down and asked me to."

V minus 76

Ikulu

Dar es Salaam, Tanzania

Some fifty miles south-west of the Sunrise Palace Resort where the Zanzibar triangle had been discovered, a starlit scene few could have ever imagined greeted the media personnel lucky enough to have been invited. Four men stood behind a wide podium at Ikulu, the State House and official residence of Tanzania's President.

He was there, proud as could be, as was the triangle's discoverer, Hassan Manula, who looked distinctly like he would rather be anywhere else in the world.

Two men more familiar to an international audience stood in the centre. The first was Ding Ziyang, just off the plane having made a beeline for Tanzania when news of the incredible find first broke. Ding's initial reaction had been one of scepticism, and this lay behind the public silence he had maintained so far.

As the inaugural President of the Earth Liaison Forum as well as the world's most populous superpower's head of state, Ding had a strong claim for the position of most powerful man in the world. And given what he had been told about the Zanzibar triangle after a full day of careful analysis, he had a strong feeling that the discovery of the object — now at a secure location further inland — would cement his position and perhaps even remove any doubt.

Ding's presence was a welcome surprise to the attendant press, but it had never felt out of the question. What caught *everyone* off-guard was the identity of the man standing at Ding's right-hand side: John Cole, the former British Prime Minister who had been forced to resign in disgrace after deciding to unilaterally reveal to the public that Earth was in the path of an extinction-level comet.

Now, Cole's brand was utterly toxic in the United Kingdom, long abandoned and disowned by even his closest former allies. A greater cause of anger than the irresponsible comet revelation itself had been its deceitful nature, a transparent 'accident', as well as the fact that it was evidently driven by self-interest and a grudge against then-GSC Chairman William Godfrey.

In the intervening time, Cole had been working as a spuriously defined 'development consultant', primarily in African and Asian states where his notoriety as the recent leader of such a powerful Western country counted for enough to cancel out the utter contempt in which he was now held at home.

Many eyes stayed on Cole while the others addressed the media, beginning with the Tanzanian President who spoke of his pride that the Messengers had chosen to bless his nation with the triangle. Unaccustomed to the global spotlight but tremendously glad to be in it, he also personally thanked Hassan Manula for putting his country before himself in alerting the authorities as soon as he discovered it.

Hassan, feeling tremendously out of place and visibly sweating buckets, rushed through the speech that had been written for him. He said that he felt blessed on an even deeper level since he had been the one lucky enough to first set eyes on the incredible object, and really did as well as anyone could have expected in delivering the pre-written words in a plausibly natural manner.

Speaking Chinese despite his well-known mastery of English, Ding Ziyang wasted no time in stressing the importance of the Zanzibar discovery. He described the triangle as the most beautiful thing he had ever seen and the most incredible gift in human history. Much as the two earlier speakers had expressed their gratitude that the triangle showed up in their country, Ding took great delight in expressing his own joy that it had arrived within the borders of a staunch ELF member like Tanzania. Details of what his expert analysts had determined while studying the object would be released in due course, he promised, and until then he begged for patience from the citizens of GCC nations who might understandably feel left out of an incredible moment in humanity's history.

In two short sentences, Ding Ziyang then greatly turned up the heat on Chairman Godfrey by encouraging such disenfranchised citizens to make their feelings known to their national leaders in any way they deemed appropriate, and by encouraging those national leaders to switch allegiance to the ELF now while the offer stood.

"Because as we can see from where they put the triangle," Ding concluded, surprising everyone with an impromptu and highly symbolic switch to fluent but heavily accented English, "the Messengers have just made *their* allegiance perfectly clear."

John Cole, pushing out his burly chest to a near comical extent, cleared his throat and leaned forward slightly into the microphone in front of him. "I'd like to echo President Ding's words," Cole said, using a title no one else ever had. The Englishman spoke in his northern accent of old, jettisoning the more 'proper' speech patterns that had been coached into him by his former confidante and partner in crime, Jack Neal. "It says a lot about the President that he's been kind enough and forgiving enough to extend the hand of friendship to those who have so far been bullied or bribed into participating in Godfrey and Slater's Argentine charade, and I dearly hope the offer is seized by many while it stands."

Just as when Cole had once stood at Godfrey's side during the political free-for-all that followed the IDA leak, making controversial points his boss wanted to get across without actually saying himself, it didn't take a political genius to know that Cole was once again being used in this way. His new master, Ding Ziyang, now stood quietly while Cole delivered controversial soundbites whose origin allowed a degree of plausible deniability, if necessary, that he had overstepped the mark of his own accord rather than as per any orders from above.

"I stand here before you delighted to announce the President's intention to initiate a rapid proliferation of ELF satellite offices in strategic locations," Cole went on, booming out the words as though addressing a packed arena with no microphone, "the first of which will open on the beautiful island of Cuba in a matter of days. I myself am greatly honoured to have been chosen as the ELF's new Western Secretary, and I look forward to taking up my residence in Havana.

"I've been here in the ELF's African heartland handling some unrelated business for over a week, and the fact that the Messengers placed their latest message of peace in this particular chunk of the ELF's vast territory makes the timing very good from my personal standpoint. I've already seen the desperate conspiracy theories and claims of hoaxes but really, this is one story that not even Richard Walker could have made up! I'll be here for the rest of today and tomorrow, keeping a close eye on what else our brainbox scientists can find out about the triangle, but none of that is going to stop me from appearing via satellite on tonight's live episode of *Focus 20/20*. And needless to say, I very much look forward to sharing my views on these exciting recent developments with Marian de Clerk and my fellow panellists. Until then, friends…"

At the end of his speech, Cole extended a hand which Ding took very gladly, posing for the press and sending a message to the world — one city in particular — that *no one* had seen coming.

V minus 75

GCC Headquarters
Buenos Aires, Argentina

"I don't know whether to laugh or cry," William Godfrey mused, watching a televised repeat of the impromptu ELF press conference in Tanzania with a suitably puzzled expression etched on his face.

President Slater, whose ability to survive turbulent times Godfrey had come to admire and whose viewpoint he had very recently come to seek in private meetings like this, was currently the only other person in his office. A third kind of reaction came to her mind: "How about scream?"

Godfrey involuntarily chortled. "We can deal with this, Valerie. After all, we're dealing with amateurs. I mean to say... *John Cole*? The only person more inept than Cole is a person who wants Cole on their side!"

"I know what we talked about," Slater said, "and I understand the strategic reasoning for letting this play out until the inevitable slip-up hands us the keys to the kingdom. But those speeches weren't just the ELF sticking its thumb in the GCC's eye, William, that was the Chinese Premier engaging in borderline sabre-rattling and holding a middle finger in the United States' face."

"Go on..." Godfrey encouraged, pleasantly surprised by the intensity of her anger.

Slater paused, shaking her head in disbelieving rage. "I mean *come on*, a new ELF office in Cuba? Fucking *Cuba*? That's a calculated move and they know exactly what it represents — they know *exactly* what it harks back to — and even if it didn't trouble me personally like it does, this is going to blow up at home. Because let's break this down to what it is: a Chinese base less than a hundred miles from the coast of Florida. It simply cannot stand!"

"I fully agree," Godfrey insisted. "Quite frankly, I didn't expect them to be like this; not in the slightest. I thought they would cagily drip-feed information about the triangle, not double-down on its authenticity and pummel us with too many provocations to count. It seems to me that they've taken our silence for weakness... because yes, warning us they're going to establish a physical presence in Cuba is a clear message, but there was a lot more than that to what they just said. Describing a large sovereign state like Tanzania as an '*ELF heartland*' is provocative in itself, but talking about '*the ELF's territory*' is flat-out inflammatory. The call for defections is similarly infuriating in its own right, but the implicit call for civilian disobedience in GCC countries is a line they're going to regret having crossed. I don't want to use the word 'war', but if—"

"It's too late for *ifs* on that front," Slater interrupted. "Elements of my party are going to see this as an act of war, and the opposition is going to seize on it, too. Whatever happens with the triangle, this Cuba thing isn't going to go away. But that's what I'm thinking... what *about* the triangle? With how firmly they just came out, it really does look as though Ding at least *believes* that this is real. John Cole has never considered the consequences of his actions before and I don't think he's going to start doing so anytime soon, but Ding must know how bad this would look if it turned out to be a hoax."

Godfrey nodded several times. "And I can't even begin to get my head around why Cole mentioned Richard Walker, or why he went as far as pre-empting suspicions of a hoax by actually uttering the H-word. We've already looked into this Hassan Manula, of course, and I just got a report a few minutes before he appeared at the Tanzanian State House. Manula has no formal education or qualifications and has worked various low-paying jobs in the hotel industry throughout his adult life. *But...* I've just learned that not only does this man speak serviceable Chinese, he actually teaches Chinese guest sensitivity classes at his current workplace. This whole thing is either the biggest coincidence in history or they're baiting us with his identity as well as their words. It's like they're begging for us to call this out as a hoax, which makes me see your point about Ding appearing to believe this is real, after all."

"So where the hell does that leave us, William? And where the hell do we go next?"

"Hold your horses," he pleaded, reacting to Slater's raised voice and evident urgency. "There is one more possibility that makes sense if you consider what we know so far. Think about it: *we* don't think this is real, but we're starting to think that Ding *does*. This has been bad for us, obviously, but if and when the hoax is exposed, it's going to be bad for the ELF, too. So the question becomes one of motive... and who do you know of that doesn't just want to embarrass the GCC, but also the ELF?"

Slater turned her palms upwards in impatience.

"The scale of this hoaxing plot is great indeed given the sheer size of the triangle," Godfrey went on, "and it's certainly reckless in its level of ambition. But that's what's in my mind, Valerie. Because when we're talking about recklessly ambitious plots on a grand scale, it's difficult to avoid thinking about *another* recent plot that brought our enemies within a few hours of a physical attack on the President of the United States."

"You think this was the *GeoSovs*?" Slater gasped, shocked that Godfrey would even consider this rather than stunned by a lightbulb-like realisation.

Godfrey held her eyes. "No, but I think it *might* have been..."

She shook her head, dismissing the relevance of his musings as much as their likelihood of being well-founded. "Whatever that stupid triangle is and whoever put it there, that's just context," she groaned, "and no amount of context is going to change the *content* of what they just said. Right now they're showing us up as fools, and with Cole having come into the picture, we can expect him to fire more and more provocation at us until we're backed so far into a corner that there's nowhere left to turn."

Godfrey placed his thumb and forefinger on his cheeks, squeezing inwards in sudden thought. "We need a Cole of our own," he announced. "We need someone who'll say the things we want to say, but who isn't us."

"Hmmm. Go on..." Slater urged.

"Or even better," Godfrey mused, "for further detachment, what about someone who's broadly on our side but who isn't bound by political decorum in the slightest? Someone, you might say, like Dan McCarthy?"

V minus 74

After filling everyone in on what he had been through and what he made of the Zanzibar triangle, Dan went next door with Emma to unpack the suitcases from their abortive pre-honeymoon. Tara followed and Emma asked Timo to come, too, so that she could grill him on exactly what he'd been told so far by his Fiore Frontiere delegates in Buenos Aires.

Within a few minutes of walking through the door, they all heard a familiar but rare chime emanating from the trend-tracker in Emma's living room. This device, which they had all first grown accustomed to in Dan's old basement, sat high on the wall and resembled a ticker from the stock exchange. For most of the day its elongated high-resolution screen was completely blank, only kicking in when a news story or post came in from the owner's customised list of sources. A further customisation option could restrict the number of alerts based on a virality threshold, with only the most wave-making posts and stories getting through.

Emma's trend-tracker functioned as a canary of sorts, only tending to cheep out its call when something was wrong. This was because her tracker was set to the maximum virality threshold, alerting her only to posts which had been shared an extraordinarily high number of times in a very short period, and nothing travelled faster than bad news.

The post which greeted their eyes as they glanced up came from an ACN-affiliated reporter in Tanzania, and could hardly have been any more surprising: "Ding has been here for ten minutes waiting for someone else. That someone else just arrived, unannounced: JOHN COLE! Something big is coming..."

Emma immediately grabbed the remote control from her couch and pressed a button to bring down the hidden projector which spent most of its time in a recess in her ceiling. A video feed from Tanzania filled the living room's main wall within seconds, and John Cole was visible within a few minutes.

They watched and listened in growing shock as the press conference continued with barb after barb aimed westward to Buenos Aires.

"What the hell is Cole's endgame here?" Timo asked, outraged by much of what he'd heard. "I can understand why Ding is using him, but what is he playing at?"

Dan and Tara, quite naturally, deferred to Emma for an insight.

"Well, Cole is different from the rest of them," she said. "His everyman schtick is the one thing about him that's real; he came into politics late, from the real world. So it's not always safe to assume he's thinking in the same way as a regular political climber would. But here, *this* time, I think it's pretty clear what he's doing. I know he's being pretty ruthless about the Western leaders, but it looks like he's positioning himself as a kind of compromise choice for when this GCC-ELF face-off eventually dies down and the dust settles. The dust might only settle after an explosion, if you know what I mean, but he's trying to set himself up to lead whatever comes next."

"Hmm," Timo uttered. "To be honest, Emma, I think you might be giving him too much credit. Cole's name is dirt in Britain and it's dirt here. My take is that he wants a semblance of power and the only way he can get it is to let Ding use him as a middle finger to Godfrey and Slater. An ELF office in Cuba... that's a message to them. But putting Cole in charge of it? That's salt in the wounds, adding insult to injury."

Emma shrugged. "I don't think he's quite as stupid as he looks — after all, he weaselled his way into Godfrey's ministerial Cabinet a few years ago with some very calculated *quid pro quo* promises. In his mind, he's going to be the frontrunner for leadership of a future unified organisation because he clearly expects that he'll be trusted by people in China... but he also knows that even as a clear Chinese puppet he'll still be less unpalatable to Westerners than an actual Chinese leader would be. So that's what I think *he* thinks... it's bullshit, but when you're dealing with idiots it's important to at least *try* to make sense of what they believe. If you know what someone believes, you can at least guess what their next move might be; and that's exactly what makes the *GeoSovs* so hard to get a handle on, because there are so many gaps in the logic of what they want and why the hell they even exist. Those people are—"

Another chiming sound abruptly cut Emma off, but this time it came from her pocket. She lifted her phone out and reacted in visible shock to the name on the screen. "What do you want from us?" she asked, picking up immediately.

The others exchanged uneasy glances.

"I'll *ask*," Emma went on, "but we both know what he's going to say. Dan... Focus 20/20?"

"I already told them no," he replied. "Why are they asking again?"

Emma held her hand against the phone's speaker. "It's not the network this time."

"Huh? So who is it?"

"It's Godfrey," Emma said.

Before her mouth had closed behind the words, Dan's hand was outstretched to take the phone. She handed it over.

Everyone watched Dan as he gazed down at the phone, all wondering and guessing and anticipating what he might say.

He took a deep breath, shook his head, and ended the call.

"Good call," Tara said. She moved towards Dan and placed a supportive hand on his back. "Going on Focus 20/20 is the opposite of keeping your head down, and Godfrey is just trying to use you the way Ding is using Cole. Even *I* can see that."

Neither Timo nor Emma looked quite so pleased, but Dan didn't see them.

"I'm going to give him a quick call," Timo announced. "I want to know where his head is on what Ding and Cole just did, and it could be a while before he convenes the delegates again."

No one argued, so Timo walked towards the kitchen and ultimately stepped outside. In the living room, Dan sat down.

"Why do they even want me to do it?" he groaned a few minutes later, the weight of the world suddenly back on his shoulders all over again. "This isn't even my fight."

"No," Emma said, "but by doing this you wouldn't be fighting for yourself. Dan... I love you, and I don't want to put you in a difficult spot. But you need to do this, and I'll be here to help you every step of the way. Ding and Cole just turned this thing up to eleven. Putting Cole in charge of an ELF base in Cuba? Talking about ELF *territory*? If Godfrey doesn't respond to this, Slater's going to have to."

Dan closed his eyes, hating Emma's words less than the feeling building within him that she was right.

"And we're thinking about all of this with a level of detachment," she went on, "because we know the Messengers warned you about the hostage plot and we know they told you something about the triangle. Everyone else just knows there's an alien triangle that only some countries are being granted scientific access to. Ding just turned that on the GCC and called for civil disobedience and national defections, and Cole was smiling like a Cheshire cat the whole time. This is going to get messy if nothing else happens; but if another triangle shows up soon or there's any serious disorder because of what they just said, those words are going to get people killed. This *has* to be defused, Dan, and no one else can do it."

"Emma, you *know* I'm out of the spotlight. That doesn't work if I do this. I can't dip in and out; I bowed out of the public arena and the only reason we have any kind of normal life is because everyone knows I'm never going to say anything so they've stopped even trying to ask. If I did *this*..."

She looked deeply into his eyes. "All of that is true, but this isn't like before. This isn't like when we were trying to get the truth out while keeping certain things back for everyone else's benefit. This *is* for everyone else's benefit, but it's not about abstract truths or conspiracies or coverups... not anymore. Dan, this is about people's lives. This is about the safety of good, innocent people, and the danger they're in because of all this tension that's being caused by people like John Cole and those goddamn GeoSovs. This is about challenging them so that—"

"I know," Dan interrupted. "Emma, I *know*. But why am *I* the best person to challenge them? Crabbe, Billy, even Godfrey or Slater themselves... they're all much better speakers than me."

"It doesn't matter if they're the best speakers in the world, Dan; they're not you. There's not another person alive who can challenge them like you can — no one. Not Godfrey or Slater, not Timo or Billy or Crabbe... not even me. I know you didn't ask for your life to bring you here — trust me, I know that better than anyone — but this is where you are and this is what you have to do. It's via satellite so you can read from notes, and most of the panel will be firmly on your side and very firmly against Cole and the GeoSov guy. I hear what you're saying about what this is going to do to the normal life we've been trying to live together, but this is bigger than us. If this keeps escalating, there's no limit to how serious it could get. Wars have started over a lot less, Dan… and if they really do open a Chinese-funded base in Cuba this week, Slater is going to have a lot of military voices in her ear. If she does nothing, the accusations of appeasement will be the end of her and a hardliner will fill her shoes in no time. And if *you* do nothing, that's what's at stake."

Dan balled his fist and pressed it upwards against his chin in thought. "And you'll be right beside me?"

"Just like always. Well, except that one time when I was in the hospital and you kinda single-handedly saved the world by summoning the Messengers to stop the comet…"

"Man, I wish I could summon them like that again today," Dan sighed ruefully. "Things would be so much easier if they would just come back and explain this triangle themselves."

Timo re-entered the living room moments later, holding his own phone in his palm. "He makes a good case, Dan, but neither he nor I can go on the show to challenge Cole on this; the GCC's founding articles don't allow for independent comment on contact-related issues without majority approval, and there's not enough time for the delegates to convene before the show. Would you hear him out for one minute?"

Dan, already having been all but convinced of his unwanted responsibility to try to cool things down, took the phone without complaint.

Emma intercepted Dan's hand. "Pretend you still need to be convinced," she whispered. "Let him think you're doing him a favour."

Dan couldn't hide his confusion, but after this long he knew better than to question Emma's strategic and occasionally machiavellian instincts. With more than a hint of reluctance, he swallowed away his doubts and took hold of the phone.

V minus 73

Maria Janzyck, ACN's senior reporter, stood outside the ELF's global headquarters for the second time in as many days.

Having arrived in Beijing to cover Contact Day from a location often ignored by mainstream US networks, the previous day's lack of activity was already out of her mind.

For today, with an apparently alien artefact having been discovered in an ELF-aligned country, the mood in China was very different.

More news crews were arriving by the minute, in scenes reminiscent of those Maria had encountered in Birchwood, Colorado when Dan McCarthy and the IDA leak had transformed a disused drive-in lot into the world's most iconic media hotspot.

If her stay in Beijing ended up half as exciting as her time in Birchwood, Maria would be very glad she came.

And if what she was hearing about the Zanzibar triangle from her low-level contacts within the ELF turned out to be true, the ride was just getting started…

V minus 72

"What do you *want*?" Dan spoke into the phone.

"Mr McCarthy!" Chairman Godfrey replied, his tone reflecting his pleasure that Dan had taken the call. "Before we continue, I should let you know that you're on speaker-phone."

"Why, who else is there with you?"

The world's most familiar female voice answered: "Hello, Dan."

Dan turned to Emma. "Slater's there," he mouthed silently.

Emma gave him an 'okay' hand gesture. She couldn't hear the other side of the call live but knew Timo's phone would have similar recording software to her own and that she'd be able to retrospectively analyse every syllable in due course.

"And we'll get right to the point," Godfrey continued. "I understand you rejected an invitation to appear on the live episode of *Focus 20/20* this evening, and I'd very much appreciate it if you would reconsider. I imagine Billy Kendrick will make a fair fist of shutting down Cole's nonsense, but he lacks a certain gravitas. Crabbe meanwhile... well, he can't be relied upon to do anything. And needless to say, whichever GeoSov rat crawls out of a sewer to say their piece will prove to be an obstacle rather than an ally.

"One of Valerie, Timo or myself would gladly do this ourselves if we could," Godfrey went on, "but as you might already know, GCC members are currently prevented from making substantive individual comments on anything within the Commission's explicit remit. And in more general terms, we really don't want this to become a shouting contest between the GCC and ELF. This isn't about two sides, Mr McCarthy, this is about one planet's security being endangered by two extremely foolish men."

Dan felt like asking if Godfrey was talking about Ding and himself rather than Ding and Cole, but he left this disdainful thought unshared. "You know I made a decision to stay out of the spotlight and leave everything to the people who have been elected to lead," he said, "and you know I didn't make that choice lightly."

"*Dan*," Godfrey said, slipping into first-name informality in a deliberate attempt to emphasise his concern, "that ship has well and truly sailed."

"He's right," President Slater chimed in. "And I know this is a lot to ask after everything that's happened, but everyone would benefit from your appearance, Dan. Your presence is unifying in a way the rest of us can only dream of. I encourage you to talk openly about everything, including and especially your recent vision and the role you played in stopping a GeoSov plot that the rest of the world doesn't even know we foiled. My only request is that you don't mention what happened immediately following your vision, with the unfortunate actions of the ground agents or indeed the fact that they were alerted by a chip in your neck. As I said, that can be removed whenever is convenient, and if you are understandably concerned about further surveillance and by the security issues that might come with a re-heightened public profile, I'm entirely prepared to grant you full Secret Service protection. Your relationship with the Messengers makes your wellbeing a national security priority, Dan, and in a personal sense I'm very grateful for what you prevented. Whatever you want or need, consider it done."

"Okay," Dan said.

"Okay?" Slater repeated. "So you're in."

"I'm in. But Godfrey, don't start thinking we're on the same side here. I don't want there to be two sides and I'm not going to pretend otherwise. And regarding the triangle itself, I—"

"Good," Godfrey interrupted. "And you can say anything other than what Valerie has asked you not to. You're a smart man, Dan. I know you don't want to bring unnecessary problems on anyone; least of all yourself. Godspeed."

The call was terminated before Dan could reply. He didn't like Godfrey's use of the word *'can'*, as though Dan had somehow agreed to be bound by their conditions, but this was a small annoyance in the grander scheme of things.

"Excellent!" Timo cheered. "Dan, you are a good man and this is the right thing."

Emma held her hand out for Timo's phone. Dan handed it over, and she immediately navigated to a recording of the call. "I'm going to listen back to this and see what I can read between the lines, as well as what we can read into what they actually said."

Timo followed her, with permission, just as keen to hear it.

This left Dan and Tara alone in the living room. He sat down on the couch next to her and leaned back.

Tara lifted her knees up on to the couch's surface and let her tired and slightly hung-over head fall onto Dan's shoulder as ACN filled the wall in front of them. Talking head after talking head appeared to say their piece on the possible implications of the controversial recent comments from the ELF's leadership, and more generally on the organisation's evident finders-keepers attitude towards the Zanzibar triangle.

"I don't think you should be doing the show," Tara said after a few minutes, sounding as if she didn't want to say it — like she didn't want to make Dan's next few hours any harder than they were already going to be — but like she really couldn't keep it in.

"Emma doesn't usually get things like this wrong," Dan replied.

"I know," Tara sighed, looking up into his eyes with visible concern in her own, "but I really don't like it."

Dan tried to think of a reply that would ease Tara's anxiety, but the truth echoed in the chambers of his mind too loudly to ignore, ultimately escaping of its own volition: "Neither do I."

V minus 71

The morning had begun like any other for Liang Fu, and as 8am rolled around he was ready to head out the door and make the short drive to his workplace. A low-level diplomat, Liang had settled well in Vanuatu thanks to the tiny archipelago's relatively sizeable population of Chinese workers.

Relations between the countries' governments were ever-deepening, benefitting one economically and the other strategically. Liang's work was purely administrative, but he had heard rumblings from some friends that a governmental building which recently closed for renovation had in fact been refitted as an ELF office which would be announced and opened very quickly.

The remarkable news from Tanzania — both the Zanzibar triangle's discovery and the comments that followed about an expanded ELF presence around the world — certainly made Liang re-think his previous suspicion that his friends had been pulling his leg about an ELF office on the remote island he called home.

"Pin-Pin," Liang called, encouraging Pinocchio, his large Alsatian, to come in off the beach so he could lock up before departing for the day. "Here, Pin-Pin, time to come inside."

The dog didn't come, which wasn't unusual enough to worry Liang but was certainly enough to frustrate him. But when he stepped outside, all of his frustration immediately turned to concern.

To Liang's horror, the typically water-shy dog was around twenty metres out to sea and still paddling away.

"*Pinnochio!*" Liang yelled in an altogether different tone. He removed his work blazer and took his phone and wallet from his pockets, running to the water and diving into the sea. "I'm coming, boy."

The dog heard its owner and, as though soothed, made a slow 180-degree turn. Liang had hold of him before long and hurried back to the shore.

"What were you thinking?" he boomed at the dripping-wet canine, as though expecting a response.

Another voice then filled the air, coming from the next house over as Liang's neighbour and colleague, Zhou, sprinted from his home in pursuit of his own dog which was dashing towards the sea.

Inexplicably, the dog went straight into the water. Liang, already soaked to the bone, dived back in and recovered the much smaller dog within seconds.

"What the hell is going on?" Zhou asked, seeing that Pinnochio was just as wet as his own dog and had clearly done the same thing moments earlier.

"I don't know," Liang panted, exhausted from his exertions, "but I don't like it. Go back inside and lock your door, Zhou... something's not right."

V minus 70

A piercing canary-like chime filled the living room within minutes of Dan's eventual agreement to appear on the evening's highly anticipated episode of *Focus 20/20*, the world's longest-running current affairs panel discussion show and comfortably its most important. He could see that Emma had wasted no time in passing the message on to the network, and the instantly viral announcement came from the desk of the show's much-respected host, Marian de Clerk herself.

Dan thought the wording was more befitting of a tabloid journalist than someone with de Clerk's gravitas, but by now he understood how the media worked. Soundbites and punchy phrases were the currency of social media in particular, and this announcement was composed accordingly:

"Dan McCarthy breaks his silence — TONIGHT! Join me for Focus 20/20, live from New York, where it's McCarthy vs Cole and the world will be watching..."

"It's not really you against Cole," Tara said, "... right? It's more about you trying to, I dunno, contextualise Cole's crap and calm everyone down?"

Dan nodded. "They're just using the angle that works for them. But

120

the point of doing this is to get people interested... and the more people who watch, the better it is, I guess. So if framing it as me vs Cole brings in even more viewers, it's probably not a bad thing."

Within no more than another twenty or thirty seconds, Clark burst in with a disbelieving look on his face. "What the hell is that?" he boomed, gesturing towards the trend-tracker whose counterpart next door had alerted him at the same time as the rest of the world. "Who talked you into this? Timo?"

"Emma did," Dan said, telling the truth. He considered leaving it there, but in accordance with his continued drive against secrecy he decided to expand on what had come next. "Slater and Godfrey called to ask me to do it, too, but Emma had already talked me round. Cole is trying to drive the world apart even more than it already is, and the things he's saying are going to cause riots all over the place because he's blaming Godfrey for the triangle having to be kept from us. Remember all the first looting after the plaques came out, and then the much worse rioting when Cole leaked the news about Il Diavolo? We were stuck here, watching from the couch, hoping it would get better. This time I have a chance to stop things from getting that bad. This time everyone else is going to be on their couch watching *me*. TV is real life; everyone saw and heard Cole speaking from Tanzania and there's going to be outbreaks of violence all over the world because of it. So when everyone sees and hears me coming at them with a different kind of message, maybe we can stop that violence before it gets out of control?"

"It's not even just that," Emma interjected, announcing her presence as she walked into the living room from her kitchen. "We live in a bubble, okay? And that bubble kind of makes us forget how important Dan is. Yeah, his words can calm a lot of everyday citizens down and hopefully prevent any civil disobedience that we might have otherwise seen tonight. But it's deeper than that. He's your little brother and he's my fiancé, but to half the world Dan's a messiah and to most of the other half he's at least some kind of prophet. Those aliens saved us all because of what he told them, Clark... we can try to get on with our lives and pretend that didn't happen, but it did. So if Dan says something against certain ELF or GCC policies, or even against the national policies of certain leaders, that's a serious amount of pressure. Everyone is worried about protests and riots because John Cole basically just called for people to pressure their governments into abandoning the GCC. And Clark, that's John *fucking* Cole... one of the most hated men in the world! So, hypothetically, if *Dan* was to call for real international unity and encourage people to protest against leaders who stand in the way, it would be a brave and foolish leader who doubles down against him."

"Dan?" Clark said, one simple word all he needed.

"I don't like it, but this is my calling," Dan replied. "The Messengers aren't perfect, but you know what they told me: '*When we can help, we do what we can*.' And that's where I am, Clark; that's where *we* are. This is what I can do. This is *all* I can do. So whatever it achieves, I have to try."

Clark knew Dan's mind was made up; even if he'd wanted to, there would have been no sense in trying to talk him out of it.

Within little over an hour, and despite the news that Dan would imminently address the world after a year-long public silence, ACN and every other news network was filled with image after image of the unrest that had already broken out in multiple locations.

Surprisingly to Dan, the worst pictures so far were coming in from the UK. Throughout the British morning and early afternoon, demonstrators had clashed with police outside both the American and Chinese embassies. Many of the primarily young demonstrators wore T-shirts adorned with the '*Now Now Now*' slogan made famous during the heyday of the Now Movement and its calls for truth regarding a perceived alien cover-up.

Both were protests rather than demonstrations, with one set of agitated citizens directing their anger at the self-serving GCC and the other at the self-serving ELF.

The flash dual-protest had been organised on social media at short notice, with participants being encouraged to attend at one location or the other based on the first letter of their surname. The protests were equal in size and reporters on the ground at both sites got very similar comments from the demonstrators they interviewed. The common grievance was that an international rivalry — petty in the context of extraterrestrial contact — was derailing what should have been another incredible moment for humanity, while simultaneously delaying the decoding of a message that could be crucial for all kinds of reasons.

One protestor at the Chinese embassy made this point in simple terms, stating that the coded message on the Zanzibar triangle could be just as important as the message on the fourth plaque, which warned of Il Diavolo's approach.

Another common complaint in London was the invisibility of British Prime Minister David Hearst, who lived in William Godfrey's pocket and had done absolutely nothing to tell the rest of the world that the GCC Chairman spoke only for his own interests — and certainly not for those of the country he had treated with the contempt of vacating his position not once but twice.

Pictures from southern Europe showed oftentimes serious violence outside American embassies and consulates, continuing a theme so recurring that few batted their eyelids.

The only protests which made it to Western airwaves from an ELF-affiliated country were those in India, where a vast proportion of the city-dwelling population had always felt their government had made the wrong choice in affiliating with the ELF rather than the Western-dominated GCC. Now that the ELF was in possession of a bona fide alien object and Indian scientists had been quietly frozen out in favour of a joint Chinese and Russian analysis team, this belief was firmer than ever. Indian police and security forces were ruthless in cracking down wherever anger arose near buildings of Russian and Chinese significance, and that these scenes of police brutality played around the world only increased the growing anti-ELF sentiment.

One large banner lay on the ground in New Delhi, catching the attention of a local journalist who managed to evade the authorities and film everything on his phone. The banner featured three words and one image. Two of the words were written in red circles and each was scored out like a cigarette in a no smoking sign: 'GCC' and 'ELF'. A third word lay between them, above a low-resolution but unmistakable image of Dan McCarthy physically connected to one of the Messengers who conversed with him at the Birchwood drive-in on Contact Day. The third word was 'Unity', and it represented all that the protestors were looking for.

Dan felt sick watching it all, and tried to focus on the point that he was going to do all he could to cool things down before they got too much worse.

For the several hours until Focus 20/20's 7pm start time rolled around, Emma ran through all the pitfalls that could emerge and generated a plentiful list of effective lines Dan could use to get around them. It felt like old times, taking Dan back to his first appearance on Focus 20/20 when Emma — then a business-only ally — had done the same thing in a studio in Amarillo.

Exhausted after two nights to forget, Dan was in need of some cosmetic assistance before facing the world through the Ultra HD camera attached to Emma's computer. Tara assisted in this regard, covering up the circles under his eyes and picking out a suitably smart shirt from his wardrobe, readying his physical appearance while Emma focused on readying his mind and his nerves.

The violent scenes he'd seen on TV steeled Dan's resolve and settled any doubts that he was doing the right thing. His old life was long gone, and his year-long attempt to bring it back had run its course. Dan McCarthy had never asked for fame, let alone the level that the events of Contact Day had brought his way, but after much deliberation he was finally ready to step into his new life with no more reservations, accepting the responsibility that had been thrust upon him and using his often-uncomfortable level of public adoration for good.

When the time came, Emma told everyone to stay out of her room no matter what they saw on the live show and no matter what they wanted to tell Dan. She encouraged them to text her if there was anything truly necessary for her to know, but stressed the '*truly* necessary' element of this instruction.

Henry, Phil and Mr Byrd were all still next door and ready to watch the show in the hope it would go well, while Timo, Clark and Tara were going to watch in Emma's living room.

Timo reiterated his gratitude for Dan having agreed to do this, and promised that he would be instructing Alessandro, Fiore Frontiere's permanent GCC delegate, to firmly push for a new approach to reducing international tensions in the coming days.

Tara, meanwhile, told Dan to be careful then tried to lift the mood of brooding anticipation by telling him to make sure he didn't mess up the makeup she'd taken so long applying in a way that made his face look as fresh as her own with a little more subtlety.

"I really fucking wish you didn't have to do this, man," Clark said, sighing deeply, "but I'm damn proud of you for taking it on."

"Thanks," Dan said from the doorway, very sincerely. "I'll try not to let anyone down."

V minus 69

From a familiar audience-less studio where countless names had been made and countless careers had ended, Marian de Clerk sat in her usual seat before an unusually sparse panel of three. Two further spots would be rounded out by the remote guests whose names were responsible for much of the expected record-breaking viewership, and the final panel of five was quite possibly the most explosive in the show's history.

Before introducing the panel, Marian de Clerk perfunctorily mentioned that Kaitlyn Judd had unfortunately been unable to attend. In truth, she had been culled to make way for Dan; her representatives were willing to accept this quietly given that his presence was doubtless going to utterly dominate the focus, and thus would have left her twiddling her thumbs. de Clerk gave a quick plug to the *Il Diavolo* movie whose home media release Kaitlyn's appearance had been booked to coincide with long before the specific topic of the show had been decided, introducing a short trailer to precede the hotly anticipated panel discussion.

"Originally, this special Saturday night episode was going to look back at Contact Day and discuss where the intervening year has taken us," de Clerk said after the thirty-second trailer ended. "Much of our panel was booked with that in mind, but the remarkable events of the past few days have brought us two more panellists of the highest profile. As well as two very familiar faces and returning guests in the shape of Billy Kendrick and Joe Crabbe, we're also joined today by Poppy Bradshaw of the anti-contact 'GeoSov' movement. The panel's two recent additions are coming to us via satellite and need little introduction. We have John Cole, the ELF's new Western Secretary, coming to us from Dar es Salaam in Tanzania, and we have none other than Dan McCarthy coming to us from Birchwood, Colorado."

Dan gave a half-nod and half-smile in recognition of his introduction, a gesture that looked effortless and organic only because of how long Emma had helped him to practice making it so.

The final pre-discussion order of business was de Clerk's explanation that today's broadcast would be one of very few in the show's history not to follow the titular format of focusing on two separate topics for twenty minutes apiece. Quite understandably, network heads had decided that it would have been unwise and likely impossible to enforce a topical division between the recent GCC inauguration and the issues surrounding the recent discovery of a supposedly alien triangle. For that reason, the live show would run on a relatively unstructured basis. It would also last for only forty-five minutes, with a five-minute commercial break between the two twenty-minute segments, to avoid interrupting the flow of discussion any more than necessary.

de Clerk explained that the single-topic nature of the episode and the fact that two of her five panellists were participating via satellite would lead to a slight change from how things normally played out, with more time for the panellists to express themselves unchallenged and with fewer aggressive interruptions than many episodes tended to feature. The satellite delays, although very slight, could make regular back-and-forth conversations problematic, she explained, and the calibre of the night's guests meant that thorough statements of their positions were what viewers wanted most of all.

She began her slow circuit of the panel with Joe Crabbe, a one-time shock-jock who had often been a lone voice of support for Richard Walker during the tumultuous days of the IDA leak. Crabbe was well known for holding American sovereignty above all other considerations, and in recent times had come to be known as a man of few words. Walker's death and Dan McCarthy's humility at his funeral had made Crabbe see some things in a new light, and the former foe was now someone Dan expected to be relatively cordial.

"Joe, to begin… your general thoughts on the GCC and ELF?"

"Even the likes of *me*," Crabbe began with a knowing grin, "even the American exceptionalists and unashamed patriots like me can see that in the face of a beast like the ELF, we need a devil we know like Godfrey. I would like to see our country leading the world and leading the way, taking our own path to handling future contact and inviting allies on our own terms. I would prefer it if we weren't in the GCC, just like I prefer having NASA to the old GSC. But if we weren't in the GCC, the GCC wouldn't exist. And if the GCC didn't exist, the Russians and Chinese would have everyone else banding together and we'd be left in the lurch. By joining our staunch allies — or dependents, as I see them — we can stand against Eastern aggression in a way that would be far more difficult on our own, in these tough economic times."

"An approach very much born of pragmatism, you might say?" de Clerk prodded.

"I *would* say that," Crabbe nodded. "I *do* say that. I'm a pragmatist who wants what's best for his country, just like Richard Walker was. He made mistakes, as we all know, but everything he did was done to protect us from the threat he saw coming from aggressive Chinese expansion. He would have predicted this, you know; I'm absolutely sure of that."

de Clerk turned next to Billy Kendrick, a popular and affable man who had carried himself with a quiet dignity during a longstanding smear campaign and who had acted with humility when he was ultimately proven right about the existence of intelligent extraterrestrial life. A personal friend of Dan since the days of the IDA leak when Dan himself was the subject of much ridicule, Billy had since carved out an exceptionally profitable niche as a tour guide to remote locations of extraterrestrial relevance. The likes of Kerguelen and Bouvet Island were no longer must-see sites now that the story surrounding the 'alien' spheres which had supposedly been discovered on their shores had been revealed as a masterful hoax by the late Richard Walker, so Billy had returned to his old pre-Disclosure career as an author and touring speaker.

Billy's latest show was built around his recent bestselling book, *The Fork*, which philosophically addressed the questions raised by extraterrestrial contact and the options such an epoch-defining event presented for an intelligent species. Its abstraction surprised many readers who went in expecting an analysis of the Messengers and a deep reflection on Contact Day, but precious few had been disappointed by the mind-expanding insights and questions posed within *The Fork*'s pages.

The Fork's tie-in speaking tour was currently filling major cities' largest arenas for multiple nights in a row, with the exhausting 100-date tour narrowly on track to reach two million paying attendees. Money had never been the main thing for Billy; even going back to the days when his sanity and motives had been questioned, he had offered his books and lecture tickets at the lowest prices he could while maintaining a reasonable standard of living. Billy's life had been driven by his tireless pursuit of truth and his burning desire to share his knowledge and beliefs with the widest possible audience, and even now that no one could accuse him of cashing in on conspiracy theories and he could comfortably charge triple what he did and still sell out arenas across the country, he steadfastly maintained his flat pricing structure.

Billy was now able to travel by plane and stay in the best hotels during his coast-to-coast tour rather than live out of a car as he had during the less-attended tours of old, but the money hadn't changed him in the slightest.

"What's your take on the split, Mr Kendrick?" de Clerk asked him. "I know you're close friends with Timo Fiore, who wrestled with his own decision on whether to formally endorse either organisation. Was your decision at all influenced by his?"

"No. My position on this is similar to Joe's, albeit for slightly different reasons," Billy said. "Like Joe I have publicly recognised the GCC — not endorsed it — and even then my limited support, if you really want to stretch the meaning of that word, has come only with great reluctance. I dearly wish that there was one truly global organisation; but with the choice that's been presented to me in reality, it's not overly difficult to consider an organisation composed of the world's largest democracies somewhat more palatable than one composed of the world's largest dictatorships. Our own kind of politics isn't perfect — Jesus, I've made a career of pointing that out! — but at least it's participatory."

Crabbe gave a measured nod of acknowledgment.

"But this chaos was utterly inevitable," Billy went on. "In the *Five Scenarios* book that brought me into the public eye, I wrote at length about how contact could play out post-Disclosure. Declarations were in place — supposedly binding ones, at that — about how we as a species would deal with extraterrestrial contact. But the real issue is this: all of the old declarations were about contact, not visitation. And now, as we all know, we're not just post-detection or post-contact; we're post-*visitation*. Our planet has been visited, but the important thing to remember here is that there hasn't been even a modicum of 'official' diplomatic contact. The only contact the Messengers have initiated has been with Dan McCarthy."

"And as far as today, Billy," Marian de Clerk began, glancing at her notes, "what do you see as the way out of this current situation of what feels like deadlock between East and West, and how do you see Dan fitting in?"

Billy considered the question. "Ideally, although the last thing I want to do is put words in Dan's mouth, I'd like to see a truly international contact-focused collective and I think he would, too. Something like a Global Contact Forum or GCF, if you will, in which Dan felt able to participate without having to choose a side. To me that is self-evidently the best way forward, but unfortunately we're currently being led by men and women of ego rather than logic; men and women who live to climb rather than to serve."

"Hmm," de Clerk mused, not quite personally involved in the discussions but seeming more so than usual. "And as for where you think things *will* go in the short-term, as opposed to your hopes for where things *should* go?"

"Life is going to be difficult for the ELF if they maintain this current strategy of confrontationalism," he replied without a moment's pause for thought. "Western culture is pretty much *global* culture, and citizens in certain large ELF countries aren't happy that they're being driven further away from the rest of the world. In many cases these citizens feel very disconnected from their governments in general terms, but this issue is going to highlight that to an all-new level. Implicit opposition to universally popular figures like Timo and especially Dan is not going to go down well. But on the point I mentioned about broader cultural shifts in those countries, I think that's something much deeper. Presenting Western powers as the devil incarnate was difficult enough for the Soviet Union thirty years ago… but now that the internet has made the world so much smaller and made Western culture even more dominant, it's all but impossible."

"Well," de Clerk grinned, "we certainly have the right man to tackle that charge. And we'll hand over now. Can you hear us, Mr Cole?"

"Hello, friends!" he began, raising ironic smiles and shakes of the head all round. "And a particularly fond hello to my two good friends in Buenos Aires, William and Valerie. I know you're both watching and I hope you've had a good day so far, because you're probably not going to enjoy the rest of the night too much…"

V minus 68

"I don't know what the problem is, he just won't sit still," Liang Fu explained over his phone to the local veterinarian. "It *is* persistent; this has already been going on for three hours! And I told you, next door's dog ran towards the sea at the same time. Something spooked them and I don't know what the—"

Liang's concerned recounting of the story was interrupted by his dog Pinnochio, who was now sitting still — all *too* still — but continuously growling in a way Liang had never heard.

"Do you hear that?" he spoke into the phone. "He's growling at the door!"

Seconds later, Pinnochio's growl morphed into an extremely aggressive and repeated bark. The Alsatian's bark resonated through the house and raised the hairs on Liang's neck. He had raised Pinnochio since he was a tiny puppy and had never expected to be intimidated by the large dog, but this sound was something he had never expected to hear.

"Pin-Pin, it's okay," he called, keeping his distance. "There's nothing there."

No more than five tense seconds later, the barking ceased and Pinnochio scampered away from the door, rushing to Liang's side and whimpering.

"This isn't normal," he told the veterinarian. "Get over here as soon as you can... please!"

As soon as the phone was down, Liang devoted his full attention to the now puppy-like dog. It didn't stay down for long, though, ringing almost immediately to inform Liang of a call from his neighbour Zhou.

Liang listened to his friend's frantic retelling of an all-too-familiar episode in which his own dog had behaved exactly like Pinnochio: a burst of aggressive barking followed by a sudden regression into a state of apparent fear.

"You don't think it could be..." Liang said, cutting himself off.

No, he thought. *Don't be stupid.*

"Maybe they're smelling a gas leak or something like that?" he continued.

Zhou wasn't saying much on the other end of the line, and Liang got the distinct impression that they were both thinking the same thing but that neither wanted to risk saying it first for fear of how crazy it sounded.

As it always did, time would tell.

V minus 67

"I'm speaking to you all from Dar es Salaam," John Cole beamed, "which translates as 'haven of peace'. Somewhat ironic, you might say, given that our triangular gift from above is as clear a signal as any can be: a clear signal that the Global Contact Commission is an affront to human decency and a threat to world peace."

"And with that, we'll get right into it," de Clerk said, unflustered and unsurprised by the strength of Cole's opening gambit. "Mr Cole, what is abundantly clear to all of us and indeed to vast numbers of concerned citizens is that this so-called Zanzibar triangle has underlined and exacerbated East-West divisions that have been brewing since—"

"I won't make a habit of this, Marian," Cole interrupted, "but since time is so tight I do have to step in to make a point here. As the ELF's Western Secretary, my office in Havana will actually be further West than the GCC building in Buenos Aires and indeed further West than the White House. So really, the talk of an East-West split isn't particularly accurate and is no longer a valid way to frame things. What's *more* accurate is the recognition of the ELF as a forum for those of us unprepared to be dragged along by the calculated self-interest of the United States and the irresponsible egotism of William Godfrey."

Astute observers immediately noted Cole's careful and deliberate choice of words, with 'calculated self-interest' being a term popularised by Godfrey himself in criticising President Slater's initial reaction to the IDA leak.

"Well, I must interject to remind you that neither President Slater nor Chairman Godfrey are here to defend themselves," de Clerk said, "so while we certainly want to hear a candid statement of your views and positions, unnecessary personal asides aren't what *any* of us are here for."

"No, Godfrey's *not* here," Cole said, unaffected by the rebuke. "And do you know where *else* he's not? London, fulfilling the position he has twice been elected to hold and has twice abandoned for a bigger paycheck and greater power! Do any of you even know who David Hearst *is*? The office of Prime Minister used to mean something. When I was Prime Minister, Britain was internationally relevant. Godfrey, too, until he abandoned the country twice."

"In the interest of balance..." de Clerk said, "I can't impartially allow any implication that your own time in office was all sunshine and rainbows, Mr Cole. We all know how it ended, in particular."

"I stepped down with dignity after what I admit was a serious error of judgement," Cole replied, "albeit one I was pushed into by Godfrey's complete lack of action in the face of Il Diavolo's relentless approach. Godfrey, on the other hand? He has stepped down from the office of Prime Minister not once but twice, and on both occasions for the sake of ascending to a position of greater international power! I'll keep repeating this until the point gets through. He is a ruthless climber and a career politician, and he can talk about being 'born to lead' all he wants. But let me make one thing clear: I was born in the gutter and I fought my way up. There were no silver spoons or trust funds in the south side of Sheffield, I can tell you that much. I didn't grow up going to the right schools or knowing the right handshakes, but I made it to the top through my burning desire to represent people like me — the *real* people, from all over this great world of ours — and I've contended with the snot-nosed entitlement of the likes of Godfrey and Slater all my life."

"You're cut from the same cloth whether you can see it or not," Billy interjected. "Rats one and all."

Cole theatrically rolled his eyes. "Only one of us is here to sell books, Billy boy, so spare us the judgement. But if you want to talk about similarities, here's one for you all. Everyone is so up in arms that Chinese and Russian scientists are currently studying an object that arrived two short days ago, but there seems to be some collective and I would argue *voluntary* amnesia as to what happened when a certain sphere was recovered from the ocean off Argentina. Since that's the case, allow me to remind everyone that it was *Godfrey* who once wanted to exclude *American* scientists from the sphere analysis process, purely because he wanted us — the UK — to be the only English-speaking nation represented. And *that* was purely because he wanted to be the only English-speaking leader making the resultant Disclosure announcement! That's the man we're dealing with, people. And yes, I've spoken some strong words against the historical and contemporary policies of certain nations, the United States and Argentina included, but at no point did I lobby to exclude anyone from the international team who studied the Argentine sphere."

Cole raised a finger to delay the inevitable interruption that always came on Focus 20/20 whenever someone dominated the conversation to this extent.

"And to illustrate this point even more clearly: Godfrey's conditions for consenting to the late addition of an American scientist, since unanimity from the initial list of nations was required, was that the American scientist's name had to go last on the jointly signed document. At that point that was the most important document in human history, and the newly inaugurated Chairman of the GCC was playing politics on a level *so* trivial that everyone else just shrugged their shoulders and let the petulant child have his way. All of this, and you ask me why I stand with President Ding? All of this, and you ask me why I stand with the leader of an inclusive international organisation that represents more than half of the world's population and more than half of its landmass? And how about this — look at the diversity in a room full of low-level GCC delegates, and then look at the racial makeup of Godfrey's inner advisory board. That's what shows us once and for all that the Global Contact Commission is not just an exercise in Western imperialism, it is an inherently white supremacist organisation."

Joe Crabbe shook his head incredulously. "Laughable," he blasted. "Especially coming from you, with all the crap you've said in the past about inferior cultures and everything else. You're a useful idiot; the Chinese and Russians are using you like a cheap whore and you're playing along because you think you're getting one over on your old boss."

"Well at least *one* of us is useful," Cole retorted. "And whatever kind of politically correct games the Western media and politicians like to play, President Ding knew they would never *truly* accept an organisation headed only by non-Westerners. Most barriers appear to be all but gone;

skin colour, gender, sexual orientation and even age don't *seem* to matter in North American and European politics anything like they once did. An African or Korean at the UN was fine, because really, a puppet is a puppet wherever it's made. But Chinese? They wouldn't stand for it. *You* wouldn't stand for it," he accused the uniformly American panel. "Richard Walker's Sinophobia, which motivated the whole fake IDA leak in the first place, is sadly the norm rather than the exception among your countrymen and those of your allies. It's a sad thing that I have to be here, but I'll do my duties as best as I can as we work towards closing the gap between the peoples of the world. There is a sizeable GCC-shaped roadblock standing in my way, I'll admit, but I'm a patient man."

Billy Kendrick cleared his throat. "I'm all for patience, too, Marian, but are we going to get a chance to challenge any of—"

"As I said," Cole butted back in, "the ELF's reach covers a majority of our planet's landmass. In order to carry out necessary duties of observation and to better engage with local populations, we are planning new offices and bases in dozens of strategic locations. In addition to Cuba we're imminently looking to open an office in Vanuatu, as well as Madagascar and also one of a few shortlisted locations in the Russian Far North. As you can tell from these plans, the future looked exciting for the ELF even before the Messengers bestowed their triangle of peace upon us."

"Vanuatu?" de Clerk asked, picking this little-referenced country from Cole's short list. "You must be aware of successive Australian governments' long-running and very public concerns regarding a Chinese military base on Vanuatu, no?"

Cole shrugged. "Well, I'm not talking about China and I'm not talking about a military base. So with the greatest of respect, Marian, if there's any relevance in those observations then you're going to have to spell it out for me."

Joe Crabbe gestured to de Clerk that he would like to take this one, and she gladly waved him on.

"You're right about something at last," he scathingly shot at Cole, "because the ELF and its aggressive strategic placement of new bases is *not* Chinese. Let's call the ELF what it really is: a joint Chinese-Russian operation aimed at redressing what they see as a power imbalance and I see as Pax Americana. I suppose you're going to tell us next that a Russian base in Cuba would be nothing to worry about, either? That this ELF incursion into our American sphere of influence is completely without historical precedent or political symbolism?"

"Not everything is as complicated and conspiratorial as you think,

Joseph," Cole said in his best condescending tone. "And even if it was, so *bloody* what? America has bases all over the world. You want to talk about China? China is surrounded by US bases on all sides and endlessly provoked with regional war-games, yet somehow China is rebuked as soon as an international organisation it's just one member of expands its physical presence into a country the Americans decide is too close to their own? Somehow China and Cuba being allies is a problem, but no one cares when Slater is eating sushi and cheeseburgers with the Prime Minister of Japan? The point is this, Crabbe," Cole snapped, real venom in his words for the first time. "American hegemony is dead — it's time to grow up and get over it."

"Billy?" de Clerk asked, favouring him over Crabbe when seeking a reply to Cole's scattershot remarks.

Billy shook his head. "I came here to talk about Contact Day and the Zanzibar triangle. When you want input on that — if you ever do, that is — I'll give it. Cole has already shown himself up for what he is, as if we needed any reminding, so I'll save my breath."

"May I?" Poppy Bradshaw asked, smiling politely at de Clerk as though butter wouldn't melt in her mouth. After a nod from the host, she continued. "John, I need to ask you one thing: Did you leak the news of the comet's approach on purpose? And be straight with us, for once in your life!"

"I did," Cole said, bluntly and finally laying to rest a question that almost everyone already knew the answer to beyond any doubt. "I knew it could and likely *would* ruin my career — of course I did — but what kind of psychopath thinks about his career when a comet is hurtling towards Earth and set to eliminate our entire species? Slater and Godfrey, I suppose, but certainly not myself. And did my actions spark disorder? Yes. But was Godfrey's GSC doing enough to save the world? Not on your nelly! And as for you, Poppy Whatever-it-was, I know why you hate me. You hate me because my actions that day contributed to the world being saved! You hate me because my actions had the side-effect of hastening the inevitable disorder, which forced McCarthy to admit his longstanding lies in an effort to bring the Messengers back to Earth, which in turn resulted in a defeat for your predecessors: those scum-sucking Welcomers who violently targeted Timo Fiore and Emma Ford in Colorado Springs."

Poppy either couldn't hide her rage or didn't try to. "There is no single shred of evidence for these slanderous comments," she yelled, really more of a shriek. "Our movement is an anti-contact movement and we have nothing to do with any of the supposed 'predecessors' that the pro-contact corporate media and the rest of *the powers that be* keep endlessly trying to link us to. Some lunatics who used to call themselves Welcomers might now call themselves GeoSovs, fine, but what do you want us to do about that? We can't disown them, because we don't own them. All we can do is disavow them, or at least we could if we hadn't already."

With Poppy getting a foothold in the conversation and Dan loath to let her come across anything close to positively, he decided it was time to reveal his vision; it was time to reveal the GeoSov plot to take President Slater hostage, which had been foiled thanks to a warning from the Messengers and which Slater herself had encouraged him to reveal on live TV.

"There's something I need to say," Dan spoke up, for the first time in a long while.

"Unfortunately we've reached the time limit for our first segment," de Clerk told him, "but fortunately we have another twenty minutes and will be handing over to you for a good number of them, Dan. Thanks again for being with us tonight. But Mr Cole, since I gather you have to leave us at this halfway point, I'll give you the final word for now."

Cole nodded curtly, wasting no time on platitudes. "I wish to join Dan in publicly calling for international unity at this important time, and I'd like to both applaud and thank him for sharing the official ELF position on that issue. Division does no one any favours, and William Godfrey's exclusion policy is a crime against humanity which could lead to catastrophic armed conflict if his irresponsible politicking doesn't end. I hereby call on the likes of Slater, Hearst, and any other GCC national leaders who can find a backbone somewhere to finally call a spade a spade and to call William Godfrey out as the reckless lunatic he is. If the GCC is to continue to exist, its members quite simply must oust the man who is driving them over a cliff because he's too busy admiring his own reflection in the rear-view mirror to watch the road ahead. With that, I bid goodnight from the haven of peace and promise to see you all from Havana very soon."

Cole's feed cut to black before de Clerk could sign him off, much less allow anyone else to address his closing comments.

"Focus 20/20 continues after the break," she said, composed as ever, "when we'll hear more from the GeoSov spokesperson Poppy Bradshaw on what the Zanzibar triangle means for her controversial anti-contact movement. And, of course... last but *certainly* not least... once we've heard from Poppy our attention will turn squarely to Birchwood, Colorado and humanity's conduit to the stars: the one and only Dan McCarthy. We'll see you after these short messages."

V minus 66

"Realistically, it couldn't have gone too much better than that," President Slater mused, still in Buenos Aires while the dust settled on Zanzibar and once again alone at Chairman Godfrey's side.

"Absolutely," he replied.

On one hand both were greatly irritated that the normally firm Marian de Clerk had allowed so much of the opening segment to turn into an uninterrupted policy speech by John Cole, but on the other both were relieved that he hadn't said too much that caught them off guard.

Some of his language was clearly inflammatory, once again, leaning on loaded terms with recent significance, and Cole had been particularly if not-unexpectedly scathing towards Godfrey.

But the GCC chairman felt sure that things would turn around in the next twenty minutes, when Billy Kendrick and Joe Crabbe, incisive men if nothing else, would doubtless lay into Cole's nonsense. Most of all, though, Godfrey felt as though he could count on Dan McCarthy. As he eloquently phrased it to the less sure President Slater: "Don't worry, Valerie; with Ford at his side, McCarthy's going to tear him a new arsehole."

But just like Dan McCarthy, William Godfrey had no idea what was coming next...

V minus 65

After a first-half segment that was so comfortable for Dan that comfort almost turned to frustration, he was looking forward to finally saying everything that was pent up inside him and everything that he hoped would halt the rapid escalation in international tensions that had followed the Zanzibar triangle's discovery.

The primary tack Emma had suggested was one whose efficacy Dan didn't doubt, but that didn't mean it was one he was completely at ease with. In short, she had essentially told him that the only way to reduce the focus on GCC-ELF divisions and indeed to reduce the GCC and ELF's focus on each other was for Dan to position himself above both organisations, acting as a lightning rod by publicly and firmly reminding everyone that he was the only person alive with whom the Messengers had ever initiated direct contact.

John Cole's departure, no doubt strategically planned because of his famed inability to handle direct criticism or even arguments, was actually something Dan was glad about. He didn't want a two-way fight with a slippery customer like Cole on live TV any more than Cole wanted a fight with someone sitting next to Emma Ford and her famously keen mind for one-liners and quick rebuttals.

When the show returned to the airwaves, Marian de Clerk very briefly recapped what had been covered in the first segment, reintroduced the panel with an understandably prolonged camera shot of Dan, and invited GeoSov spokesperson Poppy Bradshaw to say her piece.

Poppy was a complete unknown, who even Emma had been unable to pin down and identify before the show began and her name was announced. She looked to be around forty and was well turned-out without looking like much effort had been made, and there was an air of calm about her that suggested media experience of one kind or another.

"On the topic of this stupid triangle, the biggest question we have to address is the question of the aliens' motives," Poppy said. "They tried to fool humanity with the third plaque, so we know they have a history of messing us around. And all of this destabilising uncertainty over the meaning and intent of a message is precisely why we should reject contact. By its very nature, contact is divisive. And we have *Mr* Divisive sitting there in Birchwood, no doubt ready to hypocritically lecture us all from his ivory tower. But they've spoken exclusively to him, which is the absolute opposite of openness. We already know the aliens are all about favouritism, and there would definitely be more than a hint of irony if their new favourite contactees turn out to be the designated-bad-guy leaders of the ELF."

"That doesn't even make sense," Dan said.

Poppy grinned from ear to ear. "What makes no sense is humanity listening to the views of someone who is almost certainly a Trojan horse! The aliens changed you, Dan... if that even is the name of your internal identity anymore. The real Dan McCarthy would never dismiss any so-called conspiracy theory out of hand without at least giving it a fair hearing."

"There's not even a theory here!" Dan retorted, disbelieving of how inane and insane a turn the conversation had taken so quickly. "If you're trying to pretend to be smart it's not working, because everyone can see through this tired old crap."

"Dan, your own government doesn't even trust you. Why else would they have implanted a chip under your skin to monitor the neck pain they expect you to feel if there's any future contact?"

Stunned that Poppy could know this, Dan's lips and mind were frozen.

Emma typed two words: DENY QUICKLY.

"It's almost like you don't *want* anyone to take you seriously," he said after several uncomfortable seconds, forcing out a fairly convincing chuckle.

"We both know that this isn't a baseless accusation," Poppy shrugged, "and everyone else will know it soon, too. This is an accusation that can be proven or disproven whenever you want, Dan. How about tomorrow? Will you consent to some public scans?"

Dan read aloud the words Emma hurriedly typed on his autocue: "What are you trying to distract from? This is a textbook play of 'say something stupid to distract from something secret'. What's the dirt?"

"There's a chip in your neck," Poppy yelled, "that's the dirt! It was placed there by human agents — *American* agents — and that is a cast-iron fact. The only thing I don't know for absolutely certain is whether it's in there because American agents think you're an alien operative, which is what *I* think, or alternatively because you're secretly colluding with US and GCC agents."

"People have thrown a lot of crazy accusations at me these past few years," Dan sighed, not needing any autocue for this, "or at least I *thought* they had. But seriously, Poppy, if all that was crazy, I don't even know what to call this."

Poppy turned to her fellow panellists, both of whom were intrigued by Dan's long-silent views and declined to jump in. She shrugged and looked back to the screen. "Dan, you're using the exact silencing techniques they used to use against you," she said, throwing her hands up in an exasperation that was either real or incredibly convincing. "Right on cue, here comes the laughter curtain! And in just a second I'm sure Billy and Joe will jump to your defence. But what was it *you* used to say, Billy, back when you were an underdog rather than an establishment lackey? Oh yeah, that's right: consensus is collusion. And everyone watching this who has an open mind can see where the collusion is. *We* are the underdogs, fighting for a sovereign planet that can live in peaceful harmony, free from the reach of interfering aliens who see us as playthings at best and probably see us in a way that's a lot more sinister than that."

de Clerk signalled Dan's right of reply.

"You know, I reluctantly support giving these idiots a platform," he said. "Bad ideas fester and spread in the dark but they get exposed in bright light, exactly like a lot of smarter people than me have said in the past. I *was* ridiculed back in the day, but it went beyond that; some people tried to silence me, and other people supported it because they thought I was crazy. So banning anyone from speaking, even the GeoSovs, would set a dangerous precedent. Because if you don't support free speech for people and ideas you hate, you don't support free speech at all. Maybe something could or should be done about the paid ads the GeoSovs have used to target kids with anti-contact memes, because kids are—"

"Garbage," Poppy interrupted. "No such thing has ever been proven to have come from an official GeoSov account."

Dan tried not to let any annoyance show. "As I was saying… kids are kids. But *this* kind of situation, for me, is clear. This is a current affairs show for adults and no positions should be banned on principle. In the political sphere, if all speech isn't free then no speech is free; at best it would be conditionally free-for-now, until someone in an office somewhere might decide that it offends their sensibilities and has to go. I hate these people, but they should be allowed to speak."

"Dan, hate is a strong word for a man with such a warm and cuddly public image," Poppy mocked, shaking her head indignantly.

"I despise you," he hissed in reply. "I detest you. You and your people tried to kill Timo and Emma, and the one good reason you shouldn't be on this panel is that you should be in prison!"

Poppy began to reply, but de Clerk promptly stepped in with a firm insistence that Dan had agreed to come on the show with the intention of talking about more than the GeoSovs. She of course had no idea just what Dan was planning to reveal about the GeoSovs themselves later in the show, but for now she had heard more than enough from Poppy Bradshaw.

"The floor is yours, Dan," de Clerk announced. "The Zanzibar triangle's discovery coming on the anniversary of Contact Day has raised all kinds of questions, and the precise timing — during the GCC's inauguration — has proven just as controversial. No one can come at this from either side with a more complete perspective than you, so please let us in to your mind."

"The first thing I want to say is that there aren't really two sides here," Dan began, following Emma's advice to hit the political nonsense first. "The way I see it, there are *three* sides. There are a bunch of politicians in Beijing, there are a bunch of politicians in Buenos Aires, and there are seven billion people who wish those politicians would all get together, join hands, and jump into the nearest volcano. So let's all try to keep that in mind when we're talking about sides. And just quickly on that, this isn't even about normal politics. The 'sides' these politicians have created in their own minds are so binary — but again, only in their own minds — that John Cole, a hardline Western conservative, is going to live in Cuba where they're probably going to treat him like a king. This is a return to the old Cold War logic of 'my enemy's enemy is my friend'… if you can even call it logic."

Appearing surprised by both the strength of Dan's opening comment and the direction he had moved in, de Clerk pushed him back in the direction she wanted the discussion to go. "But of the two *'bunches of politicians'*, as you put it, which do you see as the more legitimate in their claims to represent humanity as a whole?"

"Neither," he insisted, "and that's the whole point. I see what you're getting at, though, so I'll say this: while I will never formally endorse the GCC or the ELF, what I will do right now is unreservedly condemn the ELF's leadership — Ding Ziyang and now, apparently, John Cole — for the pathetically divisive rhetoric they spouted earlier today. It reminded me of the posturing during the IDA leak, when Cole and Godfrey were on the same side and were more concerned about making President Slater's life difficult than they were about the contents of the leak. And I know for a fact that Godfrey didn't even think the leak was real at first, he just jumped at the opportunity to get one over on Slater and distract from his own problems. Obviously we all found out that it *wasn't* real in the end, but the point is that Godfrey pretended like he believed me long before he actually did, and purely because it was politically expedient to do so.

"And now with this triangle," Dan went on, "you have Ding telling us with one breath that it's the most important thing ever, but then what does he do with the next ten breaths? Makes it about the same old point-less political games and his stupid power struggle with Godfrey. That's one thing I want to clarify, in fact: I don't hate China... *of course* I don't. But I bet most people there like Ding about as much as I do, which is about as much as I like Slater. That's the point: this isn't *'China equals bad'* any more than it's *'America equals bad'* or even *'Britain equals bad'*, since Godfrey is still such a big part of things. This is tails wagging dogs, with great nations being led by petty children."

"And regarding the triangle itself..." de Clerk probed, trying to move things along while staying out of the way as much as possible.

"Do you mean what do I think of its origin and what do I think should happen next?"

de Clerk nodded. "Precisely."

"I'll start with the second point," he said, always cognisant of how crucial Emma had told him it was to save the revelation of his recent contact experience and the clue regarding the triangle's markings until near the end, leaving just enough time to close with the revelation of the GeoSov plot that President Slater had given him permission to expose.

"If you wish," de Clerk said, holding out a palm to encourage him along.

"Okay, well I'm not in a position to make any 'formal' declarations," Dan said, "but if Ding Ziyang and John Cole don't share access to the Zanzibar triangle within the next few days, I will be prepared to make a very firm *suggestion* of what the leaders of other ELF nations and the citizens of all ELF nations should do in an effort to convince them to change their minds. And whether Cole in particular likes it or not, my word carries a lot of weight among real people with real lives — from Birchwood, all the way to Beijing."

"You're half-right, Dan," Poppy interjected. "You're not in a position to make any formal declarations, so you're correct there. But you're also not in a position to make any requests of anyone. Proactive contact is a foolish road for humanity to take and it leads only to ruin and regret, but one thing that can at least be said of the GCC and ELF is that they're composed of people who one way or another rose to positions of national authority. But you? You're just a gullible fool from Nowhere, Colorado who fell for a hoax and dragged the rest of us into it. There wouldn't even be any talk of contact if you hadn't done what—"

"None of us would be alive if I hadn't done what I did!" Dan snapped defensively. "But we all know that's exactly what you and your demented Welcomer friends would have wanted, so you can just spare us all the crap and keep your mouth shut." He immediately took a deep breath, scolding himself for taking the bait; blame-apportioning talk of the hoax had long been his primary sore spot, and Poppy almost certainly knew this.

de Clerk stopped short of admonishing Dan directly, but did issue a general call for civility.

"And I wasn't *requesting* that they grant open international access to the triangle," Dan continued. "Request isn't the word. So everyone everywhere, if you're looking for a headline on what I'm saying about this triangle, here it is: this isn't a request, it's a demand. Ding, Cole, and everyone else at the ELF... open up the scientific analysis just like Argentina did with the sphere, or my words are going to get a lot firmer and your lives are going to get a lot more difficult."

"A demand?" Poppy scoffed. "So tell us, oh mighty one, who exactly put you in a position to make—"

"I'm the only one the Messengers talk to," Dan interrupted. "Out of seven billion people, *I'm* the one. We're talking about a triangle here... well, how about thinking about a contact triangle? There's the GCC, there's the ELF, and there's me. Two of the sides don't even matter. The Messengers have used one point of contact, and we all know which of the three it is."

Poppy raised a hand and repeatedly opened and closed it in a dismissive *'blah blah blah'* gesture.

"I'm not even talking to you," Dan said, just as dismissively. "I'm talking to Godfrey and Slater, to Ding and Cole, and I'm telling them this: you can have your little contact clubs and keep fighting over countries like they're tiles on a board, if that's how you want to spend your lives. But the truth none of you want to hear is that this is a game you can't win. And do you want to know why? Because when the Messengers want to contact Earth, they don't call Beijing and they don't call Buenos Aires. They call *Birchwood*. They contact *me*... and all you can do about that is learn to deal with it — it's not going to change if one of you 'wins' and ends up in charge of an organisation that really is 'global' or really does represent 'Earth', because the Messengers still won't want to talk to any scheming politicians."

Very suddenly, and without so much as a knock, Clark then burst through the door so quickly that he almost fell into the room.

Dan didn't think anything he'd said came close to meriting an intervention, much less one so far from Emma's approved method of a text to her phone, but Clark's face and body language were testament to the urgency of whatever he had to say. In a million years, Dan could never have guessed the words that came next:

"They just found another triangle," Clark panted. "Vanuatu. It was on the trend-tracker and it's on every other station. de Clerk's bound to mention it any second now, as soon as she hears."

Instinctively, Emma's hand had already hit a button on her computer's keyboard that muted Dan's microphone and blacked out the camera feed. She pointed to the door and firmly mouthed for Clark to get out, pointing at the computer to remind him that Dan was currently going out live to an international audience well into the hundreds of millions.

"You just heard it on the trend-tracker and our internet glitched," Emma said, slightly unnervingly effortless in the lie, "and you think maybe there was a spike because of the news. No one is going to query it, so just say that. And Dan, whatever you do, don't commit either way on this. Don't say what you were going to say about the first triangle being real, okay? Not now. Vanuatu sounds too convenient to be real but it almost sounds too convenient to be *fake*, if you know what I mean."

"I know exactly what you mean," he said, nodding for Emma to press the button to reactivate their outgoing broadcast.

As soon as he returned to screens around the world and also the giant screen in the Focus 20/20 studio, Marian de Clerk turned her attention to Dan. "Did you see it, Dan?" she asked. "The second triangle?"

In his focus on Clark and Emma, Dan had missed the moment when de Clerk heard the news and passed it on. He stuck rigidly to Emma's suggested line about the trend-tracker and internet surge, also sticking to her advice to leave all speculation at the door.

Dan was running on autopilot, adrenaline taking over and Emma's typed words the only thing keeping him afloat. His mind was a confused mess, but so was everyone else's; Billy Kendrick and Joe Crabbe looked bemused by what they were hearing second-hand via de Clerk, while Poppy Bradshaw appeared to find the whole thing extremely amusing.

Poppy's expression, which she seemed to be trying to conceal, told most of the world once and for all that she and her GeoSov friends didn't oppose contact so much as they craved chaos.

Marian de Clerk did a laudable job of listening for incoming details of a remarkable and ongoing global happening while trying to stumble through the last few minutes of the show. The unexpected development meant that this show would no longer feature the revelation of a GeoSov plot to take President Slater hostage or anything whatsoever about the vision in which the Messengers had warned Dan of the plot and also confirmed in hindsight their prescient knowledge of the first triangle.

Whether the Messengers were back or something fishy was going on in Vanuatu having already swept across from Zanzibar as one perfectly timed 'discovery' followed another, Dan was glad he had spoken out about his views on the GCC-ELF split. He spoke again a handful of times as de Clerk and even Poppy fired difficult questions at him, and he managed to dissociate — as Emma's autocue suggested — and focused on making it through some of the most difficult few minutes of his life by reading exactly what she wrote. If Dan's mind had been clear in the slightest he would have wondered how Emma could remain so unflustered, but in that moment clarity of mind felt as out of Dan's reach as the power of flight.

As the ticker counted down and Dan realised he wasn't going to have to speak again, he breathed a deep sigh of relief. Without his contextualising words — intended to disempower Buenos Aires and Beijing's dual grip on public consciousness — he expected that this second triangle would have catastrophically ignited the gunpowder spilled by the first. Coming just minutes after John Cole's mention of a soon-to-open ELF office in Vanuatu and his now-suspicious half-time departure, it was difficult not to jump to the obvious conclusion.

Because even after his attempts at sweeping the gunpowder away, Dan knew that Vanuatu was simply too much of a coincidence to dismiss out of hand.

He knew the Messengers were close — the Slater-saving vision told him that — but he didn't know what they were playing at.

If this was them, they had to stop... and if it wasn't, they had to let him know.

Without knowing what was happening, Dan was back to experiencing his least favourite feeling in the world: powerlessness.

As de Clerk signed off in a far less attentive manner than normal, Dan instinctively scratched the back of his neck.

Where the hell are you?

V minus 64

By the time Focus 20/20 drew to a close, just a few minutes after the remarkable news that a second triangle had been discovered, William Godfrey's office was a hive of activity.

While he remained at his desk, frozen in rage at the sheer audacity of what the ELF's hierarchy had just done, President Slater had risen to her feet and was in animated discussions with both her own aides and Godfrey's.

"Vanuatu..." Godfrey muttered. "Twenty minutes after that fat bastard mentions Vanuatu and disappears from the panel, *that's* where they find another triangle? And just like last time, they find it literally *during* a huge live TV event? They're not even trying to make it look real, they're seeing how far they can push us before we call this out for what it is!"

Slater rubbed her chin in thought, considering a suggestion she'd just been fed. She passed it on to Godfrey: "The only alternative, for the sake of exploring every angle, is that they might have found this triangle earlier in the day and decided to hold it back for maximum impact. Cole might have mentioned Vanuatu because the second triangle had already been found there. I don't buy this, William, but it's within the realm of theoretical possibility: the ELF could be setting us up to call this out as a hoax because they know it's real. If we fell into that kind of trap, we would struggle to find a way out of it."

"And Chairman Godfrey," one of Slater's aides boldly interjected, "this theoretical possibility is one that we *do* have to give some consideration. The security implications of this second discovery are enormous, whether it's real or not. If it's real then that means the Messengers are interfering for what they deem a good reason, but for some wholly unknown reason doing so on the wrong side. The implications of these triangles being a hoax, meanwhile, are almost as serious. That would mean the ELF — or China, if you prefer — will stop at absolutely nothing to weaken our standing. And in this context, '*our* standing' means both the international standing of the United States and the global standing of the GCC."

"I'm not buying into this 'theoretical possibility' for a second," Godfrey grunted dismissively, "so let's not waste any more time thinking about it, shall we? Like it or not, McCarthy was right when he said that the Messengers would go to him first. There's not a chance in hell they would drop gifts for those stains on humanity's undercarriage to parade before the world. And as for leaks, there's already a leak on *your* side," he grunted. "How the hell did that GeoSov clown know about the chip your men put in McCarthy's neck. Tighten up your damn ship, Valerie!"

"*I* didn't even know about the chip until McCarthy mentioned it," she replied angrily.

Godfrey threw up his hands. "What, and that's supposed to make this *better*? An enemy of the state knows more about what your people are doing than you do, and you're using that as a defence?"

"Right now our real enemy is Cole," Slater said, breathing deeply in an effort to dissuade herself from a pointless fight with Godfrey. "He's the one attacking us in public and he's the one who dropped the Vanuatu hint before he left the panel. And we're all in agreement here: he's doing this to rile you."

"I wouldn't take it from anyone, but from *him*..."

Slater, gazing out of the window, spoke in a slightly more measured tone despite her similar rage: "Are you even listening to me? They're trying to rile us, William; you in particular."

"Well then they're winning!" he snapped, slamming a balled fist into the surface of his expensive desk. "But they're not just trying to rile me, they're trying to trap me so that any move I make is a losing one. React in kind with a scathing attack on Cole and Ding that could anger the rest of the GCC? Let them keep making fools of us with these fake triangles, which would also privately anger a lot of our members? But no... I won't let it happen. Valerie, I need agility."

Her eyes implored him to go on.

"They're doing to me what I did to you after McCarthy's leak," he continued, "saying things that backed you into a corner when I knew you couldn't punch back because your hands were tied. Ding and Cole don't need majority approval from ELF delegates before they make a substantive comment, and neither should I. *My* hands don't *have* to be tied..."

"What do you propose?" she asked.

"First thing tomorrow morning, I'm going to seek special executive authority to comment as I see fit. Extraordinary circumstances need extraordinary powers, and when I put this before the delegates I'm hopeful I can count on your support. Some member states may need a gentle nudge in the right direction to vote the right way. *Can* I count on your assistance in assuring that they do?"

"Can I count on a phone call before you say anything unexpected?" Slater asked in return. "I want a personal veto. I need a personal veto."

"It's yours. And while there's no way we could swing it so *you* can speak on contact-related matters without restraint — not that your national politics would allow the same leeway that Ding's does for him — I'm more than willing to keep you in close counsel and with however public a role you wish to have. That pair might be idiots, but they make a formidable team. We need to go toe-to-toe."

As Slater considered these words, Godfrey held out his hand. She shook it with no further hesitation, quickly surprising him with a deliberately over-strong grip she seemed reluctant to relinquish. "But I'll say this once, William: if you *ever* think about going over my head..."

"Together we are strong, Valerie," he grinned, unshaken as their reddened hands parted. "Together... we are strong."

V minus 63

Just as the final few minutes of Focus 20/20 had flashed by Dan's stunned mind, so did the final few hours of Sunday.

He was surrounded by friends and family, with the rest of the Birchwood crew having come through from next door to watch developments on Emma's huge projector screen. The Vanuatu triangle was considerably smaller than the one that had been found in Zanzibar and would evidently fit within a third, still-undiscovered, mid-sized triangle.

The few blurry images that had reached the airwaves from unofficial sources presented a clear enough view of the Zanzibar triangle for its inlet grooves to be apparent, and almost everyone who believed it could be real had immediately assumed that two further objects — identically shaped but smaller in size — would fit within it. Any lingering doubts on that front had been shattered by the discovery in Vanuatu, and what was clear now was that the world was one more discovery away from a complete set... whatever that might ultimately mean.

All Dan could tell anyone was that he didn't know whether the second triangle was real or not, but that his doubts had grown tenfold due to the ridiculously convenient location and John Cole's equally convenient departure from the live TV panel just before it was discovered.

Vivid live pictures of this second triangle came in while local law enforcement tried to secure the site as quickly as possible, and Dan could once again see the same kind of familiar and conspicuous markings he had noticed on the first. These were the same markings he'd seen in his only recent vision, but he was no longer as sure of their meaning as he had been mere hours earlier.

Back then, Dan had dismissed Timo Fiore's suggestion that the Messengers may have been warning of an imminent GeoSov hoax designed to further destabilise the world. It struck Dan as senseless for the Messengers themselves to drop a second triangle within ELF territory, and this placement ran in contrast to a vague idea he had so far kept in his own head: that the Messengers may have been planning to place three pieces of a complete message-holding artefact in various locations as a means of forcing global cooperation between rival nations and organisations. But for this to have worked, he reasoned, the second triangle would have had to turn up in a GCC country or one of the world's few unaffiliated nations.

Giving two pieces of a three-piece puzzle to the ELF's irresponsible leaders wasn't something the Messengers would do, he firmly believed, so the hoax theory was starting to make sense.

Further support for this angle came from Poppy Bradshaw's incredible revelation that she and her fellow GeoSovs somehow knew about the chip in Dan's neck, which told him that they were a more serious force to be reckoned with than previously thought. How they could know such a thing was a mystery, and Dan tried to grasp at the silver lining that the Earth-shattering news which came minutes later had at least consigned Poppy's mention of the chip to the sidelines.

Billy Kendrick and Joe Crabbe both accepted an invitation from ACN to give their reactions in a 15-minute dual interview from New York, one in which Dan had also been invited to participate. The invitation went to Emma as such things always did, but she shot it down without even troubling Dan; had he known anything about this filtering action, he would have greatly appreciated it.

Tara was as quiet as Dan through a confusing and reactive few hours while everyone else tried to make sense of what was going on, and after a while she announced that she was going to bed soon. No one else heard her at first, since her announcement came shortly after ACN began showing footage of growing disorder in areas of the world where it was daytime. Things weren't quite at the level of overnight looting and rioting — at least not in North America — but demonstrations which had been underway when news of the Vanuatu triangle broke understandably swelled and grew more insistent now that the ELF's leadership was apparently in possession of *two* extraterrestrial objects and showed no sign of granting open scientific access.

Dan couldn't help but fear that his words on Focus 20/20 — intended to force Ding Ziyang and his colleagues' hands — would instead make things worse. Had he known what was coming, Dan would have chosen his words more carefully; he knew *hindsight* was 20/20, though, so tried not to beat himself up too much. And really, in the presence of so much confusion, he had little remaining mental energy to do much besides wonder what the hell was happening.

"I'm going to lie down, too," he said.

This caught everyone's attention, primarily because it was the first thing he'd said in a while and no one had quite caught it over the general noise of frantic discussions — both the discussion blaring through the projector's sound bar and that occurring between the rest of the room's shell-shocked inhabitants.

"I want to get this damn chip out of my neck as soon as I can and I want to talk to Slater or Godfrey about speaking to Ding," Dan said, justifying his need to at least *try* to get something resembling a decent night's sleep. "Because if this is a GeoSov hoax, there's a chance he's falling for it too. Walker fooled everyone, and at the time it looked like things were working out so conveniently for Godfrey that he had to be in on it... but he wasn't. For all we know, a hoaxed triangle could have turned up in Vanuatu eight hours ago and the ELF decided to keep it quiet until after Cole could mention Vanuatu on TV. And I don't *know* why, before you ask. I'm trying to get my head back into the mindset of all the bullshit meta-conspiracy crap I thought we'd left behind last year. I hate this. I *hate* this, but we can't make any assumptions about anything."

Dan, of course, had no idea that President Slater had mentioned a similar 'theoretical possibility' of the ELF falling for a hoax to Chairman Godfrey, nor that Godfrey had perfunctorily dismissed it out of hand. He watched only Emma's reaction, keen to gauge her immediate thoughts, and he wasn't sure whether to be disappointed or pleased that she seemed to see a lot of merit in the idea.

"Now *that's* interesting..." she said, "because the whole time, since Zanzibar, I've been wondering what the ELF's winning angle is if this is their hoax. And if we're starting to think this really isn't the Messengers, a *GeoSov* hoax is the other possibility that might make more sense..."

"I said it this morning," Timo interjected, no gloating tone in the words, "and now I firmly believe it. We didn't know anything about Poppy Bradshaw before tonight, but I'll have a team look deeply into her current and former associations. They knew about Dan's chip, which was essentially a US government secret, and they were hours away from an attempt to take President Slater hostage. However stupid they sound when they open their mouths, these aren't amateurs we're dealing with."

"I'll look into that, too," Clark said. "I tracked down one of the assholes who worked behind the scenes on their chickenshit attack on you guys last year, and I still have access to the database of old Antidotalist and Welcomer connections... holding companies they used for payments, low-level chumps they used for ordering the materials, all kinds of stuff like that."

Emma nodded. "But Timo, make sure you trust the people you put on that, okay? The last thing we want is the GeoSovs getting wind that we're onto them, if this *is* their work."

"Of course," he said, gesturing to his heavily scarred arm and neck. "After what the two of us went through last year, I will never take these scoundrels lightly and I'll take every precaution. I'm also going to call it a night, but Emma... Clark... if you want to get together tomorrow to talk about this investigation into Poppy and her colleagues, I'll be at Fiore Frontiere all day."

Phil Norris, Henry McCarthy, and Mr Byrd, all of whom had been animatedly involved in the post-Vanuatu speculation, made similar moves. Phil and Mr Byrd shook Dan and Clark's hands before leaving, as the pair of them always had and quite likely always would.

"What about you guys?" Tara asked Emma and Clark, who were both still anchored to the couch as reactions to the Vanuatu triangle poured in from around the world.

"Later," Clark said. Emma nodded, barely breaking her focus on the screen.

Tara then followed Dan into the kitchen, where he was pouring himself a glass of water. "Want one?" he asked.

She shook her head. "Do you think you'll manage to get to sleep okay?"

Dan instinctively chuckled, smiling warmly. "What do you think, Tara?"

"*Want one?*" she asked, holding out not a glass of water but a small container of pills. "They're just sleeping pills, but they're the *best* sleeping pills."

"Where did you get them?"

"Doctor," Tara whispered, turning the cylindrical container around so Dan could see that her name really was written on the affixed label. "I'm hardly going to fill you with backstreet drugs!"

Dan opened his palm, satisfied the pills were safe. "Why did the doctor give you these, though? Do you have insomnia?"

"Nah. Just like…." she shrugged, looking for an easy answer, "general long-term depression. But I'm trying to help *you* out here, so I wasn't looking for a chat with Dr Dan, okay? Put that down your throat and put your head on the pillow, and all these bullshit worries will float away until the sun comes up and we get to start the party *all* over again."

"Are you sure you're okay?" Dan asked; he couldn't help it, Tara really didn't sound like herself. It seemed like she knew better than to mix her own dose with alcohol, at least, but he still felt unsettled.

"You're going through a lot more shit than I am right now," she replied, "so let's just agree we're both okay. Okay?"

"Okay. Goodnight, then," he said, swallowing the pill as he walked away.

Tara followed him out of the kitchen and turned in the opposite direction. "Night, Dan."

∼

"Aaaaaaaah!" Dan screamed, grasping his neck as tears immediately welled in his eyes in reaction to what had to be the sharpest pain he had ever felt.

It was more concentrated than ever and somehow deeper, and it came with no vision or mental image.

They're close, he thought, wincing and wishing it would stop. *They're so close…*

When Dan's eyes opened as the worst of the pain abruptly died to leave a dull but still-intense sensation, he saw that he hadn't been mentally transported to a symbolic location, either. Instead, he was where he was — at home, on his knees, beside his bed.

He pulled himself up and saw Emma lying there like nothing was going on. How hadn't she heard? He called her name and reached towards her, but his hand recoiled before it made contact. Because before it made contact with Emma, it hit something else.

A forcefield, he realised. *They're not close; they're here.*

Even this realisation couldn't prepare Dan for the brilliant white light he saw when he turned towards the bedroom's door. It was a total light, captivating in its brilliance, and it dared him to approach.

"No," he spoke out loud. "If you want me, here I am."

At that point, a bluish silver hand emerged through the light like a child's puppet through a curtain.

Dan gazed on in wonder. The hand's familiarity brought a sudden and surprising serenity to his mind, with the Messenger's two double-wide 'fingers' and extremely dextrous thumb bringing back all kinds of visceral memories.

The hand then turned, palm up, and the two wide fingers unmistakably called Dan to come hither.

Entranced, and without so much as a backwards glance towards the still-sleeping Emma, Dan McCarthy reached out, took the hand, and followed it into the light.

Part 3

UPGRADE

"It is easy for the weak to be gentle…
… if you wish to know what a man really is,
give him power."

Robert G. Ingersoll

V minus 62

???
???

The white light that surrounded Dan McCarthy was warm and gentle rather than bright and harsh, almost swaddling rather than surrounding him. Although a million questions were swirling in his mind, he felt nothing but calm and anything but anxious.

There was nothing to see in any direction other than the two familiar alien beings who stood directly before him, keeping a distance of several feet as they gazed deep into his soul. They were equal in height, around a foot shorter than Dan, and once again everything but their hands and heads were covered by a seamless skintight fabric.

"Who made the triangles?" Dan asked, firing out the question that currently sat above all others.

In lieu of any kind of answer, one of the Messengers stepped behind the other and produced an item from the small pouch at the back of its full-body garment. Dan took a deep breath and readied his neck for the inevitable insertion of a sharp cable. He knew how this went.

Or, at least, he *thought* he did.

But instead of producing a cable and attaching it to Dan's neck, the Messenger produced two small matching items that looked like foldaway compact mirrors. Wordlessly, the Messenger then handed one of the items to its companion and walked behind Dan with the other.

The Messenger in front of Dan held the small black item out and very clearly mimed what it wanted Dan to do: place all five fingers of his right hand on the item's surface.

Dan did so, more than a little surprised that it felt like nothing more alien than the surface of a highly polished table. The next sensation he felt was not quite so typical or so welcome, however, as the second Messenger placed the second item against the back of his neck.

The resulting sensation was not pain as Dan knew it, but a truly paralysing assault on his nervous system. He thought he felt his legs buckle under his weight but didn't actually move a muscle, only stared into the calm and reassuring primate-like eyes of the Messenger who was holding one of the items under his fingertips.

All Dan could do was surrender to the feeling and trust that the Messengers were doing this for his own good, like everything else they'd ever done. After an unknowable length of time, the intense sensation ceased as quickly as it had begun; only in its absence was he able to appreciate just how strong it had really been, like a camel's back freed of a heavy load. His whole body was shaking, but his legs remained relatively stable.

The Messenger who had gathered the items placed them back in its colleague's pocket without any fanfare and quickly retook its side-by-side position.

"What the hell was that?" Dan asked, trying a second question despite his first having been completely ignored.

At that point, both Messengers raised their right hands in tandem. Each touched a long thumb against one of the broad finger-like divisions that made up the rest of their hands, with the other 'finger' pointed directly at Dan.

"I don't…. just *talk* to me," Dan pleaded. "Put a cable in my neck, I don't care. Just talk to me. Please!"

Still holding their right hands out in this manner, both Messengers then used their left hands to point back and forth between themselves and Dan. Eventually, he got it.

"You want me to do that?" he said, lifting his right hand and touching his thumb to his middle finger.

Exactly, came the reply. *Now… we can talk.*

～

"Did you just put something inside me?" Dan asked, instinctively speaking out loud despite knowing that he almost certainly didn't have to. "How can I hear you without a connection? And how can *you* hear *me*?"

Our interspecies communication abilities have increased greatly since our last meeting. Your brainwaves have been studied, your thought patterns have been modelled, and we are able to communicate with you as we can with each other.

Dan was stunned, not just by the content of this reply but by how much more fluently and eloquently he 'heard' it in his mind than had been the case on previous occasions. His conversation with the Messengers on Contact Day had been tremendously more detailed than that which had been possible in Lolo National Forest the first time around, but this was on another level. They were fast learners.

"That explains the clarity, but how does it work with no cable?" he pushed, still holding his middle finger to his thumb and pointing at the Messengers with his index finger; clearly, this was important. "What were those things on my neck and under my fingers... and what did you do to me, turn my body into a transceiver?"

We have enabled you to interpret the frequency of our communications and to return your own thoughts, that is all.

"Return my own thoughts? So you can read my thoughts now, but you couldn't before? And you can't read anyone else's?"

Only your brainwaves have been studied, only your thought patterns have been modelled. This is untested on other humans.

Even with the huge jump in clarity, the Messengers still had an odd syntax to their 'speech' and a flair for repetition, Dan thought.

Interspecies communication is not easy.

Dan opened his hand, breaking the connection between his thumb and finger and no longer pointing at the Messengers. "Can you hear me now?" he asked, curious rather than challenging, having momentarily forgotten they could hear his thoughts as well as his speech and thus having been caught off guard by their reply to his silent thought about their syntax.

No reply came.

Dan touched his middle finger to his thumb once more and pointed at the Messengers with his index finger.

We heard, but you could not hear our reply — not until you physically re-declared your intention to communicate. Your mental dexterity will improve in time, but for now our abilities are not equal.

"How come it's not equal?"

Our minds are well-practiced in telepathic communications. We can filter out noise, and we can typically direct our thoughts without difficulty. Without the physical filter of an 'on switch' and without a directional pointer, your mind would be overwhelmed.

"*Telepathic* communications," Dan said. Considering that word, distinct from the phenomenon itself, gave him real pause. "We're communicating telepathically. This is telepathy."

Exactly.

Dan shook his head in near disbelief, until the pressing thought of the hour returned like a boomerang smacking him in the face: "So what's the deal with these damn triangles?"

There is a problem on New Kerguelen.

"New Kerguelen?"

Isn't this the shorthand name by which you know and consider our home world? On New Kerguelen, there is a problem with our Elders. We are trying to deal with this problem.

"The Elders who tell you what you can and can't do? The ones who set the 'minimal necessary intervention' rule and eventually let you stop the comet?"

Precisely.

"So what's the problem?"

Although you think of us as 'Messengers', among our kind we are designated Interpreters. Our core task on New Kerguelen is interpreting the will of our Elders, and since initial contact our core external task has been interpreting the intentions of your kind and the level of threat those intentions may pose. But lately the clarity of our Elders' decisions has led to disagreement among our fellow Interpreters and disagreements among our wider population. Erraticism and indecision have become increasingly common in the words of our Elders, and discontent has followed.

"Tell me about the triangles," Dan said. "Who put them there: you, the ELF, or the GeoSovs?"

As Interpreters, we are unable to engage in this conversation.

"What?"

We made an independent decision to visit on this occasion. We did this in order to protect the possibility of further contact if visitation becomes difficult due to our ongoing complications in interpreting the will of our Elders. We cannot make an independent decision to engage in that conversation.

"So if the Elders aren't being clear about anything, you obviously didn't get permission to place these triangles, right? So can you at least tell me who did, since you're already here? Was it the ELF or the

GeoSovs? After all, you warned me about the first triangle in the vision, with the marking you showed me. Surely you can go a tiny bit further and fill me in on what the hell is actually going on?"

We made an independent decision to ensure the possibility of further contact. But at this stage, we as Interpreters cannot make an independent decision to engage in this conversation. Without permission from the Elders, we as Interpreters cannot interfere in such a way.

"How does that even make sense? How is it more of an intervention to tell me who's behind the triangles than it is to come into my house and give me the ability to communicate with you telepathically?"

This action was not taken lightly, and only to ensure the possibility of future contact should our complications in interpreting the word of our Elders continue, particularly if a disagreement over our interpretation prevents visitation in an emergency situation.

"So what about when you warned me about Slater being taken hostage? Did the Elders give permission for that?"

That action was taken to prevent an imminent event which would have immediately destabilised your planet in a manner which would have unacceptably increased the likelihood of atomic detonations. Such interventions are irrevocably pre-approved.

"These stupid triangles could start a war just the same as Slater being killed could have!" Dan replied. "Please, I'm begging you... just tell me who's responsible."

As Interpreters, we are not authorised to act in such instances. You were warned of a specific one-time event, which could be stopped very easily. In such cases, when pre-set conditions of specificity and urgency are met, we are preapproved to prevent catastrophes which have no immediate side-effect. We cannot engage in a conversation on the topic you raise.

"But *you* didn't put them here? We're clear on that?"

As Interpreters, we are bound by the will of our Elders and are unable to intervene in any publicly visible way without explicit permission, pre-approved or ongoing.

"Explicit permission which you've not been able to get recently, because of the problems you've had interpreting your Elders?" Dan said, drilling down on this point again. "So reading between the lines, you're telling me without telling me. You didn't do it."

The Messengers' faces, always expressionless, continued to give nothing away.

"So can I talk to you at any time from now on, and you can talk to me?" Dan asked.

We can talk to you. As Interpreters, we pay close attention. If you want to reach us, we will know. Whether we can reply is situationally dependent, and whether we can act in accordance with any requests or suggestions depends on how we fare in improving the clarity of our Elders' decisions.

"And tonight, am I going to have to deal with agents who know you just reached out to me? Because I felt the pain like hell before you showed up."

No; a forcefield was in place to prevent any communication from the device in your neck. In the future, no other human will know you have been contacted until you make it known to them.

"So am I just going to suddenly hear thoughts in my head whenever you decide to talk to me again?"

You will hear a call. We will never force thoughts into your mind. An alert will signal our intention to communicate; if you focus your mind and physically signal willingness with a digital connection, contact can commence.

"Digital as in fingers... those kind of digits? So if I hear from you with some small alert, I need to focus my mind and touch my finger to my thumb?" Dan sought to clarify. It sounded utterly insane, but only because it was.

Precisely. Until you grow more accustomed to the process, a digital connection is required. But your progress will be quick.

"Okay. I can tell you want to leave, but can you just quickly give me a one-word answer about these triangles? They're destabilising the world in a way you don't seem to understand, and they're empowering people who aren't going to use that power well."

Farewell, Dan McCarthy. Stay true to your convictions. We have gifted you this communicational ability because you chose to help your fellow man in a manner costly to yourself by returning to the public arena. When you can help, you do what you can... as we ourselves strive to do.

Dan was surprised by the nature of these closing comments; but before he could even think about replying, the cocoon of whiteness was gone and he was back in his bedroom.

He found himself on the inside of the closed door, with Emma still sleeping soundly.

Am I tripping? he wondered, sure that what he thought had just happened couldn't *really* have just happened. *What the hell was really in that pill Tara gave me?*

But when Dan turned on the light and looked at the fingers of his right hand, he saw large pin-prick like marks. Just like the initial marks on Dan and Emma's necks had convinced Clark that they hadn't imagined their physical connection with the Messengers at Lolo, these markings settled it in Dan's mind.

"Emma!" he called, shaking her legs to hasten the wake-up. "Wake up! You're never gonna believe what just happened…"

V minus 61

FORD RESIDENCE
BIRCHWOOD, COLORADO

"So let me get this straight," Emma said, sitting with Dan at the kitchen table having listened to the whole story twice. "They can't tell you anything about the triangles, but they basically *implied* it wasn't them?"

"Right."

"And they're having a problem interpreting their Elders, which might somehow stop them from being able to visit again even if they feel like they need to, but now they can contact you remotely to initiate a two-way conversation whenever they want?"

Dan nodded again. "Right."

"And they pretty much said they gifted you this ability because you did Focus 20/20, which was an active step back into the public sphere that you didn't want to take but one you took for the greater good... because they saw that as an expression of your willingness to be involved again?"

"I know how it sounds, but it happened. Just look at my fingertips."

Dan reached for a glass of water with his left hand, lifting it off the table while Emma studied his fingertips.

"And when they want to talk, you have to touch your thumb against your finger to 'let' their thoughts in?"

"Uh-huh," Dan uttered, midway through a gulp of water. He demonstrated the finger position.

Two seconds later, his left hand involuntarily released the glass of water.

As the glass loudly smashed on the floor and Emma jumped up in an instinctive reaction, Dan hurriedly backed away like a dog fleeing a hose and didn't stop until he was leaning against the wall. He looked like he'd seen a ghost.

"It's okay," Emma insisted. "I think doing the thing with your fingers just made you drop the glass with your other hand. Take it easy for a while. You've been through a lot... just breathe."

Dan shook his head and gulped. His eyes then darted around the room as if making sure no one else was there to hear what he knew was going to be the craziest thing he'd ever said.

"Emma..." he began, still holding his hand in the communication position.

"Yeah?" she asked, uneasy at a look in his eyes that seemed less like shock than terror.

"... I can hear your thoughts."

V minus 60

"That should be enough," GCC Chairman Godfrey spoke into his phone, delighted to hear that President Slater had done her part in persuading some wavering delegates to vote the right way at the following morning's emergency meeting.

What Godfrey perceived as a muzzle was soon to be removed, and he would be as free as Ding Ziyang and John Cole to make statements on any and all contact-related matters without requiring approval from his organisation's members before any substantive new statement.

With that restriction soon to be a thing of the past just in time for Godfrey to call out the ELF's outrageously obvious triangle-related shenanigans, he had no doubt that he could effectively and decisively deal with the barrage of provocation that had recently come his way from Zanzibar and Vanuatu.

"The gloves are off now, Valerie," he said, smiling to himself in the quiet hours between very late and very early. "And if Ding and Cole want to fight dirty, they've picked the wrong man to push too far."

V minus 59

BIRCHWOOD, COLORADO

"Are you guys okay?" Tara called, rushing out of the spare bedroom at the sound of smashing glass. Although she clearly hadn't been sleeping, her words were largely drowned out by the unsettled barking of Rooster, who *had* been sleeping at the end of her bed. She looked down at the dog, who was frightened rather than aggressive, and immediately cottoned on. "*Ohhhh…*"

Dan walked over to Rooster to try to calm him down. It seemed to have been the opening of the spare bedroom door that set the dog off, doubtless because this had removed the physical barrier between him and the recently-contacted Dan.

"Rooster," Dan called, crouching to the ground and holding his right hand outstretched. "It's okay, they're gone. See? It's just me."

The dog stopped barking but still didn't look sure. He looked up at Tara, as though trusting her more, and cautiously inched towards Dan only once she gave the go-ahead. He growled defensively at Dan's fingers but settled as soon as Dan closed his fist. Within a few more seconds the dog was curled up on the kitchen floor, safely clear of the broken glass that Emma was now cleaning up.

"So what happened?" Tara asked. "Tell me they explained every-thing about these stupid triangles that are causing so much trouble…"

"Not exactly," Dan replied, tipping his head in suggestion for her to take a seat. He then gave a rapid rundown of his conversation, focusing on the core point that the Messengers had explained they were unable to enter a conversation about the triangles without permission from their Elders — permission that was currently unobtainable due to a serious problem regarding their interpretation of those Elders' typically explicit will.

Listening intently, Tara tried to make sense of the logic that Dan himself was still struggling with.

"But that wasn't all," he continued. "You know how they can talk to each other without speaking…. telepathically? They touched something against my neck and my fingers that lets me do that, too. And not just with them, but with other people. Think of a name I wouldn't be able to guess. Don't make it obvious, but make sure it's only one name."

Wide-eyed at what she was hearing, Tara nodded her assent. "Okay, I've got one."

Dan pointed at her with his index finger, touching his thumb to the tip of his middle finger at the same time. "Easy. Jayson Moore."

Dumbstruck, Tara looked at Emma.

"And now you're thinking I could have guessed that," Dan went on, "because you're thinking that me and Emma might have talked about how obsessed with his TV show you used to be. And *now* you're thinking I could have guessed *that*, too. Stop thinking about that and focus on why his name was in your head. Ah, there we go: because you're going to meet him in a few days at a club opening you're both invited to."

"I… I… I only heard about that a few hours ago," Tara stammered. "Emma, this is *real*."

Dan turned to Emma. "Clear your mind; don't think about anything that's a secret you don't want me to know. Focus completely on another name, and make sure it's one I couldn't possibly know."

"Ready," she said.

Dan touched his middle finger to his thumb again and pointed at Emma with his index finger. "Leslie Fowler," he said, breaking the connection as soon as he had the name.

Tara laughed. "*Leslie?*"

"You two never shut up about Jayson Moore for that whole summer," Emma reminisced. "You made that stupid fan club and everything!"

Tara blinked several times, as though reality had just set in. "But how can this work? They didn't do anything to change *us*, so how can we send you our thoughts?"

"They said they were giving me the ability to interpret their frequency of communication," Dan explained, doing the best he could given that it was far from clear in his own mind. "They also said I'd be able to return my thoughts to them, but that they'd only studied my thought patterns and the process was untested on other humans. But I guess maybe I'm innately familiar with human thought patterns in general, in a way they're not? I don't know. I don't even know if they meant to do this. They wanted me to be able to communicate with *them*. This whole human-to-human part could be a side-effect they didn't anticipate."

"You said the Messengers don't make mistakes," Tara said. "Last year. Remember?"

Dan sat down. "Yeah, I *did*, but that was before Contact Day. That was before I knew that they're nothing close to omniscient or omnipotent. Going right back to the start, they didn't know how destabilising it would be when they destroyed DS-1 and then they had to ask Emma for advice on the fourth plaque. Okay, on one hand that tells us they're smart enough to ask when they need help and they're not too proud or stubborn to do it, which puts them ahead of a lot of people, but they're not perfect. Even just before they finally showed up on Contact Day, they thought we could deal with Il Diavolo by ourselves... so their interpretation of human problems isn't perfect, either. But more than that, they aren't necessarily *better* than us. Billy Kendrick touches on this in his lecture tour, when he says we shouldn't worship the Messengers because the evidence we have doesn't point to them being any more moral or altruistic than we are. They're basically us, just with better vehicles and better tech."

"*Much* better," Emma interjected, ponderously looking at the table as she considered Dan's words.

"Yeah," he said. "What they *have* is better than what we have, but what they *are* isn't necessarily better than what we are. Their breed of rationality is kind of indifferent... in the same way that nature is indifferent. None of the Messengers are going to be assholes like Cole or Godfrey, but none of them are going to be saints or martyrs or poets or artists, either. Their decision-making and permission-seeking processes are so linear and rational, it even stops them from saying simple things that could save all kinds of problems. I should know about these triangles by now, but I don't. They had the chance to tell me, but

175

all they did was make sure they can contact me again if they ever need to."

"The main thing is that we keep this under wraps until we have time to really consider the implications," Emma said. "Okay? And I'm not saying forever, just until we all agree."

Dan took a deep breath. "Emma… this is *so* much power."

"I know that, Dan, but so do they. And I think they must have had an idea this would happen, even if it *was* a side-effect, and they wouldn't have done that if they didn't think you could handle it. They trusted you with this because they know you."

"Wait a second, though…" Tara chimed in, raising her head slowly in deep thought. "Dan, I could be talking nonsense since it's the middle of the night and this is all so crazy that I'm not totally sure I'm not dreaming, but hear me out. I'm with Emma about them knowing this would happen. Maybe they couldn't help you directly by telling you about the triangles, but they knew that doing this could help you help *yourself*? Like, they've given you the necessary tools, kinda thing. I guess what I'm trying to say is this: to find out what those ELF guys like Ding and Cole know about the triangles… couldn't you just stand in front of one of them and read his mind?"

Dan and Emma looked at each other, simultaneously wondering how they hadn't thought of this and silently gauging each other's reactions.

"I'm just saying," Tara went on. "Whether they meant it or not, the Messengers gave you this power, so I figure you might as well try to use it for good…"

SUNDAY

V minus 58

GCC HEADQUARTERS
BUENOS AIRES, ARGENTINA

The early-morning streets outside the GCC building in Buenos Aires were bustling rather than chaotic, but the media turnout was by far the biggest yet. As the sun rose for the first time since a second triangle had been found in Vanuatu, of all places, and with Dan McCarthy having distanced himself from the GCC's hierarchy just minutes before that triangle's discovery, many expected a strong response from Chairman Godfrey.

"GCC delegates have so far been extremely tight-lipped about recent goings on in the building behind me," an American news reporter spoke into his camera, "but rumblings overnight hint that we're going to see a strong response today. I say *see* rather than *hear* very deliberately, because my sources are telling me that Chairman Godfrey feels that the time for words is over."

The reporter was Kyle Young, an ACN newsman well known to the public for one broadcast in particular. On that famous occasion, Kyle had pursued a convoy of unmarked vehicles on their way to a midnight raid of Dan McCarthy's empty Birchwood home, and his brave decision to chase the story at great personal risk had won many admirers. Chief among them were Dan's inner circle, who had already been on friendly terms with Kyle's close colleague Maria Janzyck following her discreet assistance in providing some seemingly incriminating video footage of Richard Walker.

Young in years as well as by name, Kyle was affable and well-presented yet lacking in a certain gravitas. His relatively high vocal register killed any hopes of a behind-the-desk newscaster role — he was at least grateful that the network bigwigs had been upfront about that, rather than giving him false hope — but the public's firm mental association between Kyle and anything McCarthy- or alien-related had come up trumps in securing him this profile-boosting placement in Buenos Aires.

"The same source suggests that while senior GCC officials were infuriated by John Cole's words on Focus 20/20, they would have been prepared to deal with that behind closed doors," he went on. "But I understand that both triangles are now en route to China, where further and deeper analysis will be conducted by scientists from ELF-affiliated nations *only*. The door is closed to the GCC, meaning that the door is closed to the United States. President Slater is under growing pressure to break rank and condemn the ELF hierarchy, but it's widely believed that Chairman Godfrey's response — backed by the weight of the Western world — will go further than Slater reasonably could."

Kyle's line of work made it crucial that he stayed on top of public opinion and knew which points to focus on and which to leave by the wayside. Social Media Meta Analysis made it abundantly clear that members of the public weren't quite so all-consumingly invested in the story of the triangles as they had been in the story of the original plaques, in no small part because all of their main questions had been decisively answered on Contact Day when the Messengers showed up and revealed their benevolent nature.

Despite this, however, Kyle knew that the public was far more interested in the triangles themselves than in the political machinations between two organisations that held no legitimacy in the eyes of many. His closing remarks reflected this:

"Of course, if we take a step back from all of the politics and focus on the bottom line, we'll remember that there's still another triangle unaccounted for. If this is a hoax, it'll fall apart soon enough, so I'll focus on the alternative. There could already be a third alien triangle out there somewhere, waiting to be found, or it could be just about to arrive. What I see a lot of the media doing right now is falling into the trap of over-focusing on two bald men fighting over a comb. The way *I* see it, the bald heads in Beijing and Buenos Aires should bear one name in mind while they're scrambling over the comb of contact: Dan McCarthy."

Kyle gazed into the camera.

"I hope to speak to my friend Dan soon," he said, "and I'm sure we'll be hearing a lot more from him in the coming hours and days — wherever and whenever the final triangle turns up, and whichever political faction grabs it first. For ACN in Buenos Aires, I'm Kyle Young."

V minus 57

Having spent the hours before breakfast testing the limits of Dan's extraordinary new ability, Emma and Tara both turned towards the evidently unlocked front door when they heard it opening.

"Just me," Clark called.

Rooster immediately hurried toward him, as fast as his old legs would go. Although normally relatively aloof with the elder McCarthy brother, the dog now seemed to want Clark's affectionate attention more than anything else in the world.

"What's gotten into you?" Clark asked, crouching down to pat Rooster and smiling until it suddenly clicked in his mind. He stood up and called towards the kitchen, where he assumed everyone was: "Does someone want to tell me what the hell's gotten into the dog?"

Dan emerged from the bathroom a few seconds later. "Hey," he said to the decidedly impatient-looking Clark. "Uh, you might want to sit down for this."

～

"Why couldn't they just tell you who put the damn triangles there?" Clark moaned as Dan reached the end of the very short recap of his overnight contact experience.

"You do know what telepathy *is*, right?" Tara asked in return. "Dan can read minds!"

"Hear thoughts," Dan corrected; after much consideration, this now felt like a very meaningful distinction. "But Clark, it's just like I told you: they said there's a problem with their Elders right now. It seemed like whatever has happened has *just* happened, so it's maybe messed with pre-existing plans or it's maybe just making them hesitant to say anything about *anything* right now. All I know for sure is they wanted to know they could reach me again if they ever have to. I don't know anything new about the triangles and I don't know if they even meant to give me this power, but I have it. And the three of us have an idea about using it to find out who's telling the truth and who's not. Because if I can sit down with Godfrey, with one of the GeoSovs, with Cole or even Ding… I'll know what they're thinking."

"Do you think it'll work in Chinese?" Clark asked, immediately stumping the others with a question they hadn't even considered.

They all looked at each other for a few seconds, and could ultimately only shrug in response.

"We tested a few things," Emma said. "So far we know he has to see the person directly to initiate it, but if they wander behind a wall or something that doesn't necessarily cut it off."

"We also know he can hear two of us at once," Tara added. She turned to Dan. "Want to try three?"

Dan looked at Clark. "Are you ready? I can only hear clear thoughts you're actively thinking about or things that are in your mind as something you're trying to hide. It's almost like a lie detector, I guess, but not really. So try not to think of anything you don't want me to know, okay? I hear it in your voice, like you hear your own thoughts; so basically anything *you* know you're thinking about, I'll know too. Not memories or anything, unless they're actually on your conscious mind at the time."

Clark, striking Dan as surprisingly blasé about this, gave a casual thumbs up.

"Okay," Dan said, doing his thing. "Tara, you're thinking '*of course it's going to work*'. Emma, you're thinking about using Timo to test whether I can understand foreign languages. And Clark, you're wondering if I want to tell Dad about this."

Clark leaned back and chuckled. "You know, a tiny piece of me thought you guys were messing with me. This is *big*. It can't have been an accident, man, and you *did* say they said something about noticing that you'd put yourself back out there by going on 20/20 last night. Maybe this is like a reward, or maybe it's more like a weapon to help you slice through all the bullshit and calm things down? Because God knows the world needs that..."

"Maybe," Dan said, but he was now preoccupied by Emma's thought. "That's a good idea about Timo, though," he told her. "Could you maybe call him and ask him to get here as soon as he can?"

"On it," she said, dialling right away. Barely thirty seconds later, she quickly relayed Timo's comments that he'd been waiting for their call all morning but didn't want to wake them, and that he would arrive from the city in no time.

The intervening minutes passed primarily with Clark addressing his own relative lack of amazement, which he explained by saying that this wasn't really any more remarkable to him than some of what had gone before. "Those aliens made a forcefield in Walker's bedroom door that smashed my nose into a dozen pieces, they froze me to the spot at the drive-in, and they talked to Dan through what looked like a damn USB cable connected to his neck," he said. "Oh yeah, and they also changed the path of a comet. So yeah, this is flat-out amazing... but it would feel a lot *more* amazing if it was the first time these aliens have blown me away."

Clark was looking forward to watching Timo's face as he found out, since the Italian tended to be a lot more reactive than himself or indeed the others. But when Timo arrived, he jumped straight into some news of his own.

"I have two fresh pieces of information," the affable billionaire began. "One more surprising than the other. First, my team's preliminary investigation into Poppy Bradshaw and her GeoSov associates has led to some holding companies and shell companies registered in the Cayman Islands, and the people I have on this are telling me that it all looks intentionally obfuscatory — certainly beyond what you'd usually see in tax avoidance schemes. Rather than merely hide money, it seems that tireless steps have been taken to mask the origin and ultimate destination of every penny that passes through."

Timo seemed to be talking primarily to Emma, and she was first to reply: "Do I even want to know how your people are able to dig so deeply into that kind of stuff?"

"Well, I know *I* don't," he replied without humour. "But moving on to the more surprising piece of news... and Dan, this one will interest you a great deal more than the first. I'll understand if you're sceptical, because I was, but I trust where this has come from."

"Spit it out," Clark urged, never the most patient in the group.

"My contacts in China think the triangles are real," Timo said, straight to the point. "And trust me, Dan: these aren't people who would lie to me, and they're not in the habit of getting things wrong."

V minus 56

DRIVE-IN
BIRCHWOOD, COLORADO

"You guys would do yourselves a favour catching a flight to Beijing or Buenos Aires," Phil Norris called to a news crew at the edge of his drive-in lot as he arrived to open New Kergrillin' in time for the Sunday brunch rush. "Ain't nothing happening in Birchwood today!"

Unperturbed, the reporter continued speaking into his camera, the shot framed by the world-famous backdrop of a lot where aliens had once walked.

Birchwood would have been overflowing with media types like in the old days if anyone knew how recently the aliens had been back in town, but Dan McCarthy was keeping those cards close to his chest for good reason.

No one could ever have imagined the power that the aliens had left behind just hours earlier, and nothing good could come of them finding out...

V minus 55

FORD RESIDENCE
BIRCHWOOD, COLORADO

"I'm not talking about political contacts," Timo Fiore continued, trying to add weight to a point that Dan was understandably struggling with: that people Timo trusted in China, who had seen primary data from the initial analysis of the Zanzibar and Vanuatu triangles, believed that they were the real deal. "I'm talking about scientists on the ground who have worked with some of my Fiore Frontiere staff in the past. These people insist that *everything* they're hearing in China suggests the government scientists who have actually gotten up close to these objects believe they're real. My first thought was probably the one in your minds right now: that the Argentine sphere also seemed like it was real. The difference now, to *my* mind, is that the threshold for belief has surely risen. For these scientists to say the triangles are real, there has to be something decidedly alien about them... not just something that can't immediately be explained away as a human creation. The burden of proof is higher than ever. Godfrey and Slater have heard this news, but they're sceptical."

"So am I," Dan said. "We haven't even seen any professionally produced videos of these triangles. Hell, we've barely had any clear photos. We have some amateur footage from the cameras on locals' phones, and that's it. Everything coming out of China could be a lie, just like it could be a lie if it was coming out of here. I don't trust government scientists, wherever they are, because I don't trust governments — *wherever* they are."

Timo rubbed his chin, appearing surprised by Dan's tone. "Well, short of any way of finding out who's lying, the word of these scientists is all we have for now."

"Funny you should say that..." Clark said.

As Dan recapped a remarkable story for at least the fourth time since his latest meeting with the Messengers, Timo's surprise grew and grew. His shocked reaction was far more visual than Clark's, even taking him out of his seat and leading him to pace the living room like a caged bear on a cold day.

Unlike Clark, Timo fully and readily believed the story of the Messengers granting Dan a measure of telepathic ability even before he received a personal demonstration. That demonstration quickly and unfortunately put paid to the idea of Dan being able to 'hear' thoughts in any language that he himself couldn't speak, a regrettable development but one that wasn't too unsurprising to Dan given his limited understanding of neurolinguistics.

More like Clark, however, Timo didn't spend much time pondering the incredible ability he had just witnessed. For his part, he was very confused by what the Messengers had said about their Elders and what they *hadn't* said about the triangles, repeatedly insisting that Dan must have been forgetting something.

Dan, in turn, insisted that he had told Timo everything the Messengers had told him. He understandably struggled when trying to explain something that wasn't clear to him, particularly given that the Messengers themselves had seemed like they were being very careful with the wording of the verbal thoughts they sent Dan's way. He didn't think they had been evasive because they *wanted* to keep something from him, and if anything he thought the opposite was true; that they had told him as much as they could, and perhaps even felt like they were edging dangerously close to an implicit or explicit boundary imposed by their problem-stricken Elders.

"How many people know about this?" Timo asked, shifting his weight and all of a sudden looking more concerned than ponderous.

"Just us," Dan replied. "I haven't even seen my dad since last night, so I haven't told him."

Timo nodded slowly. "You haven't told him *yet*, or...?"

"Yet; I will soon. Mr Byrd and Phil, too. I'd trust either of them with my life, and they're both smart in different ways."

"We do need to be careful with this, Dan," Timo said. "You need to fully trust everyone you tell, and they need to fully understand that it has to stay quiet. I don't know how much attention you've paid to background developments over the past year, but the vocalisations the Messengers made at the drive-in have been studied endlessly all around the world. On the fringes, there are even scientists who claim to have some idea as to the meaning of the words they spoke among themselves. They have never shared those ideas, of course, and I agree with the prevailing scientific feeling that the Messengers didn't utter anything *close* to the number of different 'words' we'd need to build any kind of understanding. Some scientists undertook their study with the goal of reverse-engineering the Messengers' speech in order to send signal-based communications back into space for them to hear, and that kind of thing has been going on practically since the sun set on Contact Day."

"That's all true," Emma said, unsure where Timo was going, "but others have been looking into telepathy, too. I don't know if *you* know this part, Timo, but there have been *multiple* attempted data thefts from the facilities where Dan's been tested and studied. People don't talk about this in public because it sounds crazy, but there's a lot of scientific interest in the specifics of how the Messengers were able to communicate telepathically with each other. There are a few discussions online about whether or not their physical connection to Dan might have affected his physiology, and the idea that the Messengers could have transferred their telepathic abilities to Dan *has* been raised. Fortunately it's a real fringe belief, but it is out there."

"I did know that," Timo said, "and it's exactly what I'm worried about. Anything that backs up those theories will be seized upon, because it's a huge story. It's the kind of theory that people don't have to believe to be interested in, because it's just so *big*."

"Well, *I* didn't know about any of that," Dan said.

Emma shrugged. "I figured at least one of us had to keep an eye on that kind of stuff, but I also figured that one of us was enough."

"Definitely," he replied.

"So I also had an idea of what we could do," Tara interjected, speaking to Timo but glancing between the others as if to remind them she was there. "We know it's not going to work with Chinese, but I think maybe Dan should meet John Cole to find out how much he really knows about the triangles. Godfrey too, in case there's something he's keeping even from you. And then, if they'll agree to it, a GeoSov like

Poppy from last night's Focus 20/20. Then we'd know what *they* know. One way or another, we'd *know*."

"I love it," Timo boomed, his voice suddenly almost as loud as the clapping of his hands that punctuated his declaration. "This could change everything. Knowing who's lying and where the triangles really came from would enable us to dampen all of these tensions that have been... damnit, the time!"

As the others exchanged confused looks, Timo pulled his phone from his pocket.

"Godfrey is addressing the press and the speech is due to start any second now," Timo said, staring at the time on his phone and sighing when he saw that it was consistent with the decorative hands-only clock on Emma's wall. "I can maybe still stop him. But Dan, if we tell him to call it off, there's no going back. Are you sure about this?"

"Call him," Dan affirmed. "And *quickly*, because whatever he's going to say about the second triangle and about what Cole said last night will probably make things worse!"

"I'll try Slater at the same time," Emma chimed in.

Clark, meanwhile, set off to get the TV remote.

The change in Timo's body language that came immediately after he made the call told Dan all he had to know. "Straight to voicemail," he reported, underlining his visual disappointment.

"Slater's, too," Emma added with a quick shake of her head.

In the living room, Clark had known before any of them. "It's too late," he called through to the kitchen. "He's already talking."

V minus 54

"I'll be brief," Chairman Godfrey began, addressing his packed-out media room. "As I'm sure you can all understand, I would rather not have to say any of this at all. But the words and even more pertinently the actions of our enemies can no longer be allowed to go unchallenged."

Kyle Young, present alongside his ACN cameraman in the hope that Godfrey might take questions at the end, was as shocked as anyone by the GCC Chairman's casual utterance of the word 'enemies', a hitherto unspoken term in reference to the ELF. The question on the tip of his tongue was a request to expand on that word, but he knew Godfrey well enough to know there was a lot more to come; if he was starting out this strong, he was going deep.

"It's time to start calling a spade a spade. If the ELF name wasn't so ingrained I'd be tempted to start calling the Earth Liaison Forum what it really is: Contact International, or *Conintern*, if you will. It doesn't take a cartographer to look at a map and see that the countries affiliated to the ELF look decidedly like those who found themselves humbled by defeat at the end of the Cold War, and those of you fortunate enough to have been born after our hard-earned victory over their poisonous ideology

190

can simply type *Comintern* — that's *Com* with an '*m*' — into your phones to see what I'm talking about. While you're at it, have a look at Holodomor and Tiananmen Square to acquaint yourself with who we're dealing with.

"On that point, you'll know by now that I consider Dan McCarthy a friend. Dan, however, is a shining example of a well-meaning individual who is simply too young to remember the Chinese and Russian aggression of the past. Perhaps the fact that their recent aggression has so often fallen upon their own people is why the rest of the world has turned a blind eye? Of that, we can only speculate. What goes beyond the realm of speculation and crosses into objective reality is the recent international aggression we've seen and heard from the ELF's leaders. No doubt there will be those who decry my mention of certain things as provocative and internationally irresponsible. To those I say this: the pathetic words of John Cole and the desperate actions of the unelected dictator Ding Ziyang go far beyond provocative and internationally irresponsible. Whether these triangles are a power-grabbing hoax or whether two truly alien artefacts are currently being deliberately hidden away from the neutral eyes of GCC scientists, I am no longer willing to stand idly by while the illiberal enemies of freedom play politics with our planet's future.

"The discovery sites in Zanzibar and Vanuatu seem too conveniently located to dismiss as mere coincidence, even without factoring in the *exquisitely* convenient timing of the triangles' discoveries. But ladies and gentlemen, citizens of the world, I live and lead with an open mind. Stranger things have happened; after all, aliens have walked among us. I rule nothing out. I stand before you not to speculate, for the next few days will reveal the truth behind these triangles and I am not too proud to say I can't be sure which way that's going to go.

"What I can't help but be sure of, however, is that there are some striking parallels between recent events and a certain 'leak' with which we're all intimately familiar. I mentioned Dan being too young to have an intrinsic understanding of how to read between the lines that come out of Beijing's spin machine, but what Dan knows more than anyone is why the late Richard Walker initiated the infamous IDA leak when he did. The answer, of course, was Chinese aggression.

"The very week of the IDA leak, they had just announced plans for a permanent lunar colony and a manned mission to Mars. That detail has faded from our recent memory, but in years to come Richard Walker will be considered a hero for stopping those things from happening. That was Walker's 'emergency stop' to halt China's nationalistic space ambitions, and it doesn't take a genius to see that these triangles came at a very handy time to halt *our* progress here at the GCC. But in any case, at this point I'm afraid I must move on from Walker and speak briefly of the cretinous and increasingly obese John Cole."

Kyle Young stifled a surprised laugh at Godfrey's very sudden and out-of-place personal comment on Cole's size. Godfrey noticed this — Kyle had a prime spot near the front — and it brought a momentary smile to his own lips.

"In John Cole we have a man who was hounded out of British politics and who resorted to working with a list of corrupt leaders that wouldn't look out of place as a list of defendants at the International Criminal Court. I heard what he said about me yesterday and I was entirely unsurprised. *Of course* he's bitter that I twice left British politics with the best wishes of my party and my people when I'd been invited to represent the collective interests of our planet's greatest nations. If I was John Cole, I would be bitter too! This is a man abandoned by even *Jack Neal*, lest we forget. But let me tell you this: none of Cole's understandable bitterness comes close to excusing his traitorous allegiance with the man he sycophantically calls President Ding."

Although sporadic tittering had filled the room while Godfrey laid into Cole, the din faded immediately as his attention turned to Ding.

"I would laugh, if it wasn't so tragic," Godfrey sighed. "My good friend President *Slater* may not be everyone's cup of tea, but she was openly elected by an educated populace who can just as openly vote her out next time round if that's what they want to do. Tell me, who elected Ding Ziyang? If you said no one, you'd be close. His politburo or commissars or whatever they want to call themselves may have chosen him over some other individuals, but the tragic fact remains that the great people of China live under an illiberal dictatorship and have no say in who represents them on the world stage. And *that*, good people of the media, is why at every opportunity I seek to clarify that our problem is not with the billion-plus industrious and hardworking citizens of Earth who call that country home. Our problem, and it's a big one, lies with the Communist Party which is currently holding those citizens hostage.

"Other leaders tend to bite their tongues out of respect for the tradition of refraining from commenting on other nations' internal affairs, so I'll say this for them: the greatest single threat to global peace — yesterday, today and tomorrow — is the Chinese Communist Party."

From his spot in the front row, Kyle gulped at these words. The laughter was gone; things had taken a turn few had expected, and Godfrey had gone into a gear none had seen coming.

"A recent vote among our delegates has granted me executive authority to comment substantively as and when contact-related developments require an immediate response," the GCC Chairman said, straightening the edges of his notes by tapping them on the table as he often did to signify the end of a speech, "so please feel free to make yourselves at home here in the media room. For now, I'll close by sharing my dream of peace.

"My hope is that some good comes from our current turbulent times, and my *dearest* hope is that the fallout from this turbulence hastens the collapse of Dictator Ding's illegitimate rule. This is not a war and China is not our enemy. My dream is therefore not a dream of Chinese defeat, and to my many friends in China I say this: my personal dream, for your sake, is the dream of democracy. My dream is the dream of a democratic revolution. My dream, dear friends, is the dream of regime change."

V minus 53

"*Regime change*?" Timo sighed, shaking his head at the screen. "What the hell is he doing talking like that? And this isn't Iraq, Libya, Venezuela, hand me an atlas and I'll name you a dozen more… this is *China*."

"Exactly," Emma said. "It's not a threat, it's a deflection. He's trying to embarrass and isolate Ding with the Cold War and communist dictator stuff, and he's trying to put him on the defensive with that regime change comment. You know I don't like Godfrey, but he almost always knows what he's doing. It would be different if *Slater* had said those words, but Godfrey isn't a head of government and doesn't command a military or anything like that. They're just words. *Stupid* words, but just words."

"But Slater must have signed off on everything he just said," Timo replied, still dumbfounded.

Emma shrugged. "Look at all the things Cole said about Godfrey and about America last night… *Ding* must have signed off on all that."

"I'm still willing to go through with these meetings if you think it's viable," Dan told her, cutting in before Timo could continue the same kind of analysis that the now-muted ACN newscasters were conducting on TV.

Emma thought quietly for at least ten seconds, commanding everyone else's rapt attention as she did. Although a lot had changed in Birchwood and it would have been a stretch to say that *anyone* was on top of things, Emma's gut instincts were still the group's trusted compass in times of difficulty or indecision.

"Definitely viable," she eventually said, a lot more decisively than the preceding pause might have suggested. "Godfrey in Buenos Aires, Cole in Havana as soon as possible, and then we can work something out with Poppy. *That* one won't be so easy... but setting something up with Godfrey obviously won't be a problem, and the ELF will jump at the chance to host you in Cuba. This would be good outreach even without the mind-reading angle, because—"

"I really need you all to stop saying mind-reading," Dan interrupted. "Sorry, but I do. I can't dive into your memories or anything like that, I can only hear thoughts that are basically on the tip of your tongue. If you set up a meeting with someone who knows about thoughts and language, I'd be able to read his thoughts and explain this thing properly. But I feel weird enough knowing you guys know I can hear your thoughts... I don't need you thinking I can rummage through your minds and read all the way down."

Smiling at what was a minor point in the scheme of things, Emma leaned over and kissed him in acknowledgment of the clarification. "Okay... so this would be good outreach even without the *thought-hearing* angle, because it gives the ELF and GCC leaderships something to think about besides attacking each other, and it also tells the public you're serious about unity and gives them hope that it's possible. I looked at the SMMA app on my phone as soon as Godfrey's speech ended, to see the live social media reaction, and it's not pretty. War isn't a real prospect for a thousand good reasons, but people are worried about it. A lot of people *here* aren't happy with Godfrey for being so reckless, and no one is happy with Cole being Cole or with Ding freezing non-ELF scientists out of the triangle analysis."

"What do people think about the triangles?" Timo asked. "That analysis app used to show you breakdowns of individual topics, didn't it, like we saw back in the IDA and Il Diavolo days?"

She turned her phone around to show Timo the relevant graphs and charts. "Yesterday it was fifty-fifty between people thinking the Zanzibar triangle was real or a hoax," she said, commenting on the visual data for the benefit of the others who couldn't quite see it from their positions. "After the second one turned up in Vanuatu, which most people had heard of for the very first time when Cole mentioned it twenty minutes earlier, the balance tipped towards a majority of people thinking it's a hoax."

"What do *you* think?" Tara asked her, very directly. "I know we've talked about it, and about how maybe Cole knew it was in Vanuatu before he *mentioned* Vanuatu… as a trap for Godfrey to call it out as a hoax when really it's not… but what do *you* think?"

"Ninety-five percent of me thinks it's a hoax," Emma said, choosing her words carefully. "But we share more than ninety-five percent of our DNA with chimps. Sometimes it's that five percent that makes all the difference."

"Should I call Godfrey to talk about setting something up as soon as possible?" Timo asked. "I don't mean to interrupt, but…"

Emma moved her hand in a horizontal motion to tell him to think nothing of it. "Let's leave Godfrey out of the setup, though," she said. "I'll go to Slater so she can broker it. I don't want Godfrey to feel like he's in control and I want him to know how pissed off Dan is by what he just said. And Dan, I also think we should tell Slater you were contacted last night, then we'll see if she wants to tell Godfrey right away or if she keeps it inside her own administration."

"Can't we just be straightforward and tell them both?" he asked.

Emma shook her head. "I want to know how close they really are, or how much of their new buddy act is just for the cameras. This is free information we can get with no extra effort. It also keeps Godfrey's ego in check if I go to Slater and not him. Okay? I know you don't like this scheming kind of stuff, but I'm not asking you to do it… I'm just asking you if you're okay with me doing it on your behalf."

"It's gotten us this far," Dan said with a knowing but ultimately warm smile.

Emma picked up her phone and dialled the number. "President Slater," she said a few seconds later, walking away from the others to focus on the call but not walking out of earshot. "Yes, it's nice to hear your voice, too. But tell me… are you alone right now?"

V minus 52

GCC Headquarters
Buenos Aires, Argentina

"I'm alone," President Slater said. "Well, just me and a few aides. *He's* not here, if that's what you meant."

Emma detected enough implied resentment in Slater's tone to think that at least some of it was for show. "I *did* mean Godfrey, but it doesn't really matter if he hears this from you or from us, I just wanted you to hear it first. I tried to call you ten minutes ago, before he got into that ridiculous speech he just gave."

In the silence Emma left hoping Slater might fill it with a telling sigh or comment, nothing audible came through her phone.

"Anyway," she went on, "I wanted to tell you that Dan was contacted again last night and that this time it was a physical meeting. They spoke to him and he spoke to them. They didn't give any explicitly clear-cut answers to some of the questions he asked, which will no doubt be the same ones you would have asked yourself, but Dan wants to tell you all about it."

"Please, put him on! After what he prevented at the Gravesen, I trust Dan fully on this and I know the Messengers are looking out for us. I can be as discreet as necessary, needless to say."

"That's the thing, he doesn't want to talk about any of this over the phone. Are you leaving Argentina in the next forty-eight hours, or is there maybe some way we can meet you there?"

"Here is best," Slater said enthusiastically. "Things are moving quickly, as I'm sure you know, and to be perfectly candid I don't particularly want to leave our esteemed Chairman to respond to them without running them through my own filter. Everything he just said was the watered-down version, if you can believe that."

Emma rolled her eyes. "Only too easily. Godfrey can be there for the meeting too, though, if you want him to be. But when are we talking... does tomorrow work?"

"Tomorrow works perfectly, and I do think it would be best if William is in on this. Will you need us to arrange a flight?"

"No, Timo's plane is still in Denver," Emma said.

"Of course. As I've said before, Dan is an important asset and I'll personally make sure you can leave tonight, if any scheduling intervention is needed. I'd very much like you both to arrive in time for an early morning meeting, because with the pace of recent developments we could be looking at another damn triangle before too much longer."

The ensuing silence, which Emma knew Slater was leaving in the hope that *she* would make some kind of telling sound, ran even longer than the last.

"But I do have one last question," President Slater said, breaking the silence and sounding slightly flustered for the first time in the conversation. "Did Dan happen to say if the aliens mentioned anything about the chip in his neck, or maybe that they removed it? I didn't hear about this contact event... so if our security services knew, then someone has decided to keep it from me."

"The Messengers became aware of the chip after last time and this time they worked around it," Emma said, deciding that allowing preventable distrust to develop *within* Slater's administration would be good for no one. "Things have changed on that front, regarding how they make contact, and that's the main thing Dan wants to talk to you about. We *do* want these chips out, though."

"Of course. And something tells me I'd be wasting my breath if I asked for more details of Dan's current thoughts," Slater said, almost but not quite chuckling, "so I'll save us both some time and not even try. But Emma, thanks for bringing this to me."

"We'll see you tomorrow," Emma replied, ending the call with no further platitudes.

Still waiting for the GCC's embattled Chairman to return to her side after his already wave-making speech, President Slater sat in quiet thought. With the third triangle still unaccounted for and tensions rising by the second, she could only hope that tomorrow wouldn't come too late.

V minus 51

McCarthy Residence
Birchwood, Colorado

Recent years had seen Dan McCarthy get used to time passing in inconsistent ways, from the painful slowness of his days spent hoping for an alien intervention while searching for the elusive fourth plaque all the way to the whirlwind gone-too-fast days he'd spent with Emma during a fortnight in the Seychelles in the cool-down months that followed Contact Day.

Never had a day passed more hazily than this one, however, when it seemed uncannily as though evening followed morning with nothing in between. The main event of Dan's afternoon had been finding out that his imminent trip to Argentina would indeed begin with a hastily arranged late-night flight, which only served to deepen the feeling of being in limbo.

The bulk of the day had involved yet another retelling of his latest contact experience and yet another attempted explanation of his new and seemingly superhuman ability. His audience was this time an audience of three, with his father Henry joined by Mr Byrd and Phil Norris. Phil had been a fixture in Birchwood since the early days of the leak but was now a closer member of Dan's inner circle than in the past, joining the ever-present Mr Byrd in rounding out a small but important circle of support.

These two men were almost polar opposites on the face of it, with Mr Byrd a clean-cut former sheriff's deputy whose door was always open and Phil a rough-around-the-edges prepper who had ground out a living in a pawnshop for many years before the IDA leak turned his derelict drive-in lot into a license to print money. Henry McCarthy, very much the median personality of the three, had always been their common link; now, though, they were friends in their own right.

Dan valued Mr Byrd's calmness and clear head as much as he valued Phil's no-filter reactions and often esoteric knowledge. If he'd been forced to guess their reactions, he would have called it perfectly; neither Mr Byrd's advice to be careful nor Phil's decision to immediately draw up a list of people who deserved to have their unspoken thoughts examined came as a surprise.

Henry's reaction had been harder to predict, but his succinct comment that he was proud of Dan for 'doing the thing that was difficult but right' meant a lot. A single-line statement of any kind of emotion from Henry was practically equivalent to a poem written in the clouds by anyone else, as a lifetime of experience had drummed into Dan, so he seized the words and carried them with him when it came time to leave.

The only part of the day when he'd felt truly present was when he had fifteen minutes with Tara and sought to make sure she would be okay being left in Birchwood without Emma again, especially since Dan had known beyond doubt she was going through a difficult time ever since she uttered the D-word. He said she could go with them if she wanted to, but Tara politely declined.

Emma had already invited her, she explained; but although it sounded like a more than interesting trip, she already had plans.

"Oh yeah, that club opening thing," he said, remembering what had been in her thoughts when he first listened. A smile crossed his face. "And that guy's going to be there, Jayson Moore."

"A lot of different people are gonna be there," Tara replied in a full-hearted but unsuccessful attempt to hide her motives. Try as she might, the smile gave it away.

Dan smiled too; it was nice to see her happy and looking like herself. "Make sure to stay in touch with Clark, though, while we're not around. Okay?"

"Oh, I'll be watching like a hawk," Clark butted in, revealing his stealthy eavesdropping. "And as you can see, I'm a good listener, too."

"Cause that's not creepy at all..." Tara chuckled.

"But seriously," he said, "just leave your phone's GPS tracking on and authorise me as a friend or whatever you need to do for me to know where you are. I know Emma's going to ask you to do that, because she already told me, so don't give her any stress about it, okay? It's not easy for her to leave you here just like it's not easy for me to let them go without me, but it is what it is."

"Why *aren't* you going, anyway?" Tara asked, wondering only now. "This isn't like their pre-honeymoon when they wanted to be alone, and after what happened then I woulda thought you'd *really* want to be there to keep an eye on them this time?"

Clark nodded. "Oh, I do. But I can't be in two places at once, and they've always got each other... plus there's going to be security at the airport and then *government* security as soon as they reach Argentina. The way the world is right now, though, things could go south in a heartbeat. And Tara, I'm not saying you *need* me to look after you or anything like that, but there's not a chance in hell I'm leaving you here with no one. I'm not the guy who's going to sit down and talk about feelings, but we all know you came back to Birchwood last month because you didn't want to be alone... and I'm also not the guy who's going to ditch you when you need someone."

"So there *is* one of you, after all," Tara grinned, deflecting emotion with humour in an effortless way that would have made Clark himself proud. "Thanks, though; for real."

The last thing Dan remembered before leaving was overhearing Mr Byrd's preferred idea for a new contact-focused United Nations body with a rotating presidency and carefully designed voting structure. It was a nice idea in theory, but Dan and plenty of others knew only too well that even the most carefully designed voting structure in the world would mean nothing the very first time China or the United States decided to ignore a non-binding resolution as both had so many times in the past within other UN bodies.

Clark insisted on driving to Denver, with Tara gladly going along for the ride and chatting to Dan in the back seat the whole time. Someone invariably commented each time a billboard for one of Tara's fashion lines or outlets passed by, which happened more frequently than she could believe.

Even Dan's goodbye to Henry and the others had faded into a hazy cloud of absent memory as soon as the car's tyres started rolling, and at one point he felt so absent that he hoped the Messengers' recent intervention hadn't changed more within his brain than he was already aware of. He didn't want to raise this now when it would worry Clark and Tara, so he kept it to himself.

His goodbyes to them were quick when the time came, but he was present enough to know that Emma's goodbyes took a lot longer. He heard her and Clark imploring each other to stay alert and keep their wits about them, each essentially and somewhat reluctantly entrusting their younger sibling to the other. Clark had never made any secret of his view that Dan was too trusting to survive in the shark-filled waters of the media and politics without Emma diligently watching his path, but for once Emma was equally concerned about Tara. She was more worldly than Dan, for sure, but she hadn't been herself recently and quite likely needed Clark's presence to ensure her mental as well as physical wellbeing.

"And Dan," Clark called from the car window as a trio of uniformed police officers prepared to guide the couple through the airport to Timo's plane, "remember what we said: five days at most, no matter what."

"No matter what," Dan replied, gladly reaffirming the promise that he'd be back in Birchwood within that time frame regardless of how difficult it might prove to get a meeting with a high-ranking GeoSov like Poppy Bradshaw and regardless of what might happen with the as-yet undiscovered third triangle.

"So what are you guys heading down there for, anyway?" a bold police officer asked a few seconds later. His colleagues could only admire the attempt.

"We want to find out what's really going on," Emma said, keeping it simple.

"You think they'll tell you?" the man pushed, sounding hopeful.

Emma looked at Dan, leaving this one for him.

He grinned. "To be honest, officer, I don't think they're going to have much choice."

V minus 50

"I'm getting too used to this seat," Emma said, leaning back against the plush leather of Timo's tastefully equipped jet.

Sitting in his own increasingly regular seat for the third time in a week, having been to Italy and back far sooner than expected, Dan knew the feeling. His seat was diagonally behind Emma's, for no reason other than habit; they moved around during flights, but their take-off positions had been set during their first time on-board in the aftermath of the Argentine sphere's discovery. On that occasion Clark had filled the seat that now lay conspicuously empty next to Emma and in front of Dan, and in Dan's mind that was still Clark's seat.

As the pilot and copilots performed their final checks, Dan sat silently and made a full-hearted but non-expectant attempt to communicate with the Messengers. He tried to focus on very specific questions, all the while touching his middle finger to his thumb just as they had showed him. He was even pointing his index finger upwards in case that would help, but try as he might, no kind of response came his way.

"Crap!" Emma cried, cursing her own carelessness as a recently opened can of soda fell to the floor from the small table in front of her.

Dan's attention naturally followed the sound, as did his outstretched finger.

Looking down at the can as gravity did its work, Emma's expression suddenly changed from one of frustrated annoyance to one of awestruck amazement. Had she been able to tear her eyes away, she would have seen the same look in Dan's. Because as his finger pointed at the can, frozen an inch from the ground, gravity's work had ceased.

Dan's heart felt fit to burst through his chest, but he fought the urge to open his hand — the urge to break the connection — and instead tried to stabilise his breathing. After a few seconds he gulped the deepest gulp of his life and slowly raised his finger.

Although a tiny part of him had thought or even known it would happen, nothing could have prepared Dan for the sight of the can positively *levitating* through the air and back towards Emma's table. He held his finger until the can reached the surface, at which point he touched it down with only a slight spillage. Immediately, he opened his hand and stared down at his fingers.

"Emma…" he uttered weakly. "What the hell did they do to me?"

Even though the reality that the Messengers had granted Dan limited telepathic abilities had almost sunk in, and even though he and Emma had seen the Messengers themselves using *telekinetic* powers on more than one occasion, nothing could have prepared *either* of them for this.

"It's okay," she said, successfully trying to sound a lot calmer than she was. "This is just like the other thing, Dan… you control *it*, *it* doesn't control *you*. Remember that and everything will be fine."

"Yeah," he replied, far less convincingly calm. "But I swear I didn't know I could do that until now. And I wasn't even trying! I think it just—"

"Let's just say you *still* don't know you can do it," Emma interrupted, cutting him off for his own good. "And let's just say no one else ever will. Agreed?"

"All the way," Dan said, gazing at his fingers like they weren't his own. "*All the way.*"

Part 4

FOREIGN GROUND

"Three things cannot be long hidden:
the sun, the moon, and the truth."

Buddha

MONDAY

V minus 49

GCC Headquarters
Buenos Aires, Argentina

Although spending a night in a plane was never ideal, the fully reclining seats of Timo Fiore's private jet had at least allowed Dan and Emma a few hours of comfortable rest.

It had been Dan's decision to stay on board for several hours after landing; but with the recent foiling of an attack at the local Gravesen hotel still fresh in her mind, Emma readily agreed. They didn't know how many more nights they would be in town — if any — but Emma had already raised the possibility of staying inside the impenetrable GCC compound itself if they did have to find somewhere.

Dan saw the logic in that point. After all, if it was good enough for Godfrey...

"Just remember what we talked about not talking about," Emma said, speaking as a convoy led them through the streets of Buenos Aires like the visiting dignitaries they were.

Dan didn't like the ostentatious level of security and felt sure it was in place primarily to draw attention to his presence rather than to protect his person. Arriving on Timo's plane ruled out any possibility of a discreet arrival, in any case, but it irritated Dan more than a little that

Godfrey was trying to seize upon his visit as a PR opportunity for the GCC.

With plans to visit John Cole in Cuba, though, Dan knew he would soon be enduring a far grander politically-motivated welcome than this. But the gain would justify the pain, he figured, safe in the knowledge that Cole's unspoken thoughts would reveal the truth one way or the other.

The one truth that Dan and Emma had agreed not to talk about in the meantime was the incredible realisation that as well as telepathy, the Messengers had recently granted Dan tele*kinetic* abilities — intentionally or otherwise.

Dan agreed wholeheartedly with the plan of keeping this close to his chest. The power at his fingertips troubled *him* deeply, and he could hardly imagine how others would look at him if they knew he could literally manipulate and move physical objects through the power of thought alone.

Emma also wanted Dan to stay quiet about the telepathy; but although he would be only too glad to do so, he was far from sure that it would be possible. Without their understanding what could be gained, he found it difficult to imagine Godfrey and Slater permitting his planned meetings with Cole and GeoSov spokesperson Poppy Brad-shaw. Dan, a natural worrier, couldn't help but foresee worst-case scenarios of being held against his will once again or simply having his passport seized to prevent further foreign travel.

Even Emma's simply put argument that Slater and Godfrey wouldn't commit political suicide by standing in Dan's way failed to ease his mind, and in the end she told him to forget all about it and to let her talk them round if any convincing became necessary.

The route to the GCC compound's high-security entrance had seen a lot of traffic in recent days, and the streamlined arrival procedures meant that Dan didn't encounter any of the protestors or demonstrators who were still gathered outside just as they were at other buildings of symbolic signifi-cance throughout the world. Whether governed by leaders aligned to the GCC or the ELF, citizens in dozens of countries were expressing their dissatisfaction at the growing schism by taking to the streets. Some Now Movement cells called for Ding Ziyang to immediately grant international access to the Zanzibar and Vanuatu triangles, which were still very myste-rious having never been professionally photographed or filmed — at least not by anyone with an appetite to make the images public.

Dan's visit, the first planned stop in a whirlwind three-city tour, was intended to begin bridging the gulf between factions and to finally shed some light on the triangles. He could hear the crowd as he stepped out of the armoured vehicle that had carried him from the airport, and he was glad of that. The gathering was peaceful but insistent, calling for dialogue and unity.

Dialogue is the weapon, Dan thought to himself as he and Emma stepped into a building they'd seen on TV so many hundreds of times. *Unity is the prize.*

V minus 48

ELF HEADQUARTERS
BEIJING, CHINA

"We've all heard the rumours," ACN's lead reporter Maria Janzyck yelled, her voice fighting to be heard over a bustling crowd outside the ELF's brutalist global headquarters, "but I don't think *any* of us could have guessed it would happen this quickly. I've just received official word that the Zanzibar and Vanuatu triangles are both en route to China as we speak and should arrive within hours. But that's not all... both triangles are going to be presented to the public on Wednesday morning local time, which is tomorrow evening at home.

"We can only speculate whether Ding Ziyang has pushed this announcement forward because of the surprise overnight news of Dan McCarthy's touchdown in Buenos Aires, but that's certainly the general feeling on the ground here in Beijing.

"And amid growing Western scepticism regarding the true origin of these triangles, one thing is for sure: Ding Ziyang and the ELF are not backing down on this, they are *doubling* down. For ACN in Beijing, I'm Maria Janzyck."

V minus 47

GCC Headquarters
Buenos Aires, Argentina

The reception area of the GCC's imposing headquarters was abuzz with activity as Dan and Emma made their way inside via the secure VIP entrance, and it was immediately clear that this activity was urgent and had just kicked off.

Dan resisted the urge to point his frighteningly powerful finger at any of the hectically occupied workers, but Emma's quick glance at her phone brought the explanation: Ding Ziyang had just announced his intention to publicly display the triangles in only thirty-six hours' time. Neither said anything, and the chaperone who led them to Chairman Godfrey's high office had been instructed to remain similarly silent.

It thus came as a major surprise when they knocked on the office door and encountered only President Slater on the other side.

"We've been expecting you," she said, speaking to Dan with a warmth that was either genuinely felt or incredibly convincing in its effort to appear so. "William should be back in a few minutes; he's gone to brief our frontline media liaison teams on how to reply to enquiries about Ding's latest comments until we issue a full response. I assume you've seen the news?"

Dan subtly placed his fingers in the initiation position, establishing a one-way thought-reading link-up with the President of the United States. He had major ethical concerns about utilising his new ability without the knowledge and consent of the other party, particularly when they weren't a hostile foe, but on this occasion he felt that the ends justified the means so completely that it would be irresponsible *not* to make the most of what he had been given.

"What do you think's going on with all of this?" he asked.

Immediately, he heard thoughts of helpless ignorance. She didn't know, and she was dearly hoping Dan could help.

"I really don't know," Slater replied, vocalising the thoughts Dan had already heard loud and clear. "I've been hoping the Messengers told you something and that you're about to tell me whatever it was. Because short of that, we're stuck."

Dan studied the President's expression. She had been openly honest, stating in blunt terms exactly what she'd been thinking. He turned his body towards Emma, then took a few steps towards her and whispered: "I want to tell her. She's being totally straight and she'll be way more likely to help us set up the meetings with Cole and Poppy if she knows why I'm really doing it. She can help us convince Godfrey without him having to know, too. For once I think we should trust *my* gut on this; we're in his office and she's here alone... let's make the most of it."

"Don't say a word," Emma replied, winking slowly before removing her phone from her pocket. She typed a message as she walked to Slater's side. "Dan will relay what the Messengers told him as soon as Godfrey gets here," she explained to her, mindful that the room very likely housed hidden recording equipment. "But here's a still image from our home security system, showing a flash. Crazy, huh?"

Slightly slow on the uptake, Dan walked over to see what Emma was talking about. There *had* been a flash, of course, but he didn't know or understand why Emma might have saved a shot of it to her phone. The expression on Slater's face didn't reflect something so relatively mundane, either, and when Dan looked down over their shoulders to look at the phone's screen, it all made sense.

The typed message from Emma was clear: "*Be cool, don't react. The Messengers gave Dan a limited version of their ability to hear each other's thoughts, and he can hear other PEOPLE'S thoughts. We can use this, together, but right now we trust you to be responsible more than we trust Godfrey. Don't tell anyone — please. Now think of a four-digit number, but don't say anything.*"

Emma handed the phone to Dan; once again, his overwhelmed mind didn't immediately grasp what she was getting at. But as Slater raised her eyebrows at him, it clicked in his mind.

Since the connection was still active from his initial listening — these were the imprecise words in his mind when considering a process he couldn't pretend to understand on any technical level — Dan didn't have to do anything with his fingers to know what Slater was thinking. His ability to control the power was improving rapidly, as the Messengers had promised, and all his index finger did was type 0319 at the end of the existing note on Emma's phone.

Although he had gotten slightly used to the amazed reactions he'd received when telling first Emma, then Tara and ultimately the others in Birchwood, this was the first time Dan had looped in anyone who wasn't a close friend or family member. And in this moment, Dan's nervous anticipation of how the reaction would play out was greatly heightened by the fact that Valerie Slater wasn't just the first 'stranger' to find out that he possessed a gift positively alien to everyone else... she was the President of the United States.

If Clark or especially Emma had viewed Dan's gift with fear and distrust, he would've had serious personal problems to work through. But if *Slater* reacted the wrong way and passed the entrusted secret onto the wrong people, Dan McCarthy knew he would have far greater problems than that...

V minus 46

DRIVE-IN
BIRCHWOOD, COLORADO

"Well well well," Mr Byrd mused, walking into New Kergrillin' for his afternoon chat. "I didn't think we'd see a press pack like that around here again unless Dan was talking. He's not even in the country!"

"But he is in the news," Henry McCarthy sighed. He peeked out of the window and saw that the number of reporters at the edge of the lot had indeed ballooned since he'd entered much earlier in the morning.

It was sure to be another long day for the two men as they tried to distract themselves and each other from the reality that all they could do from thousands of miles away was wish Dan well. They both knew better than to talk too much in public about *why* Dan was in the news, since they were among the precious few who knew the true motive behind his trip to Buenos Aires, but this only made them think about it even more.

He had Emma by his side and the power of the Messengers within him, though, so both felt justified in their firm hope that he would succeed in his mission.

With the global situation slowly spiralling ever deeper towards chaos and conflict, as looping news reports on the bar's many TVs endlessly reminded them, the alternative did not bear thinking about.

V minus 45

"Interesting," President Slater said, reacting to the news that Dan had gained telepathic abilities with the last word he'd expected to hear.

Dan gulped, tremendously glad that neither Slater nor Emma could discern the level of fear in *his* thoughts.

"This is something I didn't expect," the President continued. "I thought there would be a flash, so that wasn't overly surprising, but this second time-stamped image shows that it went on longer than I would have guessed. This part is *slightly* more surprising, but I don't think it's something we need to trouble Chairman Godfrey with."

Dan breathed the deepest relieved sigh of his life; Slater wasn't just being discreet, she was clearly on board. With the phone still in his hand, he typed again: "*I can keep listening in or I can kill the connection. If I keep it live, I can say things you want me to say without him knowing. And I CAN'T dive deep into the recesses of your memories or read your mind like that, it only lets me hear conscious thoughts.*" Gazing into Slater's eyes, he had her consent within seconds.

He typed again very quickly, this time for Emma: "*Do you want your voice to be in my head, too, telling me what to say?*"

"Definitely," Emma said, answering Dan in a way that passably sounded like it was a response to Slater. "Do we know when to expect him back?"

As if by magic, Slater's reply that Godfrey should be back at any moment was interrupted by the opening of the door and his stepping inside.

"*Fucking Ding,*" the GCC Chairman cursed as he stomped towards his desk. He sighed, exasperated, and roughly ran a palm down his face to try to push the anger to one side for now. "Dan, Emma, thank you. Now in the name of all that is holy, *please* tell me something I want to hear. Are the triangles fake?"

"The Messengers didn't tell me," Dan replied. "They *couldn't* tell me."

Without the need for words, Godfrey's expression asked what the hell Dan was getting at.

As briefly as he could, Dan recounted every recallable detail of his meeting with the Messengers other than the rather important part regarding the powers he was granted. This retelling was the first time either Godfrey or Slater had heard in any detail about the reluctantly evasive replies Dan received when asking about the triangles, and both appeared particularly concerned to hear of a problem with the Messengers' Elders.

"I'm worried about that, too," Dan said, speaking to Godfrey. At times he had to be careful not to reply aloud to an unspoken point he 'heard' from Slater, cognisant of the risk of slipping up and letting Godfrey in on the secret. He didn't quite know *why* he didn't want Godfrey to know about the powers at this stage, but his vague thoughts on the subject were mainly related to Godfrey's recurring recklessness in the arena of international affairs.

"And you're worried because their Elders tell them exactly what to do?" Slater asked, wisely speaking out loud.

Dan nodded.

"And the words they used regarding their Elders..." Godfrey said, "can you home in on exactly what they said was *wrong*? Was it illness... corruption... disagreement... some kind of decision-making gridlock?"

"I don't know," Dan sighed. "But if this isn't a hoax, which they weren't able to tell me, maybe there's a chance that the Elders told them to plant these triangles, but now they've backtracked or changed the orders... and that's why the Messengers showed up now? They didn't tell me. They *couldn't* tell me, and it's making me physically ill trying to work this out."

"Welcome to our world," Chairman Godfrey said with no hint of humour. "But Dan, you know the Messengers better than any of us could ever hope to. What does your gut say, and what would be *your* next move here?"

Dan looked at Emma, as he always did in times of confusion. She was as glad as ever to use her nimble and well-honed mind for persuasive speech, but on this occasion her words of assistance did not have to be spoken aloud.

Fighting past how crazy it all was, Dan took Emma's silent suggestions on board as they continued to come even when he turned back to Godfrey. He explained very quickly and efficiently that he wanted to meet and publicly interview John Cole and Poppy Bradshaw, to interrogate them with any questions discreetly suggested by Godfrey and Slater.

Slater, hearing of this plan for the first time despite being in on the far more shocking revelation, silenced a gasp of sudden understanding.

Dan continued by stating that his outreach could be a way of the GCC being seen to try to bridge the gap between itself and its Beijing-based counterpart, since it would be understood that Dan, as a US national, would be visiting non-aligned nations with the implicit permission of his government who could have blocked his external movements if they saw fit.

Emma butted in to name Cuba as the planned spot for a meeting with Cole; her vocal input was unnecessary, but it maintained the familiar pattern of her appearing to guide Dan's way... which she *was*, just far more subtly and privately than normal.

Godfrey, to everyone else's mild surprise, didn't look to be dead set against the idea. "That might not be as crazy as it sounds... but it has to be said that there's a conspicuous pattern we can all see, but which we all seem to understand shouldn't be mentioned in public," he mused. "If they followed the modus operandi they've established so far, Ding will probably reveal the third triangle while you're talking to Cole or being paraded around the streets; he stole my thunder on Friday night while I was talking downstairs, he stole your thunder on Saturday night during Focus 20/20, and I'd wager that the only reason a triangle didn't magically turn up last night is that there was no thunder to steal! All I'm saying is this: when you meet Cole, be prepared for an unexpected interruption. That's the kind of thing they would pull."

"But why would they want to steal any thunder when I'm in Cuba talking to Cole?" Dan asked. "That's good PR for them, isn't it?"

"Hmm," Emma chimed in, the tone offering a hint of agreement with

Dan's point. "Yeah. If that *is* what's been happening so far, which we don't really know for sure, I don't think it'll happen again this time. It would put you on the spot, and I think that's the last thing they'll want to be seen to do. Even on Focus 20/20, before they knew you were willing to talk to them, Cole didn't go into attack-dog mode on you like he usually does."

No one openly disputed this reading of events.

"And for Poppy," Emma continued, "I was thinking somewhere non-aligned. Ideally also somewhere *close*... which limits our options."

Godfrey upturned his palms. "Cuba for Cole, naturally. But if we're looking for a non-aligned country for the Poppy meeting, the obvious nearby choice is surely Honduras?"

"Honduras is a delicate one," President Slater interjected. "They depend on us for trade and we still work together on the ground to combat drug trafficking, but they've been eyeing closer links with China for years. Their post-contact neutrality was a calculated move to try to bring better 'offers' from both sides." She turned to Godfrey. "*But...* if we deliver Dan for a public appearance, that could be something of a hearts and minds victory for us."

"Us being the GCC?" Godfrey asked.

Slater nodded. "That said, I very much doubt that a high-profile event on the Honduran mainland at extremely short notice will be viable from a security angle, so we'll draft an invitation — or challenge — for a meeting on one of the Bay Islands. Roatán, most likely. Because with the best will in the world, Honduras isn't Cuba; we don't have to like the Cubans to acknowledge that they have a firm record of maintaining public order and guarding high-value individuals. Nationally, the Hondurans would definitely prefer a mainland venue... but when this is all that's on offer, they'll still jump at it. It's good press, it'll hugely boost the country's tourism profile, and it'll probably help them squeeze better terms from Beijing next time there's a deal to negotiate."

"How close are those islands to Cuba?" Dan asked, more than willing to bow to Slater's evidently superior knowledge of all things Honduran.

"Can't be much more than five hundred miles," the President shrugged. She in turn glanced at Emma, awaiting her gut reaction.

"Honduras works," she responded. "My main hesitation was about security but the island idea sounds like it takes care of that. And I think while we should *invite* Cole, we should *challenge* Poppy. Cole and Ding will jump all over this, so making it seem as cordial as possible makes sense. I'm a lot less sure that Poppy and her idiot friends will be quite so willing so I think we should issue a challenge she can't back down from without losing face. I would shoot an organic-looking video of Dan standing outside this office, saying that Godfrey has already spoken to him, that Cole is going to sit down for a one-on-one televised interview, and that he hopes the GeoSovs will have the balls to do the same. I'd name the time and place and say this is Poppy's opportunity to make the case she claims she couldn't make on Focus 20/20 because de Clerk froze her out. Done."

"Done," President Slater firmly agreed. "Cole is going to arrive in Cuba within hours, so we'll get on that invitation and the interview *will* happen tomorrow. There's no doubt in my mind. Emma, feel free to arrange the 'challenge' video for Poppy and we'll get to work on logistics for Honduras so we're ready to go as soon as she is. Ideally, that's going to be in as little as forty-eight hours... and just like that, *done*."

Everyone turned to Godfrey, who grinned and let out a slight chuckle. "Sounds like we're done."

"I want these chips out of our necks before we go to Cuba," Dan said, facing President Slater. "You said whenever we want."

"I *did*," Slater replied, "but that was when you were at home. I'm sure we could find a medical centre here that can assist, though; from what I've learned, it's a very basic device."

"I'll sort something out for you," Godfrey interjected. "We have an in-house doctor, or you can go to the university hospital. I'd understand if you have some hang-ups about using the GCC doctor, so I won't take offence in the slightest."

Dan subtly established a connection to Godfrey, immediately sensing that his intentions were pure; he wasn't trying to do anything funny with the chips. Dan also knew he would be able to listen in to the doctors to gauge *their* intentions, and he really did want the chip gone before he left for Cuba, an ELF member state where it might prove more difficult to find a doctor he could trust.

"We'll use your doctor," Dan said, nodding at Godfrey then turning to Emma. She couldn't hear Godfrey's thoughts but had seen Dan subtly moving his fingers to establish the connection so knew that *he* had already listened in.

"Works for me," she said. "We'll shoot this video first, then go to the doctor before we head back to the plane."

"Excellent. And you can shoot your video anywhere in the building you like," Godfrey said, "just please don't let anyone talk to Dan."

Emma, Dan and President Slater all thought the same thing when

Godfrey said this, but kept to themselves the point that no one would have to talk to Dan for him to hear them.

He wouldn't be listening to any lowly GCC staff members' thoughts or indeed anyone else's in Buenos Aires, though, for Dan's interest now lay solely in Cuba and Honduras. His interest, as it always had and always would, lay in finding the truth.

V minus 44

All day, Clark's mind had been fixated on what Dan and Emma were doing in Buenos Aires.

He feared nothing more than Dan foolishly telling Godfrey and Slater about his new abilities, and the fact that Emma would never go along with such a move — particularly when it came to Godfrey — was the only thing that eased his mind.

Work at the precinct occupied his hands, at least, and by the time night came he returned home relatively relaxed. Dan had called a few times by then, drip-feeding news as it came in. The trend-tracker above the couch where Clark was now reclined had beeped shortly after each of Dan's calls when the news became public, but no one had been home at the time to hear it.

At work, which had been relatively normal in recent months while Dan maintained the lowest public profile he could, Clark had once again spent the day as the centre of everyone's attention. He didn't know what to say when they asked how he felt about Dan flying to Cuba to interview John Cole and to Honduras to interview Poppy Bradshaw, because he didn't *know* how he felt. He understood and supported the reasoning, since Dan's ability to discern their private thoughts would imminently

226

blow apart the whole triangle mystery one way or the other, but a huge part of him felt that there was too much inherent risk for this to be the right course of action.

In Clark's mind, there was never *really* going to be a political escalation of the kind that would lead to a military conflict between China and the United States; there just *couldn't* be. His own instinct would have been to wait and see what happened next, but Dan's evident concerns about the Messengers and their Elders was something that couldn't be ignored. Dan knew them better than anyone and he had reported seeing genuine concern in their eyes, as well as sensing a real frustration in their thoughts over the fact that they couldn't tell him everything.

Clark could also very well understand Dan's desire to do *something*, especially after how helpless he had been temporarily rendered in the wake of Il Diavolo's discovery the previous year. If Dan hadn't taken massive and highly risky action on that occasion, Clark knew very well that neither of them would still be around to ponder the merits of such action this time.

Dan and Emma were now ready to head to Cuba with a news crew which included Kyle Young from ACN, a man who wasn't just a McCarthy ally but one who Clark knew personally and respected a great deal for the risks he had taken on their behalf in the past. This very welcome news further eased Clark's mind and made the fact that Emma and Dan were set to land in Havana the following morning much easier to handle. The only person he would have chosen over Kyle was Trey Myers, a once-local newsman and close friend who had moved out of state for a work opportunity a few months earlier. As a family man, Clark doubted Trey would have been up for such a risky-sounding trip, in any case.

In Clark's experienced mind, however, the chances of a security incident were minuscule. The Cubans knew what they were doing on that front, and Dan's telepathic advantage over Cole left Clark confident that the interview itself should go pretty damn well; after all, Dan could link-up with Emma to covertly use her PR expertise and unrivalled skill to box Cole in and avoid any lexical traps he tried to lay.

All in all, he didn't see much rational cause for concern.

Long after midnight had come and gone, Tara called to tell Clark that she wouldn't be home and to ask if he could either stay next door with Rooster or let him stay at the McCarthys' for the night.

Clark was glad to get the call, which settled his mild concern as to why she was already so much later than the time she'd expected to be home from the promotional appearance she was making at a new night-club in Colorado Springs.

In a selfless sense he was also fairly pleased to hear the *reason* she wouldn't be home: something had sparked between her and Jayson Moore, a former TV star who was now on the right side of the same kind of fame-related substance abuse problems Clark had been worrying that Tara was slipping into. Jayson had been doing the media rounds lately to promote a warts-and-all autobiography, and he spent most of his days speaking in schools about self-esteem and drug-related topics.

There was admittedly more than a slight pang of regret inside Clark when he heard Tara was staying with Jayson, which momentarily made him consider something he'd been trying to ignore for a long time, but he firmly believed Jayson would be good for her. And given how much he cared about her, as well as how clearly her troubles had been weighing on Emma, that consideration drowned out the other in his mind.

Clark opted to collect Rooster and to sleep in his own bed while the dog rested in the living room; he was never any trouble, so the still-awake Henry didn't mind, either.

All said, it was a pleasant night in Birchwood, Colorado.

As Clark McCarthy's head hit the pillow, he tried not to think too much about the day that would follow.

TUESDAY

V minus 43

Private Jet
Havana, Cuba

"Where's Emma?" Dan asked, waking in his usual seat inside Timo Fiore's plane after a far longer sleep than he realised. He glanced at his phone and gasped. "And how the hell did it get so late?"

The woman in front of Dan, wearing a government-issued security pass which identified her as an ACN technician by the name of Alice Haines, didn't look overly concerned but did seem to have something on her mind. "How much do you remember about last night?" she replied with a question of her own.

Dan thought in silence for a few seconds then uneasily shifted his weight. "Nothing."

Alice nodded. "Figures. You've been sound asleep for seventeen hours, Dan. Emma told everyone you were just mentally exhausted, and that all you needed was a good sleep and you'd be good as gold. She didn't want to wake you until you absolutely *had to* get up, and she didn't want to leave you until she absolutely *had to* head out to meet some people and make sure everything is in order. You should probably call her, though."

"Did she ask you to stay here to make sure I was okay?" Dan asked, this question rising above many others in his mind to escape his lips first.

"One of us had to," Alice said, not sounding overly resentful at having been chosen for the task. "Kyle stayed at first when I was setting some things up for a broadcast at the airport's entrance — *big* crowd — but then we swapped places so he could do his thing. I don't know how much you remember from yesterday *afternoon* but there was a lot of negotiation with the Cubans about how big our crew could be, so we're thin on the ground."

Dan's eyes widened in shock. "*Cubans*? We're in *Cuba*?"

"Dan…" Alice said, overt concern now very much filling her expression, "what's the last thing you *do* remember??

He answered without hesitation: "Falling asleep just after we took off."

"Just after you took off from…?"

"Denver, obviously. And we were supposed to be landing in Buenos Aires, not Cuba! I need to see Godfrey and Slater about something."

Alice gulped. "You met them yesterday and set up this trip. It's *Tuesday*, Dan."

Dan glanced again at his phone, this time taking notice of the date rather than the time. To his amazement, it really was Tuesday. He closed his eyes tightly for a brief moment to empty his mind. Instead of ruminating on the fact that he had somehow lost a whole day — the time for thinking about that would come when Emma rather than Alice was in front of him — he tried to focus on getting out of this situation.

He reached into an almost empty well of energy and forced the loudest laugh he could. "Aww man, Alice… you should have seen your face!"

Alice looked confused for a second before breaking into a roaring laugh of her own. "God damnit, you got me! If you can keep your cards that close to your chest when you're interviewing Cole, this is going to go great. I'm gonna check Kyle is doing okay, but be as quick as you can."

"Yeah," Dan said, very glad that Alice was already facing the plane's exit when he said this, as it meant she didn't see his face reacting to the latest shock of an apparently imminent interview with John Cole. He typed a succinct message on his phone and sent it to Emma without delay:

"*Can you come back to the plane? I really need you… right now.*"

V minus 42

"It just doesn't make sense," Dan said, still ruminating on his apparent short-term amnesia a full hour after first telling Emma about it. They were now sitting alone together in the back of a secure vehicle that was slowing to a halt at the spot where Dan would get out.

"Of course it doesn't," Emma replied, "but just try to remember what we talked about, okay? There are a hell of a lot of things we don't know right now, but we know a lot more than anyone else. The Messengers gave you a gift to help us through a turbulent time, and if these symptoms are a side effect then we just have to deal with them... none of that changes what we came here to do, and it's something the Messengers will correct as soon as they can. Try to trust them; they already saved us once."

Dan nodded. He *did* trust them, but that wasn't the problem. The problem, as he saw it, was that there might be a scenario in which the Messengers wanted to return but couldn't. If the problem with their Elders prevented them from coming back, would he be stuck like this?

One of the symptoms — plural — that Emma alluded to was self-evidently Dan's complete inability to remember any of the previous day. The other, more manageable but still unsettling, was the most prolonged migraine-like headache of Dan's life. He could only put this down to the mental exertion of having listened to Godfrey and Slater's thoughts during those forgotten hours, something Emma reminded him of in great detail, and he was therefore more than a little concerned about how he would feel during and after his telepathic cross-examination of ELF Western Secretary John Cole.

Dan couldn't remember anything about the government-implanted chip in his neck being removed by a GCC doctor before he returned to the plane to leave Buenos Aires, but Emma assured him he had listened to the doctor's thoughts at the time and had trusted her completely. Emma's chip had been removed too, so it seemed unlikely that the very straightforward and almost painless removal procedure was in any way responsible for his symptoms.

What Dan understood least of all was why the previous day was absent from his memory but the one before it wasn't. If *everything* since the Messengers' recent visit and Dan's recent empowerment had been lost to the recesses of his mind, that would have been unsettling but at least comprehensible. As it was, he didn't even have comprehensibility to fall back on.

In light of all of this, the high-profile and internationally televised interview that Dan was about to conduct with Cole wasn't playing on his mind in and of itself. He was here to find out what Cole was thinking, and particularly what he did or didn't know about the triangles that would soon be paraded in Beijing. How Dan came across in the interview wasn't even a secondary concern, because he had no motive beyond leaving Cuba with an insight he couldn't get anywhere else.

Emma, prior to knowing how little he was worrying about *this* part of the matter, had tried to ease Dan's mind by showing him some Social Media Meta Analysis data which revealed that the general public were understandably far more fixated on what was soon going to be revealed in China than what struck many as just another media appearance in Cuba. Needless to say, none had any idea that the forthcoming interview was anything but run-of-the-mill.

"My voice will be in your head and your head will be in the game," Emma whispered as a security official opened her door upon their arrival at Havana's famous Plaza de la Revolucíon. "We'll work through everything else together until the Messengers come back, but this is what we came for."

Dan nodded, trying to look and feel more confident than he really was.

"We've got this," Emma went on, squeezing his hand and smiling sweetly. "I love you, Dan McCarthy, and there's nothing we can't do."

V minus 41

McCarthy Residence
Birchwood, Colorado

"Is Clark around?" Timo Fiore asked, standing alone at the McCarthy's doorstep and asking the question of Henry.

"Not yet," Henry replied. He was sufficiently accustomed to the world's richest man dropping by in Birchwood that Timo's presence didn't shock him, but it did seem unusual for him to turn up without calling ahead. "But he definitely wanted to be home from work in time to see Dan's interview with Cole, so he should be here any minute. Come on in."

Timo stepped inside the familiar house, one where he felt entirely at ease among small-town friends who could see past his bank balance and had taken to him like one of their own. He sat on the couch and glanced at the TV, awestruck at the size of the crowd that had gathered in Havana to catch a glimpse of Dan before he ventured indoors for his high-stakes interview.

The visit was being reported internationally as an outreach mission, with the general narrative holding that Dan had persuaded Godfrey to extend an olive branch — in the form of Dan himself — in an effort to bridge the growing gap between the GCC and ELF and to ease the associated tension.

Timo, of course, knew why Dan was really there. Any detente would be a tremendously welcome side-effect, however, so he very much hoped that one came to pass.

"I got some news a matter of minutes ago," Timo announced to Henry. But just as he spoke, Clark bounded through the door.

"Did I make it?" the elder McCarthy brother asked. "Oh... hey, Timo."

Timo pointed to the screen. "You made it. And I was just telling your dad: I found out something very interesting right before I got here. I tried to reach Emma or Dan or even Kyle but I couldn't get through to any of them. I'd like Dan to know this before the interview and theoretically we *could* still go to Slater and ask for a message to be passed to them via the security team in the next few minutes, but right now I think we need to keep this close to our chest. And really, this information will still be useful so long as he learns of it before he interviews Poppy tomorrow."

Clark, more than intrigued, plumped himself down in the armchair. "What's the deal? Did you find a link between Cole and the GeoSovs, like you've had people looking for?"

"They found a link, but not that one. The GeoSovs and Poppy in particular are proving tough nuts to crack. My team has also been looking into a shell company linked to Cole's overseas consultancy business, though — and when I say 'linked', I mean indisputably so — and we've found a series of very recent and very substantial payments to an American company which is *itself* almost completely hidden by a web of holding companies. Again, this next link is indisputable and my team have one hundred percent certainty in what they've found."

"So what the hell kind of link *have* they found?" Henry interrupted. "What's the American company Cole's working with?"

"It's a media management and PR firm," Timo said, "but it's more about the *who* than the *what*..."

V minus 40

Dan McCarthy did all he could to dissociate from the enormity of the moment as he waved to an impossibly vast crowd from the shadow of an imposing monument to Jose Martí, a hero of the Cuban independence movement.

Facing the enormous tributes to Che Guevara and Camile Cienfuegos that adorned the buildings beyond the near million-strong crowd, it was all but impossible for Dan to bear the weight of history on his shoulders as he stood in the same spot from which the likes of Pope John Paul II, and of course the Castros themselves, had famously addressed equally large gatherings.

The smiling faces before him warmed his heart — the people were so glad to see him; so glad that he had come to their little corner of the world — but the tension of the day made it one he could only hope to endure rather than enjoy.

John Cole, well dressed in a subtly pinstriped grey suit, approached a podium to a smattering of seemingly reluctant applause before booming out his appreciation for Dan's visit. Surprisingly, there were no barbs at Godfrey and not even a fleeting mention of the triangles. Cole instead praised Dan's "internationalist outlook" and, although stopping short of overtly issuing thanks or giving Godfrey or Slater a name-check, went on to share his "unreserved satisfaction" that "senior GCC figures" had played a part in making the visit happen.

A local interpreter relayed Cole's words to the crowd, bringing far more applause than had the controversial man's initial stepping forward. Dan gazed down at Kyle Young, who was standing at the front of the crowd with his barebones ACN crew. Those crew members would be the only people in the room with Dan and Cole when proceedings moved into the grand Ministerio del Interior building at the far side of the plaza.

Dan's turn to address the crowd came next, and he rattled off the words Emma was giving him. He could never truly get used to this, but in a very real sense it was beginning to trouble him just how 'normal' his one-way telepathic ability was already starting to feel.

"It's an honour to be here," he began, earning raucous applause even before the local interpreter followed up his English comment with a running Spanish translation for the benefit of the largely monolingual crowd. "I don't think it will be news to anyone to hear that Mr Cole and I don't see eye-to-eye on very many things, but the fact that we're standing here together and are about to *sit down* together is indicative of a desire on all sides to work past petty divisions as our entire planet wrestles with some big questions about the Zanzibar and Vanuatu triangles. I wish I could hang around afterwards but I have to move straight on to Honduras, so until I have a chance to come back... Viva Cuba!"

One of the Cuban officials beside the podium stepped towards Dan and raised his arm before the adoring crowd. John Cole weaselled his way to the man's other side, grabbing his free hand and raising it to complete the most unlikely three-person picture anyone could ever have anticipated just a few days earlier.

"Viva Cuba!" Cole yelled, insatiably soaking in the adulation as though it was his own.

Dan forced himself to keep smiling, but the reality was sinking in that he was almost certainly in for one of the most unpleasant half-hours of his life.

V minus 39

While watching footage of Dan in Cuba, where John Cole was ingratiating himself to the locals even more shamelessly than expected, William Godfrey received a message on his phone from a high-priority contact.

He glanced at the screen, making sure Slater didn't see, and learned that it was from his doctor:

"Nothing suspicious, the chip was what they said it was and nothing more. Dan's had transmitted a signal on one occasion, Emma's on no occasion."

"Anything important?" Slater asked, wondering what was commanding Godfrey's attention more than the live images from Havana.

He turned the phone around so she could see it. "No one was lying about the chip," he said. "Not the idiot agents who told them it was only there to transmit a signal if something happened with the pain receptors in their necks, or however the science part works, and not Dan and Emma when they told us he hadn't been contacted apart from that one night in Italy."

"Dan and Emma wouldn't lie to us," Slater said, trying to figure out what motivated Godfrey to show her the text and making sure not to let slip that there were certain things the couple had told *her* but not him.

Godfrey nodded and put his phone away. "You know, Valerie, I'm slowly starting to realise that's true."

V minus 38

As soon as Dan stepped into the ELF's new Western Office, which was located in a small portion of a large building otherwise occupied by Cuba's Interior Ministry, he knew without doubt that its opening had been massively expedited. There were exposed wires hanging overhead in the semi-renovated corridor and similar telltale signs on the floor.

It reminded Dan of his first visit to the Fiore Frontiere building in Colorado Springs, when Timo had insisted the place was "ready enough" to host a press conference. After what happened to Timo and Emma that day, it went without saying that Dan hoped the similarities would end there.

New thoughts were the last thing Dan needed, but he couldn't help but ponder what this clear rush job suggested. The office had been announced when Cole stood at Ding's side in Zanzibar, so on the face of it it seemed like that first triangle's discovery — by placing the ELF in a position of strength and the GCC on the defensive — had presented an opportunity too good to miss. Of course, a pillar holding up this belief was the assumption that the triangles were indeed truly extraterrestrial, or were at the very least not part of an elaborate hoax perpetrated *by* the ELF.

Or it could all be mind games, Dan thought. *Because surely they could have tidied up better than this? Maybe they want me to think it looks rushed, so I buy their bullshit about the triangles? As convoluted as that kind of tactic would be, it's nothing compared to what Walker pulled on everyone...*

"So we all know how this is going to go?" Kyle Young asked as soon as the small and silent convoy reached the appropriate doorway. "This is live and uncensored, and I really don't want to play Marian de Clerk. I'll ask questions if I have to, but I'm expecting you both to allow each other to speak."

Dan knew Kyle had been talking exclusively to Cole so didn't take the firmness of his tone to heart; they were good friends, with Cole's behaviour their common concern.

"We're all friends here," Cole replied, speaking with such a straight face that Dan couldn't help but admire how much his lying had improved.

Before stepping into the small interview room, Dan waved goodbye to Emma. Her absence had been a condition of Cole's participation, but Dan had utter faith that the telepathic connection he'd established with her earlier in the day would continue to work despite her now being out of his sight. They had tested this thoroughly, and there was no reason for it to change; the previous day's absence from Dan's memory had no bearing on what had come before, and the Messengers' promise that his ability to mentally control the telepathy would improve was continuing to come more and more true.

For despite having forgotten everything that had happened the previous day, Dan deeply understood that he was now able to use his gift with far more finesse than he had been at first. Like a child learning to write, his dexterity was growing with each minute's practice. He subtly positioned his fingers to establish a connection with Cole and found that he was able to effortlessly shift his focus from Cole's thoughts to Emma's at will, and — quite astoundingly — even to adjust the mental 'volume' of each while listening in to both at once. The whole thing was incredible, and it took no small effort on Dan's part not to experience paralysis through analysis in wondering how *any* of it was possible.

"I'm still here," Emma told him, very deliberately sending the thought his way. *"I'm watching and listening, so if you ever get stuck just say what I tell you and this will all go well. Now go get 'em. Game face!"*

This assurance that Emma's expertise was still at his fingertips, fairly literally, brought Dan back into the moment. With her pulling the strings, there really *was* nothing they couldn't do.

Kyle read some short introductory remarks from the autocue before flinging a softball question Dan's way about the reception he'd received outside.

Smiling, Dan reiterated the honour he felt at being in Cuba and said little of substance. He had some notes on his lap in case his link-up with Emma failed for one unforeseen reason or another, and if he had needed to look down at the first bullet point he would have been advised to keep things light during the intro.

With that out of the way, he focused on Cole's response to Kyle's next question about the triangles.

Two things became apparent very quickly. First, while Cole's pseudo-verbal thoughts were no harder to access than anyone else's, they were certainly less focused and more scattershot. Second, and far more troublingly, Dan realised in no time at all that Cole fully believed that the triangles were genuine alien artefacts.

If Cole's thoughts had exposed the triangles as hoaxes, international politics would have been set to enter its rockiest period for decades. But had that been the case, Dan would have felt that the problem — a human one — was at least solvable by humans. But if the triangles were real after all... *then* what?

If the Messengers couldn't come back... *then* what?

What the hell was going on?

Dan found himself in the horrible position of clinging on to an increasingly faint hope that the triangles might be a GeoSov hoax that the ELF had swallowed hook, line and sinker and was now selling to the rest of the world in the same way he himself had sold the IDA leak after buying the bullshit from Richard Walker.

Fool the shepherd and the sheep will follow, Dan pondered, recalling Ben Gold's fateful words on the night he confessed his knowledge of the hoax before the guilt pushed him to take his own life. Tonight, Dan hoped that Poppy Bradshaw and her shadowy associates had chosen Ding Ziyang as their hoax's shepherd.

The only remotely plausible hoax-related alternative was that Ding *himself* was behind an elaborate hoax and had somehow conned Cole and recruited him as a mindless battering ram to smash into his enemies in Buenos Aires, but Dan couldn't for the life of him see any logic for such a move; and beyond that, he knew Ding was too smart to play with a fire as wild as his ELF's new Western Secretary.

Deflated and more than a little disappointed by how little Cole knew, Dan went into autopilot for the rest of the interview. He repeated questions and answers as Emma remotely fed them into his mind, which felt like it was tiring as the thirty minutes wore on. With five to go and with nothing Earth-shattering having come out as Cole struck an unprecedentedly diplomatic tone throughout, a strong headache began to build behind Dan's eyes.

The only time Cole seemed to lose his cool came with two minutes remaining, and his ire was directed squarely at Kyle.

"There's been some speculation swirling around about your personal connections to certain individuals you might not want the world to know you're connected to," the newsman boldly stated. "Do you know anything about that speculation, like why it might have come about?"

If anything worthwhile was going to come from a mind that had so far exposed itself as being as blank as most people might have guessed, Dan knew it would come now. He focused fully on Cole and heard the all-important thought loud and clear:

"He can't know that Jack's involved. We covered our tracks…"

As Cole searched for words to speak aloud, the ones he didn't say led Dan to fight a gasp. He covered his mouth and pretended to scratch his cheek.

"Is that a no?" Kyle said. "Because some people have said that you and Poppy Bradshaw seemed less at odds on Focus 20/20 than—"

At that, Cole slammed his fist into the table. "The GeoSovs are vermin and should be treated as such!" he boomed. "Apologise for that insinuation or this interview is over."

One more thing was now clear to Dan courtesy of the inner thoughts that underlined Cole's outburst: he truly *did* despise Poppy and her colleagues.

"We only have two minutes left," Kyle replied, "but I really think—"

Cole stood up. "Well, don't say I didn't warn you. Dan… a pleasure as always. Give my regards to Chairman Godfrey. We're serious about outreach, given… well, all of this. Goodbye for now."

"Sure thing," Dan replied, "and thanks for giving this a shot." Exchanging pleasantries with Cole stuck in his throat, but it was for the greater good.

Cole wasn't lying about hating Poppy — his thoughts made that much abundantly clear — and Dan's realisation that the triangles *weren't* part of an ELF hoax had further entrenched in his own mind the importance of global unity. If an Elder-related problem had indeed come down from above, a planet divided had no hope of solving whatever it might turn out to be.

Dan wanted nothing more than to push Cole on the point about Jack being involved, since the Jack in question absolutely *had* to be Jack Neal — Cole's former ally and a sworn enemy of both President Slater and GCC Chairman Godfrey. That was a complication and revelation Dan hadn't even considered possible let alone likely, but posing any kind of follow-up question was *out* of the question; without having heard Cole's thought, there would have been absolutely no grounds for such a context-lacking query.

Dan couldn't imagine that Cole would have jumped to the assumption that Dan was somehow inside his head, but the remotest chance of such a jump occurring — especially on live TV — was something that had to be avoided at all costs.

And so it went that Dan bit his tongue and helped Kyle through the final minutes of an interview that millions of underwhelmed viewers around the world would soon be criticising as something of a damp squib.

But although Dan McCarthy hadn't gotten what he went in hoping to find, he *was* coming out with *something*. Where it would lead, he didn't know. A large part of him didn't even want to consider it, and in that moment all he wanted to do was tell Emma and lie down.

His head ached, even more than it had right after he woke up. He wanted to sleep — he *needed* to sleep — and only time would tell whether he would remember any of this. This new-found uncertainty over his own powers of recollection carried Dan towards Emma as soon as Kyle's cameraman announced that time was up.

Kyle sighed, knowing full well that things hadn't gone as explosively as he or the network had hoped, but Dan was too preoccupied to offer any words of consolation or support.

"We need to get to the car so we can talk," Dan uttered breathlessly as soon as he opened the door and casually pulled Emma out of everyone else's earshot. "Cole is with Jack, one hundred percent."

Emma stood stunned for several seconds, a speechless reaction Dan could never recall seeing from her. Eventually, her shoulders sunk and her head shook slowly. "Of all the things it could have been," she sighed, "it had to be *that* one."

"What do you think it means?" Dan asked, whispering and waiting for a spoken reply having effortlessly disabled his mind's active link-up with Emma's. Her thoughts were always clearer than anyone else's, but he didn't like listening in when he didn't have to.

"I think it means everything's a hundred times messier than we thought," she replied, walking as she spoke. "I think we need to keep this to ourselves until we hear what Poppy knows and how it fits in with all of this. I think we need to keep this quiet for now because as soon as we've finished with Poppy, I *know* that we need to find that son of a bitch before he knows we're looking for him."

V minus 37

Timo, Henry and Clark sat in the living room discussing what they'd just seen, the TV muted as a series of ACN in-studio analysts did the very same. Underwhelming was the word of the day, but no one within Dan's inner circle saw that as a bad thing.

Living in hope that Dan had heard something in Cole's thoughts that would move their understanding of the situation forward, all three were eagerly anticipating the phone call Emma had promised just as soon as she returned to the plane.

Clark's phone rang before too long, but it wasn't Emma.

"Hey!" Tara's voice excitedly boomed through the speaker, effortlessly reaching Henry and Timo as though making its way into one of Clark's ears and escaping the other at equal volume. "That was fine, right? He did okay?"

"It looked fine, but are you alone?" Clark asked. "If you are, there's something we found out that you'll be interested in. If you're not, we can't talk about any of this."

"Jayson is in the bathroom right now, but yeah I guess maybe I'll wait to talk about it when I'm home. I'll definitely be back tonight, we're just heading out to look at an old cabin in the woods he's renovating. Do you still have Rooster in with you? I *will* be home, one hundred percent, but I might be late."

"Yeah, he's here. See you tomorrow. And remember, Tara: no talking."

"Love ya," she replied, ending the call in the same excited tone she'd started it with.

Clark held on to his phone, imploring it to ring again.

"She seems more like the girl I remember," Henry mused. *"Happy."*

As Clark began to speak, his phone rang again. "Dan! Hey, man!" he said, answering as quickly as he could. "You okay? That looked like it went pretty well and you might be thinking that Cole wouldn't have eased up on the GCC without Ding okaying it, but we think there's something else going on here. Timo's people found a recent link between Cole and Jack Neal's new PR firm. They're working together on something, but we don't know if it has anything to do with any of this triangle stuff."

"I just heard Cole thinking about Jack!" Dan revealed. "Do you know how many other people know? This *has* to stay quiet until I've spoken to Poppy and we get home."

Timo held his hand out, requesting the phone from Clark, and got it. "Very few people know what my team discovered, Dan," he said, "and like I mentioned before: I trust this team completely."

Like Timo had received one phone from Clark, Emma quickly received the other from Dan and proceeded to stress just how right he was that any suggestion of Cole working with Jack had to be kept under wraps for now. The strength of her words and tone surprised no one — they knew her well enough by now to know that along with her unnerving knack for identifying the right way to handle delicate situations came a ruthless opposition to any suggestion of pursuing the *wrong* ways — but the number of times Emma repeated the same point was unusual.

"We get it, darling," Henry eventually took over, realising that she wasn't listening to Timo's insistent words. "But did Dan get anything else out of this?"

"Not really," Emma said. *"Cole* thinks the triangles are real but I don't take that as absolute proof that Ding does, and we still need to find out what Poppy's thinking before we consider our next move. The world still doesn't even know about the GeoSov plot to take Slater hostage, what with the end of Focus 20/20 being interrupted by the second triangle right when Dan was about to bring that up, and I think it should stay like that until we know where we're going next. But speaking of Poppy... did Timo's team find anything on her?"

Henry answered in the negative.

"Okay, well we're getting ready to fly to Honduras so we can get a real sleep overnight, so I'll go in a second. How's Tara doing?"

Clark, hearing everything easily through his phone's overloud speaker, took hold of it again. "Great," he said, perking up. "She's been spending time with friends — ones who are good for her — and my dad was just saying how she seems a lot more like her old self."

The news about which particular 'friend' Tara had been spending a lot of time with wasn't Clark's to share, so he didn't get into any specifics.

"You mean Jayson?" Emma asked, taking it out of his hands. "Don't worry, she already told me about that! And yeah, I think you're right... with everything he's been through, he could be good for her. Keep an eye on her until we're home, though; not like *spy* on her, but just make sure you know roughly where she is. Her head can't be *totally* clear after just a few days, so... you know, it's a 'give her space but not *too* much space' kinda thing."

"Got it," Clark confirmed.

"And you guys give *us* a call when you land in Honduras," Henry interjected, almost yelling towards the phone to be heard from several feet away.

"Will do," Emma said, having along with Dan deliberately neglected to mention his short-term memory issues and the headache that was only abating now with the help of some fairly strong medication. "Everything will be a lot clearer tomorrow night... I promise."

V minus 36

ELF HEADQUARTERS
BEIJING, CHINA

"Well..." Maria Janzyck excitedly spoke into her camera, "within the next hour or so we expected to be introducing live coverage of the triangle's public unveiling, but that much-anticipated event is no longer on the cards."

The hubbub behind Maria, with international reporters fighting for position and raising their voices to be heard, strongly suggested that there was more to this story than an event being cancelled.

"And we've just been told by the ELF's press office that this postponement — delaying the triangles' presentation — has been agreed in light of the GCC's recent efforts to find common ground. It was stressed to us in no uncertain terms that scientific access to the triangles will not be extended to scientists from GCC member states quite yet, but Ding Ziyang *is* willing to sit around a table with William Godfrey to discuss the regrettable divisions that have been exposed in recent days.

"There is a natural sense of anti-climax here on the ground in Beijing," Maria continued, ready to conclude her short bulletin before handing back to the ACN in-studio analysis team, "but when the dust has settled, relief may well sink in. Around the world, interest in these triangles is understandably sky-high and the desire to see them with our

250

own eyes is something we haven't felt since the hoaxed plaques were revealed in Argentina. But these triangles are not lost; they are still in our possession, with the greatest hope of all perhaps being that 'our' possession will soon mean the collective possession of humanity as a whole, rather than the possession of one of two pretenders to a global throne which many believe should be filled by a certain and apparently reluctant third party.

"For ACN at the ELF, I'm Maria Janzyck."

V minus 35

A broad smile crossed William Godfrey's lips, the first in a long time.

President Slater, seated at his side, appeared more cautiously relieved.

"He's done it again," Godfrey beamed. "Whether McCarthy meant to or not, he's put Ding on the back foot and spared our blushes."

"This is a long way from over," Slater cautioned. Internally she was itching to hear what Dan had garnered from his conversation with Cole using an ability the rest of the world was entirely unaware of, but she knew that he and Emma were on a tight schedule and had made it clear that they would debrief only after *both* interviews were complete. "Let's see what happens in Honduras before we pop open the champagne."

Godfrey nodded slowly. "Find a nice glass, Valerie," he said in a smugly satisfied tone, "and I'll keep the bottle on ice until this time tomorrow."

WEDNESDAY

V minus 34

McCarthy Residence
Birchwood, Colorado

Clark awoke from a sound sleep and spent the first four hours of Wednesday catching up on some administrative work that had slipped by in recent days. The urgency of the reports he had to file acted as a welcome distraction from the complicated issues that had ironically distracted him from this work in the first place: chiefly the two recently discovered triangles, but also Dan's safety during the final leg of what had turned into something of a whistle-stop Latin American tour.

When it came time to leave for work, Clark called on Rooster to take him back to his next-door home. "Come on, Tara's there," he said, sensing the dog's reluctance to return to a house that had been empty when he left it. Clark opened the door. "See, her car is… huh?"

To Clark's surprise, Tara's car *wasn't* there.

The closed curtains made it clear that she hadn't just gone out, either, and rather that she hadn't come home. Given the strength of her insistence that she would, Clark was understandably concerned. He grabbed his phone and dialled her number, but the concern only grew when a recorded voice informed him that the number was currently unavailable.

Rooster looked confused when Clark re-closed the door and sat down with his phone still in his hand, but Clark's was a look of anxious focus.

He navigated to his friend-finder app in the expectation that it would show her current location as either her own place in the city or wherever Jayson Moore lived. This expectation went disconcertingly unmet, however, when the app revealed that Tara's phone was last active in the woods west of town and had cut off abruptly at 3am. Because Tara was a primary friend who shared the maximum possible amount of linked information with Clark, he could also tell that the smart lock on her home's front door hadn't been used in over twenty-four hours.

Whatever happened after 3am, she hadn't gone home. With his heart-rate ever increasing, Clark urgently switched out of that app and checked first Tara's social media and then Jayson's. He was extremely concerned to see that neither had been active all day.

"What the *fuck*...?"

Clark rapidly searched the internet for a satellite view of the woodland area that was shown in a small image within his friend-finder app. He lucked out in finding not only a satellite image but also a full ground-level view of what turned out to be a popular walking route. To his dismay, however, there was no cabin in the vicinity. Either Tara had lied, or Tara had been lied *to*.

Following his instincts, Clark began an intensive search for Jayson Moore's home address so that he could stop by to find out just what the hell was happening. The rational part of his mind told him that Tara would be there and wouldn't thank him for showing up, but that wasn't what mattered; what mattered was making sure she was okay, and in doing so keeping a promise he had made to Emma and one he had a boundless urge to see through.

Very frustratingly, however, Clark couldn't find any address or direct contact for Jayson. Even an indirect contact proved elusive; from what he could tell, the former TV star no longer seemed to be officially represented by any talent agencies. Calls weren't connecting to Emma's phone, either, or Dan's or even Kyle Young's, which Clark could only put down to a lack of coverage or a temporary signal issue on the Honduran island of Roatán.

When he needed help more than ever, he was on his own.

The sole lead Clark *did* find was the nearby address of Jayson's parents, listed in a year-old news report about Jayson's father posting bail after his son's arrest for petty larceny. Frustratingly there was no phone number listed, which was all he would have needed to reach them as a means of getting in touch with Jayson, but fortunately their home was so close that it would take only a few minutes of driving to visit them in person.

With this in mind, and with a sound alibi for stopping by in the form of his role in the police force, Clark got ready to follow through on the only lead he had. Before leaving he sent a quick text to his friend and colleague Zack, explaining that he'd finished his reports but asking if Zack could cover his shift since he didn't feel in the right frame of mind for a half-day at the precinct.

The uncertainty around the triangles, not to mention the inevitable stress that went along with Dan's high-profile absence, provided sufficient context for Zack to take this highly uncharacteristic request at face value. He replied within seconds to say it would be no problem at all — Clark had done the same for him, more than once — and made a point of encouraging him to take it easy.

Taking it easy wasn't on Clark's agenda, at least until he figured out what was going on with Tara, but he appreciated the sentiment. He then texted his boss, which he hadn't wanted to do until the shift was covered, and was glad to receive another rapid reply along the same supportive lines as Zack's.

"Coming or staying?" Clark asked the dog while he walked out of his bedroom, ready to go. He wasn't too surprised to see that Rooster was already standing at the door.

With Rooster in the back, the car sped out of Birchwood at a borderline irresponsible pace.

At the edge of town, Clark pumped the brakes at the old drive-in. He caught sight of Phil Norris's car and ran to the entrance of New Kergrillin' Bar & Grill, pausing at the door only to compose himself. He hoped to find Phil alone somewhere so that they could talk quickly, and was relieved to see him right away behind the bar. He walked over without delay.

"Thirsty already?" the rough-around-the-edges proprietor asked, surprised to see Clark in the bar at this time of day rather than at a table in the adjoining restaurant.

"All this alien shit might be getting the better of me," Clark replied quietly, eyes darting around to make sure no one else was listening in, "but I think Tara might be in some kind of trouble and I need you to check out a spot in the woods. I need you to see if her phone is actually there or if it just stopped working there, and I need *you* to do that because *I* need to spend the next ten minutes finding out where she is now. This is on the down-low, it could get messy, and you're the man I need."

"What kind of trouble do you think she could be in? And what spot in the woods?" Phil asked. Even as he spoke, he was clicking his fingers to beckon a relatively senior staff member he could entrust with the running of the bar in his absence. He laid out some brief instructions and headed for the door.

Clark talked as they walked. "She didn't come home last night and her phone lost signal in the woods at 3am. I'll give you the coordinates. I need to find the guy she was with last night, because he's either with her or he knows where she is. I'm thinking all kinds of shit, Phil, but this is the only way to do it."

"*Woah*," Phil said, stopping in his tracks. "Jesus… Clark, why are you bringing this to me instead of the police?"

"I *am* the fucking police! And I don't have time for any crap, so if you don't want to do this I'll find—"

"I'll do it," Phil interrupted. "Coordinates?"

Clark held out his phone as Phil jotted it all down. "This is probably nothing to worry about, just a dropped phone, but she said she would *definitely* be home last night. She did tell me she would be checking out a cabin with this guy she's been staying with, and he's supposed to be clean after a drug thing he fell into a few years ago, but there's no cabin anywhere near this spot. I dunno, Phil," Clark gulped uneasily. "They're almost definitely sitting in his house right now, but she parties *hard* when she's with the wrong people… so I'm worried this guy's *not* clean and they were maybe heading out there for a deal. If she dropped her phone and that's it, we can handle that. But what if there *was* a deal and it went wrong?"

"I'll be there in no time," Phil said, noting how nearby the spot was. "Whether I find a phone or not, do you want me to join you wherever you're going?"

"Yeah, here's the address… but stay at a safe distance," Clark replied. "We'll stay in touch, and if I have to go anywhere else after that I'll make sure you don't lose me."

Phil nodded. "She'll be okay, Clark. She *is* okay."

"All I want to do is find out where she is and make absolutely sure," Clark said, gratefully shaking Phil's hand before opening his car door. "And for that, I've gotta find this fucking guy…"

V minus 33

MOORE RESIDENCE
ARCHWAY, COLORADO

Clark reached the small neighbourhood of Archway within ten minutes of leaving Birchwood, and he hoped beyond hope that his stay would be even shorter. He was here for one reason: to get in touch with Jayson Moore as a means of finding Tara.

With Phil Norris set to hang back in his own car at a distance of around one hundred feet when he arrived, Clark parked right outside Jayson's parents' house and walked up the short path to their door. He didn't like the fact that he was having to do this, but he shook away his doubts and played the only card he'd been dealt.

"Clark McCarthy!" a sixty-something man beamed from the doorway. His hair was white rather than grey but his skin and posture aged him safely under seventy in Clark's eyes. "Honey, it's Clark McCarthy!"

Within seconds, Mr Moore was joined by his wife. And although she also smiled instinctively at the up-close-and-personal sight of a figure as well known and well liked as Clark, her happiness faded very quickly. "Is something wrong? Something with Jayson?" she asked.

The first thought in Clark's mind was that he wished he shared Dan's advantage of having Emma's voice rattling around, feeding him the right lines. Lacking in such a gift, he kept it simple: "Probably not, but I *am* trying to reach him. Trouble is, his contact information is harder to find than answers about these damn triangles!"

Clark's jovial tone, which took no small effort to maintain, appeared to ease Mrs Moore's mind slightly despite his implication that something *might* be wrong. That had been his intention, to make her think he wouldn't be wise-cracking with one-liners if he was majorly concerned about something.

"He changes his number pretty often," she explained. "Things have been okay lately, but in the past few years he's had a lot of problems with debts and with hangers-on looking for handouts. Have you tried reaching him through Tara? Now *that* was some nice news, wasn't it? Those two."

"I think Tara's busy," Clark said, not entirely sure why he felt driven to avoid the truth at this stage but convinced it was the smart move. "The only thing I'm worried about is that Jayson might be involved with some of the bad types you're talking about, Mrs Moore. Partly for his sake and partly for Tara's, I need to see him as soon as possible to ask him about some individuals I have reason to believe he's been associating with. He's not in any kind of trouble — yet — and an intervention is the only way we can make sure he *stays* out of trouble. If he is in with the crowd I'm worried about and we don't manage to reach him, things could get very bad as early as this afternoon. There's only so much I can say, but it really is important that I see him."

Mr Moore sighed ruefully. "That boy…"

Clark didn't care about lying in any ethical or personal sense, but it did cross his mind that he could get into serious trouble for implying that he, and by extension the police force, were worried about Jayson. In the context of his immediate and genuine concern about Tara's wellbeing, though, this particular worry faded as quickly as it had shown up.

"You see," Clark went on, "I'm a friend in this, but I'm also a cop. So if it's not too much to ask, it would really help me out if you could call him here without saying it's to see me. Is that okay? I can hang out in my car until he arrives or I'd be delighted to come in and wait with you, but I can't stress how important it is that Jayson doesn't know I'm here; if he does, he won't come. Think of a good reason for him to hurry over here — and I mean *hurry* over here — and this'll end well. I wish I could say I would be confident of a good ending if you can't get him to come here, but unfortunately I can't."

"Oh, I'll *get* him," Mr Moore insisted, setting off into the kitchen to pick up his phone. He then called to invite Clark inside and walked out back with the phone in his hand, his wife following close behind.

Clark, anxious and impatient but at least feeling like he was getting somewhere, looked around the Moores' living room at the old family photos that adorned most of the walls and surfaces.

His phone then buzzed very abruptly, alerting him to a message from Phil and sending his heart-rate soaring. Reading the message neither further raised nor lowered his pulse: *"No phone, no signs of anything else. On my way to you."*

Promptly, Jayson's parents returned to the room. They brought with them the better news that he was on his way and would be there in three or four minutes.

"Jeez, he lives close," Clark mused. He had a leverage-related reason for not having simply asked for Jayson's home address, one that he hoped to be able to keep up his sleeve. But it was there if he needed it, in the worst-case scenario that Jayson proved uncooperative with Clark's search for Tara whether through choice or, more likely in Clark's eyes, due to external coercion.

Clark made sure to stand out of sight of the front door for the next few minutes, so that Jayson wouldn't see him until the door was closed.

And more than anything he had ever hoped for in his life, he hoped that Tara would arrive at Jayson's side.

Almost inevitably, she didn't.

"You look like hell," Mrs Moore sighed solemnly as her son stepped inside. She wasn't wrong; the bags under his eyes looked like those of a man for whom sleep was a mere memory, and the ghostly pale skin looked like it belonged to someone else rather than the bronzed actor Clark remembered.

As Clark stepped forward, Jayson's expression froze. He didn't reach for the door, but his body inched towards it.

"Clark is right," Mr Moore said, "something's going on, isn't it?"

Clark strode over with six quick, huge steps, unsubtly positioning himself between Jayson and the door. "You're not getting away that easily," he said, disguising it as a light-hearted comment.

"Clark McCarthy, as I live and breathe!" Jayson said, his forced smile fooling his parents but certainly not Clark.

"Nice to meet you," Clark replied, shaking Jayson's hand in a way that looked friendly enough but quietly compressed metacarpals with alarming ease.

Jayson winced.

"Some things I've heard through the grapevine have me a little worried about some people you might be mixed up with, especially because we have a mutual friend," Clark went on, patting Jayson on the back so hard that it almost knocked him down. "You know, *Tara Ford*?"

The look in Jayson's eyes as Clark said the name was the last one he had hoped to see: primarily fear, but with a strong tinge of guilt. It took everything Clark had not to explode, but he fell back on his training and tried to keep his head in the game. Jayson was the only person who could give him answers, and certain instinctive reactions would greatly reduce the chances of him doing so.

Alas, the leverage was about to come into play.

The familial ace up Clark's sleeve, which he had dearly wished would stay there, was sadly becoming necessary.

"But anyway, Jayson... we all want what's best for you, and that's why I've got your parents involved today. *That's* why you really don't want to do anything stupid like turn around and run away," Clark said. He stared a hole in the former TV star's tired, bloodshot eyes, gesturing towards Mr and Mrs Moore as they stood uneasily beside their couch: "It's not just me who wants to help. I care so much, I even got your parents involved! See, Jayson? *I've got your parents.*"

V minus 32

PRIVATE JET
ROATÁN, HONDURAS

"Hey," Emma said softly as she saw Dan stretching himself awake in the private jet that had become his new home away from home. He had significantly overslept again, awoken by an alarm she'd set for as late as possible in an effort to give his body and mind a chance to recover from the previous day's Cuban exertions. The sheer number of hours he had slept set an expectation in her mind that a repeat of the previous day's short-term amnesia was almost certainly going to be at play. "Do you know what country we're in?"

Suddenly wide awake, Dan turned around and stared at her in confusion. "Honduras, obviously. Are you okay?"

"What country were we in yesterday?"

"Cuba," Dan replied. "Seriously, Emma, is there something—"

"Last one: what country were we in the day before?"

At *this*, Dan's expression finally reflected his tired mind's belated understanding of why Emma was asking these questions. "Oh yeah..." he eventually said. "We were in Argentina two days ago, but I only know that because I remember talking about this yesterday. I still can't remember Monday at all. My head doesn't hurt like it did yesterday morning, though, so maybe I'm getting used to the strain of the telepathy?"

Emma's tense shoulders relaxed with this answer. "So you're not any worse, and you *can* remember yesterday. Maybe you just hit a mental fatigue point or something like that on Monday? I guess you can ask the Messengers next time they show up. But as for today, the news from outside is that a sit-down meeting between Godfrey and Ding could be possible in the next few days. We might not have found out for sure where the triangles came from — *yet* — but this is working, Dan. The outreach narrative the press ran with about our trip to Cuba is actually bridging the gap. I don't want to assume too much, but maybe the Messengers knew you'd use the power for something like this?"

"I still don't think we can take it for granted that they meant to give me the power to hear other *people's* thoughts at all," Dan replied. "Because it seems pretty damn unlikely they meant to give me the *other* power; and if there's been one unintended side-effect of giving me the ability to hear them from afar, it's totally plausible for there to have been two. And after everything that happened with Il Diavolo, I'm never going to assume they can predict how people are going to react to anything… that's not exactly their strong suit."

Emma shrugged. "Yeah, maybe. I mean, I'm not being flippant or anything, but I guess time will just have to tell on that one. Right now we have one more job to do and that's finding out what Poppy knows about these triangles and ideally what the hell the GeoSovs really want. Is there something underlying all of this, or is it really just about them opposing further contact? Timo and Clark don't seem to have had any luck finding out anything about her beyond what we already know, so this is going to be important. You're going to ask all kinds of questions, and you'll hear the answers even if no one else does. *I* want this trip to be over so I can't even imagine how you're feeling when you're the one who has to do everything, but—"

"I'm the one who *looks* like I'm doing everything," Dan interrupted with a warm laugh. "Don't you ever sell yourself short, Emma Ford," he added, a direct and loving nod to a comment she'd made in the other direction not too long ago.

Emma smiled. "You're live in twenty minutes, by the way. Short drive to the TV studio, hair and make-up on the way. Ready to go?"

"I'm ready to go *home*, so let's get this thing done and get on our way…"

V minus 31

MOORE RESIDENCE
ARCHWAY, COLORADO

"Give us a minute," Clark smiled at Mr and Mrs Moore while he led their desolate-looking 23-year-old son upstairs. "Some of the things we have to discuss might be quite uncomfortable for you to hear."

Both of Jayson's parents were shaking their heads, upset and beyond disappointed that he had seemingly fallen back into the bad habits it had finally looked like he'd been able to kick for good.

Jayson, although hesitant, realised he was in no position to resist Clark's will. Once upstairs, he opened the door to his old childhood bedroom. Clark roughly pushed him inside and closed the door.

"What were you doing in the woods last night and where the fuck is Tara?" he demanded.

As Jayson's lip began to quiver and his eyes fell to the floor, Clark knew for sure for the first time that he was hiding something. He grabbed Jayson by the collar and effortlessly pressed him against the inside of the door.

"Talk!" Clark grunted, keeping his volume low to avoid alerting Jayson's parents but speaking with a breathy intensity more impactful than a shout of any decibel level could ever hope to be.

"They'll kill me! They'll kill my parents, they'll kill my cousins. They'll—"

Clark pressed his forearm into Jayson's chest, cutting off his words and causing him to take several quick gasps in a desperate effort to replenish his lungs.

In the last few seconds, all of Clark's worst fears had been confirmed; Jayson *was* in over his head with the wrong people, and he *had* dragged Tara into it.

"I'm not who you think I am," Clark said, menacingly but almost silently breathing the words into Jayson's ear. "The gentle giant, the big brother everyone wants... that's just a picture they paint. So trust me, asshole: whoever's got you by the balls and whatever they're holding over your head, there is *nothing* in this world they could ever do to you that would come close to what I'm capable of."

Clark leaned back then showed Jayson he meant business by placing a firm hand on his face before squeezing his jaw in a manner that suggested he could start breaking teeth whenever the urge struck.

In his younger years, Clark's time in the military had provided a structured and positive outlet for channelling the aggressive tendencies that had punctuated his youth. Those years had made him a better man, and the high-risk private security work he took on in Iraq after a medical issue ruled him out of active duty had continued to help keep the beast inside at bay. His current police work occupied his time and mind, but the animal inside was still there. He didn't like making grave threats to Jayson Moore or anyone else, and he liked even less that he knew the threats weren't empty.

All signs of fear then faded from Jayson's eyes in an instant, replaced at once by dejected sorrow. His body slouched forward in a way Clark hadn't seen since Dan found out the IDA leak was a hoax, and it certainly would have hit the ground had Clark's arm not been propping it up.

"I didn't have a choice, man," Jayson sobbed, abandoning his ongoing effort to keep himself in check. "Not with what he's holding over me. I took her to the woods and he was waiting."

"Who?"

"He said he just wanted to ask her some questions while he had the chance, and he promised they wouldn't hurt her!" Jayson's words, weak and low, were sometimes difficult to make out through his guilty and fearful tears. "Clark, I swear: he said they won't hurt Tara... it's Dan and Emma he wants. He'll let her go as soon as—"

"Oh, well that's just fucking *fine* then," Clark boomed sarcastically, unconsciously abandoning his strive for quietness. He grabbed Jayson's jaw again and squeezed harder than ever. "Listen good, you little shit-stain: you've got five seconds to tell me who did this and five minutes to take me to wherever he's hiding."

"It's Jack," Jayson blurted out. "Jack Neal."

V minus 30

MIRADOR HOTEL
ROATÁN, HONDURAS

For Dan McCarthy, the past few days had been a blur. Flights and meetings and debriefings had been his life since leaving Colorado, and the events of one particular day remained truly absent from his conscious memory.

The crowd that gathered to greet him outside of Roatán's Mirador Hotel was a sizeable one but nothing compared to the sea of humanity he'd encountered in Havana. His meeting with Cole had been the one he was most worried about, since Cole had a reputation for explosive revelations and the rolling live cameras would have placed Dan in an awkward spot if the ELF's new Western Secretary had made any. The meeting with Cole, though, had also been the one for which Dan had held lower expectations of hearing a major secret in his interviewee's unspoken thoughts.

The revelation of Cole's continued working relationship with Jack Neal had been entirely unexpected, but Dan couldn't even imagine what he was going to get out of Poppy.

This wasn't the first time he had conversed with her, of course, with Saturday evening's special episode of Focus 20/20 having put them in direct opposition. Dan hadn't held back at all on that occasion, outright telling Poppy that he despised her and her role in a group that was the spiritual successor to the defunct Welcomers who tried to kill Timo and Emma in a botched attack.

Today, Emma had told him to focus on getting information out of Poppy rather than attacking her cause. There was no need for that, Emma said; her Social Media Meta Analysis app showed that the GeoSovs were more universally loathed than any other tracked group or individual.

In a small conference room within the hotel, ACN's Kyle Young began proceedings with some fairly brief introductory remarks, recapping the meeting between Dan and Cole that he'd moderated the previous day and touching on some of the tension-easing political fallout.

Poppy sat at one side of a table with Dan at the other and Kyle to the side. She had several sheets of handwritten notes containing points she wanted to get across, and Dan had a few of his own for the sake of appearances. He wouldn't need them — not with Emma's voice in his head — but their absence might have raised unnecessary questions.

Dan thumbed at his notes as a way of masking the finger position he needed to use to establish a connection with Poppy.

Although she looked a picture of confidence, the GeoSov spokesperson's thoughts immediately betrayed her nerves. Dan took this as a very good sign.

"So Dan, we'll start with you," Kyle said at the end of his recap. "What drove you to challenge Poppy to meet you today, and why Honduras?"

This double-question would have been an easy one for Dan to answer on his own, but he stuck with the wording Emma sent his way. Unfortunately, the day's first meaningful use of his telepathic ability led to a sudden and sharp pain between his eyes.

It took no small effort for Dan not to wince and call out in pain, but even in the moment he knew how bad that would have been when ACN's live cameras were sending him into living rooms around the world. He didn't even want to think about what kind of unnecessary questions *that* might have raised.

Instinctively, Dan reacted to the pain by using his increasing control over the ability to reduce the mental 'volume' of the currently superfluous advice Emma was feeding him. Immediately, the pain subsided. He focused on Emma's thoughts again and felt the uncomfortable sensation once more, at which point he wisely decided he didn't need her voice right now and that it was better to focus on Poppy if — as was apparently the case — he couldn't focus on both without a severe physical cost.

Dan began by explaining that the natural limitations of a multi-person Focus 20/20 panel had prevented him from asking as many questions of Poppy as he wanted to.

This hadn't been his only frustration, of course, but he kept quiet for now about having intended to tell the world of Thursday night's dreamtime contact experience and the heinous GeoSov plot to take President Slater hostage that it had foiled. Events in Vanuatu had put paid to his plans to do so in the show's last few minutes and the pace of events since then, particularly regarding the telepathic ability Dan gained shortly *after* the show, meant that it made a tremendous amount of sense to keep his cards close to his chest until everyone's motives were exposed.

Slater and Godfrey, who had been keen enough for Dan to talk about the foiled plot, had likewise pivoted to prefer a lips-sealed approach until Poppy's inner thoughts were no longer hidden.

"And Honduras is neutral," he said, answering the other half of Kyle's question.

Kyle then handed over to Poppy. She wasted no time in launching into a blistering attack on both the ELF and GCC, following a familiar argument that proactively pursuing further contact with aliens was an approach borne of madness. She said nothing negative about Dan and even praised him for being willing to sit down in an effort to hammer out some of the issues in a way the mainstream media and high-level politicians never did.

Throughout and immediately after her remarks, Dan focused fully on Poppy's thoughts. They were clear enough, but really seemed only to mirror her words. So far, she wasn't lying. Dan recalled Emma's clear advice to never let Poppy present herself as anything close to a friend or ally, however, so he curtly told her not to waste anyone's time pretending she was on his side of any meaningful argument.

As the interview wore on with Kyle passing questions both ways across the table and Poppy stumbling over her words on occasion without ever thinking anything particularly illuminating, Dan glanced down at his notes having decided not to risk any further pain by listening to Emma at the same time as Poppy. If he really needed her, she was there. But until then, the danger of experiencing pain he couldn't keep to himself ruled out listening to both women's thoughts simultaneously.

Perhaps for the best, Dan didn't have time to stop and think about how crazy this would all have sounded if he ever had to explain it to anyone else.

But undoubtedly for the *worst*, as the minutes ticked by he felt his mind blurring and Poppy's thoughts becoming harder and harder to read. He tried to listen for Emma's voice again but came up completely blank.

When Kyle passed the proverbial microphone back across the table, Dan shifted uncomfortably in his seat and asked Poppy to repeat her last point in clearer terms. In truth it had been clear enough and as uncontroversial as anything she'd said all day, but he had to buy a few minutes.

Dan could have handled being on his own; indeed, he had been doing so since reluctantly tuning out of Emma's thoughts. But now, if he couldn't even hear *Poppy's* thoughts, the whole purpose of the interview was in ruins.

Allied to that, Dan's mind was still clear enough for him to know that any further cloudiness could lead to a slip-up he really didn't want to make.

There were two things Dan didn't want to mention: the first was his knowledge of the GeoSov plot against President Slater, knowledge which had been provided directly by the Messengers via a dream-time vision. Secondly, there was the shocking fact he picked up from John Cole using the interrogative gift the Messengers had recently bestowed upon him: the fact that Cole and Jack Neal were back in cahoots. As much as he wanted to gauge Poppy's reaction to these two pieces of knowledge, at this juncture he simply couldn't let her know that he knew.

Kyle Young's line of questioning, as well as his mannerisms, grew increasingly hostile to Poppy as the minutes ticked by, presenting Dan with an opportunity to try to compose himself. For the viewers at home, it looked simply as though Dan was keen to hear Poppy out and hope she would expose her group for what they really were; in a sense, like he was giving her enough rope to hang herself.

Dan felt the pain build every time he consciously tried to listen in, so ultimately he gulped and shook his head in defeat. He instead paid close attention to the subtle changes in Poppy's expression and body language while she answered Kyle's firm questions, particularly one regarding the presence of many former Welcomers among the GeoSovs' followers.

Kyle went so far as to accuse the group's leaders of being "agents of pure evil" for some of the attacks that had been carried out in their name, to which Poppy only rolled her eyes.

Dan's ears perked up at one particular question, though; one regarding the GeoSovs' funding and what Kyle termed "conspicuous associations with certain other groups and individuals."

On nothing more than a hunch, Dan decided to go all in and focused his pained mind as intently as possible for a few seconds. If Poppy was going to let something slip, this was it.

Fortune favoured the bold, as the intense pain Dan experienced coincided with his reception of a perfectly clear and utterly game-changing thought from inside Poppy's mind; one almost identical to the equally stunning revelation he'd heard in John Cole's:

"Stay cool, he can't know we've been working with Jack. The PR company is hidden, our companies are hidden... He can't know. He just can't..."

As the thought ended, Dan shrieked in pain like a cat with its tail trapped in a door. He pressed his hand into the aching area above the bridge of his nose as the sensation ran deep.

"Dan!" Kyle yelled in concern. "Are you okay?"

As quickly as it had come, the pain faded away. Dan didn't spend a second thinking about how his agonised outburst might have come across on TV; all that mattered was what he had just found out.

He couldn't wait to tell Emma, and he only had to hold out for a few more minutes. He muttered something about migraines and dived into a largely off-topic monologue about his hopes for a meaningful closing of the gap between the GCC and ELF. He didn't even hide the fact that he was leaning heavily on the bullet-point notes in front of him, having decided that all that mattered was getting through the rest of the interview without slipping up.

To everyone else, Kyle included, this interview had been far more enthralling than the previous day's with John Cole. Dan hadn't participated all that fully, but his presence alone added great weight to what had primarily been a showdown between Kyle and Poppy. Dan imagined it would be great for Kyle's career and was glad of this; he definitely deserved it.

But for Dan, one thing alone had made the interview more than worthwhile: the discovery that Jack Neal, as well as working with the ELF's John Cole, was apparently working with the GeoSovs' Poppy Bradshaw.

Inevitably, a new question quickly arose in Dan's mind: *Does Cole know about Jack and Poppy?*

Another followed: *And if Cole knows, does Ding?*

The ramifications could hardly have been greater. For days, Dan had been wrestling with three possibilities: that the triangles were part of a genuinely extraterrestrial message, that the whole thing was a hoax perpetrated by the ELF, or that it was a hoax perpetrated *on* the ELF by the GeoSovs.

And just when he thought he was getting a handle on things... *this.*

The GeoSovs' official raison d'être was opposing contact between humanity and other extraterrestrial races. But while the events of recent days had raised the loose-knit group's profile to all new heights, meaningful information on its structure and underlying motives were as thin on the ground as ever. Details on this front may have been within reach had Dan not experienced so much pain during his attempts to fully question Poppy on everything; but given the explosive nature of what he *had* learned, he didn't regret having prioritised his focus.

Before Dan knew it he was shaking Kyle's hand and even extending the same politeness to Poppy. She didn't deserve it, by any means, but she had made him one happy man.

Immediately upon the interview's conclusion, Dan ran to Emma and whispered the news in her ear. His words interrupted her own angry questions about why Dan had so totally ignored her live advice — naturally, she didn't know he'd had to lower the volume — and she reacted with exactly the kind of stunned silence he'd expected.

After several ponderous seconds, and taking care to ensure that no one else heard her words, she finally replied: "We should tell Timo. His people found out about Cole and Poppy, so maybe this piece of the puzzle will complete a picture we're not quite seeing yet. Because, Jesus... Dan, if the GeoSovs and the ELF are on the same page... I don't even know how this sentence ends. We need to tell Slater, too. And how does this fit in with Cole hating Poppy?"

"I don't know, but let's wait until we get home to tell Slater," Dan said. "She might tell Godfrey and he might do something stupid. Same with Timo... he could tell Clark. And according to those social media posts you were talking about, Jack's been working in Colorado pretty recently, right? Because if Clark finds out he's involved with the GeoSovs, *he* could do something stupid. He hates Jack already, but if he knew he was in with those guys..."

Emma nodded. "Right. I don't think Clark *would*, but even if there's a small chance, we can't take it. Jack is the key to everything, so God knows we need him alive."

272

V minus 29

Clark stood reeling in the childhood bedroom of former TV star Jayson Moore, stunned into both silence and stillness by the revelation that not only had Tara been abducted, she had been abducted by Jack Neal.

Mulling over how this might fit in with everything else could wait — for now, Clark had one focus.

"Is that piece of shit still in town?" he growled.

Jayson shrugged weakly. "He was around here last night, in the woods. He stayed in a car but I definitely saw him. The other guys were armed. I didn't *want* any of this to hap—"

"Spare me the bullshit," Clark snapped. "Just call that piece of shit and tell him to meet you somewhere right now. Emergency. You're the fucking actor, make something up and make it good. You're in trouble with these guys, fine. If you lead me to Jack and he leads me to Tara, we can deal with that. We can deal with *them*. But if you can't or won't help me? That's not somewhere you want to be. Make the call. One chance."

Jayson lifted his phone from his pocket and psyched himself up in front of a full-length mirror. He then showed Clark — unprompted — that the contact he was about to call really was Jack Neal. By no means did Jayson look like someone who could convincingly pull off an uncoerced voice in the present situation, but within ten or fifteen seconds a radio-quality tone filled the room with an effortless resonance.

Clark watched intently as Jayson stared at his own reflection while asking Jack to meet him as soon as possible at the parking spot nearest the same wooded area where they'd met the previous night.

Jayson's perfectly vague excuse, that he had read something online that he feared might expose himself and Jack but really didn't want to discuss it over a phone he couldn't be sure wasn't bugged, also struck Clark as good enough.

More importantly, as he found out seconds later, it was good enough for *Jack*.

Jayson put his phone down after setting up a meeting in just ten minutes' time. "Now what?" he asked Clark. "Am I done?"

Clark tipped his head towards the door. "Good work, but not by a long shot."

~

Clark came up with the next excuse; this one for why he and Jayson were leaving together.

The Moores bought it without any suspicion, thinking it reasonable and sadly characteristic enough that their son should have to identify a drug dealer from a line-up at the precinct. Jayson's visible distress was also understandable within this context, but Clark made a point of telling his parents that he wasn't going to be in any kind of legal trouble so long as he helped out. It wasn't easy to force a relaxed tone, but Clark more or less pulled it off.

"You're driving," he then boomed in a far less amiable manner once the two men stepped outside. "If we get there before him, you'll be waiting on foot. But if he's already there, you have to get out of the driver's side door or he'll be out of there in a flash."

Before making the final few steps towards Jayson's unsurprisingly flashy car, Clark waved to get Phil Norris's attention and beckoned him over from the safe distance he'd parked at.

"Where is she?" Phil asked, automatically concerned by the expressions before him.

"Jack Neal used this asshole to bait her into the woods and he's got armed goons holding her somewhere," Clark grunted. Saying it out loud made it seem even worse than it already did, but he tried to focus on what he could still control. "Now we're using this asshole to bait *Jack* back to the same place. He wanted Tara as a way of getting to Dan and

Emma and took the chance when he saw one. And Phil… if you don't want to get any deeper into this, you don't have to. But I'm doing this, and there's no time for an 'official' police response. This is the hand we've been dealt. Are you in?"

"Drive," Phil answered affirmatively.

Clark nodded curtly. "But hang *way* back. He can't see two cars. I'll keep you on a live call so we can communicate; if I need you to drive all the way up the dirt road, you'll know. And Phil… thanks."

With no further ado, Clark stepped into the passenger seat of Jayson's car and told him to hit the gas. He immediately silenced the radio host rabbiting on about the triangles and, as calmly as he could, asked Jayson to lay everything out during the short drive.

"The first thing you have to know is that I didn't plan this," Jayson insisted, his voice still weak but no longer broken by deep sobs now that the adrenaline had really kicked in. "I've been working with Jack and when he found out I'd hooked up with Tara, he jumped all over it. It wasn't the other way around, I swear! I didn't *seduce* her for this. I would never do something like that."

It angered Clark no small amount that Jayson seemed so concerned with protecting his own honour when Tara was being held against her will, but he kept quiet and listened.

"And *because* I've been working with Jack to repair my tarnished image and manage my comeback, he has every single ounce of dirt on me that exists. I did a lot of stuff I'm not proud of when I was at the bottom, and some of it is on camera. But ask him yourself when we get there: I still said no."

Clark still said nothing.

"You want to know? You want to know what he has? From my lowest low, there's a video of me with two dealers. I don't remember it, but they—"

"I don't need to know," Clark interrupted, for both of their benefits. "Skip the details."

Jayson glanced at him in acknowledgement if not quite thanks, taking his eyes off the road for only a split second. "Well, he has that video and he told me to bring Tara to the woods or else he was going to release it and my career would be over. My *life* would be over. He said no one would look at me the same way, and he was right. But listen to me here: I told him to go fuck himself. I was ready to go to the police but within a couple of minutes I got a text from Jack… a photo of my cousins' house with his two armed thugs standing at the door. Another text came through a few seconds later: '*It's her or them. And if it's them, you're next.'* And we're getting seriously close, by the way, probably twenty seconds until the concealed turn-off."

"That scumbag is going to wish he'd never been born," Clark uttered in the most ominous tone Jayson had ever heard. He was a long way from forgiving Jayson and didn't think he ever could even once Tara was safe, but he could now at least see why he'd done what he'd done.

"He said this is all about Dan and Emma," Jayson went on. "I dunno what he meant, but that's what he said. He said Tara is innocent and won't get hurt."

Clark gritted his teeth. "The only person getting hurt is him."

Just as Jayson had announced in advance, the turn-off arrived in no time. He slowed the car and Clark ducked out of sight in case Jack was already there. In Clark's mind it would be better if he *was*, and fortunately this was the way it went.

"He's there," Jayson said. "One car — *his* car, and no one else I can see. There were only ever two other guys and I don't think they'd leave Tara. Am I sticking to the plan? I go out and talk to him, get him to turn around, and you get out to grab him before he can run?"

"Yeah but don't park too close, okay? And just keep cool. All you're doing is making him turn around for a few seconds so I can rush him before he can reach his car. Oh, and Phil, are you hearing this? We need you to park sideways at the bottom of the dirt road, just in case he gets spooked and tries to flee."

"Sure thing," Phil's voice rang tinnily through the phone. "And hey, kid... this is your one shot at redemption. Don't fuck it up."

Jayson gulped and parked the car. "He's seen me. Okay, I can't hang around. But Clark, when this is done... are you gonna kill him?"

Clark answered in a tone even more emotionless than the one Jayson had used to ask: "Depends how I feel when I'm finished with him."

V minus 28

"Well, it could have gone a lot worse," President Slater mused. There was only so much she could say to Godfrey, who didn't know that Dan had a way of getting far more from questions than the answers he received out loud. It wouldn't be long until he and Emma called to share their findings, she imagined, and the nature of those findings would determine the next move — including whether to bring Godfrey in on the remarkable news about Dan's new ability.

Godfrey rubbed his chin in thought. "Poppy was just as scathing about Ding and Cole as she was about us, maybe even *more* scathing... so I have to agree, Valerie: that didn't go too badly at all. In a sense, the GeoSovs positioning themselves so clearly in opposition to the missions of both the ELF and ourselves places both organisations on the same side in the public's eyes. Before these damn triangles showed up that's the last thing I would have wanted, because the fight for global supremacy was one we were never going to lose. Since Zanzibar, though? The ELF has had the upper hand and Ding was starting to twist the knife, what with Cole's new placement in Cuba and then the planned public display of the triangles in Beijing. But McCarthy's trip has changed everything... their tone has softened and they're even

277

holding off on parading the triangles. Ford was right: sending him to Cuba did look like an olive branch, and with how popular he is, it boxed them into a corner." A grin crossed the GCC Chairman's usually stern lips. "Let me tell you, Valerie, it's a pleasant change to have that girl on my side!"

Godfrey's office, empty aside from the English-speaking world's two most powerful figures, fell silent for a few moments.

"McCarthy was our emergency stop," Godfrey went on, breaking it with a whispered tone and essentially thinking out loud. "I thought two hoaxed triangles was *their* desperate attempt at an emergency stop when we had the upper hand, but if the triangles are real after all then it's Dan who has levelled the playing field just as *they* were racing ahead. Funny how things work out, isn't it? There's a chance Ding was bluffing about the reveal all along and that the triangles *are* fake, but everything we're hearing from Chinese scientists hints against that. So the real question becomes this: just what the hell are the Messengers playing at? If there's a message we need to hear in this convoluted way of three separate triangles fitting together to make a revelatory whole, surely at least one of them has to show up in *our* territory? And if that *is* the case, why didn't one of the first two? That would have avoided these tensions, which seems like something the Messengers would want. *Doesn't* it? Stop me if I'm wrong, Valerie, please…"

She sighed. "William, let's try to stay on one thing at a time. On the face of it, it doesn't seem like the GeoSovs had anything to do with the triangles, which does put us back squarely in the framework of them being real. Because if it's not an ELF hoax and it's not a GeoSov hoax, it's not a hoax. I don't know why the triangles were placed where they were, either, but ultimately the past few days have undermined both the ELF and the GCC in terms of public opinion. That's what the GeoSovs want, but maybe it's also what the *Messengers* want for a different reason? From their perspective, humanity having two competing points of contact probably just doesn't make sense. Ding and Cole might be making the right kind of conciliatory noises right now, but they're not going to cede any meaningful ground any more easily than you are. We have to play a diplomatic game until things get clearer, whether that comes with direct contact or the third triangle being found or whatever else might happen, but in the medium to long term we're going to have to—"

President Slater's borderline rambling was cut off by the sudden opening of Godfrey's office door. Only one other man in the building had a key card for getting in, and Godfrey knew he would never dream of entering unannounced like this unless something truly couldn't wait.

The man, his trusted assistant Manuel, didn't look scared or shocked; such was the speed with which he'd run to the door upon hearing the news he'd come to deliver, he looked nothing but exhausted.

"Third triangle," Manuel panted. "Sir, they just found it... two minutes ago. The news hasn't broken yet."

Godfrey rose to his feet, a thousand thoughts running through his head. "Tell me this one is ours," he implored Manuel. "Tell me the Messengers have levelled the playing field and Ding needs something we have to complete his little set of three. Tell me we're back in the game and it turned up in Colorado or Salzburg or Kerguelen or anywhere else administered by a GCC state."

"I'm sorry, sir," Manuel sighed, still catching his breath, "but it turned up in China, and they're already clearing foreign media from the streets. This is it."

Part 5

BOILING POINT

"The future is no more uncertain than the present."

Walt Whitman

V minus 27

ELF HEADQUARTERS
BEIJING, CHINA

"The atmosphere here has transformed twice in the last few minutes," Maria Janzyck yelled into her camera, even this raised voice barely audible over the chaos on the streets behind her.

Over her shoulder, no reporters any longer stood where there had been dozens just minutes earlier. The exclusion zone, officially unannounced but visually evident, was expanding by the second as a seemingly endless line of security officers emerged from the building and spread outwards in all directions.

"News that the third triangle has been found on the Chinese coast brought fevered excitement to the streets of Beijing," Maria went on, talking as she walked backwards along with the largely Chinese press contingent who hadn't already fled at the first sign of hostility. "But all of that changed when these ELF security officers immediately began forcefully ordering all media personnel to stop broadcasting. As you can see, a large area around the headquarters has been cordoned off and the security staff are now pushing us further and further back. And this is *not* Chinese law enforcement, this is an ELF operation. An organisation which so recently seemed ready to *finally* begin opening up to the rest of the world appears to be reverting to type, and we can only guess what that means for the third trian—"

"American," a Russian-accented voice snapped. Maria turned to see a burly man in an ELF uniform. He raised a hand to capture his supervisor's attention, and quickly received a cut-throat gesture in reply.

Without any hesitation, the man ripped the large camera from the shoulder of Maria's colleague and threw it to the ground.

"German!" another officer called, raising his hand. Twenty metres to Maria's left, he threw yet another news camera to the ground.

Maria looked into her cameraman's eyes. Partly because no one was recording her words, but largely because of what had just transpired, her tone was far less powerful than before: "We have to get out of here."

V minus 26

Clark didn't have to hear what Jayson was saying to the deplorable Jack Neal to know that he was sticking to the plan. He peeked out carefully over the dashboard and saw that both men were facing in the opposite direction. Jayson held a thumb up behind his back, and Clark knew it was time.

He grabbed some tape and bandages from a first-aid kit in the glove box then charged out of Jayson's car, not one ounce of stealth, and tactically cut off Jack's path to his own car. If the rat tried to run away on foot, Clark would catch him in no time.

Foolishly but inevitably, this was exactly what Jack tried to do.

Jack lifted his phone from his pocket as he began to flee, but Jayson proved which side he was on once and for all by diving at Jack and just managing to grab hold of him tightly enough to wrestle him to the ground. He wisely knocked the phone away before Jack was able to initiate a call or send a message, then delivered several full-hearted blows to his blackmailer's head.

Jayson wasn't trained to throw these blows but Jack wasn't trained to receive them, so the effect of the wild punches was fairly significant. Clark walked over slowly, letting Jayson get some frustration out. After around five seconds he called him off and crouched over Jack's still-conscious but greatly weakened body, gazing down at a bloodied face devoid of any resistance. He taped Jack's mouth to stifle any calls for help.

"However much you hate him, you don't want to see this part," Clark whispered to Jayson. He didn't have to say it twice.

The next thing Jayson heard was by far the most blood-curdling sound his ears had ever encountered. Curiosity got the better of him, and he turned around to see Jack quite literally writhing in agony with both hands grasping his right knee. Clark crouched down again and bound Jack's hands with a long bandage, then did the same with his feet. The stifled noises coming from behind the tape covering Jack's mouth sent chills down Jayson's spine, but Clark appeared utterly unmoved as he picked the scoundrel up from the dirt and tossed him over one shoulder.

His next stop was the back seat of Jayson's car, and as soon as the doors were closed Clark ripped the tape from Jack's mouth.

"She's in a warehouse!" the rat squealed, as easily and pathetically as Clark had anticipated.

"Address," Clark demanded. Right now, nothing else mattered; there would be time to interrogate Jack about his motives and his partners once Tara was safe.

Jack hesitated, prompting Clark to slam a fist into his already shattered kneecap. In the driver's seat, Jayson fought an urge to throw up at the piercing scream that escaped Jack's uncovered lips.

Stuttering out the words, Jack gave an address that was no more than ten minutes away. Clark wasted no time in giving Jayson an order to set off, telling him not to worry about anything else. He immediately issued the same instruction to Phil Norris, who was silently and approvingly listening in on a still-live phone call.

"Your two men…" Clark said, wrapping a broad hand around Jack's pencil neck. "Get them gone. We know who you're working with, asshole… we know about the shell companies and the secret payments."

Even through his agony, Jack's expression changed with this revelation.

"Your game's over. I don't care who else goes down with you, but no one has to die today. And trust me, Jack…" Clark trailed off, releasing his neck and balling a fist over his knee once again.

"Please, no! Clark, I'll call them… please!"

"I didn't come out here without backup and I'm not going to this damn warehouse without backup, either, so if you know what's good for them you'll tell them to get the fuck out of there before we arrive," Clark boomed. "Like I told you, no one has to die today. But if anyone tries anything funny... if any of them are still there when my team rush in or if they hurt a *single* hair on that girl's head before they leave, trust me on this: with what I'll have in store for you, you'll be *begging* for death."

As Jayson helpfully handed Clark the phone he'd knocked out of Jack's hand, Clark pressed his empty fist into Jack's knee firmly enough to make him wince. He asked for and received first the passcode and then the name of the contact in the warehouse, then whispered something in Jack's ear too quietly for Jayson to hear.

Whatever was said, it immediately widened Jack's eyes and caused his lips to quiver like a child on the wrong end of a lecture. Above and beyond the pain he had earned so far, the promise of something a thousand times worse had clearly had the desired effect.

For the second time in barely twenty minutes, Clark held his breath as a phone call transpired. Once again, the caller was under duress — *his* duress — and once again the stakes could hardly have been any higher.

"No, no tricks!" Jack said after giving the initial order. "Listen to me, you fucking idiot: it's off. They're already on to the location. Leave Tara unharmed, and don't waste anytime clearing the setup because they already know — they know about the payments. If you stay there, you're dead... and if you hurt her, we're all dead. Just disappear!"

Clark exhaled deeply; Jack wasn't having to 'act' in the same way Jayson had, but he had at least been smart enough to stick to the script.

"Good," Jack said. "And don't forget what I know. If you do anything to fuck me here..."

Clark could only shake his head; Jack, an asshole to the bitter end, was even holding something over his own goons.

Never one to enjoy inflicting pain and never one to do so purely in anger, Clark took his hand away from Jack's knee.

What happened to the rat next was a decision for later.

All that mattered now was Tara.

V minus 25

Mirador Hotel
Roatán, Honduras

News of the third triangle's discovery came before Dan had even left the location of his interview with Poppy Bradshaw, and it immediately changed both the mood and his focus.

Kyle Young understandably asked for some words to broadcast on ACN — Dan's live reaction would be one hell of an exclusive — but after an interview that was physically painful as well as mentally exhausting, Dan reluctantly opted out.

Emma stepped in, partly to give Kyle something in exchange for all he'd done for them but primarily to call for a measured response. She already knew what was happening in China with foreign media being ushered away from the ELF building by overzealous security officers, and she feared that a firm reaction from GCC Chairman William Godfrey would be forthcoming.

With their ever-increasing certainty that the triangles were real after all, Dan and Emma should have been feeling excited anticipation of finally seeing clear images of them. The muddy waters of international and supranational politics made things far less positive, however, to the extent that Emma's first reaction was to fight the potential fire of an overreaction from Buenos Aires.

She said what she thought were all the right things to say: first, that it was a good thing that the triangles would be revealed to the public but a bad thing Ding Ziyang was freezing the GCC out just when it looked like bridges were being built. Second, she personally called on Godfrey not to overreact. She could and would make this point personally, but there was power in having the request out there in the open.

Kyle pushed with more questions but knew when to stop — Emma's expression made that only too obvious — at which point he continued with some thoughts of his own. With his friend and colleague Maria Janzyck out of commission in Beijing, his footage and comments were all that would fill American living rooms for the next several minutes.

Amid chaotic scenes, Dan McCarthy's mind turned to the Messengers. Where were they, and what the hell was going on?

Emma led him outside to the waiting car which would take them to their waiting plane, and she lifted her phone from her pocket to make a call. More in hope than expectation, she dialled the President of the United States.

President Slater answered the call so quickly that Emma knew she had already been holding her phone.

"Are you with Godfrey?" Emma asked.

"He's with the media team," Slater sighed. "What did Dan get from Poppy? Did she know anything about the triangles?"

Emma hesitated. "I'm going to tell you something in trust that you won't tell him, okay? Not yet. If you tell him this, he'll ask how you know. And if you tell him *that* — about Dan's power — he won't be grateful that you told him eventually... he'll be furious that you didn't tell him right away. The last thing the world needs tonight is for Godfrey to be any more riled up than he already is."

"My job tonight is making sure Godfrey doesn't do anything too drastic, so I'm already on board with that. But hurry up and tell me while I'm alone: what did you find out?"

"Cole is working with Jack Neal," Emma said.

"Son of a *fucking* bitch," Slater cursed.

Emma paused. "And so is Poppy Bradshaw."

This time, Slater reacted with a silence that spoke volumes.

"This is a mess, but it could be a *whole* lot messier than we thought," Emma said. "Somehow, I need to get Jack and Dan in the same room. I'm asking you to keep this quiet, and I'm hoping you'll bear in mind that I know Jack better than anyone — if he even thinks anyone is on to him, in any way, he'll do whatever it takes to make sure we don't find him. If he was standing on a cliff and he saw us coming, he would jump... so please, keep this quiet. The reason I'm telling you this is so you know that we've just made some major progress in finding out what's really going on here, and if this triangle hadn't just shown up and Ding hadn't reacted like this I would've said this trip had been a huge success. We have a next move, Valerie; that's what I want you to know. Whatever you have to do to keep Godfrey from going crazy tonight, *please* do it."

"I will," the President said. "And Emma... thank you."

V minus 24

"Stay in the car," Clark ordered, speaking to both Jayson and Jack. In reality, though, Jack and his injured leg were going nowhere.

At his instruction, Jayson had parked the vehicle around forty metres from the disused warehouse where Tara was apparently being kept, with Phil Norris parking around the same distance away in the opposite direction.

Before getting out of the car, Clark covered Jack's mouth with tape once again. "Don't look at him," he told Jayson. "And whatever the hell you do, don't talk to him. I'll be back in a minute."

Clark stepped outside and signalled to Phil. They'd come this far and Jack's instructions for his goons to disappear had certainly sounded firm enough to do the job, but Clark still knew much better than to go inside alone. Phil was no stranger to getting his hands dirty, and the very fact that he was still at Clark's side after everything that had happened showed that he could be counted on.

The fact that he'd come along in the first place despite his misgivings showed as much, really, but if there had been any doubts they were all gone now.

"You're going to drive her home," Clark said to Phil, pausing briefly at a door he fully expected to have to break through and refusing to even entertain the notion that he might find anything on the other side except Tara safe and well. "I don't want her to have to see either of those two again."

"Got it," Phil said. He gestured to the door. "Let's do this."

The door buckled under the effortless weight of Clark's shoulder, hinting that it hadn't been locked in any serious way.

Instantly, both men heard muffled cries for help. Neither had to search for the origin — at the very back of the desolate warehouse, they saw someone bound to a chair. The orange bucket that had been crudely placed over their head made it impossible to say for certain, but Clark recognised the muffled voice.

"Tara!" he called, sprinting over.

Her voice filled the room again, the tone this time very different.

Clark reached her and removed the bucket, revealing an understandably frightened and mascara-stained face that at the very least didn't look to have been injured. He unbound her hands from behind her back and untied her feet underneath the chair, allowing her to deal with the tape covering her mouth so that she was in control of its potentially painful removal.

She collapsed into Clark's chest before even removing the tape, however, too weak to even wrap her arms around him.

"You're safe now," Clark reassured her in a calm and gentle tone, relief and joy having momentarily overtaken murderous rage within him. He wanted to ask if they'd hurt her, but now wasn't the time; he would listen if she wanted to talk, of course, but that was for her to decide.

Tara slowly lifted her head and looked up at him. "What happened? How did you find me?"

"I'll tell you at home, but right now I just want you to know that everything is going to be okay. I know who was responsible and he's going to pay, but right now we're going to get you out of here. I have to deal with him, so I brought Phil along to drive you back to Birchwood. Ain't that right, Phil?" Clark asked, impatiently beckoning him over and simultaneously wondering why he was still standing at the entrance.

Walking with her head low, Tara reached Phil and hugged him. She didn't know him as well as she knew Henry or Mr Byrd, but he was here to help and that was what mattered.

"You're okay now, darling," Phil said. But as he spoke, he gestured over her head to Clark and pointed towards the wall to their right.

Clark glanced over and felt a flood of confusion and disbelief shake him to the core. He saw another chair sitting between an expensive-looking camera setup and a giant flag adorning the wall.

Jet black other than a small blue circle in the centre, the design was all too familiar to him as the flag of the GeoSovs.

"What the fuck…?" he mused, walking over. He had known that Jack was back involved with John Cole, but Jack and the *GeoSovs*? He then recalled Jack's tone when telling his goons over the phone that Clark knew about the payments… and now, in his mind, it seemed to Clark as though his knowledge of shady transactions between Jack and Cole might have been confused by Jack as knowledge of transactions between he and the GeoSovs.

Whatever this meant, Clark couldn't be sure. All he knew was that it also couldn't be good.

Instinctively, he took the phone from his pocket and snapped some photos of the scene before ripping the flag from the wall and lifting the camera to carry it away, too.

"Uh… any reason for that?" Phil asked, unsure it was a good idea to take anything away.

Clark shrugged. "We can always lose it. But if we don't take it now, we might wish we had."

At the doorway, by Phil's supportive side, Tara stopped in her tracks. "I'm sorry," she sobbed, turning to Clark. "They said Jack wanted Dan and Emma, so they targeted me because I'm weak. And I fell for it — for *him* — because I'm so fucking broken."

"You have nothing to be sorry for and it wasn't like that," Clark replied. "Tara, this wasn't a setup. Jayson fell for *you*, too, but Jack saw an opportunity. He's been working with Jayson to repair his image; and when he found out he could use Jayson to bring you somewhere isolated, he made him do it. This was Jack's work, and he's going to pay for it. Will you be okay hanging out in Phil's car somewhere quiet, maybe at the drive-in, until I come to get you in twenty minutes? One of us will pick your car up later, wherever you left it, but Emma's going to be home tomorrow and I really don't want anyone to know about any of this until then, so I don't want Mr Byrd seeing Phil bringing you home. Anyone includes Emma so we won't call her tonight, but I'll be back at the drive-in in no time and I'll stay with you at home all night. And Phil: when I say I don't want anyone to know… that's including and *especially* my old man, okay? I'll call you when I'm coming and you can let me know where you're waiting."

Phil nodded.

But in place of what would have been understandable anger, Tara's expression displayed nothing but confusion.

Ignoring everything else Clark had said, she glanced at the folded flag in his hand, which she evidently hadn't been able to see on the wall from her bound position. "Jack Neal… is with *them*?"

V minus 23

From the eerily deserted public square in front of the ELF's global head-quarters, a lone spokesman stood at a podium before a lone camera.

His walk to the podium was brisk and unceremonious, indicative of what was to come.

With the spokesman's ELF-branded attire very much at odds with the more common security officers' uniform, many would soon express their views that the military regalia look it conjured up in their minds was no accident.

Speaking in Chinese, with the words being translated live as they were beamed into homes around the world, the man got right into the meat of a very short statement. No words were wasted, with the succinct announcement confirming that the third triangle had indeed been discovered in Chinese territory.

Even more significantly came the news that it would be displayed before the world in a matter of hours, directly in front of the podium from which that news was currently being delivered.

Although issues surrounding the triangles' discoveries had been at the centre of feverish conjecture in recent days, the lack of clear images

297

and details regarding the physical objects themselves had led to certain elements being given less attention than they perhaps merited.

Much discussion had understandably revolved around the major questions of whether they were real and where the second and then third might turn up. What had gone largely *un*discussed so far was a question that would occupy the world until the moment of truth came: what, if anything, would happen when the three pieces of the complete object were reunited? The indentations on the Zanzibar triangle had made it fairly obvious that two more triangles would fit within it, and leaked reports from scientists who had seen the Vanuatu triangle suggested that its physical properties added even more weight to this assumption.

Citizens of the world were excited to see the triangles in reasonable detail for the first time, but many were even more excited to see them reunited as one. Speculation was rampant as to whether the triangles possessed powerful extraterrestrial properties that no one could even imagine; and as the hour drew nearer, this speculation would only grow.

One way or another, there wasn't long to wait until the world would find out.

V minus 22

With Jack Neal still restrained on the floor in the back of Jayson's car, Clark stepped out of the passenger side to bring his own car right alongside it. He bundled Jack from one vehicle to the other after scanning the quiet neighbourhood to make sure no one happened to be watching. As soon as this cargo transfer was complete, he locked his car and returned to Jayson.

"I'm sorry," the shamed actor sighed, shaking his head at the ground.

"You're lucky they didn't hurt her," Clark replied. "Now what you're going to do is go home, keep your mouth shut, and trust that this is over. Jack's done, and his goons are out of here. There wouldn't have been any problem without you, but there wouldn't have been a solution if you hadn't convinced Jack to come out to the woods. And that's what I need from you again now, understood? I need you to lie when you need to lie. When someone asks what happened, or if anyone ever says something that makes you think they might know something, you need to stick to the lie that you don't know what the fuck they're talking about. Are we clear?"

Jayson gulped and nodded several times. "Thanks."

This reply angered Clark — *what the hell was there to be thankful for?* —

but everything about Jayson screamed vulnerability and snapping at him again would achieve nothing. He was weak and had already paid a colossal emotional price for making the initial mistake of trusting his career regeneration to a maniacal PR guru who was quite possibly the worst person in the world.

"This is over, but Emma might want to talk to you when she gets home," Clark said. "If she does, I'll be there... because I was *here*, and I know what that scumbag had over you. Like I told you already: Jack is done. Your family is safe. That video thing you mentioned, I can't help you with that; but if it ever gets out, just say it's fake. Who cares, man? With the day you've just had, who gives a shit? You're alive and so is Tara. This could have gone a different way."

Jayson forced out a grunt of understanding.

"I just want to talk to your folks for a quick second before I go," Clark said, "just so *they* don't ask any questions." He was knocking on the door before Jayson had a chance to reply, and Mr Moore was there within seconds.

"We were wondering where you'd gotten to," the man said. He focused on Clark. "How did the lineup go? Okay? And him... is *he* okay?"

"He's been associating with some questionable types," Clark said, putting on a reluctant tone. "But I think he got a little bit of a fright today at the precinct, so that should straighten him up. Right, kid?"

Jayson raised his eyebrows and shrugged. "I've made mistakes, but I'm getting better."

"Come on, come in here for something to eat," his mother insisted from an unseen position. "Clark, you too!"

"Thanks, Mrs Moore, I would love to," Clark called in. "And any other time I would, but there's something else I have to take care of right now."

Mr Moore extended his hand towards Clark. "Thanks for keeping his problem today, you know, *hushed*. It hasn't been easy these last few years, and if the media had gotten hold of this..."

"He won't make a mistake like this again," Clark said, firmly shaking Mr Moore's hand before leaving their doorstep for the last time.

As Clark reached his car, Mr Moore called after him: "Oh, and Clark... crazy news about the triangle, huh?"

"Uh, yeah, hell of a crazy thing," Clark said. Once back in the car he immediately turned on the radio and proceeded to sit in rapt attention as the newsreader recounted the remarkable events that had been playing out in China while Clark was dealing with a more immediate problem much closer to home.

Even Jack perked up as he heard the news that not only had the third triangle just been discovered, but Ding Ziyang had already announced that his ELF scientists were going to publicly unite it with the other two in a matter of hours.

Clark didn't speak during the short drive home, until he arrived and breathed a deep sigh of relief that Henry's car wasn't there. This meant he could covertly get Jack into the house and down into the basement without anyone seeing or hearing a thing. "Time to move, asshole," he called into the back seat.

Jack mumbled something, repeatedly and annoyingly enough to prompt Clark to remove the tape for a few seconds.

Clark expected to hear something about the triangles, probably a bullshit lie Jack had been dreaming up during the drive to mess with his head. Instead, a simple question came: "Are you going to kill me?"

Clark placed the highly adhesive tape back across Jack's mouth. "I need you to be alive when Emma gets home," he said. "After that? I get the feeling it's going to be out of my hands…"

V minus 21

GCC Headquarters
Buenos Aires, Argentina

Seconds after stepping into Timo's private jet for their flight back to Colorado, Dan and Emma were surprised to see footage of William Godfrey standing before a large gathering in his GCC building's media room.

A text message arrived on Emma's phone, from none other than President Slater: "I haven't spoken to him. He didn't tell me he was doing this."

Emma's sigh said it all, but she tilted her phone's screen towards Dan so he could see for himself.

"I am shocked and appalled by recent events in Beijing," Chairman Godfrey began. "What should be a momentous discovery has been turned into a point-scoring exercise by a communist dictator with no regard for anything but political gain. The analysis of these triangles should have been conducted by a comprehensive international team, but what we have seen is the very opposite. The underpinning issue here is one of arrogance and exceptionalism of a kind the United States is so often accused of, but if you cast your mind back to the IDA leak you'll remember that President Slater humbly threw her weight behind the international effort. Ding Ziyang, on the other hand, has been exclusionary and triumphalist from the moment the first triangle was discovered in Zanzibar.

"Returning to the IDA leak, one particular element of the hoaxed confession of Hans Kloster sadly comes to my mind. We now know none of it was true, of course, but we all remember Kloster's claim that the Nazi hierarchy believed the four alien spheres he spoke of had been bestowed upon the party rather than upon humanity as a whole. None had been dropped in 'hostile communist lands', as the letter put it, just as none of these triangles have been found outside of ELF territory. The parallels are stark, and Ding Ziyang's dangerous exceptionalism knows no bounds.

"I don't mean to suggest that these triangles, like the spheres, are not truly extraterrestrial. But right now, whether they are taunting us with a fabricated hoax or whether they are about to complete a three-piece alien puzzle without allowing the rest of the world to analyse the triangles and the potential effects of their physical reunion, this flagrant move by the ELF is an act of international aggression which I will *not* take lightly.

"Along with the leaders of our member states, I am already appalled by the treatment of Western media personnel in Beijing. This room, right now, contains reporters from both sides of the Chinese-built divide between ELF and GCC states, and I would have it no other way! Our world, after all, is *one* world. No one wants to see any further escalation, and the door to cooperation is not locked on our side.

"But with that said, the message I wish to send to its citizens is a simple one: if tomorrow's event goes ahead, Ding Ziyang and Ding Ziyang alone will be wholly to blame for whatever happens next."

Dozens of questions were fired at Godfrey from all angles of his media room, but he ignored every last one and walked away with the calmest expression he could muster.

With the speech over, Dan sighed and reclined in his seat.

"Do you think we should tell him what we know about Jack?" he asked, waiting for the plane to take off. "I don't know how it would help, but I feel like maybe we should. And especially about the triangles being real... because he's still talking about it maybe being a hoax; but we know that neither Cole or Poppy is in on it, so it can't be."

Emma breathed deeply. "He's said it now, so we can't undo that. I told Slater so that she would have the option of telling him if she really thought it was necessary, like if he was going to do something else dangerous that he wouldn't have done if he knew this. We haven't kept this to ourselves, Dan, we've just been careful who we've told. Slater knows, so it's on her, too."

"But what are we going to do about Jack?"

"Find a way to get him to sit down with you, like I said to Slater," Emma replied. "Speaking of that stuff, does your head feel okay now? Do you want to try it on me?"

Dan shook his head. "It hurt even when I was only listening to Poppy's thoughts. I guess the one good thing about this triangle turning up when it did is that no one is talking about that sudden spasm and yelp I let out, huh?"

"I guess," Emma said, chuckling slightly before her serious expression returned. "But if Ding really is going to join the triangles tomorrow morning, and if they really *are* as real as we think... I think whatever does or doesn't happen could totally change our next move. So even if Jack is still in Colorado, I don't think we should try to make contact until tomorrow afternoon."

Dan gazed out of the window as the plane began to taxi, his mind suddenly focused in far deeper thought than before.

"What's on your mind?" Emma asked, noticing the sudden change in his demeanour.

"The Messengers," he replied without a heartbeat's hesitation. "You're talking about making contact... I'm wondering where the hell they are. They said they could talk to me from afar if they had to, even without their Elders letting them fly here. If they're watching, they must see the storm that's building, right? So why aren't they talking to me?"

Emma upturned her palms, openly out of answers. "Maybe they'll talk to you tonight, when you're dreaming," she said. The words were mainly spoken in the hope of calming Dan's mind rather than in expectation of being correct, and it looked for all the world like Dan's expectations were just as low.

"Yeah," he said, forcing the words out in a passably optimistic tone but saving the second part of the thought for himself: *fat chance.*

THURSDAY

V minus 20

McCarthy Residence
Birchwood, Colorado

Dan had a feeling something was wrong when Mr Byrd was the one to greet him and Emma from their plane in Denver, but his neighbour's repeated insistence that Clark was simply too tired to handle the drive seemed to come from a place of truth.

It did and it didn't, in reality, since Mr Byrd was repeating a lie he believed to be true. Such were the stakes and so high was the tension, Dan didn't feel at all conflicted in testing the veracity of Mr Byrd's words with a quick application of his esoteric ability, but he killed the connection as soon as he had this confirmation.

The full truth, which would come in time, was that Clark couldn't leave Birchwood while Jack Neal was locked in the McCarthys' basement. No one else knew of Jack's presence; not even Henry, who slept in the same house overnight, and initially not even Tara, who was still reeling from a horrifying ordeal perpetrated by Jack himself.

Clark had spent the night stewing over what he'd found in the warehouse and wondering what the presence of a GeoSov flag at Jack's crime scene meant in relation to the triangles and everything else. Phil Norris had so far kept everything as close to his chest as Clark had requested, not telling a soul about anything he'd seen the previous day. Jayson Moore, too, had wisely and understandably stayed quiet.

While Dan and Emma made their way back to Birchwood with Mr Byrd, Clark talked extensively to Tara about what was going to happen next. This involved telling her that Jack was in the basement in the house next door to the one in which she'd slept restlessly with Clark for company in the living room.

Emotionally shattered, she didn't react as Clark had thought she might: by running next door and descending into the basement to give him a warm slice of exactly what he deserved. Instead, she nodded slowly and said she was glad that Dan would have a chance to get inside his head.

"I think maybe when we've dealt with this and Jack is taken care of one way or another, you should talk to someone about what happened," Clark said. "Someone better at listening and talking back than me, you know? A professional, maybe?"

"*Emma's* almost home," Tara said. Something about the way she said this viscerally reminded Clark of the way Dan used to talk and think about him when they were growing up; like he could come in and solve any problem. But while Emma was as competent as they came and Tara was dealing with a traumatic experience far better than anyone could have expected, Clark couldn't shake the feeling that the emotions were bound to explode at some point.

With very little time remaining until the point at which Ding Ziyang had promised the world that the triangles would be revealed and joined together in full public view, Dan and Emma finally arrived home after a traffic-hit drive from the airport in Mr Byrd's car. He joined them inside the McCarthys' home, where he saw Phil and Henry sitting on the couch as a countdown on the TV told them there were only nine more minutes until a much-anticipated live broadcast was due to hit the airwaves from Beijing. Only Timo was missing from Dan's inner circle, with Clark having decided this was something he didn't have to be burdened with for now.

Tara took a few minutes to fix her makeup before going next door with Clark, keen to downplay things for Emma's benefit, at least for now. She explained this to Clark and in his mind it said a lot about Tara that she seemed to be worrying more about how her ordeal would affect Emma than anything else.

"Hey, guys," Dan said when he saw them.

Emma wasn't so easily fooled. Hurrying to Tara's side, she saw through the facade: "What's wrong?"

As the tears began and Clark's expression hardened like stone, he asked everyone to sit down and listen carefully, because he didn't want to tell the story twice.

$\sim$

After listening in growing disbelief and anger as the story of Tara's kidnap twisted and turned to its warehouse-based conclusion, Emma jumped to her feet and dashed across the room as soon as Clark revealed that Jack Neal was locked in the basement.

Clark caught up with her before she made it down to the chair Jack was humanely but securely bound to, ensuring that she wouldn't do anything *too* reckless before Dan had a chance to hear exactly what the scoundrel was thinking.

"Business is business," Jack said as soon as the tape was removed from his mouth, staring at Emma with a surprising defiance in his snake-like eyes.

She stopped in her tracks.

He had known she was coming, obviously and inevitably, and *this* was what he had chosen to say. Lashing out might not be something he *wanted* her to do, since he was bound and utterly defenceless, but it was more than likely what he expected.

Dan, seldom struck by violent urges, could barely resist the temptation to lunge at Jack and deal with him once and for all. Instead, he subtly touched his thumb to his middle finger and pointed at Jack.

"Does Cole know you're working with Poppy?" he asked.

"No," Jack replied, surprisingly straightforwardly.

He was telling the truth. This didn't *surprise* Dan given how clearly he had sensed Cole's hatred of the GeoSovs, but rather provided very welcome confirmation.

"And are the triangles real?" Dan asked, moving on without revealing Jack's thoughts to anyone just yet since he didn't want Jack himself to know about the power.

Jack gave a confused frown. "What the hell else would they be? And you should know, *you're* the Messengers' messenger boy!"

Whether he was right or wrong, Jack was again telling what he thought was the truth.

"One last question for now," Dan sighed, aware of how little time remained before the big moment in Beijing. "Were you in on the plot to take Slater hostage at the Buenos Aires Gravesen?"

At this, a broad grin crossed Jack's face. "Of course not," he lied.

"We'll deal with you later," Dan said, once again glancing at a clock on the wall before heading to the stairs and urging Clark and Emma to follow him.

Upstairs, with just a few minutes left, Dan quickly relayed Jack's unspoken answers to the others. There were no real surprises so far, and Emma was primarily relieved that Dan had been able to hear *anything* without feeling searing pain as he had the previous day.

"What are we going to do with him?" Henry asked, having stayed upstairs due to the lack of wheelchair access to the basement. Mr Byrd had stayed at his side in disbelief along with Phil, who didn't think he would have been able to refrain from decisive violence, and Tara, who couldn't face the thought of looking at Jack ever again. "What are we going to do once we've got everything we need, I mean. We have his phone, and Dan can hear what he's thinking."

No one else said what all of *them* were thinking.

Eventually, Emma broke the tension: "I'm not going to tell anyone to do it, but the world will be a safer place when he's dead."

Despite the weight of her words, the air in the room felt lighter once they were out. No one spoke against them.

"*We* will be safer when he's dead," she went on. "If you catch a poisonous snake in your bedroom, you don't let it out in the back yard and hope it won't come back. That man is a *virus*, and he's a virus with a grudge. If we hand him in to the authorities, there's a chance that he gets out. Even if that's a faraway eventuality, it's not a chance we want to take."

"Give him to Godfrey," Henry suggested. "Godfrey hates him already, let alone when he finds out he's working with Cole and the GeoSovs."

Emma shook her head. "Maybe my head isn't clear right now but I can't even contemplate giving him to anyone. If he's out of our sight, we're in his *sights*. Henry, he hates us so much, he kidnapped Tara... for what, to get to me and Dan? He's just... you can't think about him like you'd think about anyone else. He's working with the GeoSovs! I don't know if he really wants to see the world burn like they do, but he definitely wants to see Slater and Godfrey and all of *us* burn, and he doesn't care about collateral damage. He's given up on life... his grudges are all he has."

"Clark..." Phil said.

Clark inhaled sharply. "What?"

With an undisguised hand gesture, Phil called him over to the corner of the room. "If it really comes down to… you know, something having to *happen*…"

"Yeah?"

Phil looked at him intently. "Well if something has to be done it ain't exactly gonna be one of *them*, is it? What do you say, rock paper scissors?"

Clark studied Phil's eyes for a few seconds, trying to figure out whether he was serious. Those eyes had seen a lot, and Phil's hands had accumulated a lot of dirt over the years. Although he was a fairly warm man to those he knew and liked, Clark had grown up in the knowledge that Phil wasn't someone whose wrong side he wanted to spend too much time on.

Clearly, he was serious.

"Are you thinking that the winner *gets* to do this or that the loser *has* to?" Clark asked.

"Winner's choice," Phil replied. "*On* three, not after three. Okay?"

Out of sight of everyone else, the two men reached a highly uncomfortable decision in a way that would have felt disrespectfully flippant if it didn't relate to someone they considered on par with a viral infection.

"Rock beats scissors," Clark said, observantly rather than triumphantly.

Phil shrugged. "Well, I did say winner's choice…"

"If you wanted to do it, you would have volunteered. And I can't put this on you, Phil. You already helped out. So if something *does* have to be handled here, I'll handle it."

With a nod, Phil placed his right hand on Clark's left shoulder, then patted his left hand twice on Clark's right cheek. "You're a good man, son. A *good* man."

"Here we go, everyone!" Mr Byrd announced. "They're about to cut to Beijing!"

Everyone gathered around the TV, with Dan finding himself next to Tara. She leaned on him, quite literally, and said nothing as she breathed slowly.

"It's all going to work out," he promised. "We're past the worst of this. You *got* the worst of it, and you made it through. You're the strongest person here."

She looked up at him with a smile. "You always know the right thing to say. Is someone feeding you lines?"

Dan couldn't help but laugh loudly at this, drawing verbal rebukes from Henry and Clark along with a far-reaching punch in the arm from the latter. "Shut up!" they cried in unison.

Abruptly, the ACN studio feed finally cut to live coverage from the empty square outside of the ELF building in Beijing.

Empty of *people*, that was.

"Holy *shit*," Phil Norris gawped.

No one told him to be quiet, because he had taken the words right out of their mouths.

V minus 19

ELF Headquarters
Beijing, China

The sight was truly surreal as three metallic triangular prisms lay side by side, almost entirely filling the vast public square in front of the ELF's global headquarters. Two huge cranes were also present, evidently ready to position the smaller triangles inside the largest which had been found first of all on an unassuming beach in Zanzibar.

After around twenty seconds of silence, an ACN newscaster commented that they were receiving a raw feed from China, with all media organisations now banned from a wide exclusion zone around the building. The camera didn't zoom in close enough to reveal much detail on the triangles' surfaces, but everyone understood that there would be time for that later. The wide-angle shot framed everything nicely, giving a real sense of scale and spectacle.

"I'll let these pictures speak for themselves," the newscaster said, bowing out as a crane carefully lifted the middle-sized triangle with the help of some barely visible and fully removable attachments. This middle triangle fitted perfectly within the indentations on the largest, and its presence had an immediate effect.

Stunningly, the jewel-like markings on the outer triangle began to swirl around like a sea of shooting stars. The camera zoomed in on this, eliciting gasps from everyone in the McCarthys' living room and doubtless everywhere else, too.

As soon as the middle triangle was in place, the second crane lifted the smallest and prepared to complete the set.

Something was going to happen — that much was clear enough from what had already come to pass — but no one had any idea what that something might be.

"And now what we've all been waiting for..." the voiceover announced, punctuating an already tense moment.

At first, the effects of the triangular union were relatively low-key. Following a familiar pattern, the markings on the surface of the middle triangle began to swirl. The camera zoomed in again to capture this moment, which was still remarkable but naturally less breathtaking the second time around.

Then, however, the camera very suddenly zoomed out to its original wide-angle view as a steam-like substance began to emerge from the now-complete three-part object.

Viewers around the world gasped in awe, but this was nothing compared to what came next.

All of a sudden, the middle and inner triangles rose of their own accord, creating a tiered effect that resembled something between a pyramid and a wedding cake.

The ACN newscaster started to pass comment on this remarkable turn of events, but his words were cut off by a reactive and instinctive gasp as an incredibly bright beam of light shot upwards from the centre of the inner triangle. Laser bright and redwood wide, the beam left him lost for words.

Little did he know, the main event was yet to come.

While the man searched for some words to describe what he was seeing, the beam vanished as quickly as it had emerged. In its place, however, something even grander appeared in the sky above Beijing.

It was the single grandest sight anyone had ever seen, in both scale and meaning, and its sheer mass conjured up one word above all others. In this case, craft wouldn't do. Because for *this* craft, mothership was surely the only appropriate word.

As the colossal object descended slowly, its shadow grew wider until the whole area around the ELF's headquarters was cast into darkness.

Workers ran outside for a glimpse of the remarkable mothership, and the remote cameraman pointed directly towards it. Despite the immensity of its shadow the craft was still a great distance from the ground, highlighting just how unprecedented the scale truly was.

"There's only one thing I can think of to say," the newscaster commentated, his tone one of wonder rather than fear or anything else negative. "Ladies and gentleman... they're back."

V minus 18

McCarthy Residence
Birchwood, Colorado

"Guys guys guys!" Dan called, his voice urgent rather than pained. He waved his hand to silence the others then closed his eyes and placed his other hand across them. "They're talking to me..."

As Tara got to her feet to give Dan some space, Clark and Emma instinctively looked at each other.

"What do you mean it's not you?" Dan asked, disbelievingly responding out loud to a voice no one else could hear.

The looks around Dan, very suddenly, became grave.

Those looks, however, didn't come close to the expression of horror that fell upon Dan's own face a few seconds later.

He dropped his hand and opened his eyes. The words stuck in his mouth rather than his throat, a sudden and total dryness paralysing his tongue.

"What are they telling you, man?" Clark asked. "What did they say?"

Dan turned to Emma. "They're d-d-different aliens," he stammered. "*Hostile.*"

Part 6

THE SQUADRON

"The world is a stage,
but the play is badly cast."

Oscar Wilde

V minus 17

GCC HEADQUARTERS
BUENOS AIRES, ARGENTINA

As the screen in his office relayed the remarkable sight of a colossal alien mothership hovering over Beijing, William Godfrey nervously picked at his lower lip in a way President Slater had never seen.

"What the hell is going on?" she asked, thinking out loud rather than anticipating any informed reply. "Why are they *there*?"

The office door swung open seconds later. Both knew it could only be Godfrey's longstanding and well-trusted assistant Manuel — no one else had the access key — so neither were remotely surprised when a familiar voice announced his presence.

"Sir, Madam President, should we call on our member states to be ready for a unified emergency response?"

Slater turned to the beleaguered GCC Chairman. "I'm going to have to do *something*, William," she said. "It may as well be unified."

Godfrey shook his head. "They're in Beijing, not Buenos Aires, and that can mean one of two things: either they have a message and they've chosen to give it to the ELF over not only us but also McCarthy, which I doubt very much, or they've finally seen what we see."

Manuel, fidgeting uneasily in the doorway, shared a glance with President Slater. "Which is...?" he asked.

"That the ELF is a stain on our planet," Godfrey grunted. "Maybe these triangles were a test and maybe Ding failed by keeping them all for himself like a fat little shit with a birthday cake. And I'll tell you this, Manuel: if the Messengers are here to deal with our little ELF problem, we're not rushing to step in."

V minus 16

Quite understandably but equally overwhelmingly, everyone gathered tightly around Dan as his expression remained more focused than any they had ever seen before.

"I can't hear anything else," he said, straining his closed eyes tighter and tighter in an effort to change that. "They just said it's not them and that the Squadron aren't our friends. They're hostile, but I don't know who to. Us, the ELF, the Messengers... the connection is gone, like it just stopped working."

"Did you just say *Squadron*?" Clark asked. The question was so short and clear, it broke through many more that the others had been throwing at Dan while he strained silently. The depth of Clark's voice helped, too.

Dan's eyes opened. He looked straight at Clark and nodded. "Definitely. They said '*the Squadron*', clear as day."

"They must know the military connotations of that word," Clark said, turning to Emma and blowing air from his lips. "But either way, one craft isn't a squadron."

"*The* Squadron," Dan replied, like this distinction was a lot more important than it sounded. "The way they said it, it seems like the

Squadron is the name they use for this race or group or whoever the hell is inside that thing. Just like we call *them* the Messengers. There aren't necessarily going to be more ships."

Phil Norris, standing stoically with his arms folded, offered up a thought that had been uttered by all kinds of people in alien-related discussions since Dan first found Richard Walker's folder on Winchester Street to kick the whole thing off: "If those things wanted to hurt us, we'd already be dead."

No one immediately took issue with this, even Dan, but Emma sat down and lifted her phone from her pocket. The point Phil made was *such* a familiar one, it made her mind wonder what everyone else was saying right now. She opened her Social Media Meta Analysis app and perused data regarding the immediate public reaction.

Words like 'fear' and 'invasion' dominated the word cloud, but the presence of others like 'comet' and 'helped' suggested that a lot of users were bearing in mind that the Messengers had a history of benevolence. What they didn't know, of course, was that the Messengers had just told Dan the mothership wasn't theirs.

The highlighted top-trending post of the moment was from the actress Kaitlyn Judd: *"I've seen this movie before, and the aliens who arrive in something looking like that aren't usually the kind who challenge us to a game of basketball."*

Due to the mixed reactions coming in to the unfolding events in China, the estimated overall mood of related discussion fell within the section of the SMMA spectrum marked 'apprehensive excitement'. Had the whole world known what those inside the McCarthy family living room knew, Emma imagined the fear levels would be off the charts.

"Maybe we should tell Slater and Godfrey what the Messengers just told you," Tara suddenly interjected. "Because Dan, if these things *are* hostile…"

Dan looked at her with a conflicted expression on his face. "I know, but Phil just said it best. They're here, and they're not attacking us."

"Well," Emma said, looking up from her phone. "They're not *here*; they're in China. There is a chance — just a chance — that they're either only hostile to the ELF or they're only going to be *friendly* with the ELF, which could make them hostile to *us*. And I wasn't in your head when you heard the words, but for the Messengers to use a term like 'the Squadron'… that makes me think these things might at least be the same *kind* of aliens, you know? Race, species, whatever you'd call it. Maybe… I dunno, a different *faction*? If their Elders are dead or still just unresponsive, there could be a power vacuum on New Kerguelen."

"Jesus," Clark groaned. "Just what we need, more goddamn factions."

"I'm just spit-balling, I don't necessarily think this is right," Emma said, trying to reassure him.

With Dan no longer surrounded like the weirdest animal in the zoo now that the others knew he had lost his connection to the Messengers, he set off towards the basement neither trying to be noticed or caring if he wasn't.

"Why are you going back down there?" Tara asked, rising and rushing to catch up with Dan. She held on to his arm.

"I just want to find out if he knows anything else," Dan said. "Don't worry, I'll close the door behind me; you won't have to hear his voice or anything."

Tara shrugged. "It's not that. It's just... how would it even make sense for him to know anything else? They just arrived."

Dan searched for a response. "I... well, maybe there's..." he stammered for a few seconds before sighing deeply. Everyone was looking at him again. "I... I don't even know."

"Look!" Mr Byrd called, his ever softly spoken voice at odds with the urgent and sharp tone. Apparently having been the only one *not* looking at Dan, he had been the first to see what was happening now in China.

Whatever the newly unfolding scenes precisely meant, they were anything but a welcome sight.

Dan could only gulp.

From beside the couch, Clark summed it up best: "Well, I guess now we know why the Messengers called them the Squadron..."

V minus 15

From his new office in Havana, the ELF's controversial Western Secretary tried in vain to follow three conversations at once.

Not only was John Cole on the phone to one of Ding Ziyang's senior advisors, he was also issuing text-based orders to his media team via his computer while listening to incoming news from an aide of his own who was standing in the doorway.

The present aide had been getting the least of Cole's attention, but that all changed when he relayed a specific piece of news. Due to the position of Ding's advisor deep inside the ELF building in Beijing, Cole's aide in Havana got the news first and broke it immediately:

"Sir, the mothership just released five smaller spacecraft. We don't know what they want and we don't know where they're going, but they left in different directions."

By the time Cole had heard this once, he was hearing it again over the phone as the news of what was happening outside the building reached Ding's advisor. Cole put the phone down, stepped away from his computer, and unmuted the TV on his wall.

The screen was split, with the left side showing a live scene in Beijing that didn't look any different from what he'd seen the last time he looked up a few minutes earlier. On the right, however, ACN was showing a looped replay of the moment when five saucer-like spacecraft had emerged from the underside of their mothership's centre and dispersed for their unknown destinations.

"One has stopped at the Chinese coast!" an off-screen ACN newscaster revealed, shrieking out this development the instant it reached him. "It's hovering exactly where the third triangle was found, which gives us a good clue as to where two of the other four craft are currently headed!"

The newscaster spoke with an excitement better suited to a sports commentary gig, Cole couldn't help but think, particularly given the unclear motives of the alien visitors.

Within no more than a few minutes, which were filled by intense speculation and trance-like focus on the new live satellite-based tracking map which showed the crafts' movement, that map showed that one of the remaining four craft had stopped over Vanuatu.

Following different paths, one of the others was heading East towards the Americas while the others were heading West. Very soon after the second took up a hovering position over Vanuatu, the third craft stopped somewhere less expected: not Zanzibar, but Moscow.

"*Moscow?*" Cole asked, turning to the aide who was now by his side and gazing at the screen just as intently, rather than standing awkwardly in the doorway as he had been at first.

"ELF European Office," the man said. "Which means…"

He didn't have to finish the thought, and neither did Cole.

After the fourth craft positioned itself over Zanzibar, surprising no one, all eyes turned to the movement of the fifth.

Buenos Aires, Cole willed the still-moving craft. *Come on… just stop over Buenos Aires.*

If Cole had explored this thought he would have realised that it marked a turning point in his outlook; rather than wishing for the spotlight and attention that would come with the craft stopping directly above him, he craved the degree of reassurance that would come from knowing that the aliens weren't only interested — for one reason or another — in ELF-based sites.

Alas, the craft's direction of travel as it crossed the United States dismissed Buenos Aires as a futile hope. There was no doubt where the fifth craft was going — or coming, from Cole's perspective — and the best place to see its arrival was not on a TV set.

John Cole and his aide rushed through the still-unfurnished corridor outside his hastily opened office and continued to the edge of the building. They stepped outside without any hesitation and saw a great number of local police and ELF security officers already in attendance. Very few civilians were anywhere to be seen, with the atmosphere very much one of calm-before-the-storm tension rather than excitement.

The behaviour of the aliens piloting the mothership and its series of nested craft certainly didn't have much in common with that of the Messengers who had touched down in Colorado with little fanfare before stepping out and walking on Earth like it was something they did all the time.

On the contrary, the sheer scale of the mothership suggested, to Cole's mind at least, that the intimidation factor was no accident. They couldn't *not* know how intimidating it would be to cast such an enormous shadow over the capital city of the world's most populous nation, he reasoned, and he could think of no reason why the Messengers would ever want to act in such a way.

Cole didn't just have more questions than answers; he had *all* questions and *no* answers. Standing opposite the imposing monument from which he had addressed a huge crowd at Dan McCarthy's side just days earlier, his mindset and the external atmosphere could scarcely have been any different. No longer was there a sense of triumphalism within him and a sense of eager anticipation around him.

Now, all was trepidation.

And although he wasn't personally looking at any screens or engaged in any phone conversations as the fifth craft drew ever closer to Havana, Cole knew when it was close; the change in body language among the police and security officers — who *were* in touch with people monitoring the craft's path — made this only too obvious.

Sure enough, when shoulders tightened and weapons were raised, John Cole's life had only around fifteen seconds of anything resembling normality remaining.

Beyond that, as the alien craft first appeared as a speck and grew ever larger as it approached and descended, he knew that nothing would ever be the same again.

V minus 14

As stunned as anyone by the arrival of five small spacecraft in Havana and elsewhere, Emma hurriedly and focusedly opened a chat app on her phone with one thing in mind.

She typed a quick message to a new group containing some low-level media personnel at the GCC and also Maria Janzyck, who was still in China and had built up a series of her own low-level contacts within the ELF during her time there. Emma asked very simply what they were all hearing, and the answers didn't surprise her.

The primary fear among individuals on both sides, so typical of the political nonsense that had been frustrating the general public for so long, was how these developments could negatively impact *their* side relative to the other rather than how they could impact the planet as a whole.

Within the GCC, Emma learned, a common fear was that the arriving aliens might be set to share wisdom and technology with the ELF; a move which would decisively swing things in their favour... if the aliens' arrival over five ELF-administered locations hadn't already done so.

On the other side, meanwhile, Maria Janzyck reported that some

Beijing-based ELF sources were telling her that their superiors feared a far-out scenario involving Dan himself. Their extraordinary concern centred on the possibility that Dan — in their eyes too friendly with senior GCC figures — had used his close relationship with the Messengers to convince them to take up arms against the nations of the ELF.

Emma relayed all of this to a roomful of shaking heads, none of whom could believe the level of self-obsessed convoluted nonsense that went through the minds of their planet's political leaders.

More to the point, in fact, they *could* believe it only too well and collectively lamented how unsurprising it all was.

"Have you spoken to Timo?" Dan asked, mentioning a name that had slipped most of the others' minds. "He has contacts, too. Actually, how far out of the loop *is* he? He doesn't know we have Jack, but does he know I found out about Jack being linked to the GeoSovs? Last I heard about that, his team who were looking into all the hidden companies and payments hadn't found much on Poppy at all."

Clark shook his head. "They still haven't, at least not that I know of. And I didn't tell him about Jack… I trust him, but that was one of those things that had to stay as close to our chests as possible."

Emma, satisfied with what she'd found out via her contacts and now keen to do something about it, turned to Dan. "So we're not telling Timo anything for now, but what do you want to tell Godfrey… and when? He doesn't know about the telepathy, or about Jack working with Poppy *or* Cole — let alone being linked to *both* of them. My gut says it would be dangerous to say too much right now because he'll be angry we didn't tell him and even angrier that Slater didn't tell him after we told *her*, and right now an angry Godfrey could do something *very* regrettable and *very* un-take-backable, if you know what I mean."

Dan took several quick but shallow breaths, trying to capture enough air to stop his lungs from feeling empty. The stress and pressure of the moment — one he didn't think he could influence in a positive way — was becoming too much.

"This is my worst nightmare," he sighed, "back to having to watch something on the news and being powerless to do anything about it. But right now, this very second, I *have to* see who or what comes out of those spacecraft; if anyone does at all. I need to see if they're going to land or do anything else, because until I know what the hell is going on I can't dive in by doing something that could make everything worse and that I might regret two minutes later when I find out something new. I could tell Godfrey everything, I could tell everyone everything, or I could try to meet these other aliens if they come out. It depends on what *they* do."

"So what do you *think* they'll do?" Clark pushed. "Land and come out? Start blowing stuff up? And okay, I get that these guys aren't the Messengers, but why did the Messengers stop talking to you after they told you that one thing… and where the hell *are* they?"

Dan McCarthy could only shrug, because this final question was the one stumping him most of all.

V minus 13

"*No* emergency response," William Godfrey reiterated, this time very firmly. "Not until we see what they're here to do."

President Slater, by now talking to Godfrey via phone while she sat in another of the GCC building's many secure offices with other key members of her administration, had been on the receiving end of equally firm calls and suggestions in the opposite direction during the last few minutes. "That craft is barely 100 miles from mainland Florida!" she told him, reiterating a point that had been made to her by military and security personnel who saw allowing the continued presence of a questionably motivated vessel so nearby as an intolerable risk.

"Don't start fights you can't win," Godfrey replied, more soberly. This was a phrase he considered often in his own mind and one he had memorably used on Emma Ford during her days as an antagonist in his life's story, but never had it felt more pertinent than it did now.

Slater hesitated, listening to the words of a key ally and relaying them: "William, if a lion is slowly prowling towards you in the middle of the savannah and all you have is a bow and arrow... do you use what you have, or do you do nothing and hope the lion wants to be your friend?"

"How about you do nothing in the belief that it's really prowling towards the person next to you?" the GCC's embattled Chairman replied. "Because if these lions are hungry, they didn't come to *our* table to get their fill. Let's not make any new enemies, shall we? I can imagine the kind of pressure the war-hawks are putting on you right now, but this is the time to be strong. I'm not asking you to listen to me, I'm just begging you *not* to listen to them. Valerie, if you're going to listen to anyone right now, call Dan and listen to him. He'll be on my page here."

In the nearby office where Slater had set up shop, a few supportive heads nodded around her. Some faces were less enthused, already resentful of how much Dan had been in Slater's ear recently when certain big decisions were needed. There was no obvious hint that the aliens would emerge from any of their spacecraft imminently, but there was likewise no let-up in the tension as the possibility remained that they very well might.

Slater's allies all understood that Dan had recently prevented a catastrophic incident at the nearby Gravesen hotel, and they largely put her faith in his views down to a debt of gratitude she felt towards him. In reality, of course, she knew that he had ways of knowing things no one else could.

Hoping beyond hope what the answer would be, she dialled Emma Ford's number and got ready to deliver to Dan what was sure to be the most important question he had ever been asked…

V minus 12

With most of the world's attention focused on the alien craft hovering like a hungry hawk over John Cole's Cuban office, each passing minute took the tension to all new levels.

"The longer nothing happens, the sooner you're gonna have to do something," Clark mused, no need to specify that he was talking to Dan. "Even just *say* something... because seriously, man, people are gonna start going crazy if these things just stay there in the sky. And Beijing? Our news stations aren't showing that anymore but millions of people are stuck in the shadow of a giant spaceship *right now*. That can't go on forever with nothing happening."

"Hello?" Emma said, answering a call so quickly that the ringtone didn't even sound.

Everyone fell silent and turned to her, knowing she wouldn't have picked up unless the caller was one of the very few people she would deem worthy of attention at a time like this; not that there had ever been a time quite like *this*.

"Slater," she whispered, handing the phone to Dan.

Without reluctance, he accepted it and listened to what she had to say. After all that had happened he was well past considering how

334

surreal it was that the President of the United States not only cared about his opinion but actively sought it out in times of crisis.

The question Slater asked was one Dan had seen coming, but that didn't make it any less disconcerting to hear. The answer, though, was clear in his mind and took no thought or effort to deliver: "Under no circumstances should you order a strike or any other kind of military action against any of these spacecraft. China is China; if they do something, the aliens might only take it out on them. But if *you* do something…"

"Do you know anything else?" Slater asked. The straightforward wording and even more so the straightforward tone made it difficult for Dan not to automatically share the Messengers' revelation of apparent hostility on the Squadron's part, but then he realised that President Slater — like everyone else — wasn't even clear on the Messengers/Squadron distinction.

He gulped, looked at Emma, and decided to unload. "Well, as soon as the mothership appeared I got a—"

Mid-sentence, Dan fell to the ground.

He wasn't grasping any part of his body as had sometimes been the case during previous instances of contact, but his eyes fell immediately and disconcertingly closed.

Emma, gravely concerned, was first to his side. Within seconds, though, she was knocked off balance by a very uncharacteristic nudge from Rooster. Having rushed over as quickly as his old paws would carry him, the dog stopped at Dan and began to whimper frantically. This worrying performance lasted only a few more seconds, however, until Rooster turned towards the basement and barked furiously at the door as though he could see a cat stealing food from his bowl.

"Oh, *shit*…" Clark groaned, sprinting towards the basement. When he opened the door, Rooster surprised everyone by running down the steps. Far from scared away by an apparent alien intervention, he was emboldened by rage or something like it.

The barking got louder and louder, to the extent that Clark didn't know what he would find when the floor and Jack Neal's holding chair came into view.

His first guess proved correct: the chair was empty, and Jack was gone.

The Messengers took Walker away because he was a problem, Clark tried to tell himself. *They weren't on his side, they wanted him out of the picture. That makes sense here, too. That makes all kinds of sense…*

"Clark!" Emma called. "Get up here. Dan's moving, but we can see Jack."

"Huh?" he called back, dashing to the steps as quickly as he had in the opposite direction. "Did they put him outside or something? What the hell is going on?"

Emma took a deep breath, staring glumly at Clark while Dan pushed himself to his knees and the TV screen told the story. "Look," she said. "Jack's outside, alright, but not here. The son of a bitch is in Havana."

V minus 11

ELF Western Office
Havana, Cuba

Standing out in the open beneath a hovering alien spacecraft, John Cole turned around in reaction to a great deal of commotion and quickly saw what everyone else was looking at. Although human, the identity of the individual standing in the doorway of the ELF's Western Office was almost as great a surprise as anything else could have been.

"Jack?" Cole said, disbelieving that the man who had once served as his chief Prime Ministerial advisor was here. The building was a secure site — one of the most secure Cole had ever entered — and the relationship between his foreign diplomatic consultancy business and Jack's myriad PR firms was anything but public.

How Jack had gotten into Cuba unnoticed, let alone into the building, was one major question in Cole's mind. The other, equally strong, was *why* the hell Jack was so publicly standing before him like this when their working agreement was underpinned by a binding No Public Association clause.

Cole had fallen into high-level politics more or less by chance when his single-issue campaign pushed the right social buttons in the north of England several years earlier, but even through his many faux pas and embarrassments he had developed some degree of political where-

337

withal. He knew enough to know that his reaction to Jack's entirely unexpected presence would go a long way to determining how everyone *else* would react — including the dozens of surrounding officers with raised weapons and tense expressions. Indeed, once the initial momentary shock of seeing Jack had hit, many of their glances were now directed towards Cole to see whether *he* saw the controversial man's appearance as cause for alarm.

"It's okay," Cole said, hand-gesturing for the police and security staff to turn away from Jack and back towards the imposing craft overhead. He didn't know if anything about Jack's presence really *was* okay — he didn't know what it meant, or even how it had come about — but any sign of interpersonal suspicion, let alone conflict, was the last thing anyone needed when a direct *interspecies* interaction seemed imminent.

Jack walked slowly to Cole's side, looking far happier than anyone could understand given the gravity of the unfolding situation. He then gazed down at his own knee and smiled even more widely as he belatedly realised that the severe injuries it suffered at Clark McCarthy's hands — or feet, to be more precise — had been miraculously healed. As he stopped and patted Cole on the back, however, a deeper kind of knowing satisfaction crossed his face.

"What the fuck is going on?" Cole whispered. He pretended to scratch his nose in order to cover his mouth as he spoke, making use of a trick he'd learned from Jack himself.

Without answering directly, Jack issued a hand gesture of his own. His was similar to Cole's 'lower your weapons' downward hand movement of moments earlier, but its target and result could hardly have been more different.

More to the point, they could hardly have been more remarkable.

For in response to Jack's gesture, to the amazement of everyone in attendance and the billions watching around the world, the craft hovering above the ELF's Western Office began to descend. It moved steadily until it reached the ground, at which point a long ramp emerged; not too dissimilarly to the one so familiar from a previous alien landing at the Birchwood drive-in.

This craft was slightly larger and shaped slightly differently to the one everyone remembered so well, but there were enough similarities for the assumption to stand that the aliens inside were the same *kind* even if not the very same ones.

Confirmation of this assumption — both parts — came mere seconds later when two humanoid extraterrestrial beings appeared at the top of the ramp. They looked for all the world just like the Messengers, with the only visual difference being that their skintight tunic-like garments were shaded in a gentle sky blue rather than the more clinical white of their counterparts.

"What *is* this?" Cole asked, stunned by the sight before him. No small part of him wanted to run away and the fear within him was so great that he didn't even consider how weak he would look for doing so; the only reason he stayed frozen on the spot was his knowledge that trying to flee would be futile and might even anger the aliens.

Having ignored Cole's earlier question, Jack brazenly replied to this one with no effort to cover his mouth or lower his volume: "Don't worry, John," he said, placing a scrawny hand on his former boss's bulky shoulder. "These ones are on *our* side, and *I'm* in charge now…"

V minus 10

McCarthy Residence
Birchwood, Colorado

All around the McCarthys' living room, silence circled. Tara watched through her fingers while most of the men held a hand covering their mouths in sheer shock and fear.

The aliens hadn't just *taken* Jack, they had healed his injured knee and were seemingly following his orders. Of everything Dan had considered possible, nothing had come close to this. He was sitting sheepishly on the couch next to Tara, still recovering from a debilitating but fortunately brief lightning bolt of pain that had hit when the Squadron fleetingly intervened to remove Jack from the basement. Rooster lay at Dan's feet, looking up and clearly worrying about his friend.

Emma's words from earlier in the day echoed uncomfortably in Dan's mind, focusing his fears: Jack Neal was a grudge-driven virus, and one which posed a grave threat whenever it was loose.

Now that Jack was not just loose but apparently in command of a hostile alien fleet, the danger he posed was almost unimaginable.

"Emma..." Dan said, breaking the most uncomfortable silence he had known since first learning of Richard Walker's hoax, "it's time to call Buenos Aires. I need to tell Godfrey everything."

"Damn right," Clark chimed in, his eyes glued to the remarkable scenes in Havana. "But not just that, you also—"

"I know," Dan interrupted, gulping at the weight of the thought in his mind. "I also need to tell Slater I'm almost ready to take back my answer from a few minutes ago, because with Jack in their ears it might really be time to start thinking about a pre-emptive strike."

V minus 9

Jack Neal encouraged John Cole to stay by his side as he set off to meet the two familiar-looking aliens halfway between his starting position and their ramp some thirty metres away.

Cole stood on the spot until Jack tugged at his arm and made the case: "Come on, John, think of the visual! You and me, the ultimate thumbs in Godfrey and Slater's eyes."

Once again, the widely loathed PR man made no effort to conceal his words from the few cameras pointing his way while most of the others remained fixed on the aliens. Belatedly, Cole walked with him.

Security personnel watched the two men approach their alien counterparts and stop mere feet from their faces. The events of Contact Day had been replayed so many times that this almost felt like a rerun in a different place and with two humans set to converse with the aliens instead of one.

John Cole's heart was in his mouth as he stared into the wide, intelligent eyes of an extraterrestrial being. It was a Messenger, or at least of the same race, its identical physical makeup told him. It extended a hand for him to shake, just as one of the Messengers had done in front of Dan McCarthy a year earlier. The alien in front of Jack outstretched its hand too, and both men reached out in unison to formally greet their visitors from afar.

"We need to talk," Jack spoke to his alien. It looked at him blankly. "Talk," he repeated, pointing to his neck to suggest a cable of the kind the Messengers had used to communicate with Dan.

Although their expressions didn't change, it immediately became clear that the aliens understood. One stepped behind the other and produced a cable from an unseen pouch at the back of its tunic.

"And me," Cole said, pointing to his own neck.

Jack waved his finger in a 'no no no' motion he hoped would be galactically universal. He then put a hand on Cole's chest to stop him from getting what he considered too close to the aliens.

"What the hell are you doing?" Cole asked, mindful not to appear overly aggressive given the tension of the armed officers and the red lights of the live TV cameras but furious with Jack's desire to hog this remarkable opportunity for interspecies communication.

"Trust me on this, boss," Jack pleaded. For the first time, he then covered his mouth to hide his words from prying eyes and lenses. "There's a long game and you'll see the forest for the trees soon enough. I'm going to ask them to let ELF scientists study one of them and to let some of your people on to their craft. *I* already know they're on our side and not McCarthy's, but that's the kind of thing the world needs to see to know it for sure."

Jack's use of the word boss, as transparent an attempt at ingratiation as it would have been had Cole's head been in the right place, did the trick. It did confuse Cole more than a little that Jack referred to the 'other side' as McCarthy's rather than Godfrey's or the GCC's more generally, but that seemed like a small point in the context of the many *huge* points of unanswered confusion all around him.

But despite his own position as the ELF's Western Secretary and Jack's utter lack of any official role, Cole could see that for some reason the aliens clearly were keen to talk to Jack. His gesture had brought them to the ground, after all, and his sudden appearance remained an unexplained mystery.

Stepping aside only slightly, Cole watched on in conflicted anticipation as one alien connected the other to Jack Neal via a cable and a process familiar to everyone from the famous Birchwood footage.

John Cole's questions were many, and he could only hope the answers were coming soon.

V minus 8

Rather than Chairman Godfrey, Emma made a call to President Slater's phone; before Dan could talk to Godfrey, one thing had to be absolutely certain.

"Emma," Slater said, picking up immediately. Her words, on loudspeaker, rang through the living room. "What... the... hell?"

"We were already thinking the problem with the Messengers' Elders might have led to a power vacuum or factional disagreements," Emma replied, wasting no words or seconds, "and this all but confirms it. What we know for sure is that Jack has been working with the GeoSovs. He kidnapped Tara and Clark had been holding him here since dealing with that. All of that can wait, though. These new aliens... the Messengers call them the Squadron. Dan was about to tell you that when he got knocked out by the pain when they came for Jack, but now that Jack is in their ears, doing nothing is no longer an option. What I need to know is whether you've told Godfrey you know anything yet about Dan's power and what he learned with it — about Jack working with Cole, or about Jack working with the GeoSovs."

"No," the President said. "I'm dealing with the national security side of things at the moment because the calls for action were deafening even before the craft landed. Are you going to tell him?"

"Dan is; we just had to make sure you hadn't already, so we're singing from the same hymn sheet. I have one idea that could get us somewhere, so please try to hold off on anything irreversible for now, okay?"

"What's the idea?" Slater understandably asked.

In the McCarthys' living room, everyone else wondered the same thing.

"To tell Cole that Jack's working with the GeoSovs," Emma said. "I don't think he knows, and Jack seems to trust him. Trusting *Cole* isn't my idea of an ideal play, but if he's the only tool at our disposal right now then we might just have to use him. We could ask him to keep Jack from doing anything too crazy — at least until we know exactly what's going on with these aliens. The Messengers spoke to Dan when the mothership arrived but haven't said anything since, so we're hoping every second that they might give us more. The key thing is that Cole is going to feel betrayed, because he and everyone at the ELF hates those damn GeoSovs just as much as we do, so as much as he hates *us* he could still be receptive."

Clark nodded approvingly at this idea, as did a few others. Dan understood the logic, but the inherent risk of telling Cole too much certainly wasn't lost on him.

"I like it," Slater said, "but how about this: you two start trying to get in touch with Cole right now and *I'll* deal with Godfrey. I'll tell him everything and I'll present it as though I just found it all out... I'll say you called me because you trust me more than you trust him, which isn't even a lie. For everyone's interests, Emma, I feel as though it's better for him to bear some resentment towards you right now than for him to bear it towards me. But the main reason I think *I* should tell him is so you can try to reach Cole immediately, because that's the most important thing and it might not be easy."

Emma turned to Dan, looking for his approval. She got it in the form of a curt nod. "Agreed," she said to Slater. "You get to Godfrey, I'll get to Cole."

The sound of Emma's deep exhalation was the loudest in the room as the call ended.

"Why does it always have to get so damn complicated?" Tara lamented from the couch. "If no one lied, there would be none of this crap about keeping track of who knows what."

Dan in particular pondered these words, having thought similar things on countless occasions of late but having never been able to put it so succinctly. He didn't reply, instead sitting up straight in amazement as the TV relayed footage of a Cuban police officer and an ELF security officer stepping inside the alien craft along with one member of the Squadron.

Jack, now disconnected from the other, stood gleefully at its side and explained to the watching cameras that the aliens were granting open access to their technologies and had even agreed to be physically tested by local medical experts. This would both infuriate and terrify the GCC hierarchy, and the smug grin on Jack's face suggested that not only did he *know* this, it was the whole point.

Emma, while watching Cole's equally confused expression on live TV, wasted no time in trying to call him. She did so from Jack's phone, still in Clark's possession, having unlocked it using the passcode he'd given to Clark under more than a hint of duress.

She needed access to Jack's phone to get Cole's number — this was naturally better than going through a low-level ELF contact and hoping they could reach Cole — but she chose to *call* from it rather than use the number on another phone for two reasons. First was that she imagined a man in Cole's position doubtless used a similar digital assistant to herself, delivering only calls from the most important contacts and sending everyone else straight to voicemail. The second and supporting reason was that even if Cole *didn't* have any restrictions on incoming calls, seeing one from Jack's number would surprise the hell out of him since Jack was right there in Havana and clearly not using his phone.

With these considerations in mind, Emma made the call. She did so more in hope than expectation that he would answer, so wasn't too surprised to reach his voicemail after several rings. He probably couldn't hear it or feel the vibration among all the commotion, she reasoned.

Emma moved straight on to Plan B and sent a multi-line text message laying out the main points, delicately balancing the competing needs for brevity and clarity. She hoped Cole would at least see this the next time he looked at his phone… and could likewise only hope that his next look wouldn't be too far away. She would engage Plan C in the meantime, reaching out to low-level ELF contacts via the intermediary of ACN's Maria Janzyck and trying to talk someone into delivering an urgent message to Cole.

"These visitors come in peace and they come in need," Jack suddenly announced, facing the cameras again and this time talking in a far more self-important tone as though he himself was one of humanity's official points of contact with extraterrestrial races. "*Where* they have come is no coincidence, as I'm sure you can all understand, and more will become clear in the coming hours. The message I want to deliver to a likely suspicious Western world is that this is a positive development, and the ordinary citizens of GCC countries have nothing to fear from our alien friends."

John Cole, although particularly intrigued by the line about the aliens coming in need, was growing slightly irritated by Jack's showmanship and pomposity.

Wondering how much longer this show would go on before Jack pulled him aside to explain what the hell was happening instead of leaving him standing there like a fool before a media horde with whom he was equally in the dark, Cole instinctively glanced at the time on his smart watch. It was at this point that he saw an exclamation mark in the screen's notification bar, alerting him to a missed call and recently received text message from a top-priority contact.

Naturally, given the tremendously limited number of people who fell into this category, he checked it out. It then took no small effort for him to control his expression and broader reaction as the text message's words sank in:

"*This is Emma Ford in Birchwood. I'm watching this live and we have Jack's phone because he's been working with Poppy Bradshaw and other GeoSovs for months — he helped them kidnap Tara and those aliens just took him from Clark's custody. The Messengers just told Dan these aliens are hostile, so keep that in mind. Don't trust a single word that shit-stain says, but DO NOT LET ON that you know any of this. Call either me or Slater as soon as you can, and in the meantime please try to stop him from doing anything irreversible... WITHOUT LETTING ON that you know anything. I don't know what he has in mind but it's not going to be good. Remember: he's not on your side, he's with the fucking GeoSovs.*"

The cameras watching Cole relayed his understandably increasing difficultly at keeping his expression in check. His eyes narrowed, sending nothing but hate Jack's way.

Emma held her breath; she was ecstatic that he'd gotten the message so soon, but everything rested on the next few seconds. If Cole could get through them without snapping at Jack, he could prove to be a useful asset and the unlikeliest of allies in a situation whose outcome no one could predict.

Cole took a deep breath, and then another, before re-covering his watch with the sleeve of his blazer. He forced a smile, and although it was one of the least convincing Emma had ever seen it was also one of the most welcome. He still wouldn't be winning any awards for his acting, but for once in his life John Cole's intentions were good.

"Oh my *God!*" Dan yelped, instinctively placing a hand over his forehead and shaking his legs in agony. He waved his other arm in a plea for space. "Tara, Tara, Tara," he said, trying to get her off the couch so he could lie flat.

Everyone turned to see him and Clark rushed to help, but Dan McCarthy was out cold by the time his head hit the couch.

V minus 7

???
???

All around Dan McCarthy was white. The floor, the ceiling and the walls — if there even *were* any — merged utterly into one.

He turned around, hopeful of what and who he would see, and immediately his hopes were met.

"I don't want to hear anything," Dan said, pre-empting the Messengers' words. The two aliens stood before him, their large eyes striking him as concerned but the lack of eyebrows and the general almost-but-not-quite-human spatial layout of their faces making it difficult to be sure. "I don't even want to *see* you here. I want to hear you and see you where you need to be: on Earth, for everyone *else* to see and hear, too. Whatever is going on, we can't fix it while you're hiding... wherever the hell this place is."

The Messengers turned to each other. Dan didn't know why, bearing in mind they could communicate telepathically, but he assumed it was an instinctive or habitual thing.

A second or two later, they turned back to Dan and very clearly nodded.

"You're coming?"

A soft voice in his head relayed a single word before his senses faded to black: *"Cornfield."*

V minus 6

STEVENSON FARM
EASTVIEW, COLORADO

Within five minutes, Dan was out the door.

His immediate reaction to the atypical contact experience had been to sit bolt upright and blurt out the gist of it before his eyes were even open: "The Messengers are coming to the cornfield. Come on, we need to get out there before they show up and the police shut down the roads!"

Clark was the only one to react with physical urgency, running to grab his car keys. "You heard him, come on!"

"You're sure?" Emma asked.

Dan nodded and got to his feet, then headed towards the door to get his shoes. Tara followed, no part of her wanting to stay behind.

Henry, Phil and Mr Byrd, though no less keen to see the promised return of the Messengers, shared confused looks before Phil took it upon himself to ask the obvious question: "Any particular cornfield?"

"Ohhhh," Clark said, "shit, that's right... we didn't tell you. Uh, it's *your* cornfield, Phil. Remember how it went up for auction right after Walker died? That's because it was his old place."

Phil's eyebrows furrowed.

"Yeah..." Clark went on. "The Messengers landed there a few times, they called Dan to the cornfield twice, and they took Walker away twice. One of those times I was there and broke my nose running into a force-field. I guess it's a long story why we didn't tell you, but you loved that place as soon as you saw it and you didn't need to know. So, uh, yeah... your driveway is gonna get real busy real soon, and the government will probably seal off the whole area once this is done, just like they did at the drive-in. So if there's anything in there you'll need in the next little while, this would be a good time to get it out."

While Dan, ready to leave, clapped his hands together to restate the urgency, Phil stood in stunned shock. "The four of you have got some serious goddamn explaining to do, keeping that shit from me for the past year," he grunted.

At his side, the unusually quiet Mr Byrd smiled incongruously at the absurdity of it all.

"I'm not coming," Henry announced. "The shadow of a spaceship is no place for a wheelchair... no place for a man who can't run away."

Mr Byrd, as loyal as friends came, insisted upon staying behind with Henry. Clark didn't offer to do the same, completely set on going with Dan, while Phil had his own reasons to head out to Eastview and Emma and Tara were likewise in no doubt as to where they wanted to be.

The drive was short, filled with speculation as to what would happen next and occasional conversational lulls when the live radio news coverage of events in Havana and beyond dropped in some new information.

Nothing new had happened in China, which was news in itself; now a considerable amount of time since its arrival, the colossal alien mothership continued to cast an imposing shadow over much of central Beijing.

Clark was driving, and even through the tension of the moment he couldn't help but crack a smile as Phil Norris somewhat irresponsibly overtook at the first possible opportunity and sped towards the home he had just found out to be an unparalleled hotspot of alien visitation.

"Guys!" Tara yelled from the back seat, next to Dan. Her voice was excited rather than frightened as she pointed out of the window. "I think that's it!"

"Talk to me," Clark said, keeping his eyes on the road.

Over the next few seconds it became clear that Tara was right, with a huge uncloaked alien craft appearing larger and larger as it descended from the heavens. It didn't look to be coming down all that quickly, but this was a matter of perspective and reflected the high altitude at which it had first become visible.

Huge was the best word to describe the craft; for although the scale was difficult to ascertain, it was clearly much larger than the craft that had landed in the drive-in on Contact Day but just as clearly much smaller than the obscenely sized mothership hovering over the ELF's global headquarters.

"Emma... that's the one from Lolo!" Dan observed when the craft came low enough for the clear shape and first signs of detail to emerge. "The one we went inside first time round, when it was cloaked and Clark couldn't see."

"Definitely," she replied, recalling every detail and slowly seeing them come into view. The car took the semi-concealed turn towards Stevenson Farm at this point, temporarily blocking their view of the incoming craft. "And that was *their* mothership, right? So there's probably going to be more of them than just two..."

Although the narrow road that led the rest of the way to the house and more importantly to the adjacent cornfield was a short one, the news being discussed on the car's radio changed abruptly before it reached its destination. Eyewitness testimony and images of the incoming craft were spreading like wildfire on social media, evoking memories in Dan of the old plaque-hunting days when the California Fireball had captured the nation's attention.

This event was far more significant, with the Messengers' uncloaked return intriguing the whole world enough to tear attention away from the remarkable live images in Havana. Those images now appeared to show friendly cooperation between ELF personnel and a faction of the Messengers' species who only Dan's group and a select few others knew to be considered hostile by the Messengers themselves, with several police officers having boarded the parked craft one-at-a-time with an extraterrestrial escort at their side.

Police sirens, distant at first, became audible just as Phil's farmhouse came into view. The Messengers' mothership was close, directly above the cornfield and now moving only vertically, with its relatively and perhaps deliberately slow descent having enabled the police and likely countless others to set off with a general idea of the landing site before it touched down.

Dan rushed out of the car before it drew to a complete halt, but Clark was too awestruck by the sight of the incoming mothership to rebuke him like he normally would have. The etched details on its underside were highly visible now, and the police sirens ever more audible.

The mothership touched down gently in the centre of the cornfield, taking up a far larger area than the circle-making craft of old, but no ramp extended to the ground; because just like at Lolo, the mothership itself didn't actually rest upon the ground. Instead, a pseudo-metallic cylinder extended from its base to act as a remarkably strong support, holding the whole mothership in position at an angle that surprised everyone except the two people lucky enough to have seen it before.

"They're going to come out," Dan said, utter confidence in his voice. "I know it. We don't have to go in, they're coming out."

Every passing heartbeat and second led the others to exchange increasingly unsure glances, which progressed to fairly urgent questions as to how sure Dan was about this when two police cars arrived. Right behind them came an ACN news van and then a line of civilian vehicles.

A police officer hurried out of his car to instruct the civilians to stay back, while one of his colleagues walked straight to Dan. These men were *Clark's* colleagues, too, of course, but Dan was naturally their focus for now.

"How did you know they were coming?" the man asked.

"Not now, Terry," Clark replied on Dan's behalf.

Terry ignored Clark and asked again, but Dan responded by decisively ignoring him.

More and more cars continued to arrive, packing the narrow road like it was a drive-in itself. People abandoned their vehicles and rushed as far forward as they could, stopping only at the arbitrary point which the police had decided was close enough.

A loud collective gasp sent Dan's eyes away from the growing crowd and towards the cornfield, where he took great delight in seeing two very familiar Messengers in their very familiar all-white tunics. The aliens emerged from the field with graceful steps but stopped very abruptly when they saw a raised weapon.

Dan, literally as well as figuratively caught in the middle, gestured several times for the officer to lower it.

Despite this, the stubborn and frightened officer didn't budge.

"You need to lower your weapon," Dan snapped, wondering how the man — Terry, as Clark had called him — didn't know that was what he meant and how he didn't understand that Dan wouldn't be signalling for such a thing if it wasn't necessary.

"Terry, what the hell do you not understand here?" Clark boomed. "Put it down!"

One of the Messengers began to raise its hand, planting a seed in Dan's mind that it was about to immobilise the armed man it perceived as a threat, just as had happened at the drive-in a year earlier.

"Don't even think about it," Terry yelled at the Messenger, grasping his firearm ever tighter and adjusting his aim for its head.

A voice entered Dan's head: *"This imminent threat cannot stand. He leaves me no choice but to—"*

Dan appreciated this warning and made full use of it, taking matters into his own hands before even hearing the entirety of the thought.

Without any hesitation, he turned towards Terry with his thumb pressed to his middle finger and pointed at the weapon with his index finger. Dan then swiped his finger through the air, effortlessly emptying Terry's hand and sending the gun to the ground.

As soon as it landed, Dan used tiny finger movements to remotely — *telekinetically* — knock the weapon away from Terry.

The civilians standing beside their cars at the edge of the exclusion zone had clearly seen what happened and were standing in genuine awe following the most concerted collective gasp Dan had ever heard. His eyes briefly took in the even more stunned expressions of Tara and Clark, from whom he and Emma had kept their knowledge of his untested telekinetic ability.

This instance was far more significant than when Dan had stumbled upon the frightening power in catching Emma's falling drink on board Timo's private jet, and it went without saying that the size of the crowd was sufficient to ensure that word would spread and his already complicated life would take another decisive step away from normality.

Telekinesis was certain to be too much for many, perhaps even *burn-him-for-witchcraft* territory in some minds, as Dan knew only too well. He tried to push all of that out of his mind, but this became impossible when the rest of the uniformed police officers turned to him in response to orders received via their barely visible earpieces.

One even called for him to put his hands up, fingers spread.

"Back the fuck off," Clark yelled at them, prompting calls of '*stay out of this*' from men he had considered loyal colleagues and in some cases even friends. Dan had never done anything to hurt anyone in his life, so no part of Clark could understand why he would suddenly be seen as a threat. His telekinetic control of the firearm had been a truly remarkable sight to behold, for sure, but by no means an inherently *threatening* one. "He could've saved Terry's life by doing that!"

"Exactly," Dan insisted, as glad as ever to have Clark in his corner to the very end. He encouraged Emma and Tara to retreat into the car, and Emma accepted the safety-first suggestion; talking to the media or politicians may have been her forte, but Clark was undoubtedly better suited to talking to the police.

Even *he* couldn't seem to get through to them, though, as the attendant officers approached Dan and ordered him in firmer terms to raise his hands. When he didn't, they starkly raised their firearms in unison.

"Get back," Dan said, his voice loud but weak.

"Hands above your head!" Terry's gruff and fear-struck voice called. "Hands above your head right now or I swear to God they'll—"

With a forceful downward thrust of his hand, Dan sent everyone within a thirty foot radius flying off their feet. This included all of the attendant officers, even the off-duty Clark, and left Dan alone in an otherwise empty circle.

The ground was charred by his desperate and instinctive creation of a forcefield far less discreet than those typically used by the Messengers, and the visual effect was remarkable.

Dan glanced down at his hand and contemplated the power within it. When he looked back up, none of the countless faces that met his gaze, with the sole exception of Clark's, any longer looked as though they were meeting the eyes of a fellow human.

With two Messengers standing directly behind him and dozens of accusing expressions bearing down, Dan McCarthy very suddenly knew how it felt to be alien.

Part 7

THE ELDERS

"Courage is a kind of salvation."

Plato

V minus 5

The human faces around Dan reflected fear and unease at the decidedly alien ability he had just exhibited.

The Messengers, behind him, meanwhile appeared entirely unmoved. Their body language was approving, if anything, with the one that had looked ready to act against Clark's gun-toting colleague now standing in a perfectly relaxed manner next to its partner. Only these two Messengers had emerged from the craft despite its size having suggested a far larger crew was not only possible but likely, but that didn't necessarily mean they had come alone.

The only faces Dan cared about in a personal sense were those of Clark and Tara, the latter of whom had now stepped back out of the car for a first-hand look at the incredible sight of Dan standing with only the Messengers for company inside a forcefield of his own telekinetic creation.

Even in the heat of the moment, Dan was aware of how this would be reported and how incredible it would look from the outside. He knew the image would instantly become even more iconic than last year's remarkable snapshot of him standing at the drive-in like Moses in the parted sea, the only person able to remain inside the Messengers' forcefield.

The reason was simple: this time, *he* had generated the forcefield. This time, *he* had the power.

It didn't take more than a split second of reflection for Dan to know that once the dust settled and the understandably startled observers realised they had nothing to fear from his power, it would doubtlessly bring him an even higher level of messianic worship.

Crucially, though, with the traitorous and spiteful Jack Neal in cahoots with a hostile alien faction, Dan knew that even *having* a future to worry about could depend on his own ability to work with the Messengers to solve whatever was really going on with their Elders. Because that, after all, was why the Squadron were here in the first place and why Jack Neal was by their side in Havana rather than being securely held in the McCarthys' basement.

Dan didn't like that he'd kept this new ability from Tara and Clark, even though he and Emma hadn't kept it quiet for any dubiously motivated reasons, but right now he knew that their expressions weren't the ones that mattered; there was nothing to *forgive* him for, but they would accept his reasoning in time even if they did currently feel slighted for having been kept in the dark when secrets were supposed to be a thing of the past.

Talking to the Messengers mattered most of all, but there was certainly a pressing need to explain what had just happened so that speculative media narratives couldn't take hold. Now more than ever, the last thing the world needed was suspicion about Dan or the Messengers.

Their arrival was a beacon of hope to Dan in the face of a powder-keg situation; but with minute-to-minute public perception more important than ever given the potentially catastrophic results of any military action a government might feel pressured to take, he knew it was absolutely crucial that hope was the only feeling radiating outward from Colorado.

"The Messengers granted me some telepathic abilities so they could reach me whenever they might have to," he said, speaking very suddenly and immediately drawing everyone's attention from the general sight of the remarkable forcefield and focusing it all upon himself. "The telekinesis came with it. I didn't ask for any of these powers and I didn't even *agree* to take *this* one... but here I am. I haven't asked for any of this since the very beginning; I didn't ask to find that

362

damn folder on Winchester Street and I didn't ask to be the Messengers' conduit on Earth... but here I am."

From the side of the car, Emma subtly signalled to Dan that she wanted to tell him something. He initiated a one-way mental connection with equal subtlety and immediately heard her suggestion. It made a lot of sense in his mind and he always trusted Emma's instincts in such matters, so he acted upon it without delay.

Turning to the Messengers, Dan initiated a *two*-way connection with them — unsure if it was even necessary — and silently told them what he wanted them to do. In light of events in Havana, they agreed very quickly.

To Dan, their unhesitant cooperation to what were fairly major requests was a very clear sign that they understood the stakes... perhaps even better than he did.

"Terry," Dan called to the police officer whose tetchiness had led to the escalation, "how about you come inside with me and take a look around. These guys are on our side, and one of them is willing to undergo some non-invasive tests just like we saw happening in Havana. Scans, measurements, things like that. We're in this together and they want to show that."

"Are those the same aliens?" a voice from the crowd called.

"What's with the different outfits?" another yelled.

Dan forced a smile, trying to look more relaxed than he was. "I'll have some answers in a few minutes," he said, tracing a circle in the air to remove his own forcefield in an entirely instinctive manner. Once that was done, he beckoned Terry forward with a friendly hand gesture.

Terry stood still, shaking his head. "I don't... I... I'm not going in there."

Dan encouraged one of the Messengers to extend its hand and walk slowly towards Terry. It did so, all but screaming '*we come in peace*' as the world watched on.

When Terry unsurely glanced at Dan, Dan widened his eyes in a manner that *told* Terry to do this rather than merely suggested it.

The world is watching, he tried to stress without speaking. *Man up.*

Whether it was the weight of the crowd or something else, Terry eventually shook the Messenger's hand. His expression softened immediately at the contact, and he began walking towards the cornfield with no further reluctance. The Messenger who had walked to greet him remained where it was, striking the pose of a lost dog as it looked around uneasily at countless unfamiliar faces.

"Clark," Dan called, "look after that one while we're in there. Make sure they treat him well when they're doing measurements and stuff, okay?"

"Damn right," Clark said. He rushed to the frightened-looking alien's side and offered a handshake of his own.

The Messenger reciprocated.

"So uh… hey, dude," Clark uttered. "Can you hear me?"

Confirmation came in the form of a nod.

"Can you talk to me?"

No answer.

"*Will* you talk to me?"

A shake of the head.

Clark couldn't help but grin; the situation was so surreal he could hardly believe any of it was happening, but at least the alien was honest.

At the edge of the cornfield, Dan turned towards the crowd in front of Phil's farmhouse one more time. "I'll be back soon," he called. "Emma, I love you."

"I love you, too," she shouted back.

"And Tara…" Dan went on, "don't worry about anything; they're here to help us."

Dan McCarthy had been wrong before, but never as wrong as this.

V minus 4

???
???

Side by side with a police officer named Terry who had been a complete stranger until minutes earlier, Dan McCarthy ascended an elevator-like cylinder in Phil Norris's cornfield and emerged in a room so white that it once again felt like a dream.

He had been in this very mothership on one previous occasion, when he and Emma came face to face with the benevolent but imperfect Messengers in Lolo National Forest.

Terry stared open-mouthed in every direction, searching for a break in the impossibly total whiteness. He walked around the walls and felt brave enough to touch them, all while the Messenger before Dan — the only one in the room — paid no heed whatsoever.

The Messenger's full attention was on Dan, and it wasted no further time in letting him know what was going on.

"Our Elders are dead," it communicated silently, holding Dan's eyes with its own. "Our home world is in chaos. The calling of my kind, the Interpreters, has been ripped from our grasp. Where once we were intermediaries between the wisdom of our Elders and the rest of our race, we are now distrusted as pariahs. We have been accused of sabotaging our own Elders; we have been accused of incompetence in missing indications of their ill-health while something could have been done about it; we have had our voices drowned out by the bombast of the Squadron and their beliefs that we Interpreters failed our race on purpose."

Dan listened more intently than he had ever listened to anything in his life.

"The Squadron have not come to Earth to claim it as their own," the Messenger continued. "New Kerguelen faces an existential threat and the Squadron have come in search of assistance, believing us not only incapable of finding a solution but untrustworthy of even trying. Their distrust of us extends to our known friends and allies, so much so that the Squadron have searched for friends among the enemies of our own. Everything about the triangles was designed to divide… to thicken the line between sides and bring hidden loyalties and hatreds into the light. In the shape of their chosen conduit, they have discovered the antithesis of our own — and not by accident."

Upon hearing this truly remarkable information, Dan instinctively turned to Terry. The voice in his mind was so clear that it was easy to forget he wasn't hearing it out loud, but Terry's continued obliviousness to anything other than the totality of the white surfaces all around him reaffirmed that he couldn't hear anything.

"Let me get this straight…" Dan began, replying without actually speaking. "They chose Jack because he's my worst enemy… which is relevant because they distrust *you* and know that you trust *me*? Is that right?" The thought alone was difficult for Dan to wrap his head around, striking his overwhelmed mind as almost impossibly convoluted.

"Members of the Squadron are not raised or educated with a focus on logical thought," the Messenger replied somewhat dryly.

Dan shook his head. "But they had this plan about the triangles… all of that just to sharpen the divide and bring the fault lines into plain sight? That's elaborate scheming, almost like the kind of thing that human politicians—"

"Not almost," the Messenger cut in, essentially interrupting an outgoing thought in Dan's mind with an incoming one. "It is not *almost* like a human scheme of deceit, it was built upon observation of such schemes. They know from previous events on Earth, which we Interpreters observed and relayed, that humankind would react with great interest to the discovery of one artefact which hinted at more to come."

"But they even knew where to put them," Dan replied. "Tanzania? *Vanuatu*? That takes a serious level of planning and consideration. Are you sure they weren't in contact with Jack before all of this, and that he didn't advise them?"

"Entirely sure. Truly, without doubt. Our home world, known to you as New Kerguelen, is managed by a cross-sectional council of our kind and every other. Some time ago, when our Elders became unreliable in their dispensation of advice, the council approved a Squadron mission to independently observe the only other socially complex intelligent race we have encountered: humanity. That decision grew from a brewing distrust of our increasingly sporadic interpretations of the Elders' will, and it allowed the Squadron to paint their own picture of Earth. The Squadron are our planet's defensive security force, with sole control of energy-based weaponry beyond human comprehension. Driven by their distrust of us, the Squadron have sought assistance in the worst possible place. But the great difference between the Squadron and their earthly conduit, it is crucial to understand, is that they *believe* they are acting in the best interests of their home planet… of *our* home planet."

Dan's brow furrowed. "So they're not a *bad* faction, they're just wrong? And we just have to convince them that Jack's an asshole who only wants to use them to get one over on everyone he hates, no matter the cost? Because I can promise you this: Jack Neal isn't going to help *anyone* unless it's a side-effect of getting what he wants, let alone an alien race."

"We do not have to convince the Squadron of anything other than the need to pause their efforts to find help while we undertake one final effort of our own," the Messenger replied, the thought somehow surprising Dan with its insistent tone. "In the absence of our Elders, New Kerguelen needs unity. In the Elderless vacuum of the moment, New Kerguelen needs to embrace the better parts of human civilisation. And that, Dan, is where you come in."

So much had changed since Dan first stepped inside this mothership, both in his life and the world in general, but one thing had always remained constant in his mind: when they could, the Messengers would help.

Now, however, as he was in the process of finding out, the shoe was very much on the other foot.

~

"The Squadron will not make any attempt to block our return to New Kerguelen, even with visitors," the Messenger said.

Dan's eyes involuntarily widened upon 'hearing' the word *visitors*. He had a feeling where this was going, but opted not to interrupt.

"Our race faces very real and very urgent problems," his alien counterpart continued, "and we were in the process of handling those problems when the Elders became unresponsive. Despite their distrust of our efforts so far, the Squadron will be nothing but happy if we find a way to solve the problem and improve conditions for all. Grudges are not the same among our race as among your own; if we solve the external problem, there is no problem left. They were granted an observation permit by the council as a last resort when the Elders' responsiveness faded to a fraction of what it once was, and although they are here we are content in the knowledge that they would return home gladly once the problem is solved. Our success will regain their trust."

"What *is* this problem?" Dan asked. "The external problem you keep talking about... what is it?"

The Messenger replied very flatly, almost indifferently: "Our physical environment. External conditions have been worsening for several generations, but in the recent time since our Elders' deaths many internal and protective tasks have been neglected. Without direction many are lost, and without the Elders our words carry no weight."

The tone of the words seemed to be changing, and Dan waited eagerly for the punchline.

"We wish for unity," the Messenger went on, "such as that engendered on Earth albeit temporarily following our necessary intervention against your Defensive Station 1. A perceived threat from outside can deliver unity, but so can diplomatic outreach. Indeed, until today, your own outreach across national boundaries looked to be bridging the divide the Squadron were attempting to exacerbate with their triangles. Our own divisions are far less stark, and the unifying perspective provided by an alien visitor may be what New Kerguelen needs. We turn to you in need and ask for whatever help you can provide. *Please.*"

"You want *me* to unite *your* planet?" Dan asked, sure he must be misunderstanding. The 'please' at the end caught him off-guard, but the immensity of the broader request didn't give him any time to reflect on why that word felt so unexpected.

"A public appearance is a last resort," the Messenger told him, "but with the possibility at hand we would turn to no one else. The great majority of our race are unaware of distant lifeforms such as your own, and this revelation could be the kind of unifying moment your old enemy brought about with his initial hoax. The difference, again, is that our motives are pure."

The breadth and depth of what the Messenger was talking about surprised Dan almost as much as the core topic; it truly did have a full grasp of the twists and turns his life's path had taken in the time since Richard Walker enacted his leak sequence. The Messenger's characterisation of Walker as his 'old enemy' almost elicited a smile, but not quite.

Dan breathed deeply, having utterly no idea what his visit would entail but already knowing beyond doubt that he had to try to help. There were all kinds of reasons, but Jack Neal potentially being mere inches or hours from indirect access to impossibly powerful weaponry was certainly one of the more pressing.

"I could bring experts," Dan said. "Linguists, engineers, biologists, doctors, veterinarians... whatever and whoever could possibly help with your environmental problems or even your Elders. Because when you say they're dead, does that really mean *dead*? And don't you have successors ready to step in, or at least candidates to train? Can't one of *your* kind take up the mantel of an Elder... an Interpreter? I could bring conflict resolution specialists, diplomats, anything you can—"

"The travelling party will comprise you and at most one companion," the Messenger interjected, saving Dan from wasting any more energy on fruitless thoughts. "And no, we have no succession process for future Elders. As individuals we live and die like any others, but our Elders do not. Until now, at least, our Elders *have* not. They were not like us. Seeing is understanding... you will understand when you see."

"I'll *see* them?" Dan asked. "Last time you told me it was literally impossible for me to see them."

"Access was restricted to only our kind during the Elders' time. As Interpreters we worked with them endlessly to ensure all data was being considered before a decision was reached and relayed to the rest of New Kerguelen. Now that the Elders have passed, no such restrictions are in place."

"So what's the situation now... are they lying in state or something?" Dan asked. He briefly wondered whether 'lying in state' would be something the Messenger understood, before remembering that it wasn't listening to his unvocalised words so much as it was observing and interpreting the brainwaves that preceded them.

"Yes; as they were in life, so they remain."

Dan nodded in understanding. Well... not quite *understanding*, but certainly acknowledgement.

As for the point about a sole travelling companion, although this surprised and in many ways disappointed Dan, there was zero doubt in his mind who that companion would be; no one in any world could be better suited to the task of persuasion than Emma, and there would have been no one else in his thoughts even if he didn't know she would be so useful.

This brief thought, of how much of an interpersonal influencer Emma really was, brought a thought of Jack — another master of the art, as much as Dan hated to admit it — right back into his mind.

"Are the Squadron asking Jack for advice right now?" he suddenly asked. "Or are they asking *him* to go to New Kerguelen, too? Because we definitely don't want him to beat us there."

"At the moment they are merely gathering his perspective."

"Which happens to be the most warped perspective in the world," Dan replied with a rueful shake of his head. From the outside this conversation would have looked like two beings engaged in an endless and silent staring contest, but the only person present to witness it — Terry the police officer — was still sensorily overwhelmed in a very genuine way by the colourless uniformity of the vast room.

"Our immediate concern is that he succeeds in convincing them to take regrettable action, either here or at home," the Messenger said. "Their communications abilities are far beneath our own as you saw from their use of the cable — they have never communicated with humans, unlike our kind, so they have not developed the understanding required to forego the physical connection. The nature of their conversations will also be stilted, as were ours at first, but in time that will change. For now, complex discussion is beyond them. Our window is short, however, as their acuity will develop rapidly as they converse with their conduit further."

"I'll come," Dan said. "I don't know what you want me to do and I don't know if I can do it, but I owe you this much. I have a lot of questions about the powers you gave me, but those can wait for the journey."

Unless Dan's eyes were deceiving him, the Messenger's lips crinkled slightly in the closest thing to a smile he'd ever seen on an alien face. Evidently, it was glad he was in.

"Excellent," it said. "But there will be no journey; from your perspective, we will depart and arrive with no voyage in between."

Dan shrugged. This was another 'think about it later' point — and think about it he would — but for now there was a more urgent matter to attend to. The future of New Kerguelen and quite possibly of Earth itself depended on the de-escalation of a post-Elder schism and the filling of a power vacuum of which Dan had no detailed knowledge.

Despite a tightening in his chest, Dan tried to focus on the point that the beings he considered the smartest in the universe, if not quite omniscient, seemed adamant that he was the man to help. He was a human with alien powers; seen as an alien by his fellow humans just minutes earlier and surely a human to be viewed as decidedly alien by the struggling residents of New Kerguelen.

"Terry," he called, speaking out loud for the first time in several minutes. "Time to go."

As Terry complained about having just got there and not having seen much, Dan's mind fell silent.

The invitation to help was as humbling as the stakes were intimidating, but Dan McCarthy's mind was made up: the Messengers had come all this way to ask for his help, and the least he could do was give it a shot.

V minus 3

STEVENSON FARM
EASTVIEW, COLORADO

With a clear next move in mind at last, Dan McCarthy stepped out of the cornfield and returned to the view of the gathered crowd. No others had crossed the scorched line of the circular forcefield he had generated and removed, likely due to how prominent that line remained, but all eyes turned to Dan and Terry as they emerged with a Messenger walking just a few paces behind them.

The *other* Messenger remained with Clark, who was firmly enforcing a more remedial exclusion zone of his own with help from his colleagues in the police force. This Messenger had the benefit of being able to gauge the thoughts and intentions of those around it and was thus relatively relaxed, sensing that their curiosity and interest came with no negativity attached. It seemed to feel particularly comfortable next to Clark, gladly sticking by his side due to the protective aura he exuded.

"They want us to go with them," Dan whispered, reaching Emma and Tara at the edge of his circle. He raised a hand, non-threateningly, to encourage everyone else to give him some space. "Just the two of us. The Elders are dead, and New Kerguelen is in trouble... there's some kind of problem with their atmosphere and there's a total power vacuum without the Elders there to make the big decisions. The Messengers want to use our arrival on New Kerguelen to bring everyone together if that ends up being necessary, just like all the early alien revelations kind of brought everyone on Earth together for a while."

"Jesus," Tara said. Emma didn't say anything out loud, but Dan heard a similar reaction in her thoughts.

"But here's the thing," he went on, "the Squadron came here to get help, too. They actively distrust the Messengers because of what happened with the Elders, those Elders aren't there to keep the Squadron in line like they used to, and the Squadron think their enemy's enemy is their friend. They used the triangles to bring our divisions into sharp focus, and they saw Jack as the antithesis of me — the Messengers' conduit — so that's why they're talking to him. We're back to the old thing of trying to understand alien psychology while they're acting on their own limited understanding of ours, but this is the gist of it. I'll explain everything later, or *they* will, but right now I'm worried about the Squadron having access to weaponry we can't imagine and Jack Neal offering to help them if they do what he wants. It's what *he* might want *them* to do that bothers me, because you said it best: that man is a virus."

"We need to get the police or ELF security guys to stop Jack from talking to the Squadron any more than he already has," Tara said, interjecting with a very valid point.

"We *do* need to stop him from talking to them before he gives them any dangerous suggestions or before they take him to New Kerguelen," Emma replied, "but not like that. He could just tell them the police are hostile, the security forces are hostile, and that anyone *else* who tries to interrupt is hostile. We need him to be *willing* to hang back, and the only way to do that is via Cole. If Cole can convince him it's more beneficial to play a long game and see what happens with *us* before *they* commit to anything, at least that would give us an opening. The Squadron's ships are casting long shadows and people are worried, which gives Jack power as their conduit. And let's be real… he's a coward and the last thing he's going to care about is helping them, so he's probably not about to give up his new-found spotlight and power on Earth to get in a spaceship and blast off to a world he knows nothing about. Again, though, he has to be the one deciding this… all we can do is get Cole to push him in that direction to make sure. So that's all I can think of right now; if Cole manages to frame it in a way that makes Jack think it's better to wait here while *we* go to New Kerguelen, we have a chance of avoiding any flashpoints. I'll tell Cole there's a way for everyone except Jack to save face at the end of this, and we'll work that part out later."

Dan gulped, struggling to even *follow* Emma's plan let alone evaluate it. The one great positive, which he had never really questioned but was still glad to hear, was that she was absolutely on board with the idea of travelling an unknown distance to an unknown world for the greater good.

Just like it was for him, Emma's urge to help the Messengers on New Kerguelen and simultaneously diffuse the powder-keg situation on Earth was sufficiently compelling to drown out all fears about the risks of such a mission.

"Don't worry — *I'm* overwhelmed, too," she said, reading Dan's expression and still talking aloud so that Tara would hear, too. "I didn't explain it right, but I'll only tell Cole what he has to know. I'll deal with that, you deal with this…"

Emma looked over at the crowd and the cameras, prompting Dan to do the same.

"Say they need our help," she went on, "but don't mention anything about the Squadron or their motives, okay? If in doubt, it's better to say too little. That's what I'll be doing; we can always add to it, but we can't take words back if we say too many."

"Relying on John Cole," Dan mused, almost but not quite a question. He didn't know what else to say, and neither did Emma or Tara.

Emma stepped inside the car for some privacy and picked up her phone to tell Cole what she wanted him to do, counting on the hope that the level of betrayal he felt towards Jack would carry him through. She thought that Jack's concealed working relationship with the GeoSovs was bound to sting Cole, a man with a famously short temper and one whose hatred of the GeoSovs was not just for show, to the extent that the risk of him telling Jack about this plan — which would have been catastrophic — felt truly minimal.

Tara stayed beside the car while Emma called Cole, but Dan stepped away to address the anticipatory crowd who had been waiting patiently for the last minute or so.

Terry was already talking to news reporters about what he'd seen inside the craft — or more to the point what he *hadn't* seen, which was to say anything but near-total whiteness — and the two Messengers were now reunited in silent discussion next to Clark.

A glance in any direction presented one surreal sight or another, but all eyes focused once again on Dan.

"The Messengers need our help," he began, booming out the words due to the size of the crowd when in reality their silence made doing so unnecessary. "They want to take me to New Kerguelen to help with a problem. The other aliens could be asking Jack the same thing, and despite all of our differences I hope he goes, too. We owe this to the Messengers."

This part came to Dan only as he said it, but he didn't regret it. His gut said that Emma probably wouldn't have approved, but for all he knew she might have; for now, her position inside the car from which she was reaching out to John Cole meant that she wasn't even aware he'd said it.

Despite being content with these words, however, Dan endeavoured to be more careful. No one had to know too much, and he considered that prettifying the truth to reduce tension probably wouldn't be a bad idea.

"The Messengers and their misguided friends have come here in their time of need," he continued, prettifying more than a little with his use of the term '*misguided friends*', "and we have a positive duty to do all we can to help. I don't know exactly what they want me to do, but the only thought in my mind is that *they* came *here* on Contact Day when I called them in *Earth's* hour of need. They saved us from a problem that had nothing to do with them, and they asked nothing in return. Now, we have an opportunity and a duty to pay them back. They only want two of us to go, so there is no option for broad or international representation. To Ding Ziyang and John Cole I want to make it as clear as possible that we will not step into that spacecraft as representatives of the United States or the GCC. We are human beings first, second, and third: representatives of our species, our planet, and nothing else.

"There have been some misunderstandings of late," Dan went on, "both between and within our two species, but today we put that right. To William Godfrey and Valerie Slater I want to say thank you for supporting my efforts to build a bridge to the ELF before these complications burned it down, and to the people of this planet I want to say stay calm and remember that our only threat comes from ourselves. These aliens are not our enemies… and once we've assisted them with the problem they're facing, our two species — moving past our temporary factional disagreements — will step forward together into a brave new future as the best of friends."

Clark took it upon himself to applaud, not reactively but rather in the hope others would follow.

They did.

"*Clap*," Dan said without speaking, sending the suggestion to the Messengers.

They did.

The sight of the two alien beings awkwardly mimicking this decidedly human action was perhaps the most surreal of the day, particularly since their hands lacked multiple recognisable fingers.

The imagery was strong, however; and as Emma stepped out of the car, already looking sufficiently relaxed to suggest that she'd gotten through to Cole and that he'd been receptive of her message, she smiled broadly at the scene before her.

"The medical tests the Messengers promised to undergo are going to have to wait," Dan said, not overly disappointing anyone, "because it's time for us to go."

Some of the gathered crowd cheered now, perhaps enlivened and excited more at the prospect of the growing problems on Earth being solved by Dan's mission rather than at the prospect of the *aliens'* problems being solved. Most saw how fully the two were interconnected, though, and were simply glad that there appeared to be something Dan could do.

No one was more glad of this than Dan himself, having loathed the feelings of helplessness that had circled like vultures in his gut until the Messengers' belated return. He called the Messengers forward and they came without hesitation.

"How long is this going to take?" Clark asked, walking with them. He directed the question at Dan, knowing he would be the one to get the answer back from the Messengers.

Dan took several seconds listening to their answer and clarifying with some follow-up questions before turning back to Clark. By now, Emma was well within earshot, too. "Whatever happens, you guys won't feel like we're gone for more than a few days at most," he said, confident that this was true even if he didn't fully understand it yet.

Emma turned to face Clark and Tara. "You two are going to need to follow your gut when we're gone. Talk to Timo before doing anything if something comes up, okay? He's always on our side and he's probably on the way out here now, stuck in the traffic that'll be backed up right into the city."

They both nodded, listening attentively.

"I've told Cole you both know everything and are in a position to advise him if he needs help," she continued. "He picked up this time so I actually spoke to him… he's fixing to rip Jack's head off for working with the GeoSovs behind his back, but he's going to play dumb and make sure Jack doesn't tell the Squadron to do anything stupid. Oh yeah… if you do feel like you have to make any public comments, don't talk about 'the Squadron'. That's not a word we want to be out there."

It crossed Dan's mind to suggest that Emma should perhaps stay behind to deal with all of the things she was making sound a lot simpler than they would be for anyone else, but he stopped himself upon considering how important she would doubtless prove in his own exceptionally intimidating task.

But as Emma took a step forward towards the cornfield, ready to leave and get to New Kerguelen and back as quickly as possible, one of the Messengers placed a firm hand on her shoulder to stop her.

"Huh?" Dan asked, instinctively reacting out loud to a statement from the Messenger that took him completely by surprise. "What are you *talking* about? Emma's older than me!"

"Thanks..." she said, briefly glancing at Dan then back to the Messenger who was now holding rather than merely touching her shoulder.

"I'm talking about what they said," Dan explained. "One of them said '*no, not her,*' and the other one said '*the child will not survive*'. I don't even know what..."

Dan trailed off at precisely the same moment it hit everyone else.

Tara's gasp was the loudest by far.

"I'm *pregnant*?" Emma asked, quietly but firmly seeking absolute confirmation of something that was far too important to leave to assumption.

Dan turned to the Messenger for the two seconds this took, then faced Emma once more. "We're having a baby!" he gleefully announced.

They shared an emotional embrace, with the vast majority of the crowd utterly oblivious to what was going on.

Emma wiped away a tear as they separated and the warm smile slowly faded from her face. "But I guess that means you're going without me."

V minus 2

"It was once imagined that these streets would be abuzz with activity in any contact scenario," an aspiring student journalist spoke into her phone's camera as it captured the otherwise deserted area outside the UN building in New York.

"The original Global Shield Commission was born in the building behind me, when a perceived alien threat brought the governments of the world together like never before. Today, events in China, in Cuba and in Colorado tell the story of a planet divided to an extent few would have believed back then.

"Our visitors, who so famously stepped in during our own time of need, are in trouble. The first visitors to depart in the opposite direction will carry a responsibility and burden unmatched in human history, bearing the weight of not one world but two.

"Dan McCarthy would surely be the emissary of choice for anyone but the most rabid contrarian, but his decisive Messenger-beckoning intervention on Contact Day seems to pale in comparison to the scale and complexity of *this* mission.

"Together with the Messengers, Dan McCarthy achieved the seemingly impossible in saving Earth from the relentless and fatal path of Il

378

Diavolo. A year later, the world today holds its breath as they depart in the hope of preventing disaster on New Kerguelen. Their success now appears to present our only hope of cooling down a tempestuous showdown between East and West that threatened to break out into a costly military conflict even before an imposing alien squadron made its presence known above conspicuously chosen sites.

"It may be reckless to speculate that the Messengers have experienced bitter political division like our own, but with the recent arrival of physically similar beings adorning different uniforms — not unlike the contrast between the human security forces who surround them in each location — that does appear to be the case.

"Whatever comes next, however, one thing is certain: as the streets behind me lie empty, the nations of the world stand united in hope."

V minus 1

"I can't leave you," Dan said, holding Emma's hand. "Not now. Not when I know—"

"You have to," she interrupted. "If we want a future at all, you have to fix this. I know you want to help them but that's not the main thing… helping them is how we help *ourselves*. Helping them is how we get rid of the Squadron before someone loses their nerve and smashes the button to start a nuclear war. Helping them is how we deal with Jack once and for all, and helping them is how we make sure this child has a world to grow up in."

Dan exhaled deeply; he knew she was right, and that was the worst part.

"*I'll* come with you," Tara chimed in, surprising everyone. "Clark, you have to stay with Emma — and I mean *with* her, at all times — in case anyone tries to do anything like they did to me. But I want to do this. I need to do this. I'm not some helpless victim; I can help and I *want* to. I want to help pay them back for saving us on Contact Day, and you can bet your ass I want to pay *Jack* back for what he did to me. When this is finished, so is he… so let's get started."

Emma and Clark shared a long, thoughtful look.

"I want her to come," Dan said. "Tara is way better at reading social cues and stuff like that than I am, and I trust her like I trust myself."

Tara smiled beside him. "Thanks."

"Will they even let you go?" Clark asked. "They've never spoken to you. And are you definitely sure that *you're* not, you know..."

"Oh, don't worry about that," Tara said, her chuckle introducing a much-needed moment of levity. "That's the one kind of test I have a one hundred percent record of passing!"

"And she is allowed," Dan added, having already silently asked the Messengers. "They're glad to have her on board."

Tara looked into the cornfield. "On board..." she mused, an innocent expression of wonder breaking through the tension and pressure of the moment. "On board an alien spaceship..."

"They're telling me it's time," Dan relayed to the others. He turned to Emma and they took a few steps to the side to talk privately.

This left Clark with Tara, and he had a simple message as he pulled her in for a tight, protective hug: "Be careful."

"I don't even remember if I ever thanked you," Tara said, speaking to his chest with her head on his shoulder, "you know, for everything you did to get me out of that spot with Jack and the GeoSovs."

"Thank me by saving the world and bringing Dan back in one piece," Clark replied. "Maybe two pieces, three at most. But no more than that. Deal?"

Tara giggled and pulled her head back slightly to look up at him. Her eyes lingered for several seconds.

Clark let out a slow sigh. "Why do you have to look at me like that *now*, when you're about to fly off in a spaceship?" he asked, a light-hearted twang in a series of words that sounded like they were coming from somewhere real.

"Don't think I haven't thought about it," Tara replied, real all the way. "If it wouldn't be so weird, I—"

"Weird for who?" Clark interjected. "For you, fine. But if you mean for everyone else... what everyone *else* thinks is the worst reason ever. It's not even a reason."

"Why do you have to talk to me like that *now*, when I'm about to fly off in a spaceship?" she replied.

Clark's lips broke into a touché-tinged grin. "How about we talk when you get back."

"Deal."

Emma and Dan arrived at the cornfield-side of the circle at this point, while the police were doing a good but easy job of keeping the public well clear. Phil Norris stood on his porch, raising a hand to wave goodbye as he kept an eye on the crowd that had understandably but from his perspective *frustratingly* gathered on his property.

"Tell Dad and the guys I said bye," Dan requested, his mind turning to them at the sight of Phil.

"No," Clark point-blank refused, his tone gruff and uncompromising. "Just you fucking concentrate on making sure you get home, you hear? Get home and tell them hello, none of this hand-wringing goodbye bullshit."

Vintage Clark, Dan thought, but he wouldn't have had it any other way.

Emma and Tara's parting was predictably softer but equally brief, with both aware of the urgency they faced. What Emma also became aware of, though, was an uncertain glint in Dan's eyes. She held two fingers up to the Messengers, not even considering whether they'd understand this plea for slightly more time, and moved closer to Dan to give him a few final words of encouragement.

They had come a long way since she arrived on his doorstep chasing a payday for XPR and since she had escorted him to countless media appearances when he was viewed by many as a lunatic conspiracy theorist. It hadn't been a straight road and certainly hadn't been without its bumps, but they were still driving and now had the promise of reaching an all new destination in around eight months — with a long-planned wedding somewhere in between.

"Never stop believing in yourself," Emma told him. "Because everything that's come our way, and there's been a *lot* of it, we've always dealt with it. Even if it was Walker who chose you for the leak sequence that kicked everything off, the *Messengers* chose you for this, Dan. They didn't want *me* plus one, they wanted *you* plus one. Me staying behind means I can deal with everything else... talking to Slater and Godfrey, Ding, and especially Cole. This could work out for the best."

Dan forced a slow nod. "But don't stress yourself out by doing too much at once, okay? Things are different now."

"Yes they *are*," she replied, leaning forward to kiss him goodbye. "And they'll still be different when you come back. All we need to do is save two worlds at once; I'll handle Earth, you handle New Kerguelen. Easy, right?"

This time Dan didn't have to force anything. He smiled widely, suddenly hit by a wave of realisation of how lucky he'd always been to have Emma in his life and how much luckier he'd just gotten to learn they would soon have a family, too.

His grin widened as he had the idea to appropriately turn back on Emma the words she'd spoken to him when he was about to meet John Cole in Havana. It was the last thing he said to her before entering the cornfield for the trip to New Kerguelen, and it had her smiling just as widely:

"I love you, Emma Ford, and there's *nothing* we can't do."

V minus 0

???
???

Tara squeezed Dan's hand tightly as they stepped into the elevator-like cylinder positioned underneath the enormous mothership that all but filled the cornfield.

He reassured her that there was nothing to worry about, feeling confident that this was the case. His own concerns regarded how grave the problems on New Kerguelen might be and how much the Messengers might be expecting his arrival to achieve; but in terms of the journey and the way they would be treated, his mind couldn't have been more relaxed.

An open-mouthed reaction of exactly the kind Dan expected crossed Tara's face as the total whiteness of the craft's vast entrance room hit her eyes like summer snow on a mountaintop kissed by the rays of a high-noon sun.

"Is it all like this?" she asked.

"I've never been further inside than this one room," Dan admitted, hopeful that might change. "How long is the journey?" he then asked, turning to the Messengers but speaking out loud.

The reply, of course, came only in his mind, leaving it for him to relay it to Tara. This led to him asking the Messengers if she could receive the same kind of neurological upgrade — if that was a remotely appropriate term — that the Messengers had granted him. It would make things easier, primarily for Tara, so Dan was glad that they responded affirmatively.

"They said you can get the same telepathy they gave me," he relayed.

Tara shook her head. "Thanks but no thanks. If that's okay…"

It *was* okay, the Messengers assured Dan, and they were in fact pleased given that 'mind adaption' — their term — was an intervention they didn't want to make unless it was absolutely necessary, as it had been to ensure they would remain able to stay in contact with Dan.

Again, Dan relayed this to a relieved Tara.

"What did they say about the journey?" she asked.

"Oh yeah… they said it's not really a journey as we would consider it. We don't 'travel' the whole distance in a linear way, there's some kind of portal near Earth and another one near New Kerguelen. They wouldn't tell me if they set those up; apparently the Elders were adamant that information on things like interstellar travel was never to be shared with other races because of the potential for unintended consequences. And even with the Elders dead, all of the aliens — even the Squadron — still live by the core edicts that are ingrained in their minds; it's only new decisions that are causing problems and division because there's no one there to make them. I guess we'll see exactly what's going on when we get there."

While Dan was speaking, one of the Messengers had been holding its hands against a seemingly nondescript part of the wall which was now revealed to house two reclined seats.

"Are those for us?" Tara asked. "We're just going to sit in here?"

One of the Messengers nodded. It struck Dan only then that he hadn't heard their sing-song like vocalisations for some time, with all of their communications having occurred silently both with him and amongst themselves.

He attentively listened to the fuller answer the Messengers delivered to Tara's question, knowing that it would be down to him to follow the familiar and somewhat frustrating pattern of passing the message on.

Dan could well understand why Tara didn't want to be changed in the way he had been, but there was no denying it would have made their mission far more straightforward if she had accepted the upgrade. He did however take solace from the fact that the Messengers hadn't suggested it, much less insisted upon it, as this made him think that it wouldn't necessarily have proven all that advantageous on New Kerguelen.

"We *are* sitting out here," he said as soon as he had the full answer, "but we're basically going to fall asleep and wake up on New Kerguelen. They said we *have* to be 'suspended' for the portal part of the journey, and they're going to do it right away. We won't feel a thing."

Tara walked over to her semi-reclined chair, which had an odd angle of curvature but in general terms wasn't a million miles from the kind of things she'd sat on in beauty spas from time to time. Upon sitting down, she was pleasantly and visibly surprised by the soft comfort it provided.

Dan joined her on the other seat just a few feet to the side. It *was* comfortable, bringing to mind his usual seat on Timo Fiore's private jet.

"Now what?" he asked, out loud.

In lieu of a direct answer, one of the Messengers tapped the wall to bring forth an enclosing bubble of sorts which extended from the wall to the floor with Dan and Tara on one side and everything else on the other.

"I guess this is it," he said to Tara.

"Thanks for letting me come," she replied, turning to face him.

He likewise turned his head to look her way. "Are you joking? I always want you around. We all do."

The last thing Dan saw before the light around him rapidly faded to black was Tara's warm smile. After that, there was only darkness.

FRIDAY

impact

Dan awoke only a second or two before Tara, but this was enough for him to see that the brilliant white light had returned to the room and the bubble was gone. The two familiar Messengers stood before him.

"Are we here?" he asked excitedly, his vocalisation startling Tara upright.

She smiled when she saw that the bubble was gone then waited in eager anticipation for Dan to relay the answer.

With a broad smile on his face, Dan turned to Tara and said the words she was waiting for: "We're here."

V plus 1

The Messengers, still only a pair, led Dan and Tara towards the elevator which was now the only thing between them and the surface of New Kerguelen.

The enormity of this really sunk in during the short descent, and Dan could feel his heart racing. "Do you want to step out first?" he asked Tara.

"Obviously," she smiled, "but not as much as I think you should be first. You *have* to be first. Nothing else makes sense."

As the elevator reached the ground, all thoughts of who would go first went out of the window. All either of them could focus on now was the panel that was about to open and reveal the outside world.

A million visions rattled through Dan's mind in an instant. What was he going to see?

He had seen every movie and read most of the books. Countless nights as a child, countless lunch breaks as an adult... all spent escaping to alien worlds full of wonder and surprise. With a *real* one now just inches away, he wondered which of all the imaginary versions would end up proving the most accurate.

Would he step into a field? A forest? A city? A desert?

The much anticipated opening of the panel revealed a view full of unnatural metallic surfaces, telling Dan that 'city' was without doubt the closest of his approximations. Tara nudged him forward to remove his choice of who would go first, and his first conscious thought related to the total lack of buildings.

"I think we're still inside something," he said to Tara, although by the time he spoke she was already next to him and thinking the same thing. "Maybe like an airport type of place?"

Tara looked all around, growing progressively more certain that Dan was right. In truth, having imagined endless starlit vistas and rolling alien landscapes, she very much *hoped* he was right.

The Messengers stepped forward, encouraging their visitors to follow.

"Before we go..." Tara said. "If I get the brain upgrade to be able to hear you and talk to Dan without actually talking, can you undo it before we go home?"

Both Messengers nodded, far less awkwardly than when they had first attempted this human gesture.

Tara's eyes widened hopefully. "Can I still get it?"

Two more nods confirmed that she could, and two short if painful minutes was all it took for the Messengers to repeat the process they had used on Dan a week earlier.

Tara practiced the necessary finger positions, which Dan no longer had to worry about now that his mental acuity had increased with experience, and the near euphoric expression in her eyes when she first heard the Messengers' thoughts made him more glad than ever that she'd come along.

"Can we go outside?" she asked without speaking. Dan heard the question just as clearly as the Messengers did. "Without suits or anything?"

"Outside is no place for life," one of them replied, clearly having no problem decoding Tara's thought patterns. Dan wasn't sure if this was because they'd had plenty of recent practice talking to him or if they had overestimated the differences between individual humans, but he didn't give it too much thought.

"Air breathable to us is air breathable to you," the Messenger continued, "but you will find none of that outside. This area, Sector Zero, is the only area of New Kerguelen with a gateway to the universe beyond. The rest of our home is entirely enclosed, as is necessary to keep an increasingly hostile atmosphere at bay."

Tara and Dan shared a very different kind of wide-eyed glance, before turning back to their hosts. "So you're always inside?" Dan pushed. "We're not going to get to go outside?"

Merely feeling the need to ask this caused Dan's heart to sink before a reply even came.

All of a sudden, Dan ruefully considered that this perhaps might not prove to be too unlike his trip to the secretive facility where he was taken by inquisitive federal agents on Contact Day.

Then, as now, his eventual visit to the kind of place he'd wanted to go for most of his life had begun with an indoor arrival at the end of a journey that left no possibility of tracing its location. *Unlike* then, however, he knew there was no way he could ever hope to pinpoint *this* location unless it was shared with him, which seemed incredibly unlikely.

"We spend our lives inside, yes. This is of necessity; New Kerguelen's atmospheric conditions are far less friendly to life than was once the case, but fortunately our ancestors built the Great Shelter when there was still time. Unfortunately, in recent times the Great Shelter has fallen into disrepair. Without the Elders to direct the necessary maintenance, the situation has worsened rapidly and continues to do so. Several sectors are already uninhabitable and more are not far away. But as well as unity we lack leadership, and more tangibly we lack knowledge. The Elders held the wisdom of ages gone by, and without access to that wisdom we cannot begin the necessary repairs."

Dan's shoulders slumped. "*What*? I can't help with something like that! I thought you just wanted my presence to unite your planet?"

"Humanity continues to build ever-grander structures despite the great social divisions that permeate your planet," the Messenger replied. "Your presence can unite *our* planet, and our hope is that by fostering trust in humanity it will allow greater outreach between our races. Our hope is that we can help each other with our strengths and be helped by each other in areas where we are weak. Our area of weakness is one for which we need help as a matter of urgency, but the membership of our planetary council currently distrusts us. Their distrust is such that if you were not here, they would disregard our reports of humanity's willingness to help and they would reject the kind of information exchange that will be needed to repair our Great Shelter."

Dan pondered this for several seconds. At last he could understand the logic of why he had been invited: to show the planetary council that humanity would be willing to help in a crucial matter the aliens couldn't handle on their own due to the unexpected deaths of their Elders. A new perspective based on humanity's willingness to help would eliminate or at least greatly reduce factional divisions on New Kerguelen, if the Messengers were correct, and Dan was giddily excited by the possibilities of what could come next.

He liked the sound of an 'information exchange' between Earth and New Kerguelen, and the idea of anything close to diplomatic relations or official scientific cooperation brought his mind straight back to the once-fantastical stories that had filled so much of his youth.

"We will take you to the council at once," one of the Messengers said. "Would you like to see our Elders?"

Dan McCarthy nodded decisively.

The setting may not have been quite the kind he had dreamed of, but he was regaining hope that the ending just might be.

V plus 2

Sector One
New Kerguelen

"So where is everyone?" Tara asked as she followed the Messengers through a door which led from the enormous Sector Zero into something more akin to a hallway. "And how many of you actually are there?"

She could easily have believed she was still inside the mothership, and indeed had something of a hard time reminding herself that she wasn't. The floor, the walls and the impossibly high ceiling of the narrow passage were all as white as the interior of the craft, but most conspicuous was the complete lack of other aliens.

Tara's second question about the size of New Kerguelen's population was not something Dan had ever really thought about, but now that it was in his mind he was tremendously curious and keen to find out.

"In the region of forty thousand," one of the Messengers replied.

"Wow," Dan reacted. Although he hadn't considered the point in great depth, his guess would have been at least one order of magnitude higher than this. "And no one is fit to replace your Elders? There isn't anyone else with accumulated wisdom... even someone like one of you guys? You know a *lot*. It might not help with this exact Shelter problem you have, but it would fix the power vacuum. Because that's going to be a problem even if human engineers fix your roof in exchange for whatever information and tech you can give us."

The Messengers stopped walking, quite abruptly.

"*Lop baan, mo san shoo,*" one sang into the air, the tone rising and falling melodically exactly as Dan remembered. "*Vadda lin, booh.*'

"*Seeshoo, daab collo,*" its partner replied.

Dan enjoyed the sound — it was truly soothing — but it didn't take a genius to know that the Messengers were using their vocalisations, understandable only to each other, because they wanted to discuss something without Dan hearing it.

No more vocalisations came.

"We confirmed previously that our Elders remain in death as they were in life, in all but their ability to guide us," one of the Messengers said. As ever, everything they said was now heard equally clearly by both Tara and Dan. "There is a reason why we cannot take their place, and it is an important one to understand."

The Messengers moved to the other side of the narrow corridor, and continued only another twenty paces or so. At that point, one touched the wall in a certain spot for several seconds to bring a previously concealed doorway into view.

Dan and Tara were far too far down the rabbit hole to turn back now and each knew it just as well as the other. They stepped forward in unison, crossing the threshold like it was nothing.

The room they entered was very different from those before it, by simple virtue of the fact that it wasn't a void of nothingness. Dan's eyes took in everything, from the low chairs to the long window-like panel that ran horizontally along the far side of the room and essentially served as the upper half of its wall.

He walked over, naturally enough, and there he saw two tall metallic pillars on the other side of the glass. Clearly man-made — or *alien*-made, to be more precise — the perfectly crafted grey pillars extended at least twenty metres into the air, far higher than the ceiling of the room Dan observed them from. They had a polished sheen and a very slight bezel-like groove around each of their sides, which planted a seed in Dan's mind that they could perhaps act as screen-like displays for relaying data of some kind.

Something about them made them seem like a lot more than mere pillars, and Dan grew surer by the second that they were powered appliances or instruments of some kind.

He belatedly noticed that a similar room to the one he was standing in appeared directly in front of him, with one to the left and another to the right. The pillars were in a central quadrant observable from four different rooms, for one reason or another.

Upon closer inspection, Dan saw that the pillars were connected to each other by a cable not altogether unlike that which had once been connected to his own neck. Furthermore, four other cables ran from each pillar: one entering each of the surrounding rooms.

"So where are the Elders?" Tara asked, standing at Dan's side having sauntered over to the window more slowly after examining everything en route. The room's layout and furniture wasn't quite as 'alien' as she may have expected, but on reflection this made a fair degree of sense given that the Messengers were bipedal humanoids of relatively similar height and weight, so it stood to reason that they would find physical comfort in similar places.

To her question, the Messengers said nothing.

"Are you taking us to see them next?" she pushed. "Are the Elders in another sector?"

"Tara…" Dan said, speaking out loud and momentarily breaking his visual focus to look into her eyes, "we're looking at them right now. I wouldn't believe what I'm about to tell you if I wasn't seeing this with my own eyes, but I don't think their Elders are 'dead' because I don't think they were ever really alive."

She gasped, stunned. "You mean…"

"Yeah," Dan said. "Their Elders were machines."

Part 8

TURNABOUT

*"It is folly for a man to pray to the gods
for that which he has the power
to obtain by himself."*

Epicurus

V plus 3

Sector One
New Kerguelen

"They're like… supercomputers," Dan said, uttering the words to Tara as both gawped at the so-called Elders in stunned realisation. "I don't know what words *we* would use, maybe *AI mainframe* or something like that, but not *Elders*. When those things were operational with data scrolling or static on their surfaces, they might've looked more like something we'd have a reference point for, but this is just…"

"Insane," Tara offered, finishing the sentence with Dan's exact thought. "And I'm guessing when the Messengers tell us these things are 'dead', that means it's gonna take more than a firmware update or a call to tech support to get them back online."

Although he remained too shocked to laugh, Dan ran with her attempt at levity. "Yeah, something tells me we can't just switch these things off and on to reboot them."

"*I've* got a reference point," Tara said in a higher-pitched tone. "This is like if you always use GPS to find your way around, and then one day it stops working. Right? Because they got so dependent on asking these things for answers… when the answers stopped coming, they'd forgotten how to think for themselves."

"It's exactly like that," Dan sighed. "It's *exactly* like that. This has always been one of the hypothetical concerns about an established technocratic society. When the tech stops working, then what? Yeah, there's a power vacuum that causes problems like we're seeing here... but there's also a total helplessness and inability to make decisions that had been made by the tech. If you don't use a muscle it wastes away — you know, atrophy — and as *intelligent* as these aliens obviously are, they let themselves get totally *dependent*."

Tara nodded slowly, like she largely understood. "So technocracy is like democracy but with computers in charge, basically? But the computers didn't build themselves, so everything they know must have been programmed into them, right?"

"Not exactly," Dan said, aware that he was likely to reach the boundary of his own limited understanding of Artificial Intelligence almost as soon as he started trying to explain it. "We haven't achieved it yet but real AI, once it's established, learns and develops independently. It's like when two people have a kid... they need to 'make' it and teach it the basics, then give it decent input as it's growing up, but eventually it can overtake them and keep going and going. I can see why the Messengers came to see these machines as gods, but I don't get why they called them Elders."

At this, Tara turned away from the window and faced the Messengers to do the obvious thing and ask them outright: "Why do you call them Elders?"

The Messengers took several seconds before replying to consider both Tara and Dan's inner thoughts carefully. The distinction between bona fide Elders and a sophisticated decision-making system put in place by long-gone forefathers was an alien one to the Messengers, and it was a distinction that proved as surprising to them as its absence had to Dan and Tara.

Eventually, one of the Messengers replied, explaining that the Elders had been in place for hundreds of generations, seeded by the wisdom of the ancients, and had grown ever-wiser with time. This didn't answer anything specifically, but at least confirmed to Dan that the Messengers did on some level understand that the Elders they had described as 'dead' had never truly been alive.

Dan's lines of understanding were blurry, though; for as great as the breakthroughs in interspecies communication had been since his earlier encounters with the Messengers, his brain and theirs were still very differently configured supercomputers in their own right, trying valiantly to find an island of common understanding amid the ocean of stars that had separated them for so long.

As with when he had been rendered speechless by the Messengers' almost-but-not-quite human faces during his first interaction with them, Dan once again considered that much of the difficulty he was experiencing came not because the two races were utterly different, but rather because their broad physical and mental similarities brought the few huge differences into sharper focus than might otherwise have been the case.

"And these ancients you speak of..." Dan said, out loud, "were they *your* ancestors? Or were you seeded here by another, older race? That's important for me to understand."

The answer came quickly and clearly: "They were our direct ancestors, as the builders of your pyramids were yours, and they were born here as we were. Many generations ago, the wisest among them — the wisest among *us* — developed the Elders. More than mere repositories of knowledge, the Elders were the arbiters of all disputes and the guiding hand of all progress. An epoch of harmony endured until very recently, when the Elders ceased responding reliably and ultimately ceased responding at all."

Dan nodded, glad that the Messenger was being so open and even more so that it was able to explain things in a way he could understand. The mention of ancient pyramids and repositories of knowledge brought to his mind Alexandria and other libraries lost to time, where the wisdom of ages gone by had been burned to ash and returned to the ether. It was impossible not to see the similarity here, in a situation where too much knowledge and wisdom had been stored externally and not passed directly between generations. Tara's GPS analogy rattled around alongside these thoughts, too, bringing into sharp focus the danger of depending too much on anything but internalised knowledge.

Computers break down and books burn, he thought to himself. *The safest place is within ourselves.*

Although Dan didn't intend this as a comment to the Messengers, as a clear thought it was naturally picked up.

"The wisdom of the Elders was far greater than any one individual could hope to possess," came the somewhat defensive reply.

"Who said anything about one individual?" Dan asked rhetorically. "And I'm not saying don't write stuff down or use technology, but look at you now! You can travel the stars following the instructions the Elders gave you, fine, but now that they're gone you can't even patch a broken roof? That's basically what this 'Great Shelter' you're struggling with is, isn't it... a roof? *Birds* can build shelters. *Termites* can build shelters!

When you rely on a machine, you lose something innate. But that doesn't have to be forever; the Elders are gone, but you're still here."

Tara looked sideways at Dan, worried he was being too firm.

"And you already have a council," he continued. "What's the deal there? Why are you making *some* decisions among yourselves?"

"The council met regularly to propose questions for the Elders and to discuss the answers we received. As Interpreters, we were the go-between. That's why when the answers stopped coming, we lost the trust of our council."

Dan scratched his chin. In some ways it all made sense, but in many others he couldn't even begin to wrap his head around it. "Okay... so you need humanity's help with your Shelter, right? The Elders would have told you what to do, but they're gone. And since they're gone... what's happening, the decision of whether or not to engage with us in a full information exchange is gridlocked? Where does the Squadron fit in to this?"

"The Squadron are our security force," the Messenger replied. "They are the only other group on New Kerguelen with access to a craft capable of reaching Earth. You attack our lack of intergenerational teachings from a place of ignorance, for specialised skills and knowledge are passed routinely down the generations just as they are on Earth. The problem with the Great Shelter is of a kind we have never faced; it was constructed by individuals with the necessary knowledge — clearly — but no maintenance has ever been required. The skills and knowledge of construction were lost to time, I grant you that, but how many humans today possess the knowledge that brought your species to its apex position? To spark a fire from sticks and stones, to navigate by the stars alone... *how many?* You lean on technology just as we do! Our grave error was to consider our Elders immortal and infallible, but there is nothing we can do about that now. We called you here to help us, not to kick us when we are down."

Dan's expression changed in an instant with this reply. A wave of guilt hit him; when the Messengers saved Earth on Contact Day, they had said nothing of the political shambles and ideological infighting that had led to the collapse of humanity's own efforts to divert Il Diavolo's course. They had come to help, and help they did — without judgement.

"I want to address your council now," Dan said, stepping away from the window and gently touching Tara's shoulder to simultaneously tell her everything was okay and to encourage her to come along. "My mind is never going to be clearer about all of this than it is right now, and it's time to look forward, not back. I want to help you. *Humanity* wants to help you. Any kind of information exchange will be welcomed and something like the Shelter is, with respect, probably a fairly basic thing for our best minds to assist you with."

"No disrespect taken," one of the Messengers replied. "The benefit of an information exchange is that one party can assist in what is easy for them when the other party experiences difficulty with the same task or issue. We have methods of utilising energy that could transform life on your planet and eliminate a great deal of unnecessary suffering. The Elders urged against sharing anything of that nature, but they also would have urged against our calling you here. It is time to look forward, as you say, but first the council must be convinced of both our trustworthiness and your willingness to assist with our pressing problem regarding the Great Shelter. Success will lead to the Squadron retreating from Earth and ending their communications with the worst of your kind, allowing normality to return."

This part struck Dan as a stretch — that normality would return as soon as the aliens were gone and Jack was dealt with — but de-escalation would be a step in the right direction. And with powerful fingers on dangerous buttons while spaceships cast shadows over several cities, the urgency was as real for Earth as it was for New Kerguelen.

Dan and Tara followed the Messengers back out of the windowed room and into the corridor, where they proceeded for several minutes without passing another being. It was impossible not to wonder how big New Kerguelen was and where its tens of thousands of inhabitants were hiding, but Dan tried to focus his mind. Precisely what he had to achieve in his upcoming discussion with a potentially hostile council of extraterrestrials was less clear than had ever been the case before stepping into any other difficult meeting or interview, and the stakes had never been higher.

The Messengers stopped abruptly and one touched yet another unmarked area of the wall. Could they see things he couldn't, Dan wondered, or did they remember every single location like squirrels digging up their buried acorns?

"The council are gathered for our arrival," one of the Messengers said, standing beside the newly revealed doorway. It had a panel that would evidently slide to the side, not too unlike the door of the mothership's elevator.

"All we need to do is convince them humanity is their friend and that they should forget about the Elders they've pretty much worshipped for thousands of years," Dan said, forcing a light-hearted tone in an effort to calm Tara's nerves, which had very understandably become evident in her tense expression and shaking legs.

"Exactly," she said. "So easy, even you can do it!"

Dan laughed, caught fully off-guard by her own jovial reply.

"I want to see your game face, Dan McCarthy," she then said, suddenly serious as she uncannily mimicked her sister's voice and cadence.

As the door panel slid open and with his foot preparing to step across the threshold, Dan looked in her eyes. "Ready?"

"Of course I'm ready," Tara replied with a contagious degree of confidence. "We didn't come all this way for the weather and we didn't come for the view. We came here to do this, Dan, so let's get it goddamn done."

V plus 4

With focus in his eyes if not quite a spring in his step, Dan McCarthy walked into what was easily the most ornate room he had seen on New Kerguelen so far. There were no windows, with the four walls instead positively covered in decorative shapes and swirls in several pastel colours.

The art, if that was what it was, truly looked like nothing Dan had seen before; the best he could do was liken it to a curious cross between floral wallpaper and tribal tattoos.

What truly caught his eye, however, was the group of seven extraterrestrial beings sitting around a circular glass table on low glass stools.

All turned to see him and each wore a differently coloured tunic, seeming to indicate the specialised group they represented. Dan saw a sky-blue tunic as worn by the Squadron, but there was no Messenger-white to be seen.

As soon as he wondered about this, he heard the simple and unfortunate explanation that the representative from the Interpreter grouping to which they belonged had been suspended following the Elders' 'deaths'. As the Messengers had told Dan before, they were blamed for this catastrophic event having failed to see any signs of a problem until it was too late; until the Elders had become so unresponsive that they couldn't offer any advice on how to help them recover full function.

Dan asked quickly about the nature of the groupings and received a reply built around the term 'hereditary path' and the point that everyone on New Kerguelen was born into one of eight specialisations and was raised from birth in accordance with its specific needs. This system had been put in place by the Elders long ago, the Messenger said, but long after the passing of the forefathers who created them.

The word hereditary made Dan think of this structure as something of a caste system, and he considered it decidedly sub-optimal. Streaming citizens into set groups from birth ruled out anyone from excelling in any discipline other than that which was thrust upon them. Dan could only imagine the geniuses and breakthroughs Earth would have gone without had such a system been in place during the past few hundred years.

But as conceptually interesting as this was, he marked it down as one more thing to think and ask about once his real work was done.

"So I guess we're standing and they're sitting?" Tara said.

"Please," a Messenger said, walking to the table and tapping its surface.

"You want us to stand on the table?" Dan asked.

The reply came back that it was a platform rather than a table, but this hardly changed how bizarre it felt in his mind. He was then struck by a thought of wonder as to what the aliens might make of the layout of the US Congress or a British-style parliament when seeing it for the first time, and suddenly this elevated setup didn't seem quite so ridiculous.

Dan helped Tara up first and then took a step to join her. It was impossible not to feel like he was dreaming, and this was a feeling he didn't fight; if anything, it helped to counter the overwhelmed feelings that came with considering just how real the situation truly was.

"Our counterparts from other groupings lack the direct ability to understand your thoughts and words," a Messenger said, handing Dan and Tara a cable each. He thought he knew what came next, but the instruction that followed was for each of them to attach it to their index finger via a kind of semi-adhesive covering. To Dan, this didn't seem altogether dissimilar from the old-fashioned rubber thumbs that bank tellers used to wear when counting large quantities of money.

As they painlessly attached the cables to their fingers in the same manner, far more welcome than the invasive insertions they'd imagined, Dan and Tara watched the Messengers attach the other ends of the cables to the table. Then, to their moderate surprise, the Messengers handed each of the councillors a cable and encouraged them to attach them to their own fingers.

Dan had already known that the other aliens lacked the Messengers' communicational abilities, but he was only now coming to see that this 'table' was clearly anything but decorative.

The sight of seven aliens attaching a small device to themselves in order to hear and understand the words of two foreign visitors brought to mind old television footage from inside the United Nations, where countless delegates would listen through earphones to the speeches of others translated into their own native language.

It wasn't *quite* like that, of course, but the thought was there.

The silence in the room would have been eerie if Dan had noticed it, but the sound of his heart was all he could hear.

Although no sounds were actually made, the silence effectively ended when one of the Messengers began proceedings by thanking the councillors for allowing them back into the room and promising that they wouldn't regret it.

No replies came into Dan or Tara's minds, but they couldn't be sure whether this was because the councillors neglected to say anything or whether their brains were simply incapable of receiving their thoughts.

"Our friends from Earth would like to make a case for pursuing active cooperation between our races to an extent the Elders consistently advised against," the Messenger continued, "and we beg you to consider their words. Earth is not a perfect planet, as we know, but it is populated by many good and true beings. We come to you today with two of them."

The Messenger gestured towards Dan and Tara, who were side by side on the table rather than back to back. They each looked down at the faces on one side, forcing smiles through the impossible awkwardness of their elevated positions without even knowing if smiles would be understood.

Words were the way forward, quite clearly, so Dan McCarthy cleared his throat and spoke from the heart.

~

"We come in peace," Dan said, fighting the urge to grin at finally being able to appropriately open a conversation with this age-old classic line. He spoke out loud primarily because he figured that doing so would focus his mind on choosing the right words and would reduce the chance of any imprecision or misunderstanding. "We come to usher in an era of active cooperation that will help you with your Great Shelter, and we come at the request of your Interpreters who have already done so much to help *us*."

Upon completing this sentence and waiting several seconds for some kind of reply, it hit Dan that he wasn't going to get any feedback at all during what was clearly going to be more of a speech than a conversation.

"I don't know what your problem actually is here," Tara interjected, taking over in a fairly sharp tone that gave Dan cause for concern. "You need help with this Shelter and if it's just a technical construction thing, humanity can almost definitely give you that help. What else do you want us to say? What else do you *need* us to say? We have a problem of our own right now because your guys are causing it," she continued, pointing quite aggressively at the blue-tunic wearing representative of New Kerguelen's Squadron caste. "But your Interpreters... these are the guys you should be listening to. They saved us from the comet and they brought us here while there's still a chance to save you from yourselves. Get out of their way."

Dan glanced at Tara, wondering what the hell she was doing. But then he caught sight of the Messengers out of the corner of his eye and saw that both of them were nodding. *Was this what they wanted... passion?*

"Let me tell you a story you might not know," Dan said, following his gut. "Once upon a time, a comet almost killed us. Once upon a time, your Elders almost let it. If your Interpreters hadn't made a passionate case to the Elders in favour of intervention just like I'm making a passionate case to you right now in favour of pursuing active interplanetary cooperation, I'd be dead. Tara would be dead. Neither of us would be here to make this case, and no one on Earth would be alive to help you with your Shelter. Your Elders got it wrong until your Interpreters won them round, and if that doesn't tell you that life can go on just fine without Elders so long as you listen to and trust each other... I don't know what will."

The silence and lack of physical movement that followed what Dan had hoped would be a decisive point told him that more was needed. He took a few seconds to think of how to phrase it, then spoke again:

"You're an intelligent race with free will, bound only by the decision-making restrictions you've placed upon yourselves. Your Elders may have been wise and knowledgeable, but they were bound by limitations you don't face. Unlike the purely rational Elders, you *can* be rational but you aren't limited to *only* consider rational concerns. Ethically, morally, or however you want to frame it, you are capable of more... you are capable of better.

"You see, your Interpreters *wanted* to save Earth. They wanted to save *us*. Motivated by a desire to help for the sake of helping, they presented the issue to the Elders in a way that made a rational case for intervention: they argued that by protecting the only other intelligent race known to yours, the Elders would be keeping around a potential source of future help should the shoe ever be on the other foot... exactly like it is now. Your Interpreters were able to use rationality for good, but only because they were able to think *beyond* it. If they had taken the Elders' initial answer that an intervention wasn't justified, Earth would have been destroyed and I wouldn't be standing here now, promising all the help my planet can offer."

This time, Dan felt done. He didn't know what the hell else to say, and no one else was saying anything. Until, that was, Tara stepped back in.

"There's wisdom and there's kindness," she said, "and your Elders were only capable of the former. Your Interpreters, on the other hand, showed that kindness is stronger than cold rationality. And whether you know it or not, kindness is within you, too. Kindness is also within the people of Earth — so long as you don't pick out the worst possible example like your Squadron did — and the people of Earth want to help you. Please, get out of your own way and *let* us help you. Squadron commander, if you *are* the commander... just call back your guys before they do something they can't take back, okay?"

The alien in question, sitting bolt upright in its sky-blue tunic, offered no reaction whatsoever to being directly addressed in this manner.

"And everyone else..." she went on, "wake up and reinstate your Interpreters to this council where they belong. And while you're at it, let this council take the place of your Elders. You've already been accustomed to voting on which questions to ask the Elders and how to apply their answers, so just start asking those questions of each other! That's what *we* do. It's not perfect, but we're still around, and all we want to do is cooperate to make life better for everyone. People from this planet saved Earth when the comet was coming and people from Earth can save this planet before the Shelter is beyond repair. But that's just *saving* each other. Imagine all of the things we can share and achieve when we work together on progress instead of problems. That's the way *I* want to move forward: together."

One of the Messengers then surprised everyone, and no one more so than its human guests, by beginning a slow and physically laboured round of applause. Its partner joined in, with both looking like toy monkeys clapping their cymbals, but Dan didn't know quite whether the Messengers thought applause was a sign of approval or simply what people did at the conclusion of a speech.

Without further context beyond what they had seen at the edge of the cornfield prior to the journey, when they had first copied this human action, he could see that the Messengers would've had a fair reason to believe either.

In either case, however, they clearly thought the speech was over.

"I'm so glad you came," Dan whispered out of the side of his mouth, drawing a warm smile from Tara.

As silence returned, the Messengers removed the cables from the table. With his connection to the other aliens broken, Dan asked the first and only question in his mind: "How did it go?"

Tara waited just as eagerly for the answer.

Even before an answer came, however, the alien in the sky-blue tunic rose from its chair and left the room.

While one Messenger gathered the discarded cables from the surface of the table, the other positioned itself directly in front of Dan and Tara. Reacting to the Squadron representative's exit, a slow and very deliberate smile spread across its face.

It wasn't the most aesthetically pleasing facial expression Dan had ever seen, but it sent a flood of joyous relief coursing through his veins like none before it.

"The Squadron will be gone from Earth within minutes," the Messenger said. "It is done, friends; you have succeeded."

Tara excitedly wrapped her arms around Dan and jumped up and down like she was celebrating a last-second sporting victory. This victory was more important than any other she could imagine, and the joy was expressed with suitable physicality.

After five seconds or so she let go of Dan and turned to the Messenger, opening her arms. It rather humorously stepped back to avoid physical contact that would have been unwanted even though it fully understood the friendliness behind the offer. Then, however, it smiled again and extended its hand.

Tara shook it with mock formality, which naturally went way over the Messenger's head but amused Dan nonetheless.

The other council members were by now on their feet and heading for the door, none appearing moved in any way by the celebratory scenes before them.

"What sealed it?" Dan asked, purely curious.

The Messenger ushered them towards the door as he replied. "Well, our councillors were unaware of our role in persuading the Elders to authorise the cometary intervention, and that detail greatly changed their perspective on both our trustworthiness and the Elders' fallibility. It was an astute observation, but the point about looking forward to a progress-driven future of cooperation is what fully convinced the councillors of humanity's positive nature. Diplomatic relations depend on trust, and you earned that today."

"All in a day's work," Tara said, playfully nudging Dan's arm to gloat that her spirited words had played such an important role.

For his part, Dan paused to consider the point about earning trust. Did people like Godfrey and Cole — the people who made most of Earth's major decisions, when it came down to it — deserve trust from anyone, let alone a distant alien race?

He tried not to dwell on this, knowing that things on Earth would take care of themselves and that the future was now something to look forward to for all kinds of reasons. Diplomatic relations and a mutually beneficial information exchange between Earth and New Kerguelen were wonderful things to anticipate, but the biggest thing in Dan's future utterly dominated his mind as soon as he stepped out of the council room.

"When can we go home?" he asked, picturing Emma's face and the exciting months that lay ahead before their lives would be changed forever in the best way by the arrival of their child.

"Soon," one of the Messengers said. It stopped walking and quickly revealed a new door in the now-familiar manner. "There's just one more room I want you to see first."

V plus 5

Standing beside a newly revealed door, one of the Messengers encouraged Dan and Tara to walk into a room from which the first loud noises they'd heard since arriving rushed towards them and filled their ears like a million birds singing at the sun.

Dan led the way towards what looked like a window but was in fact an open and elevated lookout to a vast area below. On the ground, hundreds of small aliens were frolicking around in colour coded groups, chirping out their hypnotising vocalisations and looking as human as aliens could be.

They didn't seem to be *inside*, as such, but rather within a vast open area in which Dan saw water running in a stream and also some odd-looking trees that were *just* familiar enough to be recognised as such. The Great Shelter, Dan could see, was an extremely high and entirely transparent *roof*, in essence.

Roof may not have been the best word, but it didn't look domed.

In any event, beyond the Shelter — which was only visible at all due to some areas displaying slight reflections — Dan saw the mesmerising light of two suns.

Somehow it all felt real only now: he was on an alien planet, looking down at hundreds of aliens and standing next to one of their senior figures.

The ending *had* turned out to be the kind Dan had hoped for, and he felt a glow throughout his being as he gazed down in happiness at the last-minute realisation that the setting was, too. He would never forget his time on New Kerguelen and would be forever grateful that the Messengers had given him this beautiful sight.

As Tara looked down, her eyes and mouth slowly widened in a cartoon-like display of wonder. "Can we talk to them?" she asked, over-whelmed by the scale of the cuteness.

"If the council meeting had failed, we would have announced your arrival in public as a last-ditch effort to force the council's hand," the Messenger said. "But as you succeeded, we do not need to involve the general population quite yet. Your existence is not yet common knowledge, and we will carefully consider how to break that news."

"They deserve to know," Dan said, quite firmly.

"And they will, very soon," the Messenger replied without taking offence. "But as you know better than anyone, the manner in which such things are learned can have a profound effect on social stability. We will first announce that a solution has been found to our Great Shelter problem and that the council has found a way to assume the functional role previously played by our Elders, because introducing novelty to stability is always safer than introducing novelty to chaos."

Dan nodded, accepting the reasoning. He trusted the Messengers absolutely and took this one at its word that the regular inhabitants of New Kerguelen would learn the truth before long — that they were not alone.

"I brought you in here to show you who you saved today," the Messenger said, looking down at the youth of his planet. "Soon they will learn of this day — the day of the Visit — and you will both be remembered fondly."

This brought a tear to Dan's eye; not the part about being thanked and remembered, which was never what he cared about, but the fact that the Messenger had wanted them to see the alien children for such a thoughtful and warm-hearted reason.

"Thank you," Dan said.

It turned to him and slowly shook its head. "Thank *you*, Dan McCarthy... and thank *you*, Tara Ford."

Tara still looked slightly disappointed that she couldn't talk to the children, but she took one last long glance and knew it was a sight she would never forget. *"Now* can we go home?" she asked with a slight chuckle.

The Messenger gave its trademark awkward smile. "Of course. *Home."*

V plus 6

???
???

"Where are we?" Dan asked, waking up perfectly refreshed after a return journey which once again felt like it had taken no time at all. "And how long have we been gone?"

"Hovering high above the cornfield," one of the nearby Messenger's voices answered in his mind. "Totally undetectable, but we can remove the cloak at any moment. And we have been gone for less than one full day."

To Dan, this was good news on both counts. He stayed seated for a few moments, mulling things over.

He knew that life would never be the same again given his reluctant telekinetic outburst before leaving for New Kerguelen. People would look at him differently all over again, and even more so than had been the case after Contact Day.

He *didn't* know exactly what might happen as soon as he stepped back onto terra firma, but it seemed all but certain that a slew of shady federal agents would be waiting to take him away for testing.

That was déjà vu he didn't want but couldn't avoid, he figured, but it suddenly occurred to him that none of that had to happen quite yet.

"Can you take us home?" he asked, his eyes lighting up as the idea struck. "Like, just put us inside so no one knows? Then we can see Emma and Clark, talk about everything, see where can go from here... all before anyone else knows we're back. Obviously if there are any problems out there and I need to show up right away I will, and it'll be better because I'll know what I'm stepping into and Emma can help out."

"Definitely that," Tara seconded. "Can we do that?"

The Messenger closest to their seats gave its now familiar nod.

Tara stood up. "But first, can you put my brain back to normal like you said you would?"

"Me too," Dan requested without missing a beat, taking both Tara and the Messengers by surprise. "You guys are cool, but I want to be human again."

The Messenger nearest Dan looked intently into his eyes. "Are you sure? We cannot guarantee that we would be able to perform the process again should you change your mind."

"I won't," he said. "I want to be human. But with active cooperation and diplomatic relations in place, we'll be able to develop external translators by working together, anyway. Soon, language won't be a barrier at all."

With no further attempt to dissuade Dan and no attempt at all to dissuade Tara, the Messengers gave each of them the same apparatus that had been used to deliver their mental upgrades in the first place.

"I didn't even test my telekinesis," Tara said, suddenly realising.

Her Messenger stopped.

"No, keep going," she smiled. "I don't *want* to test it, I was just thinking. I want to be human, too."

Dan nodded in support of her decision. He hadn't liked the feeling of generating the forcefield or even catching Emma's falling drink on the plane... in every way, it felt like the wrong kind of power.

After enduring some painful but manageable sensations in their necks and fingers while their upgrades were deactivated, for lack of more appropriate terminology, Dan and Tara sat back down at the Messengers' request.

"This next part is gonna be so cool," Tara said, positively beaming with excitement.

Dan looked over at her and smiled. She had helped enormously — *crucially* — but primarily he was just glad to see her looking so happy. She had been through far more than anyone ever should and had come out of the other side not only still standing, but standing proud and standing victorious.

"It sure is," Dan replied. "It sure is."

V plus 7

After a sudden flash they seemed to *feel* as well as see, Dan and Tara found themselves sitting on Tara's bed.

"Hooooome," she sighed, sounding more joyous than relieved as she threw her head back onto what struck Dan as far too many pillows.

The next thing either of them heard was Rooster barking on the other side of the door.

"We should wait," Dan said. "He might get a fright if we open up. Emma or Clark are bound to hear him and be here any second."

While he waited, Dan lifted his phone from his pocket. The battery wasn't even half depleted, which confirmed the Messenger's answer about them only having been gone for less than a day even before he saw the date and time.

He then loaded up the ACN app to take a look at the news headlines for an insight into what had happened in their absence and how everything was being reported, but the door swung suddenly open before he learned anything.

Rather than Emma, they saw Clark. His expression transformed in two distinct steps: first from fear to surprise, and then from surprise to

420

relieved amusement. "Planning on coming outta there anytime soon?" he laughed from the doorway.

Emma was at his side within a few seconds, and then inside the room within a few more. "I don't know what you did, but it worked!" she told them, grabbing both at once for a reunion group hug.

Clark was crouched in the doorway, comforting Rooster even though his fear had this time faded as soon as he saw who was behind the door; the old dog's knack for sensing alien interventions was as strong as ever, but he seemed to be less distressed each time and now apparently reacted primarily to alert his human friends rather than to express his own discomfort.

"So what's the story?" Clark asked. "Are the Messengers gone?"

Dan explained the situation as succinctly as he could, starting with the last part about the Messengers currently hovering safely out of sight above the cornfield and having agreed to send Dan and Tara home until they felt ready to return to the craft for a more public arrival.

"That is *perfect*," Emma said. "In fact that is *so* perfect I couldn't have picked anything any better! I had an idea and this makes it better… this makes it so much more impactful."

"What is it?" Tara asked.

Clark interjected: "Forget that, what happened on New Kerguelen? The Squadron just up and left all of a sudden and no one knows why. Jack is in custody in Havana and none of the big guns have made any public comments except to say they're eagerly anticipating your return. Godfrey and Ding issued a *joint* statement saying that, because I think they've realised that no one can come out of this with any credibility unless they eat humble pie together — that way they don't lose face relative to each other, you know? Yesterday is going to live forever in everyone's memory but people don't want chaos and division like that ever again… people in China, people here, people in Vanuatu and wherever the hell else you want to mention. You can check out the statement and everything, but first you need to tell us: what happened out there?"

"It was *amazing*," Tara gushed. "At the end we saw all of the little aliens at school, and we had to talk to the planetary council to convince them that the Messengers were trustworthy and that humanity can help them. Their problem is this big thing they call the Great Shelter… it keeps them safe from the environment outside, which has been getting worse, and the Shelter is falling apart but they don't know how to fix it. They were totally dependent on the Elders because all of their decisions have been— and oh my god the Elders were machines!" she shrieked, interrupting herself. "Supercomputers, built forever ago by their ancient ancestors. What was it you said, Dan, technocratic? It was *crazy*."

The overwhelmed expressions on Clark and Emma's faces reflected this craziness, which was even harder to handle when it all came at once rather than one revelation at a time as it had for the visiting duo.

"So you had a fun trip?" Emma laughed, unsure where to start. "I'll tell you what though, Tara... why don't you fill Clark in on that right now, and I'll talk to Dan about this idea I have. Because we don't have all that much time, and if this is going to have any chance of working I have to start putting it together pretty much right now."

Clark sat down on Tara's bed, indicating his agreement with the plan. Their interaction immediately before her departure had changed the way he saw things between them, and the look in Tara's eyes suggested that he wasn't alone in that regard.

"So the main thing to know about the Messengers and all the other groups — which I'll get to — is that they were totally dependent on the Elders for everything," Tara said.

Dan listened to the first part of her excited rundown as he very briefly scrolled through news headlines on his phone. He took delight in seeing an image of Jack Neal in handcuffs; no one had ever deserved it more.

"Like, think about if someone's phone stops working," Tara went on. Dan headed out of the bedroom, but still heard her talking as he walked. "Suddenly they can't use the maps and the calculator and everything else they've always relied on, right? But even if just their contact list froze, they wouldn't be able to call anyone because they don't actually know anyone's number! It was like that... they can't fix their roof because no one has had to do it for hundreds of generations and the knowledge was only inside the computers that don't work anymore!"

"They can't fix a *roof*?" Clark asked, chortling in disbelief. "*I* can fix a damn roof!"

Dan and Emma both shook their heads and smiled as they reached the kitchen and closed the door to both drown out the incoming sound and give themselves some privacy.

"Before I get into this, do we have anything to worry about?" Emma asked.

"Like what?"

She shrugged. "Disagreements on New Kerguelen, grievance from the Squadron, anything like that?"

"Not at all," Dan said. "They don't hold grudges in the same way we do, and the Squadron were basically trying to do a good thing in a really bad way. They wanted help to save their planet just like the Messengers did, but they distrusted them so much that they distrusted *us* by extension. It's all water under the bridge, though."

"And speaking of water under the bridge..." Emma replied. "You heard what Clark said about the joint statement, right? Ding and Godfrey know that the split just won't stand anymore, not after the chaos of yesterday. We know Godfrey is a political survivor that would outlast the cockroaches if a nuke ever went off, but Ding has the same instincts. They're willing to work together to protect themselves, and things are in motion behind the scenes for a single agency with two offices: East and West. It's going to be a UN body specifically created to handle future contact-related issues, and they're going to ask you to be the figurehead."

Dan's eyes widened.

"Godfrey and Ding both know they can't credibly lead anything without you — not now — and they know there's no public appetite for any more competition over who's in charge. If you say yes, you won't have to live in New York or anything like that, you'll just have to show up every now and then. Your role is mainly for show, which doesn't mean it's not important. They basically need you for this to work because the public won't buy into it if you're not there, and neither will the Messengers... they just handpicked you for contact, *again*, and everyone knows that."

"I'm glad of that, because *I'm* not going to say no," Dan said, surprised by the news of this incredible invitation and also slightly surprised that he didn't feel overawed by it. "We're way past that. I can't go back to normal after what's happened in the past week, so if they want me to help out by giving it credibility or stability or anything else then I'll do what I can. I'll say no if you think I should, with everything we have ahead of us, but I think this is like what you said when I was leaving: doing this and eliminating the stupid tension we've all had to deal with recently could be the best way of making sure we bring this kid into a world worth living in. There's no parapet big enough to cover me now, anyway, so I think it's pretty clear cut. If you think this is a good idea, I'm all the way in."

"I remember when I used to have to twist your arm to get you to do a magazine interview in a hair salon," she replied, "and now you're volunteering to be Earth's official point of interplanetary contact."

Dan shook his head several times. "I *hated* that damn salon. But about this plan you have..."

Emma stood up and opened the kitchen door. "Tara," she called.

"You used to want to be an events planner… how about you start rounding up everyone on this guest list I'm working on? So far we've got Slater, Godfrey, Cole, Ding and Timo."

"Timo I can do," Tara yelled in reply, drawing laughter all round.

"You're fired," Dan chuckled.

Tara emerged at her bedroom door, feigning sadness. "But I'm still planning your wedding, right? Or are we shotgunning that now?"

"Ha-ha," Emma said, returning to the kitchen table. "We've been engaged since the day that damn comet passed by and the date has been set for months, smart ass. *But…* you *are* gonna need to figure something out for my dress. The design and measurements you were working with aren't exactly going to work in another three months…"

"It's going to be some year," Dan mused. "Three months until the wedding, five more after that until the baby."

Emma kissed him before she sat back down.

"Sure is," she said. "There's just this one tiny little other thing to get out of the way first…"

THREE DAYS LATER

V plus 8

On a sunny Monday afternoon in New York, leaders from both sides of the previously chasmic GCC-ELF divide emerged from the UN building to deliver a very meaningful announcement to the world's media.

The famous backdrop hadn't been the focus of so much attention since the muddy days in the aftermath of the IDA leak, when an emergency summit led to the creation of a Global Shield Commission with William Godfrey as its inaugural Chairman.

Godfrey was one of many leaders present again today, this time in his position as Chairman of the Global *Contact* Commission, and his expression gave little away. Those close to him knew that he was frustrated at having to share a second-tier position alongside the ELF's Ding Ziyang within the new UN body that was about to be formally announced, but they also knew that he was overwhelmingly glad to have saved face after things looked to have swung so decisively Ding's way mere days earlier before everything was flipped by Jack Neal's remarkable arrival in Havana.

John Cole was present too, and had already received unlikely words of thanks from both Godfrey and President Slater for his role in discreetly keeping Jack from doing anything irreversibly damaging before the ill-thinking Squadron returned to New Kerguelen. No one except Slater knew why the Squadron had retreated as suddenly as they had, and *she* knew it only because Emma Ford had seen no way of ensuring the emergency summit began so quickly without looping Slater in on the surprise that was in store and having her do the leg work of bringing everyone together.

Everyone had taken the Squadron's departure as a welcome sign that Dan McCarthy's journey to New Kerguelen was setting things right, with all now eagerly awaiting his return from the distant world and none understanding how important *Tara* Ford had been in ensuring everything went smoothly.

President Slater took to a podium with Godfrey and Ding each standing at one of her shoulders, and John Cole standing in turn beyond Ding. By any standard, this was quite the quartet. Astute observers recognised that all four had been present in China for the ill-fated launch of DS-1, which had of course come about as a result of the original New York Agreement, and this added just one more layer of significance.

The presence of Cole, whose very recent redemption in the eyes of other Western leaders was as unexpected to him as to anyone, meanwhile suggested that the new UN body would be a forward-looking one unimpeded by the squabbles of the past.

"By an enormous margin," Slater began, "the nations of our world have today voted to establish a new United Nations body which will unify the ELF and GCC under a common banner. This new body will be known as the UN Interspace Contact Agency."

Among the press pack, some reporters couldn't help but titter. The allusion to the late Richard Walker's Interspace *Defense* Agency was so overt that it was unquestionably intentional.

"The ICA will continue to make use of the excellent infrastructure currently in place in both Beijing and Buenos Aires, with Ding Ziyang and William Godfrey responsible for overseeing the operations of our two regional divisions from the current ELF and GCC headquarters. Our aim is not to throw the baby out with the bathwater in discarding the good work that has been done since Contact Day, but rather to work together to ensure that all *future* work is cooperative and collaborative rather than inefficiently competitive."

Godfrey nodded several times. Ding, a man who everyone knew could understand and speak English perfectly but who very rarely let it show, likewise expressed his support with a few simple nods.

"And albeit in his absence," Slater continued, "Dan McCarthy has been proposed without objection as the ICA's inaugural Chief Planetary

Liaison. Dan has in essence been carrying out this role on an unofficial and unselfish basis for more than a year, and his committed impartiality has made him not only *a* popular choice, but quite simply *the* popular choice. If Dan—

"Look!" someone yelled, organically but right on cue. Only Slater knew what was coming next, but even she didn't have to pretend to look shocked.

The blockbuster movie-worthy sight of an alien mothership descending over New York sent some reporters fleeing in instinctive terror, but those who stayed beyond the first few frightening seconds quickly saw *which* mothership it was. Without doubt, this was the Messengers'; not the one last seen casting an ominous shadow over central Beijing, but the one last seen departing Colorado with Dan McCarthy and Tara Ford en route to New Kerguelen.

The uncloaked craft stopped at a significant altitude, perhaps to avoid casting too great a shadow, and a much smaller saucer-shaped craft emerged from its hull to come the rest of the way down.

Ding Ziyang leaned over to Godfrey and said something that no cameras or microphones could pick up, but it led to both men smiling a few seconds later. A photograph of this very human moment would go on to define this momentous day of union almost as much as the incredible sight in the sky.

The craft landed without any pretence — straight down, no messing around — and its ramp extended to the ground just as straightforwardly. Dan and Tara emerged at the top within seconds of the ramp's appearance, and they walked down towards a thousand cameras like two models on a catwalk.

"What's going on?" Dan asked, pretending to have no clue in a way that had taken two full days of practice to master. He had spent those days at home while Emma and President Slater put the whole thing together; and, after some initial misgivings about the deceit of pretending to only be arriving back on Earth now, he had come to see that this moment would bring joy to a lot of people and ensure peace on a planet that desperately needed it.

President Slater stepped forward to 'explain' everything to him while Tara looked around in wide-eyed shock, a far more natural actor than Dan would ever be. Emma wasn't there and neither was Clark, so she joined Dan near the podium.

Dan stepped forward after hearing what the day was all about and delivered a few well-practiced lines to summarise his time on New Kerguelen and to stress the point that the Messengers were keen to engage in full diplomatic relations moving forward. This went down well with everyone, from the media to the politicians, but things stepped up a gear when he called the Messengers out from the craft and they made themselves visible.

None of the attendant politicians other than John Cole had ever seen an alien up close and personal, but all were aware of the power of this moment and called on their lifetimes of experience to look calm even if they weren't.

"My brain is back to normal," Dan said. "No more of the finger-zapping power they gave me that night, and I'll be happy to take any kind of tests regarding that. Our friends from New Kerguelen are likewise content to be tested — respectfully and non-invasively — particularly in the hope of developing a reliable translation device to enable deep conversation with no requirement of ongoing physical connectivity."

"Dan," William Godfrey said, stepping towards the microphone with Slater's permission. "President Slater just informed you about the new ICA that's just been announced, as well as its primary goals and operational structure. But a few minutes before you arrived, she also announced something that wasn't in that short recap."

Slater, in on this innocently-motivated stunt, was tremendously glad that Godfrey had seized this opportunity for a few minutes in the brightest of all global spotlights. She could act and she could lie — after all, her ascent to the top level of American politics had involved little else — but Godfrey's surprise was altogether more natural.

"And what's that?" Dan asked. By this point, he had encouraged the Messengers, who were also in on everything, to shake hands with the attendant leaders. These images were incredible and would be replayed endlessly around the world, but Dan did a good job of pretending to be intrigued about a 'surprise' job offer he had already decided to accept.

After lies and deceit had done so much damage in recent years, Dan almost felt as though he was drawing a line under everything by making this whole thing as perfect as possible with the whitest of all lies and deftest of all deceits.

There was no guilty conscience, because no one was losing out and he wasn't doing anything wrong. As Emma framed it, in fact, Dan was doing something very *right* by leaving his traditional insistence on *'hard truth, no matter what'* to one side and instead publicly returning to Earth in a way that would minimise any threat of future conflict while more immediately bringing warmth and joy to billions.

"National representatives have already voted overwhelmingly to offer you the position of the ICA's Chief Planetary Liaison," Godfrey grinned. "Given your present company and your revelation that they are seeking diplomatic relations, I'm hopeful your decision is an easy one."

Dan smiled right back and raised a thumb to the cameras. "I guess I'll give it a shot."

THREE MONTHS LATER

V plus 9

Stevenson Farm
Eastview, Colorado

Although dubbed the wedding of the century by a celebrity-obsessed media which had been longing for this day since the unlikely coupling first became news, the matrimonial union of Dan McCarthy and Emma Ford was a deliberately low-key affair.

Their lives had been a whirlwind in the months since Arrival Day, as the monumental day when not one but *two* alien motherships arrived on Earth had come to be known. Dan's position as the ICA's Chief Planetary Liaison brought incredible media responsibilities for the first few weeks in particular, and since then he had been back and forth to New York on multiple occasions to oversee votes on several resolutions. The most interesting and headline-grabbing of these regarded the upcoming assistance mission to New Kerguelen which would see an extensive international team of engineers and scientists directly assess the planet's so-called Great Shelter before returning shortly thereafter to assist in its repair.

Four humans currently lived on New Kerguelen as ambassadors, two leading scientists from former GCC members states and two from former ELF nations. The GCC and ELF no longer functioned as they once had, with both having been consumed by the ICA in a manner that wasn't completely unlike when Earth's major national space agencies had been consumed by the ill-fated GSC.

With the ELF serving as the ICA's Eastern division and the GCC its counterpart in the West, there was no longer a need for John Cole's previous position of ELF Western Secretary. As someone with a foot in both camps — trusted by Ding for joining the ELF in the first place and trusted by Western leaders for the role he played in subduing Jack Neal during his discussions with the Squadron — Cole had hoped to be selected as one of the ICA's ambassadors to New Kerguelen.

This was unacceptable for obvious reasons, primarily Cole's well-earned reputation for making culturally offensive faux pas and rash decisions, and it took an intervention from William Godfrey to talk him out of applying for the role. Godfrey promised to assist Cole in a return to frontline British politics, something the latter wanted more than anything but knew he couldn't successfully pursue without his former boss's support.

Crisis after crisis had conveniently befallen the lame duck Prime Minister David Hearst in the interim, and Cole was simply biding his time until Hearst — a non-entity on the international stage and barely viewed with any more respect at home — finally bit the dust.

Two very special guests of honour sat in the front row alongside Emma and Dan's closest friends and family, and no one was in any doubt that this would be the first human wedding attended by extraterrestrials.

Dan thought it might have been funny to talk the familiar Messengers into wearing specially tailored tuxedos, but although Emma laughed at the idea she quickly vetoed it. The tunics were simply what the Messengers wore; as she told him, anything else would just look *wrong*.

The wedding wasn't an official state occasion or even a particularly large gathering, but it was exactly what they both wanted. The small guest list was one of few compromises, with the only individuals present who weren't close friends or family being the un-omittable William Godfrey and Ding Ziyang — Dan's colleagues at the ICA — as well as the increasingly amiable President Slater.

Clark was Dan's best man, of course, and Tara Emma's maid of honour. Their budding and potentially life-complicating romance was the best-kept secret in Colorado, with an unbreakable agreement in place to keep it from Dan and Emma until after they returned from their honeymoon at the very least. After three months it felt like anything but a casual fling, but it still wouldn't have been fair to do anything to distract from the wedding until it was all in the rear-view.

There was no commercial media presence in Eastview and an exclusion zone was in force around Phil Norris's property, with drone-watchers on duty and a bounty on offer for any they successfully spotted in the skies overhead.

A large public security operation was also underway, even though the once-troublesome group of anti-contact terrorists known as GeoSovs had been positively routed by a unified international crackdown that left no stone unturned and left nothing to chance. Contacts and text messages from Jack Neal's phone provided many initial leads that exposed the GeoSovs' global web of cells and sympathisers, and Poppy Bradshaw was now just one of several hundred incarcerated former members having been caught red-handed by a string of messages which confirmed her involvement in the plot to take President Slater hostage.

Tara, for her part, had firmly requested that those who knew about her own kidnapping kept it to themselves. As she told the few who knew, the last thing she wanted to do was live her life as a victim in everyone else's eyes — she had survived Jack Neal's demented scheme, and she refused to be defined by it.

As the wedding ceremony continued, it became clear to the guests that the couple had written their own vows. Emma delivered hers first in a voice that almost sounded nervous, which made the sweet words all the sweeter in Dan's ears.

His second thought, after how wonderful they were, was that his own were going to struggle to follow them.

"It really wasn't easy figuring out the best way to word everything I want to say," he began, glad he'd decided to open with some humour, "mainly because my usual speechwriter has been tied up with a project of her own."

Emma's lips crinkled in amusement. She wore a one-of-a-kind TARA COUTURE dress, modern and elegant, which would become an instant classic.

"It's also difficult to know where to start," Dan went on, "because the world has thrown a lot at us in the past two years. And when that wasn't enough, the universe decided to throw a comet at us, too!"

Clark roared in laughter, wondering where the hell Dan had found all of these lines.

"But we didn't just *survive* everything that came our way. No... we got stronger, and we got closer. When you said yes, I thought I had everything I wanted. When I found out we're going to have a family, I knew that's everything I'll *ever* want. I'm the luckiest man in the world, and you make me happier than anyone has any right to be. The last thing I want to say is this: People always say we should count our blessings, and I've tried and tried and tried. But as soon as I get to one, there's nowhere left to go... because Emma Ford, you're the only blessing I'll ever need."

Emma tried not to cry and almost succeeded. She was glad she had gone first, at least, knowing now that she otherwise couldn't have gotten many words out without blubbering.

Under the watchful eyes of the warring politicians they'd brought together and the visitors from another world they'd introduced to their own, Dan and Emma looked only at each other as they waited patiently for the *I do*'s.

They felt at home among the friends and family who had helped them through so much — from Henry, Phil and Mr Byrd to the quiet but loyal Timo Fiore, as well as the friendly faces of Billy Kendrick and Trey Myers who were visiting from well out of town — and if such a bright future wasn't coming their way they would have wished to freeze this perfect moment in time.

The crystal clear sky overhead would come alive as an ocean full of stars when the day turned to night and the party kicked into gear, and there was nowhere either of them would rather be than under it together.

When they both said "I do", Dan felt like pinching himself to make sure he wasn't dreaming. Another part of him didn't want to take the risk just in case he really *was*, such was the disbelieving gratitude he felt in the moment.

With the verbal commitments made and barely a dry eye to be seen, only one thing remained.

At the edge of a cornfield where everything had changed more than once, the biggest and best change of Dan McCarthy's life was happening right now. There was no better place to make the step from one life to another, he thought; no better place to embrace a future brighter than any he'd ever dreamed possible.

This thought and every other was soon consumed by the warmth that flooded over him as Emma Ford's lips parted only slightly and she whispered two words as they moved in for the kiss:

"*Hashtag blessed.*"

Books by Craig A. Falconer

Not Alone
Not Alone: Second Contact
Not Alone: The Final Call

Terradox
The Fall of Terradox
Terradox Reborn
Terradox Beyond

Funscreen
Sycamore
Sycamore 2
Sycamore X
Sycamore XL

For more information, visit
www.craigafalconer.com

Made in the USA
Monee, IL
15 January 2020